SECRET RELATIONS

Finn O'Brien Book Three

REBECCA FORSTER

WOLFPACK
PUBLISHING
— EST 2013 —

WOLFPACK
PUBLISHING
— EST 2013 —

Secret Relations
Paperback Edition
Copyright © 2021 (As Revised) Rebecca Forster

Wolfpack Publishing
5130 S. Fort Apache Road 215-380
Las Vegas, NV 89148

Paperback ISBN: 978-1-64734-991-2
Ebook ISBN: 978-1-64734-990-5
LCCN 2021932141

Cover Design by Hadleigh O. Charles

SECRET RELATIONS

For
DOMI BRIBIESKA
The kindest soul I have ever known.

CHAPTER 1

APRIL 18

He was surprised to hear a bird singing because this place was better suited to lizards and snakes with its dry brush and tangled bushes and water-starved trees. But there it was, a little bird's happy song floating across the air right to him. The sound of it made him want to smile, but he didn't. It hurt to smile, not to mention that this wasn't the time. It was a workday and he wanted to finish before dark because his sight wasn't so good, the one eye being pretty much blind and all. Still, he could see well enough to spy a bird if it moved but nothing did, so he looked up at the giant house sitting atop the hill like a castle. There was a lot of money in Los Angeles. Lot of money. Lot of freeloaders. Lot of scum too. Lot of crazies. Sometimes the people with the money were freeloaders and scum and crazy too, but most people only noticed the money. Not him. No, no, not him. He noticed the bottom feeders and the filth. He got people's numbers. He knew about people. Oh, yes, he did.

The man looked away from the castle and ran the

back of his arm across his forehead to wipe away the sweat. He listened to the bird sing and it reminded him of the way the girl had talked, chirping in a language he couldn't really understand. He thought she understood him, though, because he had the basics down pat when he was a good-lookin' young buck. He figured that was all you needed. The basics.

Hola.

Bonita.

Ven conmigo.

No llores.

No llores!

No! Don't cry!

He said that last part in English because it was clear she didn't understand, or he wasn't saying it right, or something. Maybe he had misunderstood what she wanted, but that was all it had been. A misunderstanding. If she had just friggin' spoken English things would have gone better and turned out a whole lot different. All that was a long time ago and it wasn't the girl that weighed on his mind; it was what came after the girl. Awake or asleep, what came after the girl played out like a movie behind that damn bad eye of his.

When the memories made him tired, he let his head fall back so that the sun could shine smack dab on his face. That felt good. The same way the air felt good and the smells smelled good: eucalyptus and wild honeysuckle and the scrub and the dust and the dirt. Most people never took the time to appreciate the outside, but he did because he knew what being inside too long could do to a man.

"Es esto sufficiente?"

The man opened his eyes; he swung his head. The day was so pleasant, moving into evening as it was, that he had almost forgotten the boy who was doing the heavy lifting. It was dusty, mean work but it had to be done and he didn't really have the strength to do it himself anymore. Besides, it was more satisfying to watch.

The man tried to look friendly even though he couldn't smile. He put on his hat. It was a floppy brimmed thing made for camping. It wasn't the most handsome hat, but he wasn't the most handsome man, so it seemed that he and the hat were well suited. His companion, the one wielding the shovel, was quite handsome. Then again, weren't they all at that age? This one was *a border man*, just shy of a teenager but not quite the solid stock of real manhood. He stood so straight and looked so hopeful: hopeful that the backbreaking work would please the man who employed him, hopeful that he had dug long enough and deep enough, hopeful that he might even go home with more money in his pocket than promised, hopeful that he would be paid at all.

The man took a short hop off the truck gate where he'd been sitting. The little truck bounced some as it let go of his weight but not much because he wasn't a heavy man. He wasn't a slight man either. He simply was a man who moved through the world easily because he was neither this nor that. There had been a time when it was different. He had been a cocky cuss, full of himself, getting by, taking his pleasures. He could barely remember the pleasures of youth now. Pity. He might be a different sort if he could remember that.

Eyes hidden by the brim of the hat, he shuffled to the edge of the trench. Slowly he paced the length and breadth of it, surveying the project as if concerned that it was not exactly to his specifications, but it was perfect. He had to give the young man credit. He knew how to work hard. It was the only good thing he could say about people like him.

The worker stepped back as best he could, considering the trench was narrow. He raised a hand, inviting scrutiny, proud of what he had accomplished. The little wooden stakes with the yellow flags fluttered in the now-and-again breeze, but the twine strung between the stakes to mark out the work site were still taut. There was even a pyramid of pipe laid out just so. The man had a drawing that he had shown to his helper. The young man pretended to be interested in what looked like the sketch of a house. A forest house. A canyon house. A house far away from the hectic city traffic. The worker nodded as if he understood the drawing, but he didn't. He didn't care if this place was hidden from the main road and so deep in the canyon that the king in the castle on the hill would not be able to see it even if he deigned to look down. All he knew was that the drawing meant work and work meant money.

"*Bueno*," the man said.

The worker grinned, showing his perfect white teeth. The man hated those teeth. Why was God so generous when he made these people with their thick black hair and beautiful brown skin? Then to bless them with goddamn pearly whites to boot? It just wasn't right. The man shook his head in disgust. Good-looking they might be, hard-working if you got the right ones, but in the long run all that virtue and all those good looks meant nothing. These people could turn on a dime. They were wily that way. They were the lowest of the low hiding behind those pretty smiles and shining eyes. Barbaric. Cruel. Even while the man thought this, he smiled without showing his own teeth, without hurting his scarred face and said:

"*Muy bueno*."

He reached for the shovel. The young man gave it to him and then the man in the hat dug into his pocket. He took out money, counted it off and gave the young man thirty dollars.

"*Gracias*," the worker said.

The man peeled off another twenty and gratitude spilled out of the young man like candy out of a piñata. The man waved away such effusive thanks as if it were a little thing he had done, as if the boy deserved the tip.

While the young man put on his shirt, the older one took up the little stakes with the yellow plastic flags attached. He gathered them together, wrapped the twine around them and put the bundle in the back of the truck. He put the shovel in, too. He looked back at his helper. The young man was tucking in his shirt, so the older man went back for the pipe. He picked up two and into the truck they went. He had just retrieved the last pipe when the young man pushed out of the trench and started for the truck. He was a quick one and the man in the hat was disappointed that his own timing was off. Still, all was not lost. It wasn't as if this hadn't happened before. He followed the worker knowing there would be one more chance to do what must be done. The chance came quickly.

The boy put a knee up on the tailgate and grasped the side of the truck to haul himself in. That was when the older man gripped the pipe and swung, splitting the boy's head clean open on contact. The crack of his skull disturbed the canyon peace. That little singing bird, startled by the sound, flew out of the brush. That bird had been closer than the man thought but he was not distracted by its flight; he only had eyes for the work. The boy had been thrown forward so that his chin hit the truck bed and his arms were flung out. For a moment he was suspended like he was crucified, and in the next moment the boy slid slowly, quite gracefully, off the bed and crumpled on the ground.

There was a lot of blood but that didn't surprise the older man. The young man's head, after all, was almost cracked in two and the side that had taken the brunt of the blow was quite a mess. The cheekbone was crushed, the eye nearest the split was knocked out and the young man's handsome nose was pushed sideways. The good thing was that most of the blood fell on the ground and not in the truck. That's what made the older man so good at his work. He planned everything, including the optimum time to swing, striking just as the boy started to lift himself up. If he had a knee up at the time of impact, he would have fallen further in and the blood would have flooded the truck bed. Or, worst-case scenario, the man wouldn't have had the right leverage and would have only wounded him. That wouldn't be good, but it didn't matter. He had hit the young man correctly and the splatter of blood in the truck could be easily cleaned. The man preferred things as neat as possible because extra work didn't set well with him. That was really the bottom line; he wasn't the man he used to be.

He stood for a moment, just looking at his handiwork, before bending over and touching the boy's neck. He was a goner. The man went to the cab and fetched a water bottle. He drank half of it, and when he was done, he took the rest of the water and washed the blood off the truck. Some of the bloody water fell on the man with the split skull. When the man with the hat finished cleaning, he took off his hat, rolled up his sleeves and considered how to handle the next part so that he did not hurt himself. There was no telling when this appendage or that might go out on him, when breath would be hard to come by, so he had to be careful.

The boy was not too tall nor was he fat, but he was muscular in that sinewy way people like him could be. The man paused and looked over his shoulder at the trench. Perhaps the job wasn't as good as he had initially thought. From this angle the trench looked a bit too long. They could have cut off a half hour if he had been paying more attention. No matter now. It was time to finish up.

He took the body by the feet to keep the blood off his clothes. It was very hard to get blood out of fabric. He'd washed enough of his own blood out of shirts and pants and underwear to know that. Even though there was no one to hear him, the man was careful not to make any sound as he dragged the body to the hole and dumped it in. When that was done, he recovered his breath, rubbed his shoulders, and quieted his mind.

The body had fallen into the trench face down and that was not the way it should be. He had been so sure that the slope at the lip would allow for a slide and not a tumble, but there it was. The body had tumbled. The man climbed in and turned the boy so he was face up. He squared the corpse's shoulders, leaned back, and checked his work. He bent down again and this time he straightened the broken nose, wiped the blood from beneath it and then cleaned his hands in the dirt so blood wouldn't get on his clothes. There was nothing he could do about the cheek but from where he stood it was hardly noticeable. He stepped back again and surveyed his handiwork.

In the dappled sunlight the boy looked like he was asleep which, of course, he wasn't. Any fool would know that if they looked close. Any fool would see the dry dirt under his head was now dark with blood. And if they walked to the other side of the trench, they would see the crushed cheek and the dangling eyeball. But a fool just glancing at him might mistake him for napping.

In a hole.

In the ground.

Well and good.

Almost done.

Only the observance was left. In a way, that was the most important part of his work. He was not, after all, a monster. He had known monsters and he was not one. The man took the corpse's hands and folded them over the chest. He leaned back again. The edge of the trench hit his calves. He took a deep breath. He was tired. His left arm ached but he soldiered on.

Doubling over, the man dug in the boy's pockets and came up with a cell phone. The man snorted. The boy probably lived like a peasant, but he had a fancy phone. It would be of no use to him now, but the man could get a hundred for it easy. He dug in again and soon he had checked each pocket. He found no ID, but that was no surprise. He took back the fifty bucks that he had given the young man. He buttoned the top button of the boy's shirt and patted the collar into place before sidestepping to the end of the trench. He fixed the feet, so the toes pointed up. He thought to take the shoes, but he didn't need them, and it was hard to get boots off a corpse, even a fresh one, so he left them.

Once everything was as it should be, he went back to the cab and took a box of cards out of the glove box. Only two left. He chose one, got back into the hole and tucked the card under the boy's hands. They were already starting to cool. He patted those brown hands, looked into the boy's face and said the Act of Contrition. He did not hurry. He gave God his due. He said every word for the boy who could not say the words himself.

The man got himself out of the trench and swiped at his knees because he disliked dirt on his trousers. He went to the truck and got the shovel. When he returned, he filled in the trench. The feet were covered first. He filled in around the body next and then tamped some dirt down over the torso. He was careful around the young man's head, adding the dirt slowly. When that was done, he held the last shovelful of dirt, stared down at that dead face, and said:

"You're on the ledger, my friend."

With that, he tipped the shovel. At the precise moment, when the last bit of soil and twigs and stone covered the young man's face, a breeze kicked up and the bird chirped once more. The man planted the shovel, leaned on the handle, lifted his face, and listened. The world could be so beautiful, so peaceful. He appreciated it all so much, and he knew the beauty and the peace was the good Lord blessing the work he had done that day.

Then he looked at the spot where the young man lay buried. He looked for a long while and thought, as he often did, that he should leave a marker but then he heard a rustle and he saw a blur as the bird flew off to another bush. He took that as a sign, too. He would leave no marker. He never had. It was just his age and emotion making him second-guess what he had done.

He swung the shovel over his shoulder and walked away from the grave. For that's what it was, that's what it had always been. As he walked, he heard a cheery little tune whistling in his head. It was still there when he put the shovel in the truck bed next to the pipes and the little bundle of wooden stakes. He closed the tailgate and went around to the driver side and got in. The man started his truck, stepped on the gas, put both hands on the wheel and began to drive down the narrow, pitted road. The old truck shuddered and shook and by the time he reached the main road that cut through the canyon and connected the city with the valley, he was done in and he needed to rest and regain his strength if he was to finish the season. Sometimes, though, it seemed the task he set for himself was impossible.

He was, after all, only one man and these people? These people were like cockroaches.

They were everywhere.

CHAPTER 2

APRIL 21
WILSHIRE DIVISION
Captain's Briefing

Captain Fowler: The mayor has asked that all personnel make themselves available for the Cinco de Mayo celebrations at Grand Avenue Park and Olivera Street. That means seventy-two hours, round the clock, not just the day of.

Detective Pauly: Uniforms only, right?

Officer Shay: Screw you, Pauly.

Captain Fowler: Detective Pauly, if you do not understand the word 'all', I will refer you to Officer Shay for a remedial vocabulary lesson since it appears she has a fine command of the English language.

(mutters, groans of agreement)

Captain Fowler: Seriously, ladies and gentlemen, we have to be in top form. We have Intel that at least three major migrant rights groups are planning protests and those are only the ones with permits. Gangs are overly active of late, and the new federal 'surge initiative' to arrest parents who pay smugglers to bring their children over the border is putting a strain on everyone.

Detective Durant: 'Bout time.

Captain Fowler: You are a servant of the people, Durant. If I hear that you aren't serving and protecting every single person in L.A. on May five, you will be put on leave without pay. Is that understood? **(pause)** By all?

(nods)

Cori Anderson: In court on a personal matter, Captain. Then on call tonight.

Captain Fowler: You'll advise him, Anderson.

Cori Anderson: No problemo, Captain.

Detective Smithson: Didn't know you spoke Spanish, Anderson.

(Snickers. Cori flipping him off. Laughter. Captain Fowler stacking papers ignoring them all.)

Captain Fowler: Be safe. Specifics on Cinco de Mayo coming as I receive them. Any problems or concerns, my door is open.

Finn and Beverly O'Brien arrived punctually in Department 5, the courtroom of Judge Charlene Dubois, at eleven a.m.

For ten minutes they sat across the aisle from one another. Waiting. Silent. Finn found it curious that they had walked down an aisle on their wedding day, happy, looking forward to the future, and today they would once again walk down an aisle. This time only one of them would be happy and there would be no future together. Finn was not exactly sad about the event – he had long since resigned himself to the fact that his marriage was over – but he was disappointed, melancholy, low as only an Irishman can be. That, he supposed, was a step in the right direction being as he had passed on to the other side of pain and guilt.

At eleven-fifteen, the judge's clerk having called the court to order, and the judge herself having taken the bench, the marriage of Finn and Beverly O'Brien was put asunder.

By noon, Finn was in Mick's Irish Pub, enduring Geoffrey's teasing about his suit and tie and fancy shoes. Finn ordered Guinness and explained that he was in mourning. This was not exactly a lie, for that was what it felt like when Finn left the courthouse, holding the door for Beverly, standing atop the stairs to watch her put on the big sunglasses that made her look like a movie star. He watched her run across Grand Avenue, away from him to something wonderful and new. She disappeared into the parking garage without a backward glance. He succeeded in silencing Geoffrey, whose long face grew longer with sympathy. The Guinness was on the house, Geoffrey said, for which Finn thanked him.

At one-thirty Finn tired of throwing darts. He was scoring no bullseye and the hollow sound of the metal hitting cork gave him no satisfaction. Knowing one brew was all he could afford to drink given that he was on call that night, Finn left Mick's Irish Pub and went home.

At two o'clock he went for a run. He had no idea how far he ran but, when he finished, every muscle in his body ached, and he was sure that he had sweated off every last ounce of the one draft he had drunk.

It was five o'clock when he walked past Kimiko's house. He thought to stop and ask his landlady if she would grant him a bath in her *sento*, but he decided against it. Instead, Finn kept walking across the yard and through the garden to the building at the back of the property that he called home. The *sento* was a place to relax and reflect and Finn wanted none of that. He wanted to simply get through the day and then forget it altogether.

Taking the stairs lightly, not wanting to disturb the downstairs neighbor who he had never seen but knew to be in residence, Finn let himself into his apartment, took a shower and planted himself in front of the television. On the couch beside him sat the 'big black dog' of depression though Finn O'Brien would never admit it. Even after his little brother, Alexander, was murdered the 'big black dog' was not allowed into the O'Brien house. It was banished to the porch and chained up on the rail. No matter how it howled, his mother and father would not let it in. Finn, though, had brought that 'black dog' into his room many a time back then. He imagined everyone in his family had, but it was something that was never spoken of. Finn had thought that dog had run away years ago and now here he was again, a brute of a thing.

By eight o'clock Finn had enough of television and in-sipid shows about housewives who were no housewives at all. They were old, shrewish women who had not a happy man between them, having run off all the husbands and lovers with their bickering and greed. At least Bev had been honest when she left him. She had been unable to live in exile, ostracized by everyone they knew because of what her husband had done. It was an honest difference of opinion and one Finn would have changed if he could. Had he not drawn his gun to defend a homeless man from a rogue cop, a fellow police officer would still be alive, Finn would be dead, and Beverly would now be a lovely widow.

At ten o'clock Finn went to bed. When he lay down, he closed his eyes and found that the 'big, black dog' had settled on the mattress beside him. It took all his concentration to put the ugly thing out on the porch of his mind and chain him up. By the time he did, Finn was asleep so he did not see the text messages on his phone, urgent and pleading. Even if he had, he probably wouldn't have done anything about it. He and the black dog were in no mood. He would sleep it off – all of it – and tomorrow all would be well.

But he did not sleep until the morrow.

At three o'clock in the morning, there was a call that he could not ignore because he was the detective on call. Finn dressed, strapped on his weapon, and put his badge on his belt. He was headed out the front door only to realize that he had forgotten his phone. He backtracked and, in a moment, had it in hand. He pressed the button to check for updates but there were none, not even the step-down order he had hoped for. But he did see a text message sent so many hours ago. He read it as he went down the stairs.

I have to talk to you. I'm at work until eleven. Don't tell mom.

Finn turned off the phone and opened the door of his unmarked car. He peeled away from the curb estimating his time of arrival at the crime scene to be four minutes.

Amber Anderson, his partner Cori's daughter, would have to wait.

CHAPTER 3

APRIL 22
DISPATCH

417 – Person with a gun
246 – Shooting at inhabited dwelling
10-00 – Officer down, proceed with caution

FINN O'BRIEN
10 – understood

Finn was on scene in five minutes, thirty-eight seconds. Four black and whites were parked in a semicircle, head-lights illuminating a two-story house that looked as though it had been built at the turn of the century and then abandoned. But it was not abandoned and whoever was in there had the attention of L.A.'s finest. Finn parked between one of the four patrol vehicles and two ambulances on scene. The paramedics were out of their vehicles but waiting for the go-ahead to do their job.

Finn killed his lights, called dispatch to confirm his arrival, and got out of his car. He checked out the house as he moved through the team that had cordoned off the street, set up their posts and were protecting themselves behind their vehicles.

The place was a rambling old thing. Its once stately windows were now covered with fixed bars in violation of city code and common sense. The wood was so dry the house would go up like a straw man should a stray spark from a fireplace or a forgotten cigarette take hold. Anyone inside would be barbequed, unable to get out. The wood siding had once been white and now was of no identifiable color. Some of the slats had fallen away. Towels, not curtains, partially covered two of the downstairs windows. There were four upstairs windows, three of which were dark. The fourth window was brightly lit. None of the upstairs windows had curtains. One was broken. Above those was a third-floor dormer. It, too, was dark.

Even from where Finn O'Brien stood, he could see that the porch steps were rotted. He imagined the wrap-around porch was too. There was a chair sitting beside the barred front door. By the way it listed, one could safely assume it was missing two legs.

A matte-black low rider was parked in the driveway. A pit bull was chained to a metal post near the front steps, and on the patchy, weed-choked lawn a cop was sprawled face down, unmoving, just inches away from the snarling animal.

"Officer in charge?" Finn asked a young officer. The man didn't bother to look over his shoulder to see who was asking. He pointed east and said:

"Sergeant Van, officer in charge."

Finn went on his way. He found Van on the phone, pulled aside his jacket, and showed his badge. Van acknowledged him with no more than a flick of his eyes.

The sergeant was upset, pacing as he talked into his phone, barely able to control his frustration, so Finn gave him his space.

"Not five minutes from now. Now, dammit." He cut the conversation off and took a second to shake his head. He ran a hand over his face and then he offered it to Finn.

"O'Brien," Finn said.

"Van," came back at him and then both men looked at the house. Finn asked: "Do you know who's in there?"

"Fidel Andre Hernandez. He runs with the Hard Times Locos and goes by the name Marbles."

Finn raised a brow, "Not exactly a handle that would put the fear of God into a body."

"You wouldn't say that if you saw him," the sergeant answered. "He tattooed his eyes black. Both eyes. The entire eyeball. They look like marbles."

"Charming," Finn muttered.

"And the word is that he's off his rocker," Van went on. "You know, lost his marbles? He spent almost six years in juvenile detention for assault with a deadly weapon and robbery. He could have been tried as an adult, but the prosecutors balked since he was twelve. He's been front and center with the Locos since he got out. Some say he's the one who hit Manny Gomez."

Finn nodded, listening while he kept his eyes on the officer down.

"Who's taken the bullet?"

"Officer Shay," the cop answered. "Carol Shay."

Though Finn didn't show it, and the man he was speaking to made no mention of it, the fact that the cop who took the hit was a woman made them both wince.

"Has there been any movement from her?" Finn asked.

"Not for a while."

"How did it happen?"

"Shay and her partner were called out on a domestic disturbance; one of the neighbors heard screaming and gunshots. She saw at least three people run out of the house."

"Are those people here?"

He shook his head. "Gone."

"Where's the partner?" Finn inquired.

The cop pointed to the closest ambulance. "He fell back when shots were fired but he got winged."

"His name?"

"Tornto. Jim," Van said.

"S.W.A.T. not here?" Finn asked as he began to move.

"Not yet. Don't know what the holdup is."

"Many thanks."

Finn left him.

Ninety seconds was gone.

Tornto was inside the ambulance parked against the curb. The sleeve of his uniform was ripped, and his upper arm was neatly bandaged. He had a few years on him so what was going down didn't rattle him as much as wound him. His partner was down, and he was thinking it should have been him or that he should have done more so it wasn't her. Finn understood that better than anyone given what had happened to his own partner, Cori, months back, but he offered no condolences as he sat on the bench opposite the man.

"Officer Tornto, Detective O'Brien. On call this evening," Finn said. "How are you feeling?"

"Like shit. Have they got her yet?"

Finn shook his head, liking that this man took Finn's question to reference more than his own physical pain. Partners were like that; when one bled, so did the other.

"Not yet, but we'll be taking care of that soon. Can you

give me the rundown?"

"It had been a quiet night. We respond to this call at two forty-eight. Shay says she's going in and I stay back to cover her." Tornto shook his head. He put his fingers to his eyes and rubbed them. "I swear I was on the mark. I wasn't distracted." He lifted his head. "I've been over it a million times to see if I made one small mistake, if I just, you know, moved my eyes away for a minute. I know I didn't." He sighed. "She's got a kid graduating from high school in a few weeks."

"Then let's make sure she gets to the ceremony," Finn answered.

Forty seconds more gone.

"Yeah. Okay." Officer Tornto took a breath through his nose, but his chest heaved with it. "The door opened just as Shay took the last step up onto the porch and he shot. No warning. She returned fire but I think it was just reflex. Anyway, she fired one round and then came down the steps. She collapsed where you see her. I fell back to the car and called it in. I tried to get to her but there was fire from upstairs, and I didn't know how far that dog could get. I thought it was best to get back, stay alive and wait for backup."

"Did you hear anything from inside the house other than the shot?"

"He fired two more times upstairs," Tornto said.

"And you're sure it's the man they call Marbles?"

"I saw him at the window. Funny how clear that was, seeing him I mean. Once you've seen this guy you don't forget him."

"But did you see him with the gun?"

Tornto shook his head. "No, the door didn't open far enough, but it had to be him."

"Anyone else inside?" Finn asked.

Tornto shook his head. "Not that I could tell, but if it was a domestic violence call that kind of assumes someone else is in there."

"But you heard no one screaming or calling out to you?"

"No." Tornto raised his head and looked at Finn. "I didn't hear anything. Oh God, you think this was a set up?"

"Do you have reason to think it could be?" Finn asked.

Another sixty seconds gone.

He glanced through the open doors of the ambulance, listening to Tornto all the while.

"I don't know. I don't think so. We've been on this beat for a while. Shay is pretty tough. Doesn't take any guff. She brought in a couple of the Hard Times Locos last week, but they seemed cool with it. We took them out of a house over on 215th street…"

Before Tornto could finish, the night erupted with the sound of gunfire. Finn was out of the ambulance and back on the line. Every officer was positioned safely and well. Their guns were trained on the house. Radios squawked and crackled, and Van was screaming into his.

"Where in the hell is S.W.A.T.?" When Finn came to his side, he held the receiver against his chest and said: "We tried to get to Shay, but he doesn't want us anywhere near her."

"Sure, 'tisn't this feeling as if he has a beef with the boys in blue," Finn muttered as he took off his jacket. "I'll be needing a vest."

Sergeant Van ducked into his car and tossed one Finn's way. "You should wait for S.W.A.T."

"If that was you lying there, would you want to be waiting on them?" Finn asked. Van shook his head. Finn had another question. "Any other movement from the house?"

"We've only seen Marbles," Van said. "The idiot's shooting from the center window, second floor, the one lit up like a Christmas tree. Other than that, we have no idea who else might be in there."

Thirty more seconds down.

"It's about time we found out," Finn said and then added. "And do what you must with the dog."

CHAPTER 4

Finn hopscotched from black and white to black and white until he was at the end of the half circle. Each cop he passed gave him a look; one that said 'stay safe'. The rank and file knew about him, of course, but there were degrees of separation between him and the uniformed officers at his old division that made them more forgiving of his presence. Tonight, it wouldn't have mattered if he had betrayed the whole force; they still would have wished him well because he was putting himself in harm's way for Shay.

"Here we go, boyo," Finn whispered.

He drew his gun, crouched down, and ran toward the low rider. Once there, he threw himself against the back, left wheel and put his butt on the concrete drive. His weapon was up, clutched in both hands. He counted to three and consciously relaxed them. Soft hands he remembered his father instructing when he was just a boy. That's how you catch a ball solid, son. Relax the hands and you'll be ready for the next thing that's thrown your way. Rigid hands are useless.

Soft hands, boy.
Soft hands.

Finn relaxed his grip, but quieting his heart and mind were another matter. If this situation came to a showdown, Finn wasn't at all sure he could shoot another human being again. Evil or not, could he look a man in the eye and pull that trigger?

Having no answer to that question, Finn had no choice but to move forward. He pushed off, stayed low and then threw himself across the ten feet between the front of the car and the side of the house. He fell badly, recovered, scrambled close to the structure, and put his back up against the wall. Boots planted on the hard ground, he pushed himself up into a standing position. His vest scraped against the old wood as he slid across it and he could feel big splinters breaking off as he went. Though the early morning was cool, his shirt was soaked with sweat underneath the body armor. He crooked his arm and wiped the perspiration away from his eyes, raised his face and listened to the eerie quiet.

He knew this neighborhood. Not this one specifically, but ones like it all over Los Angeles. Every night the people who lived here drifted off to the sound of gunfire, children slept on mattresses on the floor to hedge their bet against being killed by stray bullets, drugs were bought and sold, good people were robbed, burglarized and brutalized. Tonight, though, this neighborhood was as quiet as a tomb. It was as if everybody on this block were holding their collective breaths, knowing something big was coming down and praying whatever it was it would not come down on them.

Finn raised his eyes to the second floor. There was only one small window on this side of the building. The kitchen window was on the first floor. There was a screened-in sun porch to his right but all of it was as dark as the rest of the house. Only the room where Marbles kept vigil was lit and that meant the man wasn't too swift. He might as well be on stage in the spotlight. Finn waited. Marbles had gone silent.

There could only be a few reasons why Marbles was not engaging the officers in the street. One: He had run out of ammunition. Two: He had taken himself out with the last shot. Three: He was focusing on whoever was in the house with him. There was also a fourth possibility. It was one Finn didn't like at all. Option four: Marbles had seen him coming and was lying in wait for him.

If that were the case, the gangbanger might have the advantage if he knew this house well. Then again, Finn knew something of houses like this too. His family had lived in one when they first came to this country. These old houses had steep stairs and rooms that jutted here and there – pantries and closets, nurseries and sunrooms. Not like the new houses, all sleek and open. Hopefully, this call hadn't been domestic violence at all but something more manageable like home invasion. That would mean Marbles was unfamiliar with this particular floor plan and that might give Finn a slight advantage.

Glancing up once more to confirm no other lights had gone on, Finn found himself looking at an old black woman in the neighboring house. She was white haired and seemed neither curious nor alarmed. She was simply leaning on the sill of her upstairs window watching him.

"Do you know how many people live in this house, missus?" Finn spoke as loud as he dared as he pointed his gun upward. In answer, the old woman slammed the window and disappeared.

"I'll take that as a no," he muttered.

In the distance, two dogs went at each other with a

viciousness that could only end badly. When they went suddenly silent, Finn assumed one of them had torn the other's throat out. It seemed to be a night for fighting to the death.

He looked at the apartment building behind the house. Lights were on in almost every unit and yet no one was looking out the window. There was a dilapidated detached garage on the back of the property. Part of the door had been eaten away and Finn could see through the hole. There was nothing but junk inside.

Keeping low, Finn crab-stepped the length of the house, paused at the corner and looked into the backyard. It was small and overgrown. There was a child's tricycle and an old barbeque. A vine grew up from the bottom and into the hood of the grill. The child's toy, while well worn, was newer and that worried Finn. The last thing he needed was a wee one getting in the way or being used as a shield.

He skirted around the back, went past the screened in porch and took the three steps up to the back door, leading with his weapon, eyes sharp. The door was barred. He let go of his gun with one hand, took the handle and tugged. It didn't give. He stepped back and looked up. The upstairs windows weren't barred but there was no way to access them. From the street he heard someone with a megaphone hailing the house. He blessed Sergeant Van for the diversion and hurried back down the stairs. Given the age of the house, he was hoping to find the one thing that wouldn't be found in any house built after 1950: a cellar.

And there it was, padlocked. Finn found his phone and turned on the flashlight. Had the situation not been so dire, he would have laughed at what he saw. The padlock hung onto a slat of wood but the wood above and below it was rotted. He flipped off the light, raised his heavy boot and with one swift kick the problem was solved, and he was on his way.

Dawn was creeping upon the night slowly and there was just enough light to brighten the stairs that led into the cellar. Finn took them carefully until he was standing on dirt, surrounded by footings that secured the lumber that held up the house above him. This was more a glorified crawl space than a cellar, but there was enough height for him to move around with only a slight stoop. With his phone lighting the way, Finn crossed to a flight of wooden stairs that would take him inside the house. This place was dark and damp and home to something that scurried along the far wall. He would be happy to be out of it but, just as his hand reached to open the door at the top of the stairs, he heard a shotgun blast as if from a great distance. Then he heard someone on a bullhorn.

Finally, when the only thing Finn heard was his own breathing, he tried the door that would let him get inside. It wasn't locked and moved smoothly as he inched it open and slipped through. That was the first small favor granted him. The second was that he could hear the man upstairs pacing on an uncarpeted floor. From the rhythm of his steps Finn knew that Marbles was thinking, planning, and worrying. He went back and forth and then forward quickly in the direction of the front window where he paused. Finn counted those quiet seconds and then listened as the pattern was repeated.

This was the walk of a nervous man, one who was desperately trying to reason himself out of an unreasonable situation. But even Marbles knew there were only two ways out: through a hail of bullets from the LAPD who had surrounded the place or walk out with his hands up. Marbles, he was sure, was not the kind of man to give up easily, so Finn would help him make that decision.

He stepped into the house and found himself in the kitchen. It was neat enough even though the cabinets had been rifled through. He could smell onions and rice. Finn took a look into the adjacent room. It had once been an elegant dining room with its leaded windows and wainscoting, but now it was filled with mattresses. Each had a pillow and thin blanket. Clothes and shoes were tossed about. There were a few satchels, a backpack or two.

From upstairs came a burst of gunfire and the sound of Marbles screaming in Spanish. The man on the bullhorn spoke back in English, but Finn couldn't make out any of what was being said. Not that it mattered. He knew the drill: keep Marbles talking, take him alive, don't screw up so that the next thing their captain saw was a headline screaming police brutality, decrying the murder of a person of color even if the crazy man upstairs had shot a police officer.

Such was the way of the world these days, but the politics of this situation were not his concern. Finn walked across the mattresses, stepping carefully when he got into the entry hall. There he laid up against the wall, faced the staircase, and kept his eyes on the front door. He had put his phone away because he had no trouble seeing now. Between the headlights coming through the thin sheets and towels covering the windows and the bright light from the middle room upstairs, there was enough light. Directly across from him was an empty sitting room. He was within reach of the front door. He could see the bathroom down the hall and a side entrance to the kitchen.

Confirming no one was about, Finn inched to the door and tried to throw the lock. It was old and would have made too much noise if he tried to open it, so he let it be. The risers on the staircase were steep and worn and were a straight shot to the second floor. Finn hoped that whatever was happening out front was keeping Marbles so busy he wouldn't hear his approach – an approach he suddenly couldn't begin.

For all Finn's resolve, he found himself paralyzed. He hands shook and he fell back against the entry hall wall, twirling into the dining room. His heart pounded and raced, his soft hands went slack, and he lost his grip on his weapon. His own sweat chilled him while the vest weighed him down. Finn let go of his gun with one hand and wiped his palm against his jeans. He did the same with the other hand.

He had not fired his weapon since he had drawn it in that alley in self-defense and killed a fellow officer. That rogue officer would have beaten both him and a homeless man to death had he not been stopped. Finn had never meant to kill him; he only meant to warn him. Yet kill the officer he had. Now another cop lay wounded – possibly dead – in the front yard of a dilapidated house, face down on the scruff of lawn, watched over by a hellish animal, and Finn, the man who could save her, was choking. In Finn's mind the two officers were one and the same in that the fault for their deaths would always be his. He put his head back against the wall, closed his eyes and prayed for strength. He prayed for Officer Shay and then he vowed that his indecision would not be the difference between Shay living or dying.

Weapon firmly in hand, his heart slowing to match his steps, Finn took the stairs one step at a time. Through the front windows the pink light of dawn was creeping slowly behind him and shading the upstairs a pretty shade of gray. He could see that the risers were worn, the middle of each one sagged and the wood was dull with wear. Finn walked the edges, his back to the far wall, straining for his first look at the second floor. When got to it, his gut wrenched.

Three men and a woman, bound and gagged, were propped up against the wall between two doorways. Each had been beaten. Two had perfect pistol shots in the middle of their foreheads and two had their heads nearly taken off with the blast of a shotgun. Another man lay on his stomach at the entrance to the room where Marbles kept his murderous watch. That man's feet stuck out into the hallway.

Finn clicked down a step when he heard Marbles walking, following the pattern, angry words bursting out of his mouth only to be swallowed back. Finn eased down a bit as the man came toward the hall, pivoted sideways, changed course, and returned to the window. Marbles would stay there for a good forty-five seconds if the pattern held. Finn raised his head and took the next stair. He took the next one and the next one, breathing easier as he put his foot on the landing. That was a mistake. He had not tested it to see what weight it would bear and as the boards groaned everything went to hell.

Marbles rushed to the hall, screaming profanities and God knew what else as he jumped over the body sprawled in the doorway. He went up on the balls of his feet, raised his shotgun and swung wide; pointing it at the dead as if he assumed one of them still lived. Finn dropped to one knee, trying to commit to memory the important things he saw, but only the sawed-off shotgun and the pistol in the man's belt were relevant. Finn raised his gun, hoping to get a drop on the man but Marbles had a sixth sense. He swung toward Finn, landing with his feet wide and his shotgun steadied against his hip with both hands. The minute their eyes met, Finn froze. Nothing could have prepared him for what he saw.

The man was lean like a wolf and fearless of the person who had come into his den. Finn's eyes bore into his, looking for a clue as to his intentions, but there was nothing to see and that put the detective at a deadly disadvantage. Corner-to-corner, top to bottom, those orbs were inky black, as if Marbles had shuttered himself away from the world. Finn dropped down a step, fell to his stomach, spread his legs, and anchored his feet to the riser below for leverage. He called:

"Police! Drop your weapon."

The shotgun did not drop. Seconds of silence ticked by until suddenly Marbles laughed. He laughed despite the dead man sprawled at his feet and the people lined up like broken, discarded dolls against the wall. The sound of that laughter enraged Finn. He pushed against the stair just enough to lift his shoulders. The barrel of his gun went through the spindled railing and was steadied by the lip of the floor above. He aimed at the man's chest intending to kill him because this was not an alley on a dark night. There was no moral dilemma here. This was about justice for innocents and Finn O'Brien was going to dispense it. He pulled the trigger, but his aim was off, and the bullet tore into the man's shoulder, shattering the bone, ripping through the muscle.

In that split second the world was filled with noise: the blast of Finn's gun, the thud of the bullet hitting flesh, the screams of the wounded man as he fell, the frantic calls from outside as the officer in charge directed his people.

Finn was up the stairs, kicking away the rifle, planting his boot on the man's chest as he holstered his own weapon. He tore the handgun out of Marbles' waistband and threw it aside. When he went to search Marbles' pockets, the bastard dared to grab Finn's leg and try to fight. Finn yanked away and put his boot to the man's palm. He heard the crack of bones. He saw the blood gushing from the man's shoulder, staining the old wood floor. He saw Marbles writhing and the man's mouth open to scream. Finn saw everything as if it were a nightmare and Marbles the monster. The man was tatted head to toe: cheeks, lips, eyelids, ears, neck, arms. Every inch of exposed skin was covered with angry words and demon images. The man's shaved head was not spared. There were piercings in his ears. Two of them were threaded with gold rings and one studded with a diamond.

It was only when Finn realized that the hand under his foot was beginning to feel like jelly, that he snapped out of it and went to work. He searched every inch of the bastard, his hands going up and down Marble's legs and into the pockets of his jeans. He flipped Marbles onto his stomach and yanked his arms behind him, taking great pleasure in the man's howls when the cuffs were ratcheted a click tighter than necessary. He raised his voice and read the vile thing his rights. Then the detective left him lying in his own blood on the floor and stepped back intending to go to the window to give Sergeant Van a sign that it was secure in the house. He never made it to the window. Through all the noise inside and out, Finn heard a sound coming from the next room down. Drawing his gun once again, he went around Marbles:

"Who's in that room? Who, you bastard?" Finn hissed.

But Marbles only cursed and wailed and demanded that he call a doctor, so Finn left him and crept down the hall to the closed door without knowing what he would find. He put his hand on the knob and determined that it wasn't locked. Listing to the right, he was barely breathing as he turned that knob in full and threw the door open. It swung wide, banging against the wall as he fell back, out of the line of fire. When nothing happened, Finn split-stepped in the doorway, arms locked as he went into the room, keeping his back to the wall. He flipped the light switch and an overhead glowed lemony yellow, not bright enough to blind him but bright enough to see the room was bare of furniture. He targeted twelve o'clock. He snapped to three o'clock. He had his sights on nine o'clock. Finn covered every corner of the room and in the last one he saw what had made the noise that caught his ear.

Two children, bound, gagged, and beaten, were lying on the floor. Their dark eyes were frantic and bright with fear. Their little bodies were bound in such a way that, had they not moved, he would have mistaken them for trash.

Had anyone asked Finn what happened next, he would not tell the truth because what he did was wrong. He did not go for the children, gather them up and comfort them. He did not loosen their bonds. He did not check their wounds. He did not call out to Sergeant Van. Instead Finn strode back to Marbles, stepped over him and grabbed up the shotgun he had kicked away when the man went down. Finn took a knee and grabbed Marbles' face. He pressed his fingers hard into the man's cheeks until his lips opened. Marbles tried to snap his head back and shake Finn off, but the detective's fingers were like a vice, holding the skintight against the sharp teeth beneath it. Marble's drooled and bled and made guttural sounds of terror as Finn shoved the barrel of the sawed-off shotgun into his mouth.

"Look at me," Finn growled as the fingers of his right hand tightened on the trigger and the left ones pinched Marbles' ink stained face harder.

He could do it and no one would be the wiser. He could say Marbles took his own life and everyone would believe it because of who Finn was and because of who Marbles was. There would be no contest.

"Look at me!" Finn shouted, knowing God would thank him for sending this man to hell. "Look at me because I'll be the last boyo you see before you stand for judgment."

But when the man did as he was told, when those black eyes met Finn O'Brien's ice blue ones, the detective went limp. With a groan, he fell away. The barrel of the shotgun slid out of the man's mouth. Finn sat upon the floor, the gun in his lap, cradled in his arms like a baby as his heart drained of hatred.

Marbles would live because the one thing Finn wanted – to see fear in this man's eyes before he left the world – was the one thing he could not have. There was nothing to see in those ink-stained orbs.

Nothing.

CHAPTER 5

KTLA News Anchor, Wendy Walsh: *We turn now to John Jordon, on the scene of a brutal multiple murder that was allegedly committed by a member of the Hard Time Loco gang. John, what are you hearing?*

John Jordon (adjusting earpiece): *Wendy, this is one of the most gruesome crimes I have covered in all my time in Los Angeles. Four alleged illegal immigrants were murdered inside this house you see behind me. Usually a quiet neighborhood, it seems that there has been major gang activity of late but those who live here were afraid to tell the police about their concerns. I don't have much for you except that one police officer is severely wounded, four illegal immigrants are dead, and two children were found in the house. I'm hearing that there was another man who has yet to be identified except by his gang affiliation. I'll be following this one closely. More details when I have them.*

KTLA News Anchor, Wendy Walsh: *Thank you, John. That is a sad story to start the morning with. Once again, we have to shine a light on the vulnerability of immigrants coming to our country. The California Attorney General has filed suit against the federal government in a bid to declare*

*the entire state of California a sanctuary. The legislature be-
lieves that this will allow those undocumented immigrants
to come forward without fear of reprisal when crimes are
committed against them. But the debate about the constitu-
tionality of such a move is heated. As a sanctuary state, California stands to lose millions of dollars in federal funding
that accounts for twenty-two point five percent of the hard
goods spending budget of the LAPD, funding that includes
weapons, bulletproof vests, body cameras, and cars. We
have reached out to both Mayor Post and Governor Munie,
but their community relations staffs decline to comment
given the pending lawsuit. The LAPD public information
officer also declined comment.*

(turning to another camera, smiling brilliantly)

*Next up, cats! One lucky woman tells how her feline
friend chose the numbers that won her a pile of cash in the
lottery. So, grab your morning coffee and stay with us.*

The man rose at three-thirty as he always did and was
in his truck by four-thirty. He never remembered exactly
what happened between the moments his eyes opened and
the time he found himself sitting behind the wheel of his
truck, but there were things he could assume. He could
assume that he had dressed himself because he had clothes
on. He could assume that he had shaved because he could
feel the sting of the razor on his face. He could assume
that he had put in the eye drops that the doctor said would
make a difference because his milky eye felt wet. He had
put food into his stomach because it felt full.

The man looked at the clock inside the cab and was
not surprised to see that it read four thirty-two. He had
been dressed and shaved every day for twenty years by
four-thirty in the morning. For all the years after that, the

extra two minutes were needed for the eye drops and the salve that was put on the long, tight scars at the side of his mouth, the dentures that must be adhered properly, and, of course, the many pills he had to swallow. So, like Groundhog Day, here he was again.

In the truck.

Hands by his side.

A little confused.

A little astonished.

And, like every other day, the confusion passed, and he got to work.

First, he looked at the maps. There were three of them: a detailed county map, a map of the Los Angeles park systems and a surveyor's map that showed rights of way, utilities, and such. Each of the maps had circles and crosses on them. He used a red marker to identify places to explore and green ones to mark those places he had seen and rejected. He used a black marker to draw the crosses on the work sites. The crosses were very important because his memory wasn't what it used to be. The crosses reminded him of where he had been, what he had done, and they reminded him not to go there again even though the temptation was great. To return to those places would be both slothful and dangerous. The beauty of his work was that it flew under the radar: a body here, a body there, a mark, a cross. *Don't go back.* Don't create a cluster because a cluster improved the chances that someone would take notice. *Take caution. Take care.* That was how he must proceed if he were to continue his work. He took a green marker, made two circles on the county map, and folded it neatly, circle side up for easy reference. The other two maps he put in the envelope and then he put the envelope in the glove box.

The next thing he did was open the Bible that was always on the seat next to him. He read Galatians 6:7 *Do not be deceived: God is not mocked, for whatever one sows, that he will also reap.* That was so true. These souls he sought out were reaping what their brothers had sewn. Pity, but someone had to pay. Then he took up his journal and wrote a bit.

Finally, he pulled down the visor above the steering wheel and there they were, the men he never wanted to forget. He tried to remember their names. Eventually he would and then their names would be lost again in the night. Some of the men in the pictures had beautiful black hair, and others had shaved their heads. Some had wide eyes and others narrow. None of them smiled but some smirked. All of them were young and oh-so-healthy. Yes, every morning it was like meeting them again. The one thing he never forgot was what they had done. When he was finished looking, the man flipped up the visor and he turned the key in the ignition.

He drove away not having spoken to a living soul.

It was four fifty-two in the morning.

Right on schedule.

* * *

Finn O'Brien watched cops cordon off the house and the yard. He watched the coroner's van load the last of the bodies, and he watched a forensic team skitter about with bags and brushes. He took note of the people who had come from surrounding houses to watch before they tired of the show and went back to bed. A social worker took charge of the children. Finn heard her say that, thankfully, the children weren't badly harmed. Bruises, really. Contusions. Finn thought to point out that being tied up like pigs and beaten by a man who looked like Lucifer and having, perhaps, watched their parents being killed might be considered harmful, but he did not.

Two ambulances had left long ago. One held Officer Shay who, though not dead, was hanging on by an angel's hair strung between heaven and earth. Her partner was by her side. In the other ambulance was Marbles. A third had arrived for the children. Steve Van came up beside Finn.

"He's going to be make it, O'Brien."

"More's the pity," Finn murmured.

"He'll get the death penalty. The trial's only a formality," Van said and Finn snorted.

"This is California. The man will live like a king while the appeals go on for thirty years." Finn reached for the straps on his vest. "He'll die of old age and have been housed grandly at the taxpayers' expense while you and I shall die with our pitiful pensions."

Finn pulled the vest off and handed it back to Officer Van who passed it into the car, exchanging it for Finn's jacket.

"So there's no real justice," Van said, understanding the need for O'Brien to get the bad taste out of his mouth. "At least you dealt out a little tonight."

"Not as much as I would have liked," Finn replied as he put on his jacket. "I'll be upstairs if you need me."

"You sure you don't want the EMTs to look at that before they take the kids in?"

Finn looked down at his hand. He had almost forgotten about it. It hurt like the dickens. After granting Marbles his life and before taking the children down the stairs, Finn had taken a moment to put his fist into a door. The door was of poor quality and that fist of his had gone straight through, the splinters scraping and cutting him as he pulled it out.

"No. Nothing broken. I've work to do. Thanks all the same." Finn started off for the house, but Officer Van stopped him.

"He's scum, O'Brien. You really should have killed him."

Finn lifted the edge of his lips. What was there to say to that? Admit Van was right or debate a man who had seen one of his officers go down? No one would win so Finn raised his hand and turned one way. Supervising Officer Van shrugged and turned the other way.

For three and half more hours Finn walked through the house. He had already made meticulous notes in his little book: measurements of the hallway where the dead people's sightless eyes had watched him come and go, squat and stand. He noted the positions of the bodies with a caveat that he had stumbled on the woman accidentally. Whatever evidence was taken from her body would be contaminated by the contact, but it wasn't to be helped. He picked up the cigarette butts from the bedroom – all sixteen of them. There were ten downstairs. If Marbles had smoked them all, he had been in that house a good long time. Perhaps the D.A. could add assault with a deadly tobacco weapon to the list of charges.

The man lying in the doorway of the middle bedroom was also tatted, a *compadre* of Marbles Finn imagined. Fingerprints would tell. The only question was why had Marbles killed him? Then Finn thought again. If Marbles was as crazy as Sergeant Van said, why not kill a friend? Crazy knows no boundaries and needs no reason. Downstairs Finn looked under the mattresses and went through the clothes but found little to help him identify the dead people upstairs. He noted the address of the house and would find out who owned it.

He knocked on neighbors' doors. Few opened them and, of those that did, fewer still had anything to say. When Finn finished for the morning, he took a moment and looked at the house. Finn wondered why it hadn't been a man like Marbles standing in the way of his bullet that long-ago night? If that had been the case Finn would not have been reviled by his fellow officers and he would not have lost his wife. He knew that was a selfish thought and there was no excuse for it except that man was flawed and Finn was a man.

In need of a shower, food, and time alone to make peace with what he had seen and done; Finn O'Brien left the crime scene. It was eight when he passed Kimiko's house. Her drapes were open, and he could see her in the kitchen. Her blind daughter, Junko, was at the piano and the music she played was beautiful. The kitten that had started showing up in the wee hours each morning, seeming to belong to no one, crossed Finn's path and he gave it a little pat. His downstairs neighbor had opened the curtains but there seemed to be no one home. The sky had turned a lovely shade of blue; the clouds were high and fluffy. That meant it would be a beautiful day in Los Angeles. Finn intended to sleep through the best of it. Unfortunately, his plans were not meant to be.

When Finn turned the corner to take the outside staircase that led to his apartment, he saw a woman with a child in her arms sitting on the top step, waiting for him.

CHAPTER 6

KTLA Weather, 9:00 a.m.: *It's going to be mild in the greater Los Angeles area today. Temperatures only reaching the high eighties in the valley. The commute is moving but get on the road fast because there's work on the shoulder of the 405 between Wilshire and Skirball exits starting at eleven. Have a good one, Angelenos!*

Finn braced himself against the tile wall in front of him: arms out, one leg back, the other crooked, head down like a sprinter ready to bolt as soon as the starter pistol popped. But he could no more run through the tiled shower wall than he could transport himself to the moon which was where he would prefer to be rather than in his own apartment with Amber Anderson and her son, Tucker, waiting for him in the living room. He turned the water to cold and put his back to it so that the frigid spray stung his shoulders and the top of his head. Gritting his teeth, he put his face under the spray and stood there until he could stand it no longer. Finn shut off the water and shook himself off like a dog. He was more awake than he had been twenty minutes ago, and he could only hope it was enough to get him through whatever trouble Amber brought with her.

Finn grabbed his towel, rubbed himself down and then wiped away the moisture from the mirror to see if he looked passably human. Passably was the key word since looking back at himself was a dodgy bloke if he ever saw one: pale at the gills, eyes dull, the scars upon his neck and shoulders shriveled. He dared not look any lower to see the damage done to the family jewels given the cold-water blast he had subjected himself to, so he wrapped a towel around his waist, opened the door cautiously, did not spy Amber and made his bedroom with a short sprint. The only thing that was going to bring him back to the land of the living was sleep and food. Sleep was out of the question now that Amber was there. Food was also questionable since he couldn't remember what was in the refrigerator. He was just stepping into his jeans, pulling on a Tee-shirt when he heard:

"You about done in there?"

Finn closed his eyes and shook his head. Amber took him to task in the same way Cori did: sharply, surely, even if she had no right to do so. In answer to her question, he opened the door and went into the living room hoping that whatever hit was coming his way would be quick and painless.

* * *

The *shoji* screens just behind the sofa and in front of the corner windows glowed pale gold and that, in turn, made the pitiful furniture in Finn's abode look quite inviting. In the kitchen – a small efficient room in which there was a tiny table and two chairs – two mugs were set out, coffee was brewing, and Amber was searching the cabinets. Tucker had been let loose to play as he pleased. He was currently under the table near the door where the mail sat, unopened.

"There's no sugar nor cream, miss," Finn said. "You're lucky to be finding coffee."

He walked toward the toddler, drew him up with both hands, held him high and gave him a shake. Tucker giggled as he swiped at Finn's chin.

"And you, my wee man, will be pulling the table over on you so let's sit somewhere else."

He deposited Tucker on the floor near the coffee table – a solid structure – and gave the boy a stack of coasters to amuse himself. Finn settled on the sofa, laid back his head and put one hand upon his brow. He didn't have long to rest. Amber was on a schedule and he was expected to get on the train.

"Here."

He raised his head, looked up at her and then at the coffee she was holding out to him. He wrapped both hands around the mug and thought he had never made coffee that smelled so good. After a long drink, he sat up and leaned his forearms on his thighs, holding the mug between his knees. He said:

"Thank you. 'Twas a long night."

"You're welcome," Amber answered back. He noted that she didn't apologize for surprising him nor did she catch the hint about his long night. Instead, she looked around the apartment with a critical eye.

"Little light on furniture."

"I wasn't planning on staying long when I moved in," Finn answered.

"Maybe it's time to change up that plan," she said.

"I'll get around to it." He had no wish to discuss his private matters with her. She wasn't interested anyway.

The girl was itchy and as anxious as a dog circling before it settled in.

"So, what brings you here this time of morning?" he asked, hoping to hurry her along.

Amber wasn't listening. She had taken the easy chair that was kitty corner to him and was attempting to scoot the chair closer to the couch. When she found it too heavy, she gave up with a huff, kissed Tucker on the head, and plopped herself on the end of the sofa opposite Finn. She wore a tee-shirt that was too big for her and jeans that seemed too small. On her feet were purple flip-flops with little jewels running up the thongs. Her toenails were painted a creamy yellow. Finn thought she smelled of pepperoni, sunscreen, and baby lotion.

"Is Cori alright?" he asked.

"Why wouldn't she be?" Amber tilted her head and her hair rippled against her shoulders.

"Sure, I'm thinking that's why you're here."

Amber said, "Mom's fine. Tucker's fine. I'm fine."

"Then I'm happy to hear it."

Finn set his coffee aside. He cocked one knee up and put an elbow on the back of the sofa. He rested his head on his upturned hand and set her a look with blue eyes that were a bit faded from lack of sleep but still sharp enough to see clearly.

The girl was a beauty, to be sure. Blue eyes of a deeper blue than his, long straight blonde hair that shined the way a young girl's will. Her face was oval, her eyes almond shaped, wide and long lashed. Her lips were generous and naturally pink. Had he been a man of a different sort, it would have been unwise for her to be sitting as she was, her long legs tucked beneath her, her fingers twining about one another, her teeth biting just at the edge of her lips.

But Finn was not that sort of man. Because he was not, he saw something that would have stopped any man from his wayward thoughts: what had brought Amber to him was serious. She had looked this way in the hospital when Cori had been beaten and left for dead in a restaurant in Little Ethiopia. Amber had found a deep strength then and it had triumphed over her fear. This morning strength was once again trumping fear, but the fear was still there – and so was something else. Amber was as tired. Something had kept her up at night, invading her dreams and making her sleep restless. It was then a thought occurred to Finn that made him drop his hand and sit up straighter; it was a thought about the one thing that would make her desperate enough to seek him out and not her mother.

"Amber, you're not here to tell me you're in the family way, are you?"

"Oh, lord. Really? That's the first thing you thought?"

Amber rolled her eyes; she shook her head and put her mug on the table beside his. When she sat back, she gave him a look of such disdain that Finn would have laughed had he not feared she would do him bodily harm.

"No, the first thing I thought was of your mother. This was the second thing I thought," he said.

"Well, screw you, Finn. One mistake and you'll paint me with that brush forever." Amber got off the couch and sat on the floor opposite him, her legs crossed. Tucker toddled over and she scooped him up and set him in the leg-nest she had made. "How would you like it if people kept calling you a cop killer until the day you died?"

Finn took her point. In the literal sense, that label was correct so he couldn't object to it. He may not like it, he may be sorry that it cost him his wife, but he would prefer the label fade and peel away from him.

Finn admitted. "I do not like it."

"Fine. Then we're on the same page."

She leaned over and reached over her purse. Tucker giggled and tried to crawl up into her arms. Like a mama bear with her cub, she put him in his place and held tight while she dragged her purse close, opened it, took something out. Before she showed Finn what it was, she said:

"Sorry about the divorce. I really am."

"Thank you," he said.

"She's an idiot, so I'm not sorry you're rid of her. I'm sorry because I know that it hurts to be left." Amber flipped her hair. "Anyway, I need your help."

"Sure, I doubt I can do anything for you that your mother couldn't do. I'm not one to be knowing about the difficulties of young women," Finn answered.

"Don't worry. This is right up your alley." Amber looked at what she had taken from her purse and then she slapped it down on the table in front of Finn, nearly bending Tucker in half as she did so. "My friend is missing. I need you to find him."

Finn looked at the picture from where he sat. When he didn't move, Amber nudged it closer until he had no choice but to pick it up. It was a photo of her and a young man. She looked the happy and healthy golden girl. The young man was the yin to her yang; black haired, dark skinned, and a bit older than she. Their faces were close together; the picture was taken from an angle that was easily identified as a selfie. While Amber smiled brilliantly, the young man looked straight into the camera. Defiant? Angry? Unhappy? Protective? Cautious? Finn couldn't tell. The one thing he knew from looking at this picture was that the California goddess, Amber Anderson, was fooling with the wrong mortal.

CHAPTER 7

"His name is Pacal Acosta. I wrote his name on the back of the picture. He's twenty-two. I put that on there, too."

Amber waved a finger his way. Tucker grabbed for it. Not wanting to be distracted, she set him aside. Finn turned the photograph over. Her handwriting was neat, that of a girl who had paid close attention in school. She had also added his height and weight.

"I know those things are important for an investigation, but I think the picture is the most important. He's been gone…"

"Amber. Amber," Finn stopped her. "I can't just investigate something on your say so – especially a missing person. It doesn't work that way."

"But you have to. He hasn't been at work for three days," she insisted. "I know something is really wrong."

"This friend works with you, then?"

"Yes," she said, calmer but hardly relaxed. "He started about six months ago and bussed tables. He hasn't missed a day in six months. He works other jobs too. You know, day labor. I've never seen anyone work so hard. And now he's just gone. Disappeared."

"Have you asked your boss if the boy has called in?"

"He hasn't. Mr. Romero is so mad he doesn't want to talk about it. He's been bussing himself when we're busy. I've been doing my own tables, trying to pick up the slack so Mr. Romero won't notice so much, but he does. I don't think he'll give Pacal his job back if we don't find him soon."

"If, as you say, he's an ambitious sort then maybe he took another job. Or maybe he was just tired of picking up dishes—"

"Stop it. Stop it," Amber wailed. "He would have quit the right way if he found another job. That's the kind of guy he is."

"Then maybe you should check with his family. A girlfriend. Have you seen—"

"Oh, give me a friggin' break, Finn."

Amber scrambled up, standing so abruptly it took Finn aback. She took a breath and then two. They came so quickly upon one another they sounded like a sob. But if the girl was going to cry, she wasn't going to do it now and she certainly wasn't going to do it in front of him.

"Are you dense? I'm his girlfriend, Finn. If he got a better job, he would have told me. Me." She put both her hands to her heart. She held them away and then let them fall against her chest again as if she were patting that heart back in place before it fell out onto the floor and broke.

"Ah," he said and then once again. "Ah, I see. And your mother doesn't know."

"I didn't want to tell her until Pacal had enough money to move us out. He wanted to show her that he was a good man who could take care of us."

In that moment Amber looked small and vulnerable

and much younger than her eighteen years. Her son was tugging at her leg, but Amber just stood there as if she too wished she had a leg to tug on, a stronger human being to lift her up in her time of woe. She was trying to make that wish come true, and Finn had drawn the short straw. It was his leg she was tugging at. They both knew Cori would have blown her stack if Amber confessed to loving a busboy, a boy who stood on corners as a day laborer, a boy who…

"Pacal is a good guy." Amber's chin went up. "He is honorable. He wouldn't just walk out. He would have let us – me – know."

For a second, they looked at one another, the only sound in the room was Tucker's cooing and babbling. Finally, Finn waved her over to the couch. She didn't move so he pointed until Amber sat down. She crossed her arms, but she lowered her eyes. Finn decided the miss was not quite as confident as she believed herself to be.

"All right, then," Finn said. "Alright?"

Amber gave him a slight nod to thank him for his time, his patience and for not dismissing her out of hand. It was slight enough, though, that he understood she would not be there unless she was desperate.

"Please. Look for him. Find him for me, Finn." She raised her pretty, blue eyes and there were tears on the tips of her long lashes.

"The place to start is with his family. Does he have family?" Amber nodded. Finn went on. "Then it is for them to file a report. If they haven't done that, then it could be because they know he's not missing." Finn paused and then asked. "Do they know about you, Amber?"

She shook her head. "Not really. I mean, yes, but we haven't met. I'm pretty sure they know I exist."

Finn breathed deep. Romeo and Juliet on their way to a no good end was what this was. Cori didn't know about Pacal and Pacal's family didn't know about Amber, Finn was sure of it. Or maybe it was simpler than that. Maybe Amber wasn't important enough to mention to his family. Perhaps Pacal had his way with her and then had enough of her. Hadn't he heard Cori talk about her daughter often enough for him to know that she put her faith in men too quickly.

"It doesn't matter if they know about me or not. They wouldn't report him missing," she insisted. "I'm the only one who can get help. Why can't I file a report?"

"You can, but it would get no further than filing for a good long while. You have no standing, Amber. You're not family. He's an adult. You're not living together and—"

"And mom might find out." Amber finished for him.

"There is that," Finn answered.

"So that's why I need you to just look for him off the record," Amber said. "I know you can do that. It's not like you haven't broken a few rules before."

Finn rubbed his jaw, ignoring her comment, weighing his options. He looked at the picture. The boy was young and handsome and had obviously turned Amber's head, but he clearly had nothing to offer her – not even a family who would lift a finger for him.

"I'm needing to be at work, Amber."

Finn got up, walked behind the sofa, and put his hand on her shoulder. She turned her face up to him. If this was what it felt like to be a father, Finn was glad not to be one. To have a young girl look to you with such hope made a man understand his limitations. He wished he could do something for her, but he couldn't do what she was asking.

"Leave it be. That would be my best advice. Leave it

to his family."

For a moment Amber stared at him. Her bottom lip quivered and then just as quickly steel came into her eyes, but he missed it. He was already headed to the door to see her out when she shot off the couch, took the picture from the table and flew at him. Amber grabbed his arm.

"Look. Look at this picture." She held it in front of his eyes, but all Finn saw was that her fingers were trembling.

"What, Amber? What is it you're wanting from me?" Finn pulled his arm away. "I have looked, and I don't know what it is you want me to do? The boy has gone off."

"No. He hasn't gone off and don't tell me he isn't worth looking for or worrying about. He is not some lazy little shit. He's not a criminal. He's sweet and kind and treats me nicer than any guy I've ever known," she cried. "His family won't report him missing because they can't. He's illegal. They are all from Guatemala and they are illegal. Get it?"

"Oh, lord, Amber," Finn groaned.

"Don't you oh lord me, Finn. I could get that from my mother," she snapped. "I don't know any boys like him. I don't know anyone as brave. He rode a train for three weeks. Half the time he was hanging on to the top. And he had nothing to eat...and his mother..."

Amber stopped talking. With each word her head lowered, her words were lost in the breath that was getting harder to take. Her shoulders shook. Her long hair fell over her shoulders and hid her face, but she did not let loose of the picture nor did she crumble under the weight of her emotions. When she raised her head again, she was defiant for both of them.

"His father left four years after they got here. He came first with Pacal's older brother and then Pacal and his mother and his little sister came. Pacal was only ten then. His mother had two more kids so there are five kids altogether. I know the oldest doesn't live at home. I know Pacal took care of his mother and brothers and sisters. He loves them. I'm lucky he loves me. He does, Finn. We haven't even slept together because he wants to marry me first. He would not leave his family after all they've been through. He would not leave me."

"Alright. Come on now, Amber." Finn covered her hand with his, careful not to crease the photograph that meant so much to her. Amber pulled away but she didn't move far. She wanted him to know everything and the story tumbled out of her mouth because it had been held in too long.

"His mom cleans houses. The little kids go to school. Pacal lost his job at a restaurant in East L.A. when it closed, and he came to work at Romero's. Then he started doing day work on the weekends and in the mornings before he had to be at the restaurant. I don't even know when he slept. He took every last cent back to his family.

"I don't know where to find his family, but you could figure it out. You could find Pacal, too. That's all I want. Maybe he's sick and in a hospital or maybe he got arrested by mistake. Or maybe ICE picked him up. Whatever it is, it has to be awful if he hasn't called me. Can you imagine how scary it must be for his mother? My mom would be crazed if she didn't know where I was." Amber stopped talking. The mention of Cori brought her back to her plan, a precise plan that included a promise from Finn. "You can't tell my mom any of this. Okay? Not until we know Pacal's all right. You have to promise. Okay?"

"Oh no, Amber. I'll not be lying to your mother."

Finn shook his head. What she was asking was against everything he knew to be right and good. He did not want to be a conspirator. His loyalty was to his partner, to Cori, to all the things that would keep her from harm including harming her relationship with her daughter. He tried again to reason with her.

"Look, there's no reason to tell your mother anything. Pacal is probably a fine young man but he lives in a shadow world, my girl. Is that what you want for yourself? For Tucker? No, you must move on. You must..."

Finn's words trailed off. Amber's head swung slowly back and forth as she laughed softly to herself. When she realized he wasn't talking anymore, she looked up with those beautiful, exhausted and now disappointed eyes of hers.

"I'm sorry for you, Finn. You just don't understand about real love."

"No, Amber," he said. "I don't understand why you would put yourself in this position."

"I'm not in a 'position'. We care about each other," she said. "It's that simple. He wouldn't have left me without saying goodbye; he wouldn't have left me without a good reason, and I can't live not knowing what happened to him. I seriously can't live that way."

With that she walked into Finn and laid her head on his shoulder. Finn's arms rose to hold her away, but when she started to weep, he patted the air around her shoulders instead. He was afraid to touch her and afraid not to. Certainly, he had no idea what the best in such a situation would be, and certainly he was now in a situation.

He hadn't promised to stay silent about Amber's problem and yet he knew he would be keeping this conversation to himself. Cori and Amber would both damn him if he breathed a word. He hadn't promised to search for Pacal but he was already thinking of where he could start looking for the boy so that he could give Amber some peace of mind. Yet if he did that, if he actually found Pacal, Finn would have to do something worse than looking for him in the first place. He would have to tell Amber that Pacal had come to a bad end or he had left her. Neither would be welcome news.

He closed his eyes and, as Amber stood against him weeping, Finn's jumbled thoughts went to his long dead brother, Alexander. The little boy had waited for Finn to pick him up from school on a sunny day and met his end in the dark of night at the hands of a person who had never been found. Now here was another mother's son missing. Perhaps, this was Finn's chance to make things right for the sin of forgetting his brother.

Before he could consider that this was Fate stepping into his life, Tucker began to cry because his mother was. Amber, hearing her child's wails, turned to him. Finn watched, helpless in the face of such sadness. Then he thought to comfort Amber by telling her that she was wrong. You can live without knowing what happened to someone you love. He had done it for years.

Luckily, he was a sensible man and kept his mouth shut.

CHAPTER 8

"Aren't you just the talk of the rodeo, O'Brien? Takin' down a truly bad dude all by your lonesome. Bravo."

Cori swept into the office at one o'clock. She tossed her purse on the table she used as a desk and whipped her chair out, turned it backward and straddled it. She wore a blue jacket and a white turtleneck top. Her pants were grey and the earrings peeking out from under her cascading hair were gold hoops. When Finn didn't respond, she tapped his desk with one long fingernail and asked:

"You doin' okay, partner?"

Finn lifted his eyes, paused his writing, and smiled at her. That was not the easiest thing to do because when he looked at her he saw Amber, and when he saw Amber all he could think about was the secret he was keeping from his partner.

"Thank you, Cori, I'm good. A little tired."

"How long have you been here?" she asked.

"Not long." He went back to his paperwork as he said, "I went home for a bit."

"You should have stayed there," Cori clucked. "Given

your court date and what went down last night, the captain would have understood."

"I'll be saving the favor for when I really need it. Besides, it wasn't just me that got everything under control last night. Everyone did a fine job. Very solid."

"I heard you were epic. I think I would have killed him after what he did to Shay. God that was cold." Finn wrote. Cori waited and then she got tired of waiting. "Okay, then. I might as well get me a blanket and take a little snooze for as much as I'm getting out of you."

Finn sat back in his chair, taking his pen with him, and passing it through his fingers. Cori often laughed at him saying it took twice the time to write a report his way: first in long hand and then copying it to the computer, but he found the process gave him clarity. Even now, he could hear the growling and snapping of the loathsome animal standing over Officer Shay, straining at its chain, wanting nothing more than to tear her throat out.

Sadly, Officer Shay had not made it. Sergeant Van, upon discovering this, shot the dog that continued to snarl and strain at its chain even in its death throes. Every officer stood and watched. Though no one said a word, they all rejoiced because they needed an eye for an eye. If it couldn't be Marbles, it would have to be the demon dog. Finn would not put that in his report, he would only write that it was necessary to neutralize the animal. He would not put in his report that Marbles was a miserable piece of shit. Finn would point him out as the man suspected of executing three men and a woman, shooting another man in the back and assaulting two children – even though in Finn's mind there was no doubt he had done these things.

Cori plucked Marbles' rap sheet off Finn's desk. She held up the picture for him to see.

"This him?" she asked.

"'Tis," Finn answered without looking at it. "Fine specimen of a human being, don't you think?"

"He looks like an alien. Who tats their eyeballs, for God's sake? Bet his mama's proud." Cori set it aside. "So, you want to go out and get coffee? Maybe head over to Mick's and see Geoffrey?"

"For the love of God, woman, why don't you get a pillow for my head?" Finn laughed without joy. The last thing he wanted was her mothering. He had a pile of guilt about his anger the night before, not to mention Amber's little visit. He hated secrets and now he had two. Finn wanted to tell Cori about his meeting with Amber but to what end? Why put either Amber or Cori in an untenable position when the chances were good that Pacal Acosta would never be found? Finn began to work again.

"Okay, cowboy." She unsaddled from her chair, tired of trying to crack the code that would get him to talk. "I just thought you might want to take a load off."

"No but thank you." Finn didn't raise his eyes. "There is nothing to talk about for now. You can read the report."

"It's your call. Long as you're good to go." Cori almost turned away but then she put her hands flat on the desk and tried once more. "You give me a jingle if you start getting night sweats or anything. I'll give you a shot and a beer and a talking to. You'll be right as rain."

"You're a gnat, Cori," Finn chuckled. "But I appreciate the concern. I truly do."

"Hey, if you can't count on your partner, who can you count on?" She smiled, picked up her chair and righted it. She hung up her jacket and then headed out the door. "You want coffee?"

"No, thanks," Finn said. Before she left, he asked:

"Cori, how is Amber – and Tucker, of course?"

"Fine. Shouldn't they be?" Cori tipped her head and furrowed her brow at the question that came out of the blue.

"No reason," he answered. Silently cursing himself for saying anything at all, he backpedaled. "'Tis only that she did well when you were hurt. I was just thinking about that. She's a fine young woman."

"The apple doesn't fall far from the tree, my friend." Cori gave him a wink and a nod. "But you're right. She kind of grew up. Lately she's been a lot more – I don't know – thoughtful or something."

"Then that's good." Finn stood up and took his jacket off the hook. "I'll walk part way with you."

"Before you finish your paperwork?"

"I'm feeling a bit antsy," he admitted. "Just not talkative."

He stood aside to let Cori out the door first. They went down the hall in silence, listening to the sounds of the precinct getting its second wind after lunch. They parted ways but only Finn went on his. Cori stood in the hallway, watching him, knowing something was amiss and it wasn't just about what happened the night before. She was staring at the door that was closing behind him when Detective Smithson came down the hall and stood beside her.

"Heard your partner pulled a Rambo last night," he said.

"What's it to you?" Cori snapped, remembering the misery this arrogant son of a bitch had caused Finn since the day he stepped into Wilshire Division.

"Geeze, Anderson. He did a good job, that's all. It was clean. Far as I'm concerned, he could take out all of East L.A." The man pushed past her, complaining. "Can't a guy give a compliment around here?"

Cori colored, ashamed of herself for thinking the worst but she was worried about Finn. She knew how he felt about using his weapon. The shooting on top of the divorce was a one two punch that would be hard to take. Cori also knew about 'walking with the black dog'. Depression was an evil thing, and she didn't want him enduring this guy's nonsense too. While she was thinking all this, while she watched Smithson saunter down the hall, he did a pirouette. Never missing a step, he walked backwards and raised his voice and held up his hands. There was a shit-eating grin on his face.

"It's not like I said anything untoward, Anderson. I mean, I could have said, nice sweater. Now that would be a shit thing to say."

He turned around and went on his way, chuckling all the while. Cori went the other way to get her coffee.

"God save me from your Manure, buddy."

CHAPTER 9

APRIL 23
WILSHIRE DIVISION

Captain Fowler: Just a heads up. Force Investigation Division is going to be looking into what went down last night.

Detective O'Brien: No problem, it was by the book, Captain.

Captain Fowler: ACLU attorneys are already on it and they beg to differ. The suspect says he was surrendering. He says you stuck a gun in his mouth and broke his hand after he was down.

Detective O'Brien: (silence)

Captain Fowler: Nothing to say?

Detective O'Brien: If you'll be kind enough to read my report.

Captain Fowler: I have, O'Brien. I just wanted to let you know what's coming your way. They won't be speaking to anyone else because no one was in the house with you.

Detective O'Brien: I'm pretty sure I'll be handling myself in a way that will make you proud.

Captain Fowler: I'm sure you will. **(pause).** It's going to be intense around here until after Cinco de Mayo. **(pause)** And O'Brien?

    Detective O'Brien: Yes, sir?

    Captain Fowler: Job well done.

    Detective O'Brien: Appreciated, Captain.

"So, a few weeks ago, Amber helps me with my profile thingy. I didn't think going on a dating site was a good idea, but then I figure there ain't nobody knockin' down my door as it stands now, so what can it hurt? A cup of coffee? Maybe I'll meet someone interesting. And I'm telling you, O'Brien, interesting men are about as scarce as hen's teeth in the LAPD. I need to branch out. No cops, though. Uh-uh. They are dumb as rocks and dull as my daddy's rusted knife."

Cori had her sunglasses on, her head was back, and her shoes were off. It was the end of the day after and whatever worry she had entertained about Finn was now good and gone. She turned her head to look at him.

"Present company excepted, of course. Oh, and Fowler. Fowler's a keeper. Kind of Harvard meets CSI. Love the way he dresses. So, what do you think?"

"I'm thinking Captain Fowler is a fashion plate, for sure," Finn laughed. "And I'm further thinking to be a wise man and not engage in this conversation."

"Come on," Cori whined. "An opinion. That's all I'm looking for. Are you going to go online and spread your wings a little now that you're free and clear?"

All Cori got for her prodding was that small O'Brien smile. It really wasn't a smile at all but an expression that made him look mischievous and made her feel like his little sister. She gave him a punch in the shoulder, scooted herself up to sitting position and put her shoes back on.

Something had happened in the last months, something good and solid for both of them. Cori would be hard-pressed to put a name to it, but it was like the boat they'd been sailing on had finally reached calm waters and they were comfortable with their stations on deck.

They had been good partners before his troubles, but when those troubles came, she had to distance herself. She had a child and a job to protect. But now they were together, better partners than ever. She and Amber were doing good and all that meant was that she, Cori, could get on with her own life.

"So, are you going to do it?" Cori asked again.

"'Tis a bit early for me to be thinking of dating, Cori."

"Hardly," she said. "And if you keep carrying that torch, you're never going to find a woman who will put up with you."

"I'm carrying no torch," he answered truthfully. "But sure, wouldn't I be doing penance for the next forty years if I didn't at least wait for the official papers before I started dating? No, I think I'll be taking a little time before I inflict myself on another woman."

"Yeah, like you'd be such a hardship," Cori snorted.

"You go first, with my blessing. You always were the brave one," Finn teased.

"I'm taking it slow. I'm starting with Lapinski. He's taking me to dinner tonight."

Finn threw back his head and this time laughed aloud. "Thomas, is it? Our Thomas?"

"You have a problem with that?" Cori asked.

"No, no," Finn snickered, trying hard to control his laughter. As much as he admired the attorney, Thomas Lapinski, and as critical as he had been to their last investigation in Little Ethiopia, he was not the right man for

Cori. "You're playing with fire with Thomas."

"Stop. Stop," Cori demanded. "He's a little shorter than I am—"

"A bit," Finn laughed.

"And he talks a lot—"

"I hadn't noticed," Finn answered.

"And he's a really thoughtful guy in case you forgot how he took care of everything after I got out of the hospital. That's worth giving him a shot."

Cori folded her arms. She wanted to hear no more of Finn's laughter. She was about to start up her defense of Lapinski again when Finn changed lanes and took a hard right on DeLapore off Wilshire.

"And we are going where?" she asked. Finn raised a finger, and her eyes followed his direction to a shopping center anchored by a home improvement store. "What? Your landlady needs someone to fix her hot tub?"

"*Sento*, Cori. *Sento*. It's a spiritual experience to get in that wooden tub. I'd ask her a special favor if you're wanting to try it."

"I don't want to be alone with my thoughts in a place like that. I want to be there with Lyle Lovett."

Finn snorted, "You'll forever be a mystery, Cori."

"To each his own," Cori answered.

It was late in the afternoon, but the big parking lot was three-quarters full. Opposite the home improvement store was a long, squat, nondescript building and Finn parked in front of it. Over the double glass door was a sign that read Labor Ready. In a city where the corners on any major street overflowed with day laborers waiting for work, Labor Ready was a bid to control that transient force. Workers were registered, guaranteed a living wage, provided insurance, and had access to a staff that actually drummed up business. This was not the LAPD's usual stomping ground.

"So? What's the deal?" Cori asked.

"I'm wanting to check on a contact that's gone missing." Finn set the brake.

"Something to do with last night?"

"Maybe. Who knows?" Finn answered.

"I don't think any of the Hard Time Locos are going to be working for ten bucks an hour," Cori scoffed. "Heck, those guys aren't going to be working at all."

"Just a hunch." He took off his sunglasses, opened the car door and said, "I won't be long if you want to stay in the car."

"I'll come." Cori opened her door. "Never been a fan of twiddling my thumbs in a hot car."

Together they walked to the front door. Cori went through first and Finn swung in after. They found themselves in a big room, bare save for the folding chairs set out in eight neat rows of ten chairs each. It would be quite a party should they all be filled, but only two were. Sitting in one chair was a big and burly fellow and in the other a man younger and more fit. Both wore expensive boots and new work clothes. They were no more day laborers than Finn was, and these two were so intent on their paperwork they didn't bother to look up when the detectives came in.

"Doesn't look like there's much ready labor hanging out here," Cori muttered.

"It's late in the day." Finn headed to one of the counter windows. "I'll see if I can raise someone."

Cori gave a nod and went to a bulletin board that ran the length of one wall to see what work might be available in a city that seemed to be perpetually building. Finn looked through the counter window and saw no one. He stepped back and went for the door on the far side of the room. Cori was reading about a project on Genesse Street at the same time Finn knocked and a woman opened the door.

She was neither short nor tall, neither blonde nor brunette, neither happy nor sad. She was slightly curious, perhaps, because Finn O'Brien looked just a tad more interesting than the hundreds of men who came through the door every month. She was dressed with nary a hint of style: slacks, a tee-shirt and a cotton shirt over that. She was a workingwoman who saw the finish line of the day just a few steps ahead of her, so she was quick to get to business.

"We're not taking new registrations until tomorrow." Her eyes shot to the men in the chairs and then back to Finn. "Those two started before three. You have to start before three. Come back before three tomorrow."

Cori had come up behind Finn and the woman's eyes flicked to her, but she wasn't much interested in either of them now.

"Before three." She started to close the door. Finn put out a hand.

"We're not here about work," he said. "I'm Detective O'Brien. This is Detective Anderson. I'm inquiring about a man named Pacal Acosta. Twenty-two years old. Guatemalan."

"The name doesn't ring a bell, but we get hundreds of men through here—"

"I'm sorry," Cori interrupted. "Is there a ladies' room?"

The woman pointed across the way. "Women's is broken but you can use the men's room."

Cori nodded and Finn blessed his good luck. When she was gone, he pulled out the picture Amber had left with him. The woman eyed it.

"No. I don't recognize him," she said. "Frankly, I don't

think he'd be coming in here."

"And why would that be?" Finn asked.

"We're really more like a placement service, so we get the real deal in here now: plumbers, electricians, dry-wallers. Some are even union. There's a lot of building going on, but there are still a lot more tradespeople than there are jobs."

"And how could you tell Pacal wasn't one of them?" Finn asked.

"You want the politically correct version or the honest one?" she laughed.

"Honest, if you'd be so kind," Finn answered.

"I guess it's okay as long as you're not recording me," she said. "That's all I need is someone coming in here trying to trip me up so they can sue for discrimination or get on my case about the poor undocumented workers. That's not what we do here."

Finn opened his jacket and gave her a woeful look. "Not wired for sound."

She chuckled again, crossed her arms, and leaned against the door.

"Look, here's the thing. Times have changed. The ones without papers are nervous. Even if we promise we're not going to call ICE, they don't believe us. If they do agree to register, they give us fake names and addresses and that screws up my reporting. Our whole purpose is to create a decent work environment and hand out some benefits. Forgive me, but one look tells me your guy doesn't have a work permit, visa, or anything close to documentation. Not to mention the people we serve like to have things above board and want their guys to speak English. I've got enough vetted workers to fill every site in L.A., so I wouldn't be sending him out for much anyway."

"I knew it was a long shot, Ms.—"

"Henry."

"Ms. Henry," Finn repeated.

The woman opened her mouth and was about to say something when her eyes flickered the slightest bit. Finn put the picture back in his pocket assuming Cori was returning but it was only one of the men who had finished filling out the paperwork. Finn stepped back. Ms. Henry took the application and gave the man a nod just as Cori appeared. Finn pulled out his card, wrote the name Pacal Acosta on the back and handed it to her.

"If you do cross his path, I'd be appreciating a call," Finn said.

"Don't hold your breath."

They bid her goodbye, and on the way out the door, Cori asked: "Did you get anything?"

"Nothing."

Finn put his sunglasses on and took out his keys, happy that he had made a good faith effort to inquire after Pacal with Cori none the wiser. He would stop for pizza on the way to Mick's and, though it would be a wee bit of an exaggeration, he would tell Amber that he had done his best. He would let her down easy and promise to keep an eye out for Pacal. The days would go by and little by little she would forget him. One day a new love would walk into her life, Pacal would be a memory, and he would be off the hook. By the time they got back to the car Finn was pleased with his plan. He opened the door but rested his arms on the top of the car.

"What do you say? Call it a day or go back and slave another hour?" he asked.

"Let's pack it in. Go take a hot bath in your landlady's magic hot tub," Cori said. "Besides, you've still got to drop me at the car repair shop."

"Just tell me where I'm headed," Finn said.

"Straight down La Cienega to fourth." Cori got into the car. Finn did the same and they were on their way. While Finn drove, Cori called to report that they were off for the day and got their messages in return.

"We've got a call from the lab on the George case, and a return call from the woman in the house next door to where that girl was assaulted over on Bundt Street. Your buddy with the black eyeballs is out of surgery," Cori said. "And social services called. One of those kids from last night is talking."

"You take the children and I'll start off with Marbles in the morning," Finn said.

"Sounds good. Send me whatever you've got, and I'll read it when I get home tonight."

"Unless Thomas keeps you up late."

"He won't be keeping me up that late, I promise."

Cori settled in, smiling, and pleased until they stopped at a light on La Cienega. Out of the corner of his eye Finn saw Cori's head shaking. She had crooked her elbow on the window and was tapping one finger against her lips. He looked to see what had caught her interest. Though it was late in the afternoon, three men were on the corner, lingering there in the hopes of picking up work.

"Poor bastards," she muttered and then raised her voice as she turned away, dropping her arm. "They'd be better off going back where they came from."

"We don't know that, Cori," Finn said. "I'm better off than if I had stayed where I came from."

"Apples and oranges, O'Brien. You got here the right way," Cori sniffed.

"And you're sure they didn't?"

"They wouldn't be standing there hoping for a gig if they had." She cocked her head. "Don't you be looking at me like I'm a red neck bitch on wheels. This is about right and wrong. It's about legal and not legal."

"Nothing is ever that black and white." Finn stepped on the gas, anxious to be away. Looking at those men brought him only guilt for keeping Amber's secret.

"Says you." Cori laughed.

Finn didn't see the humor, but he did understand that Cori was as much a product of her Texas upbringing as Finn was of his Irish immigration experience. His family had been welcomed and yet it had still been hard for them to make their way. For the souls on the corner he could only imagine the true horrors they were escaping. Not just economic downturn, not just a desire to give their children a better future. Most of these people ran from real poverty and corrupt and brutal governments. How could he blame any one of them, yet how could he not condemn them for breaking the laws he was sworn to uphold? Concluding that there was no good answer, knowing this was not their problem to solve, Finn decided all of it was better left to roil in the media and with politicians and ICE. He and Cori would deal with crime on the street and not across any border.

"There it is."

Cori pointed to a sign that read Jerry's Car Repair, Foreign and Domestic. It was a small, grungy place packed with cars in various stages of repair. When traffic allowed, Finn pulled across four lanes and into the driveway. He let the car idle as Cori got herself together.

"Want me to wait?" he asked.

"Naw." Cori released her seatbelt and it snapped into place. "Jerry's always got it ready to go. I'm just not looking forward to the bill."

"Sure, no one ever wants to pay the piper."

"You got that right." Cori opened the door and swung her legs out. Before she closed the door, she stuck her head back inside the car. "You know if you really want to find this guy you should try CHIRLA. Labor Ready is too corporate. If you don't find him at CHIRLA and you really need to track him down, I'll help you hit the corners."

"I won't be going out of my way," Finn said. "Give Thomas my best."

"I will," she said.

"And have a good time."

"I will do that too." She started to close the door, but Finn stopped her. "Cori. I'm just curious. Do you think if a body loves someone who's wrong for them the relationship is doomed?"

"Geeze, O'Brien, I'm standing in the lot of a car repair and you want me to answer something like that?" Her eyes narrowed. "Whoa, wait a minute. You're not thinking I'm hot on Lapinski, are you? It's just dinner…"

"No. No. Just with the talk of dating and such. The divorce, you know," Finn said. "Off the top of your head, what would you be thinking?"

Cori raised one shoulder and tilted her head. "You can't help who you fall in love with, O'Brien. You can only help how you deal with it when you tumble down that well."

She raised an eyebrow, gave him a sweet, soft smile and then Cori Anderson slammed the car door and went off to give Jerry a grilling about her bill.

Finn chuckled a little. Should Cori ever find out about Pacal, he would have a bit of ammunition when she went to war. Finn backed out onto La Cienega and when he passed the corner again, it was empty. The men were gone as if they had never existed.

CHAPTER 10

It was late and the man in the small white truck was frustrated. He had seen the three men on the corner but by the time he doubled back they were gone, giving up on work until the next day. But the next day would be too late. The man in the truck had a timetable and he became anxious when something disturbed it. Anxiety was noticeable. It would be reported. Once it was reported it was so hard to make things right. But it wasn't his fault that he had been late getting back to the city. There had been traffic. They had kept him an extra half hour at work.

He took a deep breath to calm himself. He must do his chore today because the next day he had drawn the mid-day shift at his ridiculous job. A real job they called it. A second chance. Bull.

No illores.

Don't cry.

Se agradecido de que vivirás.

Be grateful you'll live.

He shook those words out of his head and drove a little further, complaining to himself that the city had become too big and unwieldy. He listened to every word he mumbled since no one else did. He was his own best friend; he was the only one who cared about the great pain inside him. His lips moved against teeth that didn't feel right because they weren't his. If he opened his mouth too wide, the scars on the side of his face where his lips had been sewn back together were unbearably painful. And there were the other places on his body that hurt; places too intimate to speak about.

Sometimes he would have flashes of those horrible days and nights. When that happened, when he felt himself starting to shake and tremble, when he felt the ghost pain, he bucked himself up like a man. Nothing hurt as much as humiliation and helplessness and all that was behind him. Now he was in charge.

He was mentally conversing with himself in this manner when he saw them. His mouth went dry and his hands became moist in his excitement. His eyes darted to the traffic that penned him in. People drove like maniacs, slamming on their brakes flipping him off. Him! As if he had done something wrong. Just like before. He had never done anything wrong and still he was blamed.

Before his anger got the best of him, he took a deep breath and amended the conversation in his head. All he had to do was change lanes. There was always a way to get where he was going if he remained calm. His head swung to the right and he saw his opening. It was nothing short of a miracle that he made it across the lanes and coasted to a stop on the side street.

The five men on the corner fell upon the truck. They did this with desperate respect and that pleased the man. If there had been a little respect all those years ago, a little understanding, none of this would be necessary. But one could not rewrite history so here they were, face to face, the tables turned.

The oldest one of the bunch had a deeply lined face, proud eyes, and a fine bearing. Those eyes made the man in the white truck want to laugh. Proud, indeed. Proud of what? He was a speck of dirt, the leader of more specks of dirt. He nodded in greeting. The man in the truck nodded back and then pantomimed like he was shoveling. Two of the men turned away. They did not shovel.

Screw them.

The man's lips barely moved when he dropped his hands and said:

"*Quince dólares la hor*a."

Ah, he had them now. Fifteen dollars an hour was too good to pass up. Even the one with the proud eyes looked hungry for that payday. If they had a brain between them, they would know it was too good to be true; if they looked into his eyes they would know. The proud man held up three fingers and said:

"Go faster. *Tres hombres.*"

He pointed his finger at each man in turn. The man in the truck saw the logic of that and he was tempted. Perhaps if it had been the end of the season, he would have challenged himself and taken two, but it wasn't. He shook his head and the two younger men backed off as the older one went for the passenger door.

"No!"

The man shouted and the pain he caused brought tears to his eyes. He shook his head, shook away the tears, and shook away the anger. Anger would scare them off and this wasn't about anger. It never had been. He pointed to the youngest man, skinny and haunted looking. That one was truly hungry.

The older man stepped back but the young man shook

his head. The driver pulled his thumb toward the back. When the worker hesitated, the older man spoke to him and the younger one nodded and nodded. His eyes went to the truck and then down to the ground again. Finally, the skinny young man agreed. He clambered over the gate and into the bed. He sat among the shovels and stakes and yellow tape. He sat next to a pile of pipes.

The older man stepped back as the truck pulled away, happy that one of them would have money in his pocket soon. The man in the cab looked in the rearview mirror and saw the man in the bed of the truck waving and waving.

Goodbye.

Oh yeah.

Hasta la vista, baby.

* * *

Finn saw no reason to do it, but he did it anyway. He Googled CHIRLA – Coalition for Humane Immigrant Rights, Los Angeles – to determine if there was an office within the boundaries of Wilshire Division. He did this out of curiosity and because the memory of Sister Stella, the fifth-grade teacher in his village school, was bright.

"Ah, Finn O'Brien," the good sister would say. "I will burn God's lessons into your wee soul even if it kills us both."

Sister Stella had won the battle for that soul of his, and his brain, and his conscience and now those lessons were leading him down the path of the better man. A good man, Sister Stella would reason, would make up for the secret he kept from his partner by honoring the unspoken promise made to her daughter.

Finn, being a man of conscience, would not lie by omission or shading to Amber as he had to Cori. Conscience also told him that there were more Coris in the world who looked at the poor souls on the corners and saw an amorphous cloud of humanity than there were people like Amber who were ready to see the one human being in their midst.

So, to keep his soul from going to the hell if he was not charitable, Finn drove himself to the offices of the Coalition for Humane Immigrant Rights, Los Angeles. The place was not so much out of his way as annoying to get to at that time of the day. To him, the name of the establishment was distasteful, a condescending mouthful. The place itself was even worse, filled to bursting as it were with good, sweet, arrogant intentions. It was enough to make one's teeth ache.

The goodness, sweet intentions and arrogance were wrapped up in the person of a man/boy who went by the name of David. He was wound as tight as a spring, ready to fight for his undocumented, downtrodden, illegal men if the LAPD brought that fight to his doorstep. He seemed disappointed when Finn didn't present a challenge to his authority but only showed him the picture of Pacal and asked if he knew the young man's whereabouts.

"Oh, yes. Yes. Of course. Well, let me see."

David reached for the photo. While he took a good look at it, Finn took a good look at him. His hands were parchment white and his fingers long and bony. He wore a short-sleeved shirt, the sleeves of which seemed more like wings fluttering about his reed thin arms. Finally, he flapped the photograph against a fingertip and said:

"No. No. I honestly can't say that I remember him, and I try very hard to know everyone who comes through the door." He gave the picture back. "He's a nice-looking young man. You say he has family?"

"That is my information, but I don't know where to find them."

"And you're not likely to…"

He paused, his attention caught by a man whose presence Finn had registered but not really attended to. He was neatly-dressed, middle age, strong, and if Finn had to guess, under-employed. He was sweeping David's office.

"Gregorio! Gregorio!" David put fluttery fingers on Finn's sleeve as an apology for his distraction, but he directed his words at the janitor. "I am sorry but you need to move the desk so you can get right under it. Yes, move it."

David bent his knees and made a sweeping movement with those skinny arms of his, pantomiming so that the man understood he was to move the extraordinarily large and heavy desk. It was an impossible task for one man and, since David seemed not to realize that, Finn went to help.

"Here you go, my friend."

Finn lifted one end of the thing. When the man was done sweeping and the desk was in place, Finn found himself looking directly at the janitor. They locked eyes for no more than a second, but something passed between them. Before Finn could put his finger on what it was, the man muttered:

"*Gracias.*"

He went on his way. Finn looked after him, but he didn't look back. Instead, David came to his side.

"Really, you have to let these people fend for themselves, Detective. That's how they learn the way things are done in this country."

"I'll remember that should you ever find yourself in need of a helping hand," Finn answered and David laughed.

"You are so funny. And I am not reprimanding you. That was a lovely gesture, Detective. I'm suggesting you give them more time to figure it out on their own."

"I'll keep that in mind," Finn said and pocketed the picture. "I won't be taking up any more of your time."

Finn started for the door. Like the geeky kid in school who follows the cool kids around just to say he hung out with them, David stayed tight, chattering, not understanding that his every word set Finn's teeth on edge.

"There are so many reasons why you won't be able to find this young man, but I imagine you've thought of most of them…"

Finn palmed the door. It flew open with such force that David took a step back. Sadly, it did not deter him. He caught that door and raised his voice.

"He could have simply gone back to where he came from. Maybe he's gone to Canada. Our political climate is spooking so many of these poor people. Don't you agree?"

Finn turned back fearing that if he didn't the man would follow him all the way to his car. David grinned, happy that his audience hadn't fled at intermission.

"I'm sure I don't know," Finn said.

"Well, it is. We're a sanctuary state but these people don't trust us. That's a pity. It's a pity they are afraid of people like you."

"Not like me," Finn answered. "And I don't think Pacal would leave his family."

"Oh, Detective, the survival instinct is very strong. If that were what this young man had to do, he would do it no matter who he left behind. Believe me."

Finn opened his mouth, but he had nothing to say that this man would understand. Pointing out that Pacal held two jobs, cared for his family, and loved a girl who had a child that was not his seemed to speak to the young man's character. It took a good man to do those things, but David was on a roll and barely breathed between his ever-so-deep thoughts.

"Of course, he could have fallen in with a gang. Easy money. I've seen more than one go that way." He put a finger to his chin. "And, well, there is one other thing."

David took two steps forward and lowered his voice to a dramatic whisper. He stole a glance behind at Gregorio who was now sweeping under the chairs and within earshot.

"The girl in the picture. She's not...well...you know. Those types of relationships seldom work out. Perhaps that's all it really is. The boy is trying to get out of a bad relationship."

Finn stared in disbelief. This man had no idea that he sounded like the people he professed to stand above: racist, bigoted, condescending, intellectually bereft. Finn did not wish to debate him so he did the only thing he could think to do; he smiled.

"Sure, your insights have been most enlightening," he said.

"So glad to help. Feel free to come back. Maybe I'll have something for you. *Las paredes tienen orejas.*" David said with a flourish. But his face dropped when Finn was not impressed. David touched his ears as he whispered. "The walls have ears? You know. I might hear something."

"Ah, of course. That's fine." Finn bit his lip. He nodded. He smiled. "You have my card. Thanks again."

"Oh, I didn't think to ask," David called. "Have you checked County? That's where they take most of these people if they're hurt or sick. Better, yet, check the morgue. I'm surprised you didn't think of that."

"'Tis an optimist I am." Finn raised a hand over his head. He was done with CHIRLA and David.

Finn pulled out his phone and put on his sunglasses as he made his way back to his car. Once there, he rested his backside up against the fender, crossed one boot over the other and banished the arrogant do-gooder from his mind. It was a perfect L.A. afternoon, sunny and bright and mild. There was a little breeze that he swore carried the scent of the sea even though they were miles from it. He used his thumb to scroll through his messages, tapping the ones that interested him. His sister had written to remind him of dinner at their mother's on Sunday. He was welcome to come early and join them for mass. Mass was an invitation often extended and seldom accepted but he wouldn't miss Sunday dinner.

He tapped on a message that indicated it was of some urgency, but it was only a company suggesting it was time to change the filter in his refrigerator. They provided him with a convenient link to order it. He deleted that one though he had a healthy respect for whoever wrote the subject line that got him to open it in the first place.

Pocketing his phone, Finn took one last look at the CHIRLA building. The day was done, and he was glad for it. His conscience was eased now that he had put a bit more effort into the Pacal mystery than he had originally intended. It would have been lovely to have drawn a bead on the man for Amber's sake, but now he could honestly say that he had asked and come up empty. He thought to call Cori and ask if she made it home safely, but then he remembered that she had plans.

His own plans suited him well. He would stop at Mick's for dinner and a pint and then spend an hour or so with the dartboard. If Andrew were there that would be a good day's end, for the man had a nice touch with the arrows. After that, home to catch up on sleep for certainly he had no more than four hours the night before and tomorrow would be another long day.

His eyes roamed over the landscape as he opened the door to his car and took off his jacket. Apartments were built in rows and businesses smashed willy-nilly between them. Laundry hung on lines strung across windows, balconies were rotting, and the metal railings were rusting. The balconies were crowded with old bicycles, dead plants, and children's toys. There was a furniture refinishing shop that seemed to be open but there were three times as many storefronts that had long ago been abandoned. And there was CHIRLA. If that didn't make for a depressing sight each morning, Finn didn't know what would.

He tossed his jacket into the passenger seat and then got behind the wheel. He had the key in the ignition, one hand on the wheel and was thinking that perhaps he should check the morgue and hospitals before he spoke with Amber. It would take no more than a few minutes, and he could fit it in during the next day or the one after that. Finn was thinking that if he found Pacal at either of those places it would be hard news to deliver to the girl, when there was a knock on his window.

Keeping his eyes forward, Finn hit the button to lower the window and waited to hear David's sanctimonious voice waxing poetic about the poor downtrodden sots he served, but it wasn't David at all. It was Gregorio, the man with the broom. He put his hands on his knees and leaned down so that Finn could see his face.

"Can I help you?" Finn asked.

"I hear what you say," the man answered. "There is a boy missing."

"Yes. A friend wanted me to try to find him." Finn hesitated and then added: "I'm sure he's fine."

Suddenly, Finn realized how much he did not want to have this conversation. Until that moment he had driven the narrative, asking his questions, showing his picture of Pacal, expecting little and getting little back. But now here was a worm working its way out of the can. There was only one way to solve the problem of the worm. He must chuck it back in the can. Finn pulled out his credential.

"Just so you know. *Policia*."

Gregorio nodded, his expression grave and his gaze steady. Finn reached for his jacket and pulled out the picture once again. The man barely glanced at it but Finn asked:

"Have you seen him? This is the missing boy."

"Not that one," Gregorio said. "My son. My son is missing."

CHAPTER 11

"Something to drink? Eat?"

Gregorio Sanchez shook his head. "No, *gracias*."

"Alright then." Finn draped his jacket over the back of his chair and sat down at the small table. They were in a restaurant four blocks from the CHIRLA offices.

Gregorio had not hesitated when Finn motioned him into the car. Neither of them wanted to be within eyesight or earshot of David, the prince of CHIRLA, the man with big ears and a small mind. Finn had not asked Gregorio if he wanted to talk in a restaurant, but he was hungry so here they were.

There were six tables neatly laid with placemats that were printed with cartoon pictures of people and food. Each one was defined in both Spanish and English. Salt and pepper shakers and a bottle of hot sauce were put out on the tables. Two sombreros and three piñatas hung from the ceiling. There was a statue of Our Lady of Guadalupe near the register, holding her palms up in prayer. The woman who waited on them wore jeans and a tee-shirt emblazoned with the Tecate logo. She brought chips and salsa and put them on the table along with silverware wrapped in paper napkins. Finn leaned back so she could do her work, and saw a man in the kitchen, wearing a white paper hat and tending to a grill. Finn smelled pork and fresh tortillas.

"I'll be treating, Gregorio. I think we'd be missing some fine food here if we didn't order something."

A muscle in Gregorio's cheek flinched. His right eye twitched. Those were the only signs that he was uncomfortable, so Finn played the only card he had.

"'Tis on the city of Los Angeles. How often do you get a free ride from the city?"

Finn winked. A white lie was nothing compared to a man's honor. He asked the woman:

"Are your tamales homemade, missus?"

She looked at him curiously. When Gregorio translated, she laughed.

"She asks, is there another way?"

"Wonderful. Then would you kindly ask for a platter of tamales and beans and rice? Oh, and *cervesa*." Finn made a gesture to the woman indicating he wanted two of everything. "I've had a very long day, so we are going to eat, and drink and you will tell me what it is you think I should know. After that I will go home and sleep soundly."

Finn put aside the chips and salsa and placed the picture Amber had given him in the center of the table.

"This is Pacal Acosta and he is the man I'm looking for. Just in case you didn't get a good look at it back there. This isn't your son, is it?"

Gregorio took the picture between his short, thick fingers. His hands were calloused. His skin was deeply bronzed as if he had worked his whole life outside. His face was square and weathered. His black hair was swept away from his broad forehead. He was not a tall man, but he was solid, all muscle and no stranger to hard work. It seemed odd to Finn that such a man would be content to sweep up after the likes of David. Finn watched Gregorio's eyes flick from the image of Pacal to Amber and back again. He shook his head.

"No, I knew it was not my son. It is sad to look at this one."

Gregorio put the picture down and then reached in his back pocket for a photo of his own. He put it next to Finn's.

"This is my son," he said. "His name is Miguel."

"He is a handsome young man," Finn said, noting the resemblance between Miguel and Pacal. "When was the last time you saw him?"

"Two months ago. He call me. He always call me. He say he have a late job. He say he come home when it is done. He say it pay good so we go out to hear music and dance when he get back." Gregorio smiled, thinking of the night that had never happened. The smile didn't last long. "He a good boy, a good man."

"Did he get this job through CHIRLA?" Finn asked, pausing when the woman brought their beers, setting a bottle in front of them both.

"No, not CHIRLA." His fingers touched the edges of the picture as if he were afraid it might disappear, but he looked at Finn and smiled a little. "No one like CHIRLA too much."

"And why would that be?" Finn asked even though he could think of one huge reason.

"It is a lottery," Gregorio explained. "A hundred men come for work and fifty go to jobs."

"Sure, isn't that the way of the world, Gregorio?" Finn said. "Sometimes there are jobs for everyone and sometimes not."

"We know this," Gregorio said. "There are enough who want to work that way. For others, the corners are better. Five, six men stand together. There's a better chance to work when there aren't so many. And we talk. We are friends." He raised one shoulder as if to say Finn might not understand, but he did.

"Point taken," Finn answered.

Gregorio smiled gently but Finn did not take that to mean he was a meek man. If there was one thing he knew, it was that there was a huge difference between gentility and weakness.

"Mr. David try very hard to make things fair," Gregorio went on. "But if life was fair, we would not be in this country begging for work. Mr. David thinks to be fair means always to go in order of the lottery. He don't ask who has six children to feed or if another's old mother needs medicine. On a corner, it is different. The men know one another. If someone is new, then he tells us what his life is. The men decide who takes the job, Mr. David's number don't decide. That is fair."

"I had no idea the men who worked the corners were so democratic."

Gregorio laughed a little. "No peoples are perfect, but Miguel try. The men he stood with tried."

"Your son sounds like a fine man," Finn said. He did not point out that even good men had their limits and breakings points and prejudices.

On the corners, there were too many men with too many mouths to feed, too many sick mothers to care for, and too many fearful wives waiting at home. It would be hard to choose who had the greater hardship if push came to shove. Not to mention the corners were like an exposed flank, naked, indefensible. There were those who preyed upon the men who stood there: angry shopkeepers, dishonest employers, politicians who used them as punching bags or cause celebs. Even the police harassed them, moving them out of any neighborhood that the citizens wanted to spruce up. Maybe Cori was right. There is more that stands between those who have and those who don't have than a border. Maybe the only way to get the blessings of safety and freedom was to walk through the gate with the permission of the gatekeeper.

"So, your son is pretty reliable, is he?" Finn picked up his beer and took a drink.

"*Si*. He work every day. He work any job. Dig, clean, build. It don't matter. We both work to send him to school."

"Do you have a wife? Do you have other children?"

Gregorio shook his head to both questions and Finn was disappointed. An extended family meant more information. Often a son would tell a mother something he could not bring himself to tell a father; a sister or brother would share confidences no parent was privy to.

"It is Miguel and me," Gregorio said. "That day he call me, he was on Chestnut and La Brea. That is where he work mostly. Miguel say..."

Once again, their talk was interrupted. Their dinner was delivered on hot platters filled with creamy beans and fluffy rice and homemade tamales. The woman also brought them a round plastic container of fresh tortillas with butter. Finn tucked his napkin at the throat of his t-shirt. Gregorio did the same.

"Sure this is a feast," Finn said to the woman.

Whether she understood his language or not, it didn't matter. She grinned wide and he was sure she blushed. Finn took his first bite and said to Gregorio:

"This is wonderful."

But when he looked up, he saw Gregorio had not moved. His fingers were hooked on the table, and his eyes were on the pictures. He took the napkin from under his chin, set aside the plate, put his elbows on the table, clasped his hands and laid his forehead against them. When he dropped his hands on the table, he looked worn out with his worry.

"When Miguel was four years, I carry him on my back through the desert. My wife, she walk beside us. My wife, she die when Miguel is seven."

Gregorio blinked but it wasn't enough. Finn could see his eyes were moist with tears of frustration and anger and sadness.

"I was a good farmer, but the cartels came to my village. They chopped off the heads of people and leave them in ditches for us to find when we go to the fields. We are afraid to bury them. The bad men would say we were their enemies if we do.

"The priest, he try to bless them but they kill the priest. Another priest come and he try to talk to the men, and they kill him, too. If they kill two men of God, what hope was there? And my Miguel? They would want him to work for them. I do not want that for my son. Then we come here. People don't like us, but they want us to work. There are the gangs here too and some do the things like the cartels. Miguel do not go with the gangs. I made him afraid, and when he was old enough, I made him brave, and then he made himself a good man."

"I have a father like you, Gregorio," Finn said. "I love him very much. I know Miguel loves you too."

"*Si.*"

"But did he have any run-ins with anyone? Did he tell you that?" Finn asked, his fork on the table, the food growing cold.

Gregorio shook his head. "I don't think so."

"Have you ever heard of a person named Fidel Andre Hernandez? His nickname is Marbles? He's with the Hard Times Locos."

Gregorio shook his head again. "*No.*"

Finn reached across the table and nudged Gregorio's plate as he picked up his own fork and pointed to it.

"Sure, you don't want the lady to think you don't like her cooking."

Gregorio picked up his fork too. Finn knew the man wasn't hungry. He probably hadn't been hungry since his son disappeared, but he had to eat.

"That's better," Finn said, but when he reached for a tortilla, Gregorio's hand suddenly clamped hard over his wrist.

The detective's eyes narrowed, his muscles tensed but he did not move. It was Gregorio who was half out of his chair. His face was hard, and his jaw trembled. For a moment, there was panic in his eyes and then it was replaced with the look of a man who had nothing to lose.

"Food no make this better. You think it is easy to stay away from gangs when they come after a boy? When they say they will kill him? When they steal his shoes when he goes to school. His shoes..." Gregorio's voice shook with the shame of this, his son robbed of the only precious thing he owned.

"Sit down, Gregorio. Sit down now."

The man trembled at the sound of Finn's voice. He looked first at the detective and then over at the woman and the cook who were watching from the kitchen. He looked at the table and realized he had knocked over his glass of water when he lunged for Finn. The hand that held Finn's wrist began to shake so Finn put his own over it. Seconds ticked by as Gregorio tried to relax his hold. Slowly, he opened his fingers, but at a certain point he became paralyzed. Finn put Gregorio's hand away but held it when he said:

"Sit down, man. Sit."

Gregorio did as he was told. Finn motioned for the woman who came to the table to wipe up the spilled water. Gregorio looked away, through the window at the sad, dirty street. When she was gone, Gregorio spoke with a heaviness that came from carrying too much worry and fear for too long.

"I speak to you because you are looking for a missing boy. I think he is my boy. If you send me back to *Mexico* then that is what you will do," Gregorio said. "But you find my son. I don't care what happens to me."

Finn had a hard time looking at this man's anguished face and a harder time hearing those tortured words because he had heard them before. His own father had begged a policeman: *Find my son. Find my Alexander. I will do anything.*

Finn raised his chin and held Gregorio's gaze. "I will look for your son. I promise."

Finn set aside his own plate of food. He had made a promise that would be difficult to keep because Gregorio's situation was no better than Amber's. Miguel had no real friends. He lived in shadows. He worked. He dreamed of the future that would probably never be realized. One in which hard work would let the son do better than the father and the son's son after that. Finn was thinking about all this – how families are families no matter where they hail from – when he realized Gregorio was speaking.

"...I have a list."

"I'm sorry," Finn said. "What is this?"

"The ones who are missing."

Gregorio slid it across the table and Finn picked up the piece of paper. Written there were three names, all of Hispanic origin.

"I thought it was Miguel we were going to look for."

"There are more. See? Esteban and Santos and Miguel. Esteban is gone four months. Santos a few weeks after Esteban. I hear about Santos at CHIRLA. A man tell me his cousin never come home from a job. Santos had a new baby. He would not leave a new baby and a new wife. Santos had a job most days but then he work the corner when the lumberyard have no work for him. Esteban have no family, but the men knew him. He went to church. Then he don't go to church no more."

"Did they all work Chestnut and La Brea?" Finn asked.

"Only two. This one and Miguel," Gregorio pointed to the last name. "Santos somewhere else."

Finn held the list and then he picked up the two photographs that had been wedged between the salt and pepper shakers to save them from the spilled water.

"I'll be keeping this." Gregorio nodded and Finn put them in his pocket. "What about age? Height? Weight? From the picture it looks like Miguel and Pacal could almost be twins. What about the others?"

"Young. Yes, all young and strong," Gregorio said. "I will find out what Esteban and Santos look like."

"Were they all undocumented?" Finn asked.

"*Si*," Gregorio said as he looked at a clock over the kitchen counter. "I go. I have more work."

"CHIRLA is open at night?" Finn asked.

"There are more places to clean than one," Gregorio said.

Finn motioned for the waitress who brought a container for the uneaten food.

"We don't want this to go to waste. Keep it for later."
Finn put up his hand. "I promise, if I find anything, I'll
let you know right away. But, Gregorio, it will be hard.
It's a big city."

"And we are small people. I understand." Gregorio
stood up. He took Finn's hand. "*Gracias.*"

"I have to be asking you something, Gregorio. If you
all believe the corners are dangerous, why are the men still
going to them?"

"We all must take chances to survive, to eat," he said.

"You have a job," Fin reminded him.

"*Si*, but I take chances too. I speak to you." Gregorio
started for the door but paused as he passed Finn. "Maybe
this is no chance. Maybe God send you because I pray. *Sí?*"

Finn watched him walk out. He could only hope
that the man would be happy with God's choice. As for
himself, Finn would have preferred God left him out of
this altogether.

* * *

The man leaning against the white truck wasn't arrogant,
mind you. He had always tried to be fair and do his best.
Even when he was that young buck making trouble, he
hadn't really meant to make trouble. When he screwed up,
he tried to make it right.

No llores.

Don't cry.

Lo siento.

I'm sorry.

But there were times when he did everything right, and
today everything was right because he had planned so
well. For weeks he had pored over the maps until his good
eye was tired and the one that looked like curdled milk was

so scratchy he had to put a towel over it so that it would rest. But the hours of study had paid off. On the map, this site looked good; when he got there to scope it out, it was better than good. No hills, easy access, signs of life but no people. He went back twice more to test it out. Once he sat in the truck and watched and listened. He saw no one and heard nothing except the drone of machinery. The second time he got out of the truck and walked ten minutes east, ten minutes west and ten minutes north. He saw a man in a blue truck driving between the derricks that pocked the landscape, but he was far away and didn't stop.

After that, he got his shovel and tested the ground. It was dry but not unmanageable because it was very sandy. It was on that visit that he set out his stakes with the little yellow flags. He put out three lengths of pipe. He took the rolled-up blueprint, noted the edges were fraying and that soon he would need to make another copy, and put it inside one of the pipes so it would be easy to get. All he needed after that was a man to dig for him, and here he was. Digging. Everything was going according to plan.

They had driven to this place, the young man had been shown the blueprints as if they were official and then the man gave him the shovel. The laborer worked and the man with the milky eye enjoyed the still warm afternoon. He found peace as he watched the oil derricks dipping up and down into the earth.

When he was a kid, before the freeways were built, when Disneyland was a twinkle in Walt's eye, derricks like these used to line the highway from Long Beach to Anaheim. Orange trees and oil derricks, that's what he saw on the long, hot, lazy rides with his parents from their house in the desert to his grandmother's house near the beach. The orange trees were nice but when he spied one of those derricks he would holler and wave because they were big mechanical things that little boys loved and in the desert nothing moved. His mom would shush him, but his old man would shush her. It was good for the kid to be excited by machinery, dad said. It meant he was going to grow up to be a real man. Damn real man, that's what mattered to his father.

Good thing his old man was gone now. His father would have helped him with this work if he knew what had been done to his son. The old man would go to hell and back for his kid. He would have…

It didn't matter.

The old man wasn't around. Still it was funny how being in this place reminded him of when he was a boy, funnier still that he got a thrill from watching those derricks. He had a toy once, a plastic bird with a big yellow beak. If you put the darn thing near a glass of water, it seesawed up and down. The big yellow beak touched the water like it was drinking, and then it rose up like it was swallowing. That's what those oil derricks looked like: plastic birds, their beaks perpetually dipping down into a glass of water. These birds pulled up oil. Right here in the middle of Los Angeles, all of them on acres and acres of dirt. Yep, this was a desolate place smack dab in the middle of ten million people.

It took the dip of the sun and the sky changing from a hazy blue to the pinky gold of sunset to bring him back to the here and now. When the man realized the hour, he pushed off the truck and picked up the shovel, walked ten feet and raised it over his shoulder. The boy, dusting himself off, still standing in the trench, looked up to see if the man was pleased with his work. The man smiled like he was, at the same time he swung the shovel and damn near decapitated the brown-skinned boy.

It was almost dark when the man got home. He was right on time.

* * *

It wasn't that late, and she hadn't had that much to drink, but Cori started disrobing the minute she stepped inside the house: scarf, jacket, shoes, belt. She tossed that stuff onto her bed and then padded down the hall in her stocking feet and tiptoed into the room Amber shared with Tucker. There was a streetlamp just outside the house that beamed a soft yellow light through the slit in the curtains. She could see her daughter's silhouette huddled under the covers. Because the crib was near the window, she saw Tucker clearly. The light haloed the little boy's head. His hair looked like spun gold, his lashes looked impossibly long and his baby skin gleamed. Cori went to the crib and put her hand atop his head as she did every night.

She had spent many a night like this with Amber after her husband took off, when the future looked bleak. The feel of her child, the sound of her breathing, the way her daughter's fingers curled around one of hers gave Cori strength. That bastard had left her and Amber with a bushel full of grief, left them penniless to live in motels a whore would have turned up her nose at and, for a while, in her car. It had been a struggle to survive, but at least Cori had known why she was still duking it out. It was for her girl and now everything she did was for her girl and Tucker.

"Did you have a good time?"

Cori smiled before she swung her head and looked past her shoulder to see Amber looking at her.

"Yeah. It was nice," Cori whispered, still stroking Tucker's hair. "But Brazilians don't know shit about barb-que. They just carry around hunks of meat on swords and slice you up some when you point at it. No sauce. No eating with your hands. Still Lapinski liked it, so I told him it was awesome."

Amber chuckled and then turned on her side. She pulled the covers up and rested her head on an upturned hand. Cori laughed a little too. Thomas Lapinski, attorney-at-law, LLC was a character and a half, a head shorter than Cori, completely smitten with her and one of the finest men she had ever met. He was kind, crazy-smart and had stepped up to bat when Cori had been beaten to within an inch of her life in Little Ethiopia. He loved Tucker, appreciated Amber, was respectful and just the kind of man Cori needed. Sadly, though, he was probably not the kind of man she would ever want.

"Mr. Lapinski really likes you," Amber said.

"I like him too. He's a stand up guy," Cori said. "But he's not the only bull in the pen. Now that you put all that stuff about me up on the internet—"

"Your profile, mom," Amber sighed.

"Yeah, that. I guess I'm committed. You never know. Maybe Lapinski's the one, but maybe I could find someone who isn't…"

"Short? Loud? Busy?" Amber suggested.

"I was thinking not a lawyer," Cori snickered. "And don't you go running him down. He has a heart as big as Texas and for a Texas gal that means a whole lot."

"I agree. A big heart is worth a whole bunch," Amber said almost to herself.

"Yes. Yes, it is," Cori admitted. "But it ain't everything."

She swung her head back and looked at her grandson. Cori went on her tiptoes over to the side of the crib, gave Tucker a peck on his cheek, then straightened up and walked over to her daughter's bed. She waved her fingers. Amber moved over and lay back on her pillow, her blonde hair spilling over her shoulders. Cori sat down on the mattress next to her.

"I think Lapinski and me are just two buckets full of possums," Cori muttered.

She tucked the covers under Amber's chin. When her daughter didn't shoo her away, Cori picked up a lock of her long hair and smoothed it behind the girl's shoulder. Times like this – peaceful, quiet times – didn't come often enough for them.

"How was work?" Cori asked.

"Good. Fine," Amber said.

"Did the sitter work out okay?" Cori asked.

"Yeah. She had Tucker all fed and washed and in bed when I got home."

"So you wouldn't mind leaving him with her if I paid for some of it when I was out on a date and you had to work?"

"No, I wouldn't mind. It's about time you got out there," Amber said. "You've been alone awhile."

"I have," Cori reiterated and then went silent for a minute. "But what do you really think? I'm not everyone's cup of tea, you know. Maybe it's better to just let things be."

"I can't tell you what to do. I just know you deserve someone to love you. I think we both do," Amber said. "Don't give up, because sometimes you find love in the weirdest place."

"If that ain't a fact."

Cori put her hand on top of Amber's head. Her hair felt thick and womanly and Cori missed the silky baby curls. Time had gotten away from her. She dropped her hand into her lap.

"I'm talking down a well, honey; nothing coming

back but a sad echo. I'm going to hit the hay and let you get some sleep."

Cori stood up but paused to look at her daughter. They had both changed in the last few months. Cori had a new-found respect for this girl who had seen her through her recovery after she was attacked. She had made good friends in Thomas J. Lapinski and Detective Morrow – another strangely brilliant man with a lovely heart – and she had put Finn O'Brien in perspective. They cared for one another as deeply as they could, but their timing sucked. She was wanting a whole lot more from him than he could give just then. The nice thing was that Cori was good with that. Yep, it was all good when you were old enough to know what was what.

"I'm proud of you, sweetie pie." Cori leaned down and kissed her daughter's brow. Amber settled down again but before Cori left, she called out:

"Mom?"

"Yep?"

Cori stuck her head back in, but Amber hesitated. If there was ever a time to tell her about Pacal, it was now when her mom was tired, and the night was deep and dark. But night was no promise of understanding, and they could just as easily end up in the kitchen fighting. Amber was too tired, too sad, and too worried for that. She turned over, put her hands under her cheek and said:

"Nothing, mom. I'm just glad you had a nice time."

"Thanks, baby."

When Cori was gone, Amber turned on her side and stared across the room at the crib. She thought of Finn O'Brien and prayed that he was the stand up guy she thought he was. Then she prayed that, once Finn found Pacal, Cori wouldn't kill all three of them.

CHAPTER 12

KTLA News, Mr. Meteor, weatherman:
Look for temperatures to rise dramatically starting
tomorrow and reaching their peak on the fifth of May.
We're looking at triple digits then, so make plans to stay
cool.

KTLA News, Shana Taylor, morning anchor:
Good advice, Mr. Meteor, but it's looking like the
weather isn't the only thing that's going to heat up the
Cinco de Mayo holiday. While restaurants are stocking
up on Margarita mix, the LAPD is gearing up for
demonstrations against the tightening of immigration
laws. While permits have been issued in Los Angeles
for three groups – CHIRLA, SIEU and Citizens for
Lawful Immigration – we are told that outside agitators
are expected in the mix. In an exclusive interview with
Mexican television personality, Miguel Morenas, our
very own Sheldon Turner asked how the more than
ten million undocumented immigrants in the U.S. are
feeling about the coming holiday.
Miguel Morenas: No one is illegal and yet these

people are made to feel like criminals. They are afraid
to show their faces. They are afraid for their lives. I
think Los Angeles must prepare for the worst. It is time
for open borders.

"So Julie says to me, 'I really, really want to go to Paris'
and I say to her, 'well, honey, we'll try to swing that,
but work's been crazy and I don't know when I can get
off', and she says to me, 'no, I mean alone'. I'll tell you,
I almost dropped my teeth, Finn. Not that I would stop
her. She's a grown woman, and I must admit I'm not one
for museums and such, and she loves that stuff, so I say…
Oh, wait, here you are."

Paul Craig, Chief Medical Examiner of Los Angeles
County, found the paperwork he was looking for. He hadn't
noticed the tapping of Finn's foot, or the fact that the detective had been squirming in his chair as he listened to Paul's
latest trials and tribulations with a wife he adored and who
adored him back. Now the good doctor held up the paper,
squinting at it while he patted his pockets for his glasses.

"On top." Finn pointed to the readers nestled in Paul's
fine crop of hair.

Paul looked at him quizzically. Finn pointed a finger to
the top of Paul's own head. Paul mirrored him and grinned.

"Of course. Always. You'd think I'd know by now." He
chuckled and dropped his glasses to his nose. "Okay, it
looks like we've only got two of them done. Terrible thing.
Five people dead in that house. I'll tell you, I don't know
how you do what you do, but I'm grateful that you do."

"The feeling is mutual, Paul. Sure, I wouldn't do well
cutting open bodies all day."

"Then I suppose we're exactly where we should be.

That being said, it has been hugely busy so if you don't mind, I'll dispense with the chit chat."

Finn refrained from pointing out that Paul had been the one chatting a good ten minutes and waited for him to get on with it.

"We started with the woman in the hall. She had been bound a good long while. I'd say at least five hours. Lots of abrasions, horribly bruised, raw, rope-burned skin. She had tried to pull her hands out, but your perp knew what he was doing when it came to hog tying someone."

"If those children were hers, I imagine she would have eventually gnawed her hands off to get to them," Finn said.

"Possibly hers. She's had at least one birth. We'll do a DNA once we get swabs from the children. Anyway, death was instantaneous when it finally came. The bullet went right through her brain. Here—" Paul pointed to the center of his head. "Came out here—" he pointed to the back near the base of the skull.

"She saw it coming. The muzzle was literally right up against her forehead. But whoever shot her was standing above. Powder burns were bad. The shooter had to have blood on him. The man who was not bound—"

"The one in the doorway," Finn said.

"Yes. He was also covered with blood from different sources. All over his shoes, pants, cuffs, shirt. Since he had a clean shot through the back, it wouldn't account for the splatter. I'm thinking he was pretty close up to the hall victims. That doesn't mean he shot them. He could have been standing next to whoever did. I have his clothes; you can take them. Still, it could be that he killed the people in the hall and then your man killed him."

"Was there powder residue on his hands?"

"Yes," Paul answered.

"Marbles', too," Finn said.

"That will make it interesting for the D.A. I mean, who do you charge with which murder?" Paul said. "Anyway, not my problem. On to what is. The lady didn't have much in her stomach. She was dehydrated. Her clothing appears to be homemade except for the underwear. That had sizing labels consistent with a foreign country. I have everything ready to go. Fingerprints have been taken, hair samples, but I don't think you're going to find out who the hall-people are. They were fresh off the boat."

"And how would you know that?"

"Finn, please, how long have I been doing this job? I can tell just by looking how long they've been in this country. This one was only here hours. I promise."

"We'll see," Finn said even though he knew Paul was probably right. Still, there were procedures, and he would follow them.

"Did you find any passports when you were putting things right in that house? Any paperwork of any kind?" Paul asked.

"A few passports, but none that matched these people," Finn said. "I doubt we'll find the people they do belong to. They could be forgeries. Still, we'll run them down."

"Did you find any phone numbers? Purses? Wallets?" Paul asked.

"I've got a diaper bag and two backpacks with clothes and water bottles in them, and I found a very, very bad guy," Finn answered.

"I'm sorry for that, but I am happy that you are not in the queue for my table given the fact that he seemed not to mind who he put a bullet into."

"That makes two of us," Finn said.

"Alright then. I'm off to search some real estate records

and visit my friend Marbles. Cori is away talking to the children at social services."

"I didn't know she spoke Spanish," Paul said.

"She doesn't, but she's fluent in child speak. I fear I frighten them a bit when they see me in full light."

"You frighten me a bit in full light." Paul laughed and handed Finn copies of the reports and the evidence bags. "You have any questions, give me a call. I'll get to the rest of them as soon as possible."

The coroner started to stand up, but Finn stopped him. "Actually, Paul, I would like to be bothering you with one more thing."

"Make it quick, my friend. I'll be here until midnight clearing up all the work you've brought me. If I have a wife wanting to go to Paris on her own, I should really spend more time with her."

"Moments, I promise. Two young men. Hispanic. One is seventeen, the other twenty-two. One has been missing three days, the other two months." Finn snapped the photos in front of Paul. "I know they look similar, but they aren't related. I'm wondering if they've found their way into your fine establishment. The names are Miguel Sanchez and Pacal Acosta. Can you do a quick run through and see what's in your inventory?"

"That's no way to talk about our clients," Paul muttered but turned to his computer and mused. "Three days and two months?"

"That's it," Finn said as Paul scrolled.

"Three days ago. Three days ago..." Paul ran a finger down his computer screen. "I've got three women, two are forty-plus and one of those was an O.D. There's a seventy-eight-year-old woman who was found dead in her home. No foul play suspected. I've got sixteen men backed up, various ages. ten black, two Asian, four Caucasian. Oh, wait. Here's one. Came in four weeks ago. Hispanic – a little out of your time frame – looks to be about the right age and height. Let's go take a look, shall we?"

In the next second Paul was out the door with Finn following. He checked in with one of the pathologists along the way and then they went on to the room where the bodies were kept. Gurneys were lined up, the bodies waiting for either autopsy or an associate to make a couple of calls to confirm that a death was the result of natural causes. Paul went to the back of the room and down an aisle checking tags.

"Got him!" Paul raised a hand and unzipped the body bag. One look told Finn this wasn't who he was looking for.

"No, mine have no tattoos. But this one appears to be the right age and physical build." Finn inclined his head. "It looks like a wrecking ball hit him in the head."

"The face is a mess but the rest of him looks pretty good. He was dirty when he came in, almost as if he'd been buried."

"Construction accident?" Finn speculated.

"Farming?" Paul countered. "Maybe. Or maybe someone killed him and tried to cover it up. Let's see who brought him in." Paul checked the toe tag. "Typical. They left off half the information." Paul zipped the bag back up. "I'll take a closer look at the records when I can."

"Sure thing. I'd appreciate a picture of this one."

"Stop by the front, give Nancy the number and she'll pull it up for you. Give me a day or two on the other stuff, okay?"

"No, problem. I've a few things to keep me busy too."

* * *

With six hundred beds, County USC Medical Center is the largest public hospital in the country. Like any other hospital it is a busy place. It offers clinics, imaging, labor and delivery, heart, and neurology services – like any other hospital. The original building, damaged in the Northridge quake, had been rebuilt and expanded to include fitness trails, walking paths, and a courtyard.

The campus is bound by Zonal Avenue (East and West), Marengo Street, Chicago Street and Mission Road (north and south). It is east of downtown Los Angeles and squats just at the top of East L.A. South L.A. is within spitting distance. According to the hospital's website, the facility is associated with the Keck School of Medicine of the University of Southern California and the Los Angeles County College of Nursing and Allied Health. Even more impressive, it is one of the nation's leading teaching hospitals and boasts of a world-renowned burn center, level III neonatal intensive care unit and HIV/AIDS clinic. What is unusual for a hospital is County's violence intervention program that offers medical and mental health help as well as protective and social services to over twenty thousand victims of family violence and sexual assault each year. Even for a city of ten million people, that is a staggering statistic and speaks to the temperament of Los Angeles. There is also a special clinic for children at risk or already in foster care. And, on the thirteenth floor, County USC has a secure unit, a jail ward.

Finn knew of the facility but in all his years as a cop he had never stepped foot inside it. There was a first time for everything so he pushed the button for the thirteenth floor, and when the elevator doors opened he saw another large metal door, prison bars and a sheriff's deputy at the desk behind them.

"Detective O'Brien." Finn presented himself and his credentials. "Here to see Fidel Andre Hernandez."

"Print your name. Date. Time. Just fill it out so we can read it."

Finn did as he was told and was promptly buzzed in. The metal door open and then closed and locked behind him.

"Detective O'Brien?" Finn turned at the sound of his name. The young woman who hailed him introduced herself. "Deputy Jerome."

Her smile was bright as were her eyes and her attitude. Her blonde hair was pulled back into a bun at the nape of her neck, but a few strands had escaped and floated around her temple and just behind her ears. She wore her uniform with pride, shoulders thrown back. Her handshake was firm.

"Good to meet you," he said. "I'm here to interview…"

"Marbles. Yep. I already found out he's not too thrilled with the name his mama gave him. Come on." They fell in step, Deputy Jerome simultaneously nodding to nurses and being polite to Finn as they went. "Is this your first time visiting?"

"Yes, 'tis an impressive place," Finn noted.

"This unit saw over seven hundred patients last month and had eighty-three inpatients. It's kind of tough when we only have twenty-five beds, but we manage. Seems to be getting worse every year though. Sometimes I think the world's gone mad."

"You aren't far wrong," Finn agreed.

"That's why I love this assignment, the madness is localized and manageable. Your man's got a room all to himself." She guided him with a lift of her finger.

"A big grand room for the likes of him?" Finn asked as they turned the corner and started down another hallway.

"Nothing to do with special treatment, Detective. We've got to isolate the juvies—"

"This is no juvenile," Finn assured her.

"He's three days shy of his eighteenth birthday. The law considers him a juvenile. Chronology shouldn't be the gold standard, but I don't make the rules," she answered. "Anyway, this ward takes men and women and juveniles, but the kids have to be segregated – out of eyesight of the old folks. God knows what they're afraid of. If we got them in here, they are all in bad shape."

"Well then, let him have his comfort because he won't have much where he's going."

"We'll see," Deputy Jerome laughed.

"Don't be telling me you have no faith in the system."

"I'm of the I-believe-it-when-I-see-it school. As far as I'm concerned, we all would have been better off if Mr. Marbles in there—Oh, here we are."

Finn never heard exactly what Deputy Jerome thought should have happened to Marbles, but he had a feeling her heart was a little darker than the sunshine she presented.

"Deputy Swanson, this is Detective O'Brien. O'Brien's going in to see Marbles."

"Lucky you," the man said as he went for the door.

"No need for you to put yourself out," Finn raised his hand. "I know what shape he is in and I doubt I'll have any trouble."

"I doubt you will either, but you're going to have my company whether you like it or not. Thanks, Jerome, I've got it." Deputy Jerome went on her way without a backward look. Now it was just the two men and Swanson laid it out. "Sorry, but this is as much for your protection as ours. We don't want a he said/she said and we don't want one of these knuckleheads going at you. We've got booth deputies, desk deputies, booking officers, escort deputies. You're never going to have a problem here."

"But it's still a hospital, correct?" Finn said.

"The best," Swanson said. "So, it's you and me if you're ready."

"I'll be happy for the company," Finn said.

"You're the one who shot him, right?" Swanson asked.

"I am."

"If you ever feel like it, I'll meet up with you at the range. I think your aim is off. The heart is right about here."

Deputy Swanson tapped his own chest just above his heart and then opened the door to the room where Marbles lay.

* * *

At first glance everything appeared normal: blinking monitors, blips dancing around horizontal lines, a small bedside table on which there was a cup and a pink plastic pitcher and a small box of Kleenex. Finn also noticed what was missing. There were no pictures on the walls, no chair next to the bed, no balloons or flowers wishing the sick person well. There were no blinds on the windows so the cords couldn't be used as a weapon or to the advantage of an inmate intent on suicide or escape. The bed was standard and in it lay Fidel Andre Hernandez, aka Marbles, cruel but not crazy in Finn's opinion.

He appeared smaller than he had two nights before when he stood in that dark house, backlit by a bright light, keeping company with dead people and tortured children. Then again, anyone with a sawed-off shotgun in their hands looks bigger than life, in the same way any person who has proven life means nothing to them grows in stature when he sets his sights on you. Ask any cop. They won't speak of it, but it is the truth.

Now here he was, lying in bed, sleeping like a baby and Finn saw him for what he really was: a very young man. His upper body was muscled but lean. His skin was obliterated by some very good and some very bad tattooing. His head, resting on the pristinely white pillowcase, looked a bit like a bullet and it carried his calling card. The letters HTL, declaring him a member of the Hard Time Locos, were tattooed on the top of his head, near his ear and, Finn imagined, on the back of his skull or his neck. Coming or going, Marbles would be identified for what he was. There was a tatted spider web covering Marbles' crown. Circling his neck, the words Hard Time Locos had been spelled out in block lettering. Finn winced at the thought of the pain the intricate neck ink had wrought.

Marbles was dressed in one of those hospital gowns that made a grown man cringe. Sleeping as he was, the little dress made him appear strangely vulnerable despite the tats, the muscles, and the shaved head. Perhaps it was the sea foam green color that created that illusion. Maybe it was the little pattern of polka dots or the fact that it had slid off one shoulder and didn't cover his arms. The little gown even made all the tats seem silly. It was as if Marbles, bored in his hospital bed, had decorated himself with crayons like a child.

Finn walked over to the bed, but Swanson motioned him to the other side.

"Never put yourself between them and the wall."

Finn changed course. As he was doing so, the door opened, and a nurse dressed in purple scrubs appeared. She looked at Finn and smiled, unconcerned by his presence. She went to the bed and put a new drip bag in place on the I.V. stand and left the room. Finn stepped up again.

Marbles' exposed shoulder was bandaged, and his arm

was immobilized. The hand Finn had accidentally 'stepped on' in the commotion was not as badly damaged as he had assumed. Only two fingers were splinted and taped. Up close he could see not only the tatted crosses on Marbles' closed eyelids, he could see the man was not sleeping at all. His eyelids were shivering just a little, a sure sign he was playing possum and not deep asleep, dreaming about puppies. Finn put his hands on the bed railing.

"Time to open your eyes and talk to me, Fidel, my boy."

Swanson watched. Finn waited. The man in the bed weighed his options and then he opened his eyes. Every muscle in Finn's body tightened at the sight of those black-ened eyes. He thought he had been ready to look into them again, but the terror, the fury and the anger he had felt the night before came flooding back. Finn wanted Marbles to see none of this, so he forced himself to look deeper into those eyes and get past it all. Though there was not a speck of white to be seen, Finn was close enough to make out that Marble's irises were dark brown and that some of the blackness was fading to a deep grey. In the dark, though, those people he killed would not have had the chance to see that he was just a cruel, sadistic piece of shit. To them Marbles would have looked like Satan and that was a sad thing to take with you on the way out of this life. Marbles' smile spread slowly as he said:

"Yo, you be the 5-0 who shot me."

This boy's voice was manly and deep, his body was strong, his evil was old and ingrained. There was a slight pop where his Spanish met his English. He was no more a juvenile than Finn.

"And you murdered a police officer, killed five inno-cents and beat children. I would say you win," Finn said.

"Dat be no 187." Marbles sniggered like a kid and shook

his head back and forth on the pillow, disavowing the murders. He held up his good hand and he wiped his palm over his brow. "We just be in the mix. Gotta protect the turf, you know, 'cause Florenzia 13 be slippin', and it ain't right."

Finn straightened up to his full height hoping the prone man would feel what those people in the hall had felt: threatened, terrified, terrorized. Sadly, Marbles was a pro, and he knew there wasn't much that should worry him at this stage of the game.

"It was murder, Marbles, so don't give me any of your bull," Finn said. "What are you going to plead, self-defense? Those people were bound and gagged. Kind of tough for them to go at you."

"No, man. No. I won' lie to 5-0. I swear on God," Marbles said. "I be holdin' the pump, but I weren't the one who killed them. It was Smiley. He done it and I killed him for doing it. He be the hater, man, not me. Fuck, I was goin' down when you come at me all vigilante. I swear, that's the way it went down."

"Yeah, I'm a vigilante and you're a choir boy."

"I tell you, it was my homie done it." He shrugged as if he didn't care if Finn believed him. "I be in the mix. You know, scare 'em off. That be it for me and I want my lawyer. I want my lawyer, so you don' be puttin' the wrong words down. You hear me? I want my lawyer. You," he turned those black-hole eyes on Swanson, "you hear me?"

Deputy Swanson looked back, stone-faced. Marbles pushed his head further back into the pillow and rolled his black eyes. Finn kept on him, even toned, unconcerned.

"Well, then, doesn't that just make things better. It was Smiley who did the killing, and you were the white hat. Is that it?"

"Damn straight." Marbles head went up and down. "He

said we was just goin' to scare 'em off and I'm good with that. F13 be tryin' to put the move on us. Quiet like. They get that house and they be movin' busloads of wetbacks, bro. I swear. That's it. We just want to get F13 out 'cause they set up house on our territory. That way something bad goes down we get the blame but none of the cash. Just get 'em out of our turf and we be all good. That's all, man." Marbles narrowed his eyes and looked at Finn. "Where you from? You look like a bad dude, but you don't sound none."

"I could say the same about you," Finn said. "But let's not get off topic. What are you talking about? What is it you're telling me F13 is moving in on?"

"Coyote packs, 5-0. Coyotes shippin' 'em across the border, puttin' 'em in the house tellin' them they be safe. But they don' let 'em move out 'til they get their change on this end," Marbles explained.

Finn's eyes flickered to Swanson. The deputy raised an eyebrow as if to ask, 'why are you surprised.' Finn would answer that he was always surprised by criminal creativity. Instead he said:

"So, you're telling me that people are paying coyotes to smuggle them across the border, and when they get here, they're held prisoner until they can pay their way out of the house? Payment before and after the journey, is that it?"

"You got it, man," Marbles said.

"And you were just there to help the people in the house because you and your homies were outraged by this? Is that correct?" Finn asked.

"Fuckin' A."

Marbles grinned, pleased with the narrative he was weaving. Suddenly, he pulled down his gown and showed Finn his ink. The centerpiece of his chest armor tat was a picture of a naked woman being straddled by a gangbanger holding a gun to her head. Finn would have liked to look away for certainly it was an awful image, the kind that revisited a man in his nightmares. Instead, he said:

"Lacks a bit of style, Marbles."

"They prick all that with a staple in juvie." He chuckled, amused but disappointed in Finn's reaction. He tried again. "A staple man. Took right out of the warden's office. I didn't cry, man. I didn't say nothin'. A staple's hard stuff, you hear me. I can take it."

"And after you got done with art class, did you learn how to add two and two?"

"What you sayin'?" Marbles narrowed his eyes.

"Math," Finn said. "Your story doesn't add up. You've got quite a reputation. You like tying people up before you kill them. Maybe it's because you're not that good a shot. Could that be it, my man?"

"I be the best, I tell you. With that pump."

"Any fool can hit a mark with a shot gun." Finn put his big hands on the bed rail once again and then got into the man's face. "The next part of that equation is your friend, Smiley. He was shot in the back going into the room."

"So?" Marble narrowed his eyes, the only sign he was wary.

"So, I'm thinking that you weren't supposed to kill anyone in that house. Just scare them a little, just let F13 know that was your territory. But you couldn't help yourself. You and Smiley tied up those people and they were scared, but you didn't think it was enough to warn off F13. So, you little horror, you shot them…"

Finn put his finger on Marble's forehead. The man tried to jerk away only to cry out when his shoulder wound pulled.

"Hey, hey, you be threatin' me. He seen it. He seen it." Marbles cut his eyes to Swanson. The deputy didn't twitch.

"I'm only trying to soothe your misery, Marbles. This will help you focus." Finn drilled his finger deeper into the kid's skin. "You shot those unfortunates, and it was Smiley who freaked. That wasn't the plan, but you were trying to be a big man. Or maybe you lost it because you're a crazy son of a bitch. So crazy they won't put you in jail, they'll put you in a psyche ward all wrapped up in a straightjacket for the rest of your life."

"Smiley did it. Smiley." He looked over at Deputy Swanson. "You get me my goddamn lawyer and don' let this 5-0 touch me. I got my rights."

"And I know something you don't." Finn leaned ever closer, his finger gun sliding across Marble's forehead until it rested between his eyes. Finn leaned over the railing. He whispered hard. "I know Smiley's prints aren't on the pump. It's only your prints, Marbles. Yours alone."

"You ain't the only one knows somethin'," Marbles said through clenched teeth. "I know somethin' and it's gonna bite you big, 5-0."

"I'm shaking in my boots, boyo," Finn laughed and Marbles' eyes hardened in his anger.

"You got no idea, bro. You be goin' down. My lawyer is good, man. He be real good; know what I mean? He's a goddamn magician, my lawyer."

He lifted his bandaged hand and pulled Finn's finger away from his head and threw it aside. In the next second, he did something Finn had not expected. Marbles spit on him but the poor man in his weakened state didn't have much of a range. The glob of vile fluid fell on the sleeve of his jacket. Finn pulled a Kleenex from the box on the bedside table and wiped it away.

"Deputy Swanson, I believe we're done here. I wouldn't want to wear this gentleman out."

Swanson moved away from the window. Finn had one more question.

"When did F13 start smuggling people?"

"What do you give me?" Marbles shot back.

"I'll talk to the prosecutor, but he's the one to make the deals."

Marbles thought about it and then decided he would take a chance. "It's a new biz, bro. A year maybe."

"Same house?"

"That one and two more somewheres," Marbles said.

"Business must be good," Finn said.

Marbles chuckled.

"It ain't the only one that does good. They been shakin' down the wetbacks bad. The ones hawkin' on the corners too."

"Are they doing anything else? Maybe killing a few of those men for good measure?"

Marbles shook his head. "Naw. Shakedown is all. Been doin' it all over L.A. F13 are greedy bastards."

"'Tis the way of the world, Marbles. The strong prey on the weak," Finn said. "And then they meet up with someone stronger still."

"Florenzia 13 ain't stronger than me," Marble snorted.

"I meant me," Finn answered. "I'm stronger than all of you. Count on it."

* * *

Finn took leave of deputies and County USC. He checked his texts. Cori had interviewed the children from the house. She would fill him in later as she was rushing to her court appearance to testify to the chain of evidence in the assault with intent investigation she had handled at Westside. It had taken a year and a half to come to trial and, once it had, the judge had no patience for any witness unable to clear their calendars to appear before him.

Finn scrolled through and saw there was no follow-up message so he could only assume that Cori was still waiting to give her testimony. He texted to say he would see her the next day. He was eager to hear what those children had told her given what he now knew about Florenzia 13 and the Hard Time Locos. If what Marbles said was true, there was an ugly new side to human trafficking going down. Once it got a foothold, there would be no stamping it out. Kidnapping, blackmail, extortion of people who were already bewildered and afraid was not a thing the PD would be wanting to deal with. It would make the fine line they walked between the Feds and the local politicians worse. More troubling still was the insinuation that F13 was preying on the day workers.

Finn drove back to the office to see who might be looking for him and checked on lab reports he was expecting. He called the gang unit downtown and left a message for Sergeant Faulk saying he had information on Florenzia 13 that might interest him. Finn put his head into Captain Fowler's office, wanting to give his boss the basics on what was going down in that house.

"Does he have a minute, Tina?" Finn asked.

"Not here," she answered, without looking away from her computer screen or turning to face him. "Is it urgent?"

Finn said, "Better sooner than later."

"I'll let him know, O'Brien," Tina said.

"Sure, you must have eyes in the back of your head to know 'twas me," he teased.

"Yeah. That's it," Tina drawled. "Everybody around here sounds like an Irish Spring commercial."

"Don't be working too late."

He took his leave and then went on his way to his small office at the end of the long hall only to detour to the missing person unit. The officer behind the desk was a short redhead who Finn had seen around but had never been formally introduced to. He rectified that.

"Finn O'Brien."

She pointed to the nameplate on the desk. "That says it all."

"Officer Barnes," Finn said.

"Sheila is fine. It says that there, too."

She clasped her hands on her very messy desk and looked at him. The good news was that she smiled. Not welcoming, not flirty, just the kind of smile he saw Cori give a body now and again. That look said 'I'm all business and I'm not going to chew your head off unless you give me good reason'. Finn pulled a chair over and sat down.

"What can I do you for?" she asked.

"I've got two missing men."

"What's the case number?"

"No case number, they haven't been reported. I'm just looking into it for a friend of one of them. In doing that one, I came across the other."

He pulled out his pictures and put down Miguel's first.

"I just found out about this one. His name is Miguel Sanchez. Last seen two months ago on the corner of Chestnut and La Brea. Last contact with his father was around five in the afternoon. He said he was headed out for a job. And this one…"

Finn put down the second picture.

"His name is Pacal Acosta. He's been out of touch three days, so I'm thinking he just may not be checking in is all. Again, last heard from leaving his work at a local restaurant and on his way to pick up additional work."

Sheila Barnes picked that one up and gave it a look-see and Finn was delighted to see her taking the interest. Sheila put the picture back on the desk.

"Who were they working for?"

"I have no idea." Finn said.

"Day labor, right?" Sheila countered.

"'Fraid so. And before you say it, I know. They could be anywhere. But reports are they're both good men. Neither has done this before. I know the family hasn't made reports, but maybe you've received information on someone who matches the general description. I'm thinking it's odd that two young men, both approximately the same age and looking quite similar have up and disappeared. I didn't think it could hurt to see what you've got."

"That's what I get paid for." Sheila fired up her computer and tapped away at her keyboard. She paused. She ran the mouse, twitched her lips one-way and her nose the other. Finally, she swiveled back to him. "Nope. Nada. Closest I've got on a young Hispanic male is a twelve-year-old in the last month or so but that was a family dispute. They still haven't found him, but they think he's with his father in Mexico. If they're undocumented we're not the first place they go to for help."

"Then that, as they say, is that." Finn stood up. She gave him back the photos after taking one last long look.

"Sorry I couldn't help."

"As I am," Finn said. "Thank you."

Officer Sheila Barnes got up from her desk, went to the door and watched until Finn O'Brien was well down the hall. When she was sure he was gone, she went for her telephone and dialed. When the call went to message, she left one without hesitation:

"I need to talk to you ASAP."

CHAPTER 13

The man parked his truck in front of the house. It wasn't his house of course; it was just where he lived. More precisely, it was another place on a list of places he had lived. He had been here for a little more than a year and it was as good as any. The house, like him, was of no interest to anyone. It just existed in this neighborhood, unchanging, unremarkable, unnoticed. No one painted the house. No one tended a garden. No one hung Christmas decorations. The people who lived in the other houses on this street didn't do those things either. This house was a holding pen and the people in it cycled through until they were finally cut loose and forgotten.

So here he was again, parked in front of the house, luckier than the others because he had a truck left to him by his father. Luckier than most because his face set him apart and pity had its privileges. Pity got him a job and it got him his own room. Everyone wanted to make up some for what he had suffered. They couldn't make it better, of course. Only he could do that.

The man got out of the truck and walked up the strip of concrete that led to the front door. It intersected with a perpendicular strip of concrete that, he believed, was intended to be a porch. Really, it was just a slab of concrete.

The man did not lock his truck because no one in this neighborhood had the energy to steal it or vandalize it. Tired after their hard day of labor, their only ambition was to eat and sleep and get on with the next day. They also knew that the neighbors next door were poor and had nothing worth stealing so why bother. Except for him, he had his shovel. Then again, the shovel was probably only precious to him, so it was safe in the truck.

He opened the front door, stepped inside, took off his shoes and put them neatly against the wall. There were three pair in the hall already. His pair made four and now everyone was accounted for. There was a hole in the toe of one of his socks and he could feel the old carpeting scraping against his skin. It felt stiff with all the years of dirt and grime. Tomorrow he would buy a new pair of socks. Tonight, he would wash his feet well.

He went to a table in the entry hall and touched the top of the silver bell. It was the kind of bell you rang to summon a shopkeeper or that a teacher rang to call an unruly class to order. He liked the ting. It was so much better than the grating bray of an alarm. He hated the sound of alarms. Of doors closing. Of metal on metal. He hated voices that echoed off concrete walls. He hated the cruel laughter of men.

He touched the little bell again.

It tinged.

The woman who came at the call was a worn-out person. She didn't smile when she saw him. In fact, he was almost sure she didn't really see him. She just knew that he was on his side of the table at the right time and she was on her side as they had been every evening for a long time. She picked up a pen and looked at her watch. She noted the time in a big book with the date at the top of the page in bold letters.

"Here you go." She turned the book. He initialed the time she had written down. "Are you hungry? You're a little late, but I have leftovers."

He shook his head. He preferred not to speak. He liked to rest his face so that the scar at the side of his mouth didn't pull and pinch.

"Okay. Just don't come looking tonight. I'm still locking things up. Mr. Franks ain't got no self-control. I'll give you 'til eight then the kitchen's shut down for the night."

He shook his head again and mumbled that he wouldn't want any food. She didn't know how he kept going; he ate so little.

"Night then."

She went back to her kitchen and he went on. He passed the living room where three of his housemates were watching TV, not talking, not looking much entertained. Not much living going on in that living room he thought as he climbed the stairs. His back hurt so he paused now and again. There was no decoration of any kind in this place. Women decorated houses and there were no women here, so the house was not decorated. The person in the kitchen didn't count. Any womanly allure she had ever possessed had been beaten down, or drained out, or used up years ago. Not that the plainness of the house bothered him. It really was better this way. There were no distractions so he could spend his time planning, and reading his maps, and marking in his book, and reading his Bible. Unlike the others, he had plenty to do. He had a purpose.

In his room, he hung up his jacket and put aside his hat

as he always did. He went back down the hall to the bathroom and did his business. After he showered, he put his clothes back on. He was careful to always have his clothes on when he wasn't in his own room. Even though the other three men in the house were of an age and experience, one could never be too careful. He had learned that lesson in spades. No one would catch him off guard; no one would get him down on his knees ever again.

Back in his room he undressed once more, shook out his clothes and put them in the dresser drawer. They were a bit dirty, but not bad. Since the door had no lock, he put the chair up against it. He would know sure enough if someone tried to come in while he slept. If anyone did that, he would be ready even if there were a lot of them.

The man dressed in his pajamas and then he sat on the bed. It was a surprisingly good bed and he slept well in it even though it was small and narrow, like a child's bed. Perhaps it had been a child's bed. One time when he had been unable to sleep, after the Spanish man came to live in the house, he watched and waited all through the night. He even brought his shovel inside and held it at the ready. He even took the gun out of its hiding place and put it under his pillow. That's how afraid he had been. The Spanish person did not come for him, but still the man couldn't sleep, so he passed the time by peeling away little bits of the rose-printed wallpaper. Underneath that paper was more wallpaper. That wallpaper had yellow ducks on it. *Little duckies.* He had thought those words and he suddenly remembered being a child. Rubber duckies in the bath. The sight of that wallpaper made him smile because it was so unexpected. His mouth hardly hurt because he was concentrating on the duckies.

He had fallen asleep then, feeling safe in his child-sized

bed. Even now he could still see the little patch of yellow duck wallpaper when he turned over to face the wall, but it no longer made him smile. The Spanish person had gone away after a week and soon after, the man forgot all about him. That came as no surprise because his memory was getting worse. He only remembered the brutal things that had been done to him, his mission, and dates. People on the outside were big on dates. Still, the man knew there would come a time when he would forget the mission and why he had the maps. That was why he worked so hard now. He had to do as much good as possible before it was too late.

Sitting on his bed, the man took a book from under the pillow and made his notes for the day. They were very good notes. He looked back at the beginning of the book and read through the journal. Had there really been so many? It pleased him that he was able to be so meticulous and that he had accomplished so much.

When he was done, he got up and went to the dresser, an unnecessary piece of furniture. He could have put all his worldly possessions in a small box but, since it was there, he used it. His few clothes were in the second drawer, and the envelope he brought in each night was put deep into the top drawer. He put the maps and journal inside that envelope and tucked it away. Should he die or lose his memory someone would find this envelope and they would mail it because he had put postage on it, and it was addressed. And there was a note in it that said 'please mail'. He only hoped that he would remember to put everything inside when the time came.

On top of the dresser were his medicines. He put in his eye drops and rubbed the salve onto the scars on his face. He took out his teeth and put them in the water glass. There was no mirror, so he wasn't tempted to look at the odd reflection of a face grown old, collapsed in on itself, scarred, and ugly. When he was finished with all this, he opened the top drawer again and took out a pack of cards that had come in the mail the day before. Just in time since the pack in the truck was now almost empty. The woman downstairs had opened his package and that was fine. That was her job after all. When she saw what it was, she looked a little embarrassed. She said:

"Sorry. It's the rules to open stuff," she said. Then she added, "God bless you."

He mumbled at her and for a minute they were almost friends. Now he shuffled through the cards, admiring each in turn. It had cost him a pretty penny to get a combo pack, but he didn't mind. The printing was beautiful, the colors rich and the gold details bright as a celestial light. He probably wouldn't be able to use all of them in his lifetime, but no matter. It had been money well spent. He chose one, held it between his folded hands, knelt beside his bed and said his prayers. When he was done, he put the card in the pocket of his pajama shirt.

That was it. The day was done. It was eight o'clock and the sun was down. He closed his eyes and he slept well, as does any man who has put in a good day's work.

* * *

"'Tis the game shot, Andrew! My arrow flew straight and sure, it did."

Finn slapped Andrew, Mick's resident wannabe movie star, on the back as he went to collect the darts. He was inordinately pleased with himself since Andrew was an opponent to be reckoned with.

"Pure luck. Besides, I'm handicapped. I can't see straight. My eyes feel like they're going to fall out of my head," Andrew complained.

"Is it a cold you have? I thought your eyes looked a little bloodshot."

Finn pulled the darts from the board and placed them on the ledge where they were kept for anyone who had the urge to try their luck. He turned back to Andrew who had seated himself and was nursing his scotch.

"Nope, my friend," Andrew said with the air of a world-weary traveler dying to recount each step of his impressive journey. "I have been on set all day being dunked in a tank of water that was doctored to look like the ocean. They've got more chemicals in that stuff than Monsanto has patents."

"And what is it you were doing in the tank of fake sea water?"

Finn took a chair at the table, grabbed up his Guinness, stretched his legs and crossed one booted foot over the other.

"I was dying," Andrew said matter-of-factly.

"You didn't do it very well, now did you?" Finn answered. "You're sitting here having your cocktail, after all."

"Very funny. Dying is harder than it looks. I mean you can't be all jerky about it until the director tells you to panic. I've got this assistant-assistant director or something holding my head down—" Andrew held up a finger so Finn would attend to the most important part. "—Oh, and that's supposed to be Jack Nicholson's hand. Did I tell you that I booked a Nicholson flick? Not that I met him, but when you see the movie, you'll think it's him. We'll both be in the credits."

"Seems like you're coming up in the world. Booking a lot lately." Finn nodded and smiled so Andrew could see that he was full of admiration.

"I am finally paying the bills with my art," Andrew said

and Finn swore the lanky man's chest broadened another inch. "Yep. Yep. I think it's all going to work out. I really do. Anyway, here's the deal – this is where the acting comes in – I'm supposed to think this drowning thing is like a prank and be all smiling and having fun while I'm held under. Then the director gives the cue and I'm supposed to react: *oh, God, he's seriously going to kill me!* That's when I panic. The director wants my eyes open all the way 'till I'm dead. This director is a real SOB because he likes to hold out 'til the last minute for that transition. Well, I can tell you, do that whole scene ten or twelve times looking through that chemical water and your eyes would be bloodshot too and your aim would be off. Not to mention, it's scary. I mean really scary, but I couldn't let on. I have to show them that I can take it; I'm a real actor."

"Andrew, my friend, let me give you a bit of advice." Finn leaned forward so that he was half over the table. He cocked a finger inviting Andrew to do the same. When Andrew was close, Finn said: "Next time, die right the first time."

Andrew snapped back up and muttered into his drink. "Big help you are."

Finn chuckled, stood, and raised his glass.

"Sure, I'm pulling your leg. I'm honored to know a man who has been done in by Jack Nicholson. I think we should be talking to Geoffrey about a party the night the movie comes out."

"Naw, that's okay. I wouldn't want him to go to any trouble."

Finn smiled. Andrew, thirty years old, had blushed at the thought of being celebrated by the neighborhood folks. Finn wondered if he would remember them when he was a star. He hoped he would find out one day, for surely, he wished Andrew the best.

"You should go home and rest those eyes," Finn suggested.

"You're probably right. Except I have plenty of time to rest tomorrow. I don't have any calls, no auditions and, now that I'm dead, I'm finished with this project." Finn was about to assure him that his vacation wouldn't last long, but Andrew's attention was elsewhere. "There's Monica. Man, she is gorgeous. I'll see you, Finn."

Andrew was off. Finn glanced at the dartboard thinking to practice a little and then decided he'd had enough of the darts and ambled over to the bar. He crossed his arms on the gleaming surface, put his boot upon the brass railing, and kept a finger on his glass, trying to decide whether to shove it Geoffrey's way for a refill or call it a night. Geoffrey took the matter into his own hands. When the glass was filled up and back in front of Finn, Geoffrey crossed his arms on the bar too. They were silent as they looked over the patrons, both thinking the same thing: the ladies that night were particularly fetching. Finn looked at Geoffrey and realized he was quite the dandy tonight, too. His spectacular dreads were on full display. He looked a bit like a lion with his long thin face and that mane of twisted ropes.

"You've no beanie tonight," Finn noted.

"De spirit be movin' me, O'Brien. It say, 'show de glory of you, Geoffrey'."

"Well, the spirit was right, my man. Not that I don't like the beanies, but change is good."

"So, you be okay wit de funeral and all?"

Finn furrowed his brows and took a drink. It took him a moment and then he remembered sitting in this bar, wearing his dark suit, and coddling his morose attitude after his court hearing.

"Ah, Geoffrey, I'm sorry. No one has died. I was in court. My divorce was made final. It only felt like a funeral."

"Ah," Geoffrey raised his chin. "Like de death. Gotta mourn; gotta let it go."

"Yes, my friend. That is the truth," Finn agreed. Tired of standing, he slid onto a stool. He was getting hungry but didn't feel like a burger. He would finish up his drink and be going on home; perhaps he would pick up Chinese on the way.

"Der be a reason," Geoffrey went on, embracing the roll of philosophical bartender. "De reason is der be another lady just waitin' on you, O'Brien. See me? I know my woman be de only one for me, but we don't be livin' wit each other and dat makes it good all around. I go home, and we be happy; I leave, and we be happy. Dat's good for us. Everybody be different. But you, O'Brien? You be needin' a good woman in your bed every night sayin' sweetness. Dat's good for you."

"Sure, that is the truth," Finn answered back. "I'm an old-fashioned sort."

Laughter erupted from the end of the bar and they both turned to look. Andrew was holding court and not just with the lovely Monica. Two other ladies had joined their group. Finn smiled.

"You know, Geoffrey, here's the thing," he said. "It was hard standing there and having fewer words said to separate us than were said to bind us together. We went off as if the years had not mattered. The woman I married would not have been so carefree about such a thing as divorce."

"That not be de woman you marry," Geoffrey said.

"Agreed. That's why I am fine. I'm more disappointed, I think. I truly believed those vows, my friend. I don't know where I'm going to find a woman who…"

Finn never finished his thought because at that moment Mick's Irish Bar and Grill came under attack. The door was ripped open so violently that the women surrounding Andrew scattered, laying themselves back against the bar so that whoever was coming through the door would go for the actor first.

But the woman with the big blonde hair, the woman who had Finn's back every waking minute of the day, had no interest in Andrew or his beauties. Instead Cori Anderson stormed through Mick's and stopped a foot from Finn. She threw back her shoulders, raised herself to an impressive height and, as her nostrils flared, she barked:

"Who in the hell do you think you are, you Irish son of a bitch?"

CHAPTER 14

As with all establishments, there was a room at Mick's Irish Pub that few people ever saw, and management seldom used. That's where Geoffrey hustled Finn and Cori. He didn't mind Finn's neck in a noose, but he refused to swing along with him. Finn, after all, was only one customer. As much as it might hurt Geoffrey's heart to lose him to Cori's ire, he needed the other twenty people in the bar more.

So, here they were. Finn was sitting on an old chair that had a spring coming out of the upholstery just far enough to poke him in the back of his thigh. By the time he realized how uncomfortable it was he was cautious of bringing more of Cori's notice, so he endured the pain. Inside the room, there was a desk, the kind that would be found in schoolrooms in the fifties. There were boxes stacked against the wall. A life-sized, 3-D, plastic Santa Claus was propped up in the corner, not quite on his feet, grinning and looking as if he had imbibed a bit too much at Mick's. A glittering garland of green and silver Mylar fluff spilled out of a bag too small to hold its glory and a string of Halloween lights shaped like Jack-O-Lanterns snaked across the floor. There was an old coat tossed over a box, a mirror with a Budweiser logo painted on it, a broom and dustpan, and there was Cori pacing like a filly in a burning barn.

She had screeched like a fishwife and not even Finn had got the gist of what she was saying. Now she was silently fuming, cutting her eyes his way with each pass, shaking her head. Sometimes she paused to snort at him like a bull before she started to walk again. He waited it out and thought it a pity that he had not had the presence of mind to bring his drink with him. Better yet, he should have taken a bottle of Jamieson's, for certainly it appeared his was going to be a very long night.

Finally, Cori put her back up against the door. She splayed her legs as if she were sure he was going to try to escape. Her arms were crossed, her color high and her eyes blazing. Had Finn had one drink more he would have told her she looked beautiful. Since he valued the family jewels, he stayed silent.

"You couldn't tell me yourself? Seriously, you didn't have the guts to come to me with this?"

"Sure, Cori, I'm sorry, I don't know what you're talking about," Finn said.

"Oh, yes you do and don't be like every other lying SOB on the planet. I did not fall off the hay wagon yesterday." Her eyes narrowed, she snapped a hand his way, palm up, fingers twitching. "Give it to me. I want to see it right now."

"If you would just be giving me more of a hint as to what it is you're wanting, Cori, I'll be happy to oblige."

"The picture." She crossed the room, palm out, like a teacher waiting for the note passed in class. "The picture of Amber that you're waving all over town."

Finn closed his eyes and put a hand up to cover them.

He shook his head. Surely no good deed went unpunished.

"Don't look like you're the aggrieved party here, boyo," she mocked. "Sheila over at missing persons called me. Her kid and Amber went to high school together. She said you were in asking about two guys and one of them looked pretty damn cozy with my kid." Cori took one more step forward. "Give it to me."

Finn dropped his hand and looked up at her. Cori Anderson was an imposing figure in normal circumstances. Furious as she was, he could easily be convinced that she had dropped down from Mt. Olympus with marching orders from Zeus to incinerate the poor excuse for a mortal man that he was. Having no choice, he gave her the picture. Her jaw set as she looked at it. Her lashes were so long they brushed the tops of her cheeks. There was a fine black line above those lashes and above that was the blue shadow she favored. Her body betrayed none of what she was feeling. There wasn't a twitch of her arched brow or a tremble of the lips she held so tightly together.

"Cori, I…"

She waved the picture and turned away from him. Walking to the corner of the small room, she put her hand atop Santa's head. Her shoulders rose and fell as she collected her thoughts, tamed her anger, and dealt with her disappointment. That, Finn knew, would be a Herculean effort because she felt betrayed by the two people she most loved and trusted. Cori turned around and leaned against the wall. Santa, at his odd angle, seemed to be trying to chuck her under the chin to buck her up.

"I don't even know where to start." Cori's head swung back and forth. "I mean, really. Do we start with why my kid went to you with a problem instead of me? Or maybe we should discuss why you thought you were goddamn lord of the manor and could keep a secret like this from me? And you're not just keeping it from me, her mother, but from me, your partner. Or maybe we should just start with who in the hell is this guy and why are you looking for him?"

She flicked the photograph so hard with her nail that it sounded like the crack of a rifle shot. Cori bit on her bottom lip and settled her eyes on Finn.

"No, never mind on the last one. I can tell you who he is. He's an illegal…"

"Undocumented worker. He has two jobs…" Finn began.

Cori's free hand moved fast, and she slapped it into the plastic Santa hard.

"Cut the crap. It's just the two of us here and, unless you're going to be offended by my lack of political correctness, I can speak my mind."

"For goodness sake, woman, that's absurd," Finn said.

"Fine. Then it's you and me, but we're not partners right now. I'm not even sure we're friends. Got it?"

He nodded.

"What we are right now is this: I am a mother and you used to be a friend of the family. As such, I can tell you that I don't need to pick and choose my words like I would if we were on the clock." She held out the picture. "Illegal. Snuck in. Brought in. I don't care. That's what he is. Now tell me I'm wrong."

Finn shook his head. "You're not wrong."

Her hand fell to her side, her shoulders rounded and the pain in her eyes was almost too much for Finn to bear.

"This is what Amber has come to? This is what she wants? This is a future?"

"She says she loves him, Cori, and I believe her," Finn answered.

"She thought she loved the guy who knocked her up," Cori snapped. "She thought she loved the guy she met at the beach."

"This is different. I know it in my bones."

He started to get up, but she shot him a look that told him to stay, so he did.

"After you were hurt, Amber changed. She…" Finn paused until he had the right words, "she grew up, Cori. I watched her take care of you. I saw her handle work and Tucker and nursing you. She isn't the same girl. She's given this thought."

"You are so gullible," Cori said. "I've been fooled before. There's something about her that just begs for man trouble and this is the most trouble ever."

"Perhaps not."

"What's wrong with you?" Cori was stunned at his naiveté. "Let's play this out a little. How about that? You're the sheriff in town and you do your job, and you find this sucker and bring him back. Amber decides she can't live without him and they run off. If he stays with her but doesn't marry her – and that's a big if – they live in the shadows for the next five years, have four more kids and one day there's a knock on the door and the feds pick him up and send him packing to Mexico—"

"Guatemala," Finn corrected.

"Shut up," Cori snapped. "So they send him back and what happens then? Looks like the choices aren't all that great. In fact, there are only three. Amber marries him and he's now legal but that doesn't exactly guarantee he stays with her. Or, they aren't married, he goes back to where he came from and Amber hangs out with mom who's a tired old woman and not much help taking care of a bunch of kids. Or – married or not – she follows him back to a country where she can't speak the language and they're scratchin' out their living like chickens in a drought. Don't that just make a mother's heart burst with joy and pride."

Cori leaned back against the wall, she crossed her hands crotch level, the picture dangling from her fingers.

"Why didn't you tell me? After all we've been through, this is where you decide to screw me over?"

"Sure, it wasn't like that. I promise."

"Yeah, well you just go ahead and try to sell me this wagon like it's new, but I'm telling you it's so broken down it won't make it across the prairie much less through the mountains."

"Amber was afraid to come to you because you might react badly," Finn said, not adding that Cori was proving the point.

"Facts not in evidence," she said. Her eyes flickered to the left and then went down again. "Okay. I might have gone a little ballistic, but eventually I would have listened. Maybe I wouldn't have put on the kid gloves, but I would have helped."

"And kid gloves is what she was needing, Cori. She's afraid and worried. The boy's name is Pacal Acosta," Finn went on. "He started working at Romero's bussing tables about six months ago. They became friends—"

"With benefits, no doubt," Cori muttered.

"Actually, no. No benefits, Cori."

"Small favors." Cori colored, both with shame at jumping to the conclusion about her daughter and that Finn should know something like that. She waved a few fingers. "Go on."

"He has family here, but they are all under the radar. She hasn't met them. Amber doesn't even know where they live. So you are not alone in not knowing about the relationship.

"Pacal was working the corners as a day laborer as well as at the restaurant. He wanted to make something of himself so he worked every job he could get. He and Amber planned on telling you about their relationship when he had a way to support her and the wee one."

"Oh, God, Tucker. Did she bring Tucker around him?"

"I don't know, Cori, I'm only saying their intentions were good. Four days ago, he disappeared without a word."

"Big surprise."

"That's what I thought, but now I'm not so sure," Finn said.

That was all it took to bring her around. Mother she may be, but cop she was. The signs were subtle, but Finn saw them: a pricking of her ears, the softening of her mouth and the emergence of three furrows between her brows. Finn leaned his elbows on his knees, he clasped his hands, raising a finger for each point he was making.

He filled her in on everything: that Pacal supported his family after the father's desertion, that he worked two jobs, that he was kind and considerate. He told her about Gregorio and his missing son. Finn told Cori about Marbles implicating Florenzia 13 in the shake down of the day workers. He told her that he had talked to CHIRLA and Labor Ready and everyone offered him the same advice – the boys were jumped into a gang or had just moved on – and then dismissed him.

"So far there's one body at the morgue that comes close but it's not Pacal or Miguel and no one matching their descriptions has been noted at County," Finn finished.

"If they were hurt, they could go to any walk-in clinic in East L.A. Where does he live? We'll check it out," Cori said.

"Amber didn't know."

"Not even the general area?"

Finn shook his head. Cori twirled a finger.

"What else you got?"

"I was not putting much stock in any of this. I was going to tell Amber that I'd made inquiries – which would not be a lie – but then Gregorio gave me a list. It had his son's name and two others that have gone missing. That means four, Cori." When she didn't stop him, he went on. "Pacal and Miguel look very similar. The other two are in the right age range and Gregorio is going to find out what they look like."

"And you're thinking, what?" Cori asked.

Finn unclasped his hands. His shoulders went up. "I don't know. I'm only thinking 'tis a strange coincidence."

"How long has the janitor's kid been gone?"

"Two months."

"That's a long time for a kid who calls his daddy to say he's going to be late for dinner."

"Agreed. And if you take Amber's personal relationship out of the equation with Pacal, you've still got a responsible young man who has gone missing. Responsible young men usually don't just up and disappear for no reason at all."

"Okay, it's curious," Cori agreed.

"Don't forget F13. According to Marbles it's nothing more than a basic shakedown, mostly sport, but it's interesting that he should mention it."

"I see what you're getting at, but the bottom line is that this isn't our problem. If F13 is messing with them then that belongs to the gangs unit. Anything else is for ICE to worry about. The kid is gone. Leave it be and everything will be fine with Amber. That's the way I want it. That's the way it's going to be. I'll take care of her."

"Cori, I wouldn't—"

Before Finn could finish his counsel, the door opened, and Geoffrey put his head in.

"I be needin' some—"

Cori was on it. She pushed the door closed saying, "It will wait."

She turned back to Finn.

"What is your problem, O'Brien? I would seriously like to know 'cause I'm as confused as a gander in a hen house right about now. We've known each other a good long while, and I don't exactly recall you wanting to be Uncle Finn to my kid. Now you're in cahoots with her, keeping secrets, trying to find a boy that she thinks she's in love with. You do this even though you know it will bring nothing but heartache. Not just for Amber but for me too. You might as well have just put a goddamn knife in my heart."

Cori twitched her lips. Her palms hit against the door and she turned her head, showing him the profile of a profoundly wounded woman.

"Are you done?" Finn asked.

"For the time being," she said quietly.

"Do you want to sit down?"

She shook her head and her curls bounced around her shoulders, but the teased crown held tight as a helmet. She pursed her lips. Today they were the color of peaches with some sort of glaze on top like that of the pies his mother made. The color in her cheeks was high but it was not make-up that made them so rosy.

"Fine then. I'll be letting you in on my thinking. First, the girl took me by surprise. I found her sitting on my stoop, and what kind of man would I have been to turn her away?"

"A smart one," Cori said.

"But I didn't, nor did I promise not to tell you about this affair—"

"Bad choice of words, try again."

"Friendship," he revised. "I listened to her because she gave me no choice. I might point out that this seems to be a family trait. Be that as it may, what I heard was a young woman who had great admiration for the boy in question. She was not hysterical, she was truly wounded and worried, and I only promised to look into the matter. If I told you and nothing came of it, then a war between the two of you would have been for nothing. Things have been going so well, Cori, I didn't want to tip that balance. It's true, isn't it? Things have been going well between the two of you?"

Cori offered a curt nod.

"And if I did find something was amiss, then a boy would be in trouble, and when I told you, that would make a difference, would it not? You would want to do your duty first. Isn't that so?"

"Yeah, I suppose."

"And if you take this raging fury home and make Amber choose between Pacal and you, what do you think will happen? She's as headstrong as you. Do you really want her to take Tucker away because you've drawn a line you'll later regret?"

"No." Cori's bottom lip disappeared under her top teeth. She twisted her head. Her hands pounded lightly, open palmed, on the closed door.

"What if he just wants her so he can get a green card?" she asked.

"What if he marries her and takes her back to Central America because you're unaccepting and you never see them again?" he countered.

"What if he's just messing with her head for the fun of it?" Cori countered.

"What if they truly love one another?" Finn suggested.

"Oh, Jumping Jehoshaphat, what if he comes back? What then?"

Finn got out of his chair and walked halfway across the room, stopping at a respectful distance from his partner.

"Then you'll ride out the romance or you'll have a son-in-law. It will be up to you how you handle whichever it is, don't you think?"

"I suppose," Cori answered.

"A few days is all I'm asking. With this other boy missing, it seems that something is amiss. It's our job to try to make things right."

Cori narrowed her eyes and pursed those peach colored lips as she considered what he was saying. Finally, she took a deep breath and when she spoke again, she was reasonable.

"Two days. Three tops," she agreed. "But if you don't figure out how to shut Amber down, I'll do it. *Capisce?*"

"Three days, it is," Finn agreed.

Cori turned around and opened the door. Finn was on it, reaching over her head to pull it back. She sailed through only to come face to face with Geoffrey.

"You two bein' good wit' each other now?" Geoffrey grinned in the way one will when they are in dire straits and still have faith that help is on the way. Finn put his arm around Cori's shoulders.

"We're fine, Geoffrey. Just a misunderstanding."

Cori swiveled her head and looked him in the eye. A second later, she took his hand and dropped it away.

"Don't be counting your chickens, O'Brien," she said. "And don't patronize me."

With that, Cori Anderson marched out of Mick's Irish Pub, leaving Finn to wonder how on earth he could get out from behind the eight ball where Amber put him.

* * *

Cori was supposed to be on a date. Some guy had swiped right or left on her – she still wasn't sure how that thing worked – and he looked okay, so she'd agreed to meet him for drinks. Instead, after Sheila called and gave her the news about Amber, Cori sent a text telling him that super-secret police business was keeping her from accepting his kind offer.

She wasn't exactly lying. She'd been sitting surveillance on her own house for two hours. Amber had come home, paid the sitter, and changed out of her Italian Alice-in-Wonderland waitress uniform and into her other uniform: low slung jeans, a tee-shirt and flip flops. A half hour after she got home Amber came to the front stoop with Tucker. It was a family tradition, spending quiet time outside with your kid after work. Cori had done it with Amber and it put her right after a long day on the beat. If she closed her eyes, Cori could conjure up the feel of the grass under her feet as she pretended to chase her toddler. She could still hear the giggles of the little girl who always circled back to her mom.

But Cori's eyes weren't closed. She was looking hard at Amber sitting on the porch, elbows on her knees, chin cradled in her hands as she watched her son. It was warm so he only had on his diaper and a shirt that had Baby Hunk embroidered on it. When he went to his mom, hanging on her knees, crawling up the stairs and pulling himself close to her, Amber didn't move. It wasn't until he crawled into her lap that Amber seemed to even notice he was there.

"Snap out of it," Cori muttered.

But Amber didn't. The sun was going down and the girl was on remote control. She scooped Tucker up and put him on her hip. The little boy batted at her lips and babbled at her. Amber made the appropriate expressions and Tucker laughed. He didn't have a clue that his mom's heart was breaking; he didn't know that she wasn't thinking about the littlest man in her life but about the grown one who was missing.

Cori waited until it was dark and the lights in the house had been turned on. Amber walked back and forth – through the living room to the kitchen and back through the living room again. She went to the bedroom she shared with her son. Cori would have to remind her to close the curtains.

It was only when Amber had been out of sight for ten minutes that Cori started the car and pulled into the driveway. When she got out, she kicked at the crack in the concrete. It hadn't bugged her until now. After she kicked at it, she was truly ticked because she had scraped the toe of her shoe. She hitched her purse, opened the flap, and dug for her keys but found her gun first. One of these days she was going to have to holster the damn thing. She pushed it aside and got her key ring only to stop and pull out the hose. She turned on the faucet and gave the tomato plants a drink. They were covered with little yellow flowers and soon there would be tomatoes to pick. She didn't even like tomatoes that much, but she planted them so that Tucker could pick them. Amber had loved picking tomatoes when she was little. She never knew that there were times when that was all they had to eat.

Cori turned off the hose and coiled it once more.

Rubbing the water off her hands, she plastered what she believed was a normal expression on her face and went into the house. It was time to see what kind of actress she was.

* * *

From the back room, Cori heard the sound of the mobile they had put over Tucker's crib. It played *Mary Had a Little Lamb* and she knew that six plastic lambs hanging from their strings would be twirling over his head. He was two and he loved trucks and the little bat and ball Amber got him, but he still loved the little lambs, so they kept the mobile over the crib.

Cori dropped her purse on the chair and started for the kitchen but hesitated. She wasn't hungry. She wasn't even angry anymore. Okay, that last part was a lie. Long ago she had promised never to lie to herself since everyone else was so willing and able to do it. She was damn mad at Finn even though she understood his reasoning, but she was really devastated that Amber felt she had no choice but to go to him. Cori turned her back on the kitchen and went down the short hall, stopping long enough to toss her purse and jacket on her own bed before she planted herself in the doorway of Amber's room. She crossed her arms and leaned against the jamb.

"Hey, I'm ho—"

Amber looked over her shoulder and put her finger to her lips before she looked back at her child.

Cori's grin faded at the rebuke, but not her resolve. She walked into the room and stood beside the crib watching Amber use two fingers to rub the little boy's brow. His eyes were closing. The lambs were circling. Cori had her eyes on her daughter, and she wondered, as she always did, how this gorgeous creature could have come out of her body.

When it seemed that the baby was asleep, Amber stood up, but she didn't move away from the crib.

"You're home early," she whispered.

Cori shrugged, remembering that she was supposed to have been on a date.

"He wasn't really my cup of tea, I guess."

"Sorry," Amber said.

"Yeah. Me, too," she said just before she went on a fishing expedition. "It's damn hard finding a good man."

Amber stayed quiet, looking at her son, thinking far away thoughts of a boy named Pacal who washed dishes in a neighborhood restaurant.

The silence, her look, was enough to confirm everything Finn had said. Amber was hurting. She was scared. And she was mute. Unable to look her mother in the eye, she went to her bed where she had dumped out the laundry to be folded. Cori hesitated. She put her palm over Tucker's head for luck, and then turned from the crib and went to sit on Amber's bed. She plucked a tee-shirt out of the pile of laundry, but before she could fold it Amber took it from her, drawing it through her fingers.

"I can do that," Amber said. "You've had a long day."

"I want to help." Cori reached for the shirt again, but Amber pulled it back.

"Really, Mom, I've got it."

"Okay." Cori said. "It was kind of a disappointing evening. I guess I thought we could, you know, talk."

Amber's eyes flickered to Cori and away again. She worked slowly, petting the little tee-shirts and pants into tiny rectangles before putting them in a pile.

"Okay." Cori hitched up a knee, pretending she didn't notice that Amber had pretty much ignored her invitation to a gabfest. "So, how was work?"

"Fine. Same old," Amber answered. Suddenly she picked up the pile of clothes and dumped them back in the basket. She turned away. "You know, Mom, I'm really tired. I'll do this tomorrow."

Cori ran a finger under her nose. She tossed her head back and pushed at her hair. She bit her lip; bit the darn thing until it hurt. Keeping her mouth shut now was the hardest thing she would ever do, but she was determined to play this out. She got off the bed, pausing once to ask:

"Can I fix you something to eat?"

"No, thanks, Mom. Really. I just want to get to bed."

Cori nodded.

"Sleep well then. We'll talk in the morning."

"Close the door, will you?" Amber asked.

Cori leaned in and got hold of the doorknob. In all their years she had never had a closed door between them, but this was a week of firsts: a secret and now a closed door. There was nothing to be done about it that wouldn't unleash a storm of bad things, so Cori pulled the door closed and said a final goodnight.

In the kitchen, Cori fixed herself a sandwich, cleaned up and climbed into bed by nine-thirty. She picked up the remote, thinking to find an old movie to fall asleep to. Instead, she heard something she hadn't heard since Amber found out she was pregnant, and her boyfriend didn't care. It was the sound Cori had hoped she would never hear again. It was the sound of her daughter's sobs.

Cori Anderson tossed the remote on the bedside table, beat her pillows into submission and then pulled up the covers. She went to sleep cursing the thin walls of the dump she lived in. Oh, and cursed Finn O'Brien too.

He shouldn't have lied to her.

CHAPTER 15

APRIL 26

Marjorie Landly, Internal Affairs: It was a clean event. I just don't see that anyone is going to have a leg to stand on if they bring a complaint. This guy, Marbles, he's got a rap sheet that reads like a novel – of course none of it's public record because he was a juvenile. That changes now. You've got his prints on the shotgun, five people dead in the house and Shay is dead. Seems open and shut to me. I'm sorry I even had to interview O'Brien. **(head shake)**

Captain Fowler: Was there any problem while you were talking to him?

Marjorie Landly: He was cool, a real gentleman. Given his history with my department, I was kind of surprised to tell you the truth. He gave me what I needed. Nice accent too. Is he single?

Captain Fowler: That's on a need to know basis. **(smiles)**

Marjorie Landly: Probably too young for me anyway. **(gets up)** I'm sorry about Shay.

Captain Fowler: (nod) She was a good officer.

Marjorie Landly: Okay, then. Unless something

crawls out of the woodwork, I'm not thinking the force investigators are going to bother much with it. I will tell you the same thing I told Detective O'Brien; a civil lawsuit will be filed. That's all the rage these days. It will probably die on the vine unless this guy's attorney pushes the envelope somehow, but he'd have to get really creative. Still, everybody knows the city usually caves and makes some kind of payout.

Captain Fowler: It won't do Marbles any good in jail. He can't profit from his crimes.

Marjorie Landly: (pausing before opening the door) Just to be on the safe side, you may want to keep Detective O'Brien out of the fray on Cinco de Mayo. If there's trouble downtown and someone gets hurt, you don't want any finger pointing his way given what happened in that house.

Captain Fowler: A man as experienced as O'Brien standing down doesn't make sense. If someone has a problem with him on Cinco de Mayo, it's their problem alone.

Marjorie Landly: Whatever you say. Good to see you again, Bob. You take care.

Captain Fowler: (smiling) You, too. Thanks.

Marjorie Landly: (gone)

Finn knocked on the door of a small house four down and across the street from the place where he had shot Marbles, and where Officer Shay had lost her life. There was no indication that anything horrible had happened on the street. The matte-black low-rider was gone, towed to the city pound and held as evidence. The yellow tape that had been strung on the perimeter had been wadded up and tossed away, the chain and post to which the pit bull had been tied was still there near the steps but the pit bull had been dispatched. The bodies found upstairs were in the morgue, and Marbles, having satisfied his doctors that he was healing nicely, had been transferred from County USC to L.A. County Men's jail. Soon he would be sent on to Clara Shortridge Foltz Criminal Justice Center to await trial. Finn planned on being front row center for that. After that – after his conviction – Finn didn't care where he went just as long as it was as close to a hellhole as the bleeding hearts in the California Legislature would allow.

This morning, with Cori in tow, Finn had revisited the place to make one last sweep in case there was something he had missed, and to talk to the neighbors given the information he now had about F13's activity with the day laborers. The only thing he hadn't seen in the house – the thing Cori pointed out – was a hole in the closet where the children had been found. He promised to make note of it, but she seemed not to care if he did or not.

It was Cori who walked out of the house first and stayed a step ahead of him. It was she who answered him with one word each time he tried to break the ice that had not thawed. It was she who stared at the doors upon which they knocked in the hopes of getting anyone to speak with them. This was the eighth door that morning and if anyone was home, they were taking their own sweet time about answering the door.

"How long will you be giving me the cold shoulder," Finn asked.

"A while," Cori said.

"And is there nothing I can do to speed up it, then?"

"Nope." She moved her purse to her other shoulder. "No one's home. I've got better things to do."

It did not escape Finn's notice that she turned away from him as if he was so low she couldn't deign to look upon his countenance. Finn put a finger to the side of his nose and rubbed it as she stomped down the wooden stairs. He shook his head and looked up at the porch overhang.

"What are you sighing about?" Cori stood on the walkway looking at him with narrowed eyes and speaking at him through tight lips.

"I'm not sighing, Cori. I'm not smiling. I'm befuddled is all." He took the steps down to ground level and stood a foot away. "Sure, I've explained myself being put between a rock and a hard place as I was. I have apologized. Save for opening my wrists for you, I've not got a clue what will put me back in your good graces."

"You'll know what to do after I figure it out." Cori turned on her heel only to pivot back again. "Look, I just want to put this in some perspective here, bucko. Okay? Do I have your ear for a minute?"

"For as long as you like if it will help," Finn said.

"Good," she snapped. "So listen up. You're thinking like a man. You know how men think when something really big happens? They think, wow, something real big just happened. Take sex for instance. You know when you have really good sex and you say 'thank you ma'am'? You know that?"

"I think I remember," Finn said, amused but daring not even a smile.

"Okay, then what do you do? What do all men do? They roll over and go to sleep and the moment passes 'til it happens again." She moved a step closer and leaned into him. "And what's the lady do? Huh? Huh?"

"Sure, I'd be afraid to speculate," Finn answered.

"She lies awake wondering about stuff. That's what she does. I mean, maybe the sex was good. Maybe it was better than good. But she's left with all sorts of stuff on her mind like does he love me? Does he like me? Is there a future? Well, that's what this is like."

Cori's shoulders rose and fell, she rolled her eyes, and then went back at it.

"The other night you went home and went to sleep? I went home to my kid who is being torn apart. For two nights I've been listening to her cry her eyes out and I can't say a damn thing. I can't ask 'do you love him?' 'How do you know he loves you?' I couldn't even ask how I could help her. It was like having this huge secret that I can't share with the one person who needs to hear that I know it.

"So, in answer to your question, no. There is nothing you can do to make me less pissed off at you because I am in a horn-tossing mood and it's going to take something big to tame it. Are we clear?"

"Definitely," Finn said, unable to argue with her reasoning. "And can we get on with our work together, or is the sight of me so distressful that you want to…"

Finn stopped talking because Cori was looking past him. She forced a smile, and it wasn't for his benefit.

"We got some interest. Curtain's moving."

Finn looked over his shoulder and then turned toward the house.

"Then let's knock one more time and see where it gets us. That is if you can bear to stand next to me."

Cori flipped her hair and breezed past him.

"Don't be ridiculous. Every woman knows how to fake it."

* * *

When the door of the small house opened a crack, Cori and Finn stood tall. They were ready for anything – an angry man, a frightened woman, a defiant teenager – but what they got was a little Asian girl.

"Good day to you, miss," Finn said. "Is your mother or father home?"

The door opened a little wider so that they could see her in all her wary, scowling glory. She was no more than nine or ten and dressed in pink pants and a green shirt with white buttons. Her hair was shiny, and her clothes were neat. She wore sneakers with blinking lights embedded in the soles. She shook her head and her long black hair swung down her back.

"Do you speak English, honey?" The girl nodded as Cori got down to eye level. She held out her badge with one hand and pointed at it. "We're from the police and we need to talk to an adult, so I think we better come back when your mom and dad are home. Do you know when they'll be back?"

The little girl stared at Cori, her face wadded up into what Finn assumed was a threatening expression. Then he decided it must have been her confused expression because she was looking at Cori but her head was tilted as if she was listening to someone inside. When her head tilted back, she recited:

"My mom will come back later. What do you want to know?"

"Well, we were wondering if you know who lived in the house down the way. The two-story house," Finn said.

"Where the people got shot?" she asked.

"Yes," Cori answered, holding onto the side of the house to push back up. She shook one leg out just a little and her pant leg fell into place. "What's your name?"

The girl tilted her head again. Cori and Finn exchanged a look and a smile. Finn motioned his partner down again and she got to one knee, knowing what he wanted her to do. She was in front of the open door and from her knees she had an angle to see inside the place that he did not. She got the girl's attention again.

"You know, I'd worry if you were home alone. Do you want us to call your mom?"

She shook her head hard like little girls do and that black hair snapped.

"Oh, then you're okay? Is there someone home with you now?" Cori leaned right and so did the little girl. She leaned left. And so did the girl. "It would make us feel so much better if we knew you weren't alone."

The girl kept her eyes on Cori and then she looked up at Finn. He showed her his best smile. It seemed acceptable.

"My name's Marciella," she said and pushed the door open fully. Behind her and off to the side stood a very old woman with a toddler clinging to her black clad leg. "This is my grandmother."

Cori got up. Her knees cracked this time. She nodded to the old lady and held out her badge. Finn moved to her side.

"Do you mind if we have a word with you, missus? About the house down the way?"

"No good. Bad boys." The old woman waved her hands.

"I've seen them," Marciella chimed in. "I seen them beat some boys up."

"Really," Finn said. "Can you tell us about the boys and the people who beat them up? Is that alright, Grandmother?"

* * *

Twenty-minutes later, Finn and Cori were back outside, walking shoulder to shoulder down the street toward their car. The damn thing stood out like a sore thumb parked up against the crumbling curb. It might as well have the word 'cop' stamped on the hood. Cori hadn't forgotten her ire, but it was tamped down in favor of curiosity about the business at hand.

"So, what are you thinking?" Cori asked.

"I'm thinking we have confirmation that people came and went and that bad things have been going on for a while, but a child and an old woman are not going to be figuring into the prosecution for those murders. But they did see young men being brought in. They saw three running away."

"That could be anything. Guys they're trying to jump. Younger men who got caught up in the sweep." Cori swung herself around and stood in front of him. "You're trying to fit a square peg into a round hole. You're trying to make your missing guys fit into this scenario but it's not working."

"You're right." Finn hooked his thumbs in the pockets of his jeans and looked down the street as if hoping, by some miracle, the answer would come to him. "There is no margin in taking men off the corners and holding them for ransom. If they really are harassing the day workers, then it's a bit of bullying and nothing more. What they're doing at these houses is a sophisticated operation. The people or their relatives pay up, they're released, disappear into this huge city and no one is the wiser."

"And if they don't pay up?" Cori asked.

"Human trafficking, perhaps. They can be sold as indentured servants, sex slaves." Finn shrugged as if to say they were only limited by their imaginations. "There's nothing here that will help me find Pacal or Miguel."

"Well then, I say we make peace," Cori said.

"What will it cost me?" Finn asked.

"Tell Amber you're done. Today. You said to give it

three days. You've had two. You've asked all around. You've hit the hospitals and the morgue and you're coming up empty." Finn shifted his weight. He started for the car again. Cori stopped him – again. "That boy–"

"Pacal," Finn said and went on walking. He was not willing to let Amber's friend go unnamed. Cori fell in step.

"Whatever. He's a dead end for her. Amber cries herself to sleep every night, O'Brien. Let her get on with her life. Admit there's no there there."

Finn put on his sunglasses. He did a quarter turn and looked at his partner's hopeful face. Then he looked past her and tried to imagine Amber here, living behind bars, frightened all the time. It would be a sad thing.

"Perhaps you're right. I'll talk to her and Gregorio, too." Finn sighed. "Sure, I'm not liking the prospect of either chat. They had faith in me, Cori, and I let them down."

"Don't beat yourself up, O'Brien. It was a needle in a haystack. You did your best."

"Then why don't I feel as if I did?" Finn muttered knowing that he would wonder about those men every time he saw day workers. Worse, Amber would wonder.

He opened the driver side door of the car; Cori went to the passenger side but kept eyes on her partner. He looked back and shook his head. The woman had a way of asking a question without ever opening her mouth.

"Yes, I promise," he said. "I will talk to her tonight."

"'Preciate it," she said.

Before Finn could say she was welcome, his phone rang. He answered it, listened and when he hung up, he motioned for Cori to get in the car. He was already heading south before Cori got her seatbelt on.

"Well you ain't burning no daylight," Cori said. "Where we going?"

"The oil fields between La Cienega and La Brea."

"You mean that area off Stocker in Baldwin Hills?" Cori asked. Finn nodded. "A little out of our jurisdiction, don't you think?"

"But right up our alley," Finn answered before adding, "unfortunately."

CHAPTER 16

Baldwin Hills is home to 127 miles of parkland and scrub interspersed with homes, strip malls and a dam. The other thing Baldwin Hills has is seven hundred acres of oil fields studded with twelve hundred wells. Many are out of service, many others are abandoned, but that still leaves four hundred and thirty wells actively pumping away at the stores of oil and natural gas in the middle of the largest, most heavily populated county in the country.

The specific area Finn and Cori were looking for was just off Stocker Street, a winding boulevard that savvy commuters used to cut through the hills between La Cienega and Fairfax to La Brea just before the street dead-ends into the actual park. They turned off Stocker at a dirt driveway cut into the glorified shoulder on the edge of the busy, paved thoroughfare. They bumped over it for a few seconds and then passed through the long, low gate that had been swung back and left open. They continued up the dirt road, stopping beside a black and white and an unmarked unit. Just beyond the cars was a knot of three men standing between two wells and behind a small area cordoned off with yellow tape.

Cori chucked her purse under the seat and together she and Finn walked over the dry ground, sidestepping an irregular swath of wet earth that had come from a point higher than where the men stood.

One of the men wore jeans, a work shirt and heavy boots, the uniformed man was in full regalia with his proper gun belt, knife pleated shirt and badge. The third man wore brown slacks, a short sleeved blue shirt and a tie that was too wide to be considered fashionable. That man was slender but moon-faced. His thin blond hair seemed to ruffle despite the fact that the air was still. That man was the one Finn wanted.

"Detective Crane?" Finn called to the moon-faced man when they were within polite hailing distance.

Detective Crane looked up, said something to the other two men and walked around the yellow tape to greet them.

"I saw your communiqué—" Detective Crane said.

"You sent an alert when there was no jacket?" Cori muttered.

"And I thought this might be something—" Crane went on.

"Only after you knew," Finn whispered back.

"—that would interest you."

Crane shook their hands and then led them back to the others.

"This is Officer Friedman who responded and Mr. Brison."

The man in the work clothes said: "Tim. Tim's fine."

"Good to meet you." Finn introduced himself and Cori as they moved around the taped perimeter. He pushed his jacket back and put his hands on his hips. He raised his brows when he looked Tim's way. "I'm thinking it is you who found the body?"

"I did," he answered. "And I have to tell you it wasn't the way I wanted to end my day."

"I'm sure he feels the same way." Finn hunkered down to view the body lying in the shallow grave.

"That's got to be cop humor, right?" the man said without appreciation.

"A little ha-ha gets us through the hours," Cori answered, finding it interesting how civilians reacted when faced with a situation like this.

Some were so unsettled that they fell apart, were rendered speechless or became befuddled. Others wanted to be important, so they dogged an investigator, plying them with information that usually had no basis in fact. By the time cocktail hour rolled around they would be boasting that they had been indispensable to a criminal investigation. Still others, like Tim, were pale and wide-eyed, ready to do their civic duty but hoping they didn't have to do it too long.

"How is it you found him?" Finn asked.

"I come out and do a couple checks once a month on the wells that are still in service. These weren't on the schedule until next month, but there's a shack a ways up where we keep paperwork and maps and stuff. It's got electricity and a bathroom.

"Anyway, I stopped to hit the John and then I was headed over there." He pointed away from the area in which they stood. "That's when I noticed the ground was wet. I thought maybe a water pipe broke, but that would have seeped up, not run down. There are other water supplies for fire hook ups and such. I saw one of them was broke, so I did a temporary fix. I start back to where I was going but changed my mind and followed the trail. I figured that it would be better to know sooner than later if the water damaged anything. Not that there's much around here that could be water damaged, but never say never. Anyway, I followed the flow and that's when I saw him. There had been just enough water to wash away some of the topsoil. I only saw his nose and part of his head and I gotta tell you, I seriously freaked out. I called you guys. I guess he's all yours now."

When Tim was done speaking, they all looked at the dead man lying on his back in the hole. Most of the dirt covering him had been cleared away but they could see that the water had penetrated the hole slightly below chest level. They could make out the precision of the grave's edges where they had not been damaged by the flow.

"Did you touch anything? Move anything?" Finn asked.

"No. I retraced my steps exactly when I went to make the call," Tim said. "I know it's dumb, but I remember hearing that on T.V. You know, go back the way you came?"

"Sometimes television gets it right," Finn assured him.

"We uncovered the rest of him," Detective Crane said.

"You got pictures?" Cori asked.

"We did. The photographer's already come and gone," Detective Crane said. "I'm assuming you'll be wanting a copy or two."

"You assume correctly. Thank you," Finn said.

Cori moved to stand behind him, her eyes on the man in the grave. One look and she knew exactly why they were there. The deceased was Hispanic, young, dark haired, between the ages of fifteen and twenty-five and very dead. She leaned over Finn's shoulder.

"Is that him?" she asked.

Finn shook his head and then stood up, "No, it's not Pacal."

He reached into his breast pocket and took out the

picture of Gregorio's son. He held it for Cori to see.

"Not him either," she sighed.

"But still not good. They could all be brothers." Finn turned to Detective Crane. "So what are you thinking, sir?"

"I'm thinking someone here needs to make sure that gate is locked so people can't get in and do their mischief," Crane said. "Whoever did this must have driven right up. There would be too many people passing on Stocker if the perp tried to lug a body over the fence. Even if it were midnight, there would be too many cars to chance it."

"Is that gate ever locked?" Cori looked at Tim.

"It's supposed to be." He moved from foot to foot, in an anxious little dance that took him further from the grave with each step. "Mostly it's not. There are so many warning signs we all figure nobody's going to come in here and do anything."

"Who would have reason to be here?" Detective Crane asked.

"Eight or ten people that I know of. Geologists are out here some. The oil company people. The city people – regulators – you know. I come once a month to inspect fifty wells on a rotation."

"Can we get the names of those people?" Detective Crane asked.

"I'll give you the site manager's name. He'll know them all."

Detective Crane nodded. The uniformed officer walked away to answer a call in his car while Cori and Finn huddled over the body with their counterpart.

"It was done here, in the trench. There are no drag marks, no blood trails," Finn said.

"Yeah, but look at the ground," Cori pointed out. "The topsoil would blow away so fast if there was a wind, and we don't know how long the body's been out here. He could have been dragged and we'd never know it."

"Except the blood pooled under the head and shoulders," Finn pointed out. "There's plenty of it, so I'm thinking he was standing in there when someone split his head open. If he'd been moved, there would either be blood on the ground over there or he would have been drained if he'd come a distance. As it is, the blood is contained right here, in the hole."

"So you think he was forced to dig the grave and then just stood there waiting to have his head taken off?" Detective Crane asked.

"Maybe," Cori muttered, and then she looked at them. "Think about it. If he's like the two men we're looking for, he was waiting for work and someone offered it."

"Then they drive here," Finn said. "There would be no reason to be suspicious. This is a work site; he's told to dig and he does."

"And whoever had him do the digging, takes a shovel or a pick-ax or something and wham." Crane put his hands together and raised his arms, bringing them down at the angle that would have caved the man's head in. "Look at the blow, how the skull is cut on an angle. I'd say whatever hit him came from above for sure. If he had seen it coming there was plenty of room to run here, lots of places to hide behind, but he didn't do any of that."

"Charming," Cori drawled. "We've got a lazy, crazy killer. Make 'em dig their own graves and do the deed while they are knee deep. Very clean. There's no struggle. No trace evidence because there's no contact."

"This one is dressed for work." Finn noted the worn jeans, the work shirt buttoned up to the chin, the heavy boots. He also saw that the man's clothes were clean underneath the bloodstains and the mess the dirt and mud had made. That meant one of two things: either this young man took great pride in his own appearance or he had someone looking out for him. A wife? A mother? A father like Gregorio? A girlfriend like Amber?

"Was he just like this? With his hands crossed that way?" Finn asked.

"Yep," Crane answered. "And that would lead me to believe he might have known his attacker. Maybe it was someone close to him like family. I don't think you'd have a random assault where the killer would take that kind of care."

Finn took a few steps to the edge of the grave and looked down the slight incline between where the digging had occurred and the well that continued to pump about fifty feet away. He looked behind him and could not see the shack. The machinery was huge and far enough from the gate to hide any activity from the cars driving by on Stocker. Still, it was close enough to the entrance that, once the deed was done, the getaway would be easy. If the person knew anything about the workings of this field, he would know that there were seldom people around. All this meant that the act had been well planned, and it was pure luck that the body had been found.

"Any tracks?" he asked.

"Not really. The ground is dry so it would be like driving in the desert. That's why the body is in good shape. It looks like it happened yesterday, I swear."

"Maybe it did," Cori said.

"I don't think so," Tim said. "Yesterday there was a team up here taking samples. Three guys. I know that for sure 'cause I saw it on the schedule. Oh, and I saw a guy in a white truck about a week ago, maybe less. I'm pretty sure he was alone, but I don't know who he was working for. I think he was over in this area. Honest, I can't be sure."

"Do you know what kind of truck?"

Tim shook his head, "I don't. It was small. I remember that. Small and white. The guy had a hat on. Not a hard hat though, so I'm thinking one of the geologists or someone from the city."

"Was there anything that gave you pause about him?"

"No, not really. He waved. I waved back. That was kind of it. You know how it is when you're working."

"No worries, we'll sort it out. Thank you." Finn turned to Detective Crane. "Looks like you have more people to talk to than it would seem."

"A man may work from sun to sun, but a detective's work is never done." Crane grimaced and his two colleagues laughed politely. "Anyway, I've scoured the area. I don't see anything that could really help me. Clean as a whistle. I'm hoping when the coroner pulls the prints, we'll get a lead. Then we can work backward from there to see if he fits into your investigation."

"I wouldn't count on you finding out much about him," Finn answered. He pulled out the photographs to show Crane, but Cori didn't join them. She didn't want to see Amber in Finn's picture again, so she perused the body while her partner filled Crane in.

"I can see the similarities," Crane said. "This will be a bitch of a thing to solve if we've got a serial killer who's after undocumented folks. If we can't track the victims, we can't find the killer."

"No." Cori spoke so loudly she surprised the men. She clicked her neck and inclined her head. "No, he's not thinking that there's a serial killer. There's a long way to go before we step into that pile."

Finn stayed silent. Until he saw this body and how closely the dead man resembled the other two, the possibility of a serial killer had not entered his head. Even now it wasn't top of mind, but his list of possible outcomes was getting longer by the minute: gang jumps, runaways, return to country of origin, accident, new job, new woman – murder, serial murder.

"Did you see that?" Cori asked. Finn shook off his thoughts when he saw that Cori was hunkered down beside the grave again, pointing at the man's hands. "Right there, under the hands. I'll grab the sleeves if you can snag it, Crane."

"Will do."

From his back pocket he pulled an evidence bag and tweezers. Cori got on her knees. The grave was shallow enough that she could reach the corpse without disturbing the perimeter. She pinched the shirtsleeve on both the top and bottom arms, pulling up gently to give Crane enough wiggle room.

"Got it," he said and held up the tweezers. They could see that the thing he had slid from under the dead man's hands was a piece of paper. Finn moved in closer. Cori stood up to take a look.

"Excuse me, do you need me anymore?"

All heads turned. They had forgotten about Tim.

"No, you can take off," Detective Crane said. "I've got your statement. I appreciate the help. If you think of anything more, give me a call."

Tim waved a hand, not so much an expression of adieu as one of relief that he could put this behind him. Detective Crane dropped the rectangle of paper into the evidence bag.

"May I?" Finn asked and the bag was passed between them.

He held it up for a better look. The light was still decent but, as luck would have it, the water had seeped through to the body where the paper was placed. Most of it had disintegrated and there was little to see. Still, he could make out what appeared to be gold scrollwork on one edge and a spot of what had once been a red color in the middle.

"Any ideas?" Detective Crane asked.

Finn shook his head and handed back the bag even though there was a niggling thought that he did know what this was.

"Have you taken anything else off him?" Cori asked as the coroner's van rumbled up through the oil fields.

"Give me a minute," Detective Crane asked.

He went to meet the van and as he passed Officer Friedman, he said a few words. A second later the black and white was gone back to patrol. Cori and Finn stepped aside to let the coroner's assistants do their job. On his way back, Crane stopped at his car and when he got to Cori and Finn, he held out two more evidence bags. Cori took one and Finn the other.

"I've got a picture of a girl in a gown." Cori said and turned it for Finn to see. The girl was beautiful and very young. She wore a full white dress but no veil. "Looks like a *Quinceneara* picture. You know, a coming out party for Hispanic girls when they reach fifteen. What have you got?"

Finn held up his bag. "A receipt from a McDonalds – on Chestnut Street. The same corner where Pacal picked up work."

CHAPTER 17

APRIL 28

Father Daniel Day, St. Catherine's Church, South Bay: I look out today upon this sea of faces and I see grief for a fallen comrade. I look to Officer Shay's family and I see grief for the passing of a beloved wife, mother, and daughter. But in all your faces, I also see pride and I see faith. Pride in the fact that Officer Shay conducted herself with honor. Each and every one of us should be thankful that we knew this woman, this police officer who thought nothing of her own safety and whose selfless actions and sacrifice changed the lives of so many for the good. What she did led to the capture of a man who preyed upon the innocent and the feeble and those who have no voice. Her courage is a legacy left for each of you. When you step up for those less fortunate, those who live in silence and shadows, you will have Officer Shay on your shoulder guiding your hands and living in your hearts because you are the protectors and the peace keepers. I bless each and every one of you. I bless Officer Shay's family and I commend her soul to the heaven she so richly deserves.

Let us pray. **(hands parting, palms raised, turning to the altar, away from the casket.)**

"I seriously do not want to hear it, O'Brien. Not today. Show some respect for Shay."

They were in arrowhead formation walking down the narrow hall at the precinct: Bob Fowler at the point, Cori and Finn slightly behind flanking him at the elbows, keeping up with his brisk pace. All were in their dress blues, looking sharp from the tips of their shined black shoes to the tight knots of their black ties that hung down the front of the bluer-than-navy-blue wool long-sleeved shirts. Their gold badges were shined and pinned above their hearts; their hats were snapped under their arms. It was a sad event that had them dressed so, and it was this sad event that made it imperative for Finn to have this discussion with his captain now.

"That's precisely why we should be talking about this, Captain. Sure, isn't this why Officer Shay lay dead in her coffin today? It's because there are those in need of our assistance in the Hispanic community. Shay gave her life for those people."

"Shay was on a domestic violence call and walked into a gang problem. That's not what you're talking about, O'Brien."

"We don't know what we're talking about, Captain, and that's the point?" Cori put in her two cents. "Maybe what we're looking at is tied to the house and the shakedowns and maybe it isn't, but there's no way to know without a full-on investigation."

"We've got four men missing and a body," Finn reminded his captain. "Maybe two dead if the one in the morgue can be tied in."

"Two bodies, both out of our jurisdiction," Fowler answered. "Let Baldwin Hills deal with theirs and wherever the other one in the morgue came from. It's not our problem."

He made a hard right and sailed past Tina who swiveled just in time to hand him a stack of mail. He took it and pushed on into his private office, put his hat on the coat rack in the corner of his office and sat himself behind his desk. Cori and Finn were on his heels. He scowled.

"I don't remember inviting you in."

"Nor did you shut the door," Finn pointed out.

The two detectives stood at attention in front of him. Fowler came as close to huffing as Finn had ever seen him, then he raised a finger and motioned to the chairs in front of his desk.

"Thank you, Captain." Finn shot a small smile at Cori. She gave him one right back and let him run with it. "Two of the men went missing within our territory. Baldwin Hills is hoping to identify their John Doe. Once they do that, we can figure out if he was working the corners in Wilshire Division, too, or hiring out from someplace like CHIRLA. We may not be able to find out who the man in the morgue is, but he fits the profile so we're going to keep him on the list. Maybe we can find a link to a job site. All we're asking for is the go ahead to look into this officially and expand our inquiry throughout the county. If we come back with more hits that fit the profile, we want to know that you'll be behind a task force."

While he listened, Fowler planted his elbows on the arms of his chair, folded his hands and put his fingers up against his lips. When it appeared that Finn was finished, he dropped his hands and asked:

"Why do you do this, O'Brien? You're always chasing

after some hard luck cause that just sucks the energy out of this precinct."

"It's a curse, Captain," Cori piped up. He shot her a withering look, but it bounced off her. "Come on, you've got to admit that it seems like there's a yellow jacket in the outhouse."

"Anderson, the only yellow jackets making a buzz in this office are you two. I was counting on you to talk some sense into him." He blew out hard through his lips and put his hands atop two stacks of paper. He patted the first one. "This is my day's work, right here. I've got complaints, requisitions, budgets, memos from meetings with the city council and the mayor, and we're having plumbing problems that are making it none too pleasant in the men's locker room."

He patted the other stack.

"And here? I've got long-term planning, speeches, strategic planning for the Cinco de Mayo celebrations – or confrontations depending on how you look at it. I have to figure out how to pay you guys for the overtime you'll be incurring, schedule who is going to be on what duty and what shift all the while making sure the precinct is staffed and the daily business is attended to. Not to mention that I have to figure out a way to get to my kid's little league practices because my wife volunteered me to be an assistant coach." He fell back in his chair and did what neither detective had ever heard him do before. He complained. "I don't even like baseball. I'm a tennis guy."

He gave one little chuckle and smiled a smile that was weary and resigned.

"And you two want me to raise a red flag and tell the powers that be at city hall that you think a serial killer is preying on undocumented workers. Just before Cinco de Mayo. Just when we've assured everyone that what happened in that house the other night was an anomaly and that we do not have gangs murdering immigrants en masse. Good grief."

"Aw, Captain, 'tisn't like that at all. We're not thinking of broadcasting this investigation. We just want permission to officially coordinate with other agencies and divisions. The two bodies we're talking about were both buried in dry ground. Both were killed with blows to the head. We'll still handle the jacket for Marbles but reassign the Webb matter and the Andrews killing and let us dig our teeth into this. We'd like to go as far as Palmdale and down to Palm Springs – any place with large expanses of desert or scrub – but we need your blessing to get those departments to sit up and take notice."

"There's precedent we shouldn't ignore." Cori caught the fever and leaned into her argument, looking fierce in her dress blues with her hair pulled back in a tight bun. "The Morning Stalker Killer, remember him? He took out ten prostitutes in ten days in the spring and again in winter. We pulled out all the stops. LAPD, Sheriff's even the Marshal's got into the act on that one."

"Apples and oranges, Anderson," Fowler answered. "There was community assistance with the Morning Stalker. The girls on the street knew one another and they served a consistent enough clientele that they could compare notes. They shared their information with us. Some of them had families that gave us backgrounds on the victims.

"What you're talking about is an ever-changing landscape of people who come and go. They aren't going to put themselves in jeopardy of deportation to help us out, not even to help out their families."

"One did," Finn reminded his captain.

"And who's the other one? Some west-sider whose gardener's gone missing?"

Cori stiffened at the flippant reference to Pacal. She may not like the situation her daughter found herself in, but she sure as heck didn't like Fowler dismissing him with a stereotype. Finn shot her a look to quiet her. She gave one back that said she'd let it pass. It would do them no favors to have Fowler know there was a personal angle to this.

"A friend of one of the young men came forward. A citizen," Finn said. "There are community ties, Captain. Certainly, they are a little harder to piece together than others might be, but we will find them. The gentleman who told me about the three missing men is going to meet us at the morgue and hopefully identify the body found in Baldwin Hills and one other that hasn't been claimed." Finn paused. He held Fowler's gaze, seeing the tug-of-war the man was having with himself: duty versus daily grind, compassion versus realistic chances of success. Finn gave him a nudge. "So, have we your permission, sir?"

Fowler ran his hands through his perfectly trimmed hair. Even in uniform he had the air of man better suited to a yacht club in Nantucket than an office in the middle of L.A., but his heart and soul were all cop, and he was intrigued. He knew what Finn had brought him was not frivolous, and he knew the right thing to do. He only wished this request hadn't landed on his desk now.

"This is a political nightmare, Detectives. And I am not just talking local politics. Something like this could get way out of hand and wreak havoc in the state. It could be plucked up and used as a football across the country. Can you imagine the headlines? Half the country would be cheering the perp hoping he'd drive ten million people back across the border, and the other half of the country would be taking up arms to protect them. Sorry, it's just not something I want to spearhead."

"'Tis a hard time to be a cop, I agree," Finn argued. "But that doesn't mean we should cherry-pick our battles based on the chance of an outcome we don't like. Every action has a consequence as does every inaction."

Fowler's eyes narrowed in annoyance. Finn O'Brien's righteous heart was his own business, but his logic was all about being a cop and that was exasperating. O'Brien knew he was right. Anderson knew he was right and so did he, the man who had to make the decision.

"Alright, but here's the deal." His eyes flickered to Cori. "Anderson, you babysit your partner, or I'll hold you responsible if this goes wrong." His eyes went to Finn. "No grandstanding, no public statements, no hot-dogging. You are still responsible for the jackets you have; they will not be reassigned. If you can look into the missing persons without compromising any of the open investigations, if you can do so without affecting the extra duty at Cinco de Mayo, then you have my permission to move forward. You drop even one thing and it's done, is that understood?"

"Yes," Cori said and nodded. "I can keep O'Brien in line."

"O'Brien? Your word that you will not go full court press on this?"

"And if we find we've a serial killer on our hands?" Finn countered.

"You bring me hard evidence, a lead on a perp and people willing to give their stories for the record, and I'll request an interdepartmental task force," Fowler conceded. "But I'm telling you right now that evidence better be air-tight, and it will only be done with the approval of the chief."

Finn grinned at Cori. She looked back, unsure if this really was something to celebrate. To her, Fowler was giving them a great big maybe, but O'Brien was hearing it differently.

"Thank you, Captain. We'll…"

Finn's assurance of discretion was never finished because the door opened, and Tina cut him off mid-sentence. She headed for the television in the corner of Fowler's office and picked up the remote.

"I think you'll want to see this." She pointed the remote. They all heard a click. "O'Brien's on TV – sort of."

CHAPTER 18

KABC-TV, Six O'clock News, Kelly Lampert, anchor:
Now we turn our attention to a disturbing story that is
unfolding. A week ago, we reported that six people were
killed in a house in the mid-city, one of them a police
officer. Four were immigrants and the man accused
of pulling the trigger is a known member of the Hard
Times Locos who was, himself, injured in the standoff
with police. Fidel Andre Hernandez, seventeen years old
and going by the name of Marbles, was wounded in the
shoulder and his hand was broken during the incident.
But his lawyer is throwing new light on what happened
that night. Our own Doug Johnson was at the press
conference this afternoon.

(Cut to press conference)

David Torres, attorney
(reading a statement at a podium)
In the early morning hours of April 22, my client
Mr. Hernandez, was in the house where, sadly, four
undocumented immigrants were killed by an associate

of my client. My client attempted to stop these horrific murders, and we will be presenting irrefutable evidence to that in court during the preliminary hearing.

It is distressing that Mr. Hernandez found it necessary to defend himself and kill the man he had called a friend since childhood. By taking these heroic actions, Mr. Hernandez saved two small children who are now in the custody of child services.

Before Mr. Hernandez could surrender himself to the police and explain the situation, Detective Finn O'Brien, Wilshire Division, entered the house and assaulted my client. With no attempt to verbally communicate with my client, with no provocation, Detective O'Brien shot Fidel without warning. Thankfully, in the dark, that shot did not kill my client but rather shattered his shoulder. Even as this boy, not quite yet eighteen, lay bleeding on the ground, Detective O'Brien, again without provocation, broke Fidel's hand. Finally, using the same shotgun that Mr. Hernandez had wrestled away from the real killer, Detective O'Brien sadistically terrorized my client by putting the barrel of the shotgun in my client's mouth and threatening to, and I quote, 'blow your head off.'

(going off script)

This is another instance of police overstepping their bounds, acting as judge and jury, assuming the worst because of the way my client looked and because of his race. We cannot have rogue officers like Detective O'Brien preying on the weakest among us. Detective O'Brien has a history of being quick to pull the trigger and—

Doug Johnson (calling a question):
Do you have any evidence regarding the incident?

Another Reporter: (simultaneously)
Wasn't your client already convicted of—

David Torres, attorney:
We'll address our evidence in court for all to see. Rest
assured, this evidence is irrefutable and will be used to
protect Mr. Hernandez as well as the entire immigrant
community of Los Angeles from officers like Detective
O'Brien. Thank you. Thank you all.

Doug Johnson:
Are we talking about video? Was someone alive to
film—

Another reporter:
Your client's record. The police report—

David Torres (smiling, waving, leaving podium)
Thank you. Yes. Thank you.

(Cut to studio)

Kelly Lampert:
Mr. Torres did not divulge the nature of the evidence he
referred to, but an anonymous source has told us that it
is possibly a video, taken by a concerned citizen...

Cori turned off the television with one hand while her
other clamped over Tucker's pudgy arm before he could
grab a fistful of mac and cheese.

"Spoon." She held up the spoon with its big, soft plastic
handle and put it in his little fist.

"Poon," he said just before he tossed it across the room and grinned.

Just like a man, so darn pleased with himself after making a mess. Cori checked out the spoon over near the fridge and then slid her eyes back to her grandson.

"I'll give you this. You've got quite an arm," she muttered as she got up to retrieve the spoon.

Cori washed it and listened to him giggle and babble. Any other night the sound of his little boy laughter and his dinner antics would have made her pert as a cricket, but tonight Cori's mind was on problems – hers and Finn's. Her partner was in a shitload of trouble and it didn't even matter if what that jerk on TV said was true or not. Which it was not.

She had watched that interview four times. The first time had been with Finn and Fowler, Tina in attendance. Tina had been sent off with a polite 'thank you, close the door behind you.' It seemed like an eternity that they sat in silence, their eyes on that dark television screen. She had looked at Finn, but Finn and Fowler only had eyes for each other.

"O'Brien?" the captain said, giving him the floor.

"There is no video. There was no one alive in that house. Marbles killed them all. 'Tis lawyer talk," Finn said. "I did nothing undeserved."

Cori's heart had damn near burst in the seconds it took for Fowler to assess her partner. As much as she wanted to come to his defense, she couldn't. She hadn't been in the house, she now knew that her partner was capable of keeping secrets, and she couldn't defend Finn because she wouldn't be in the room to do it.

"Anderson, you can go," Fowler said.

Cori opened her mouth, thinking to object, thinking

to say they were partners and that whatever came down on him was bound to come down on her, but she changed her mind, kept her mouth shut, left the room and hung in Tina's office. The two women pretended to be busy, but it was the silence that had their attention. The silence timed out at two minutes, twenty-two seconds. Finn was out, cap under his arm, back ramrod straight as he walked past. Cori went out the door too.

He turned into their office; she executed a precise turn and followed. Truth be known, she would have followed wherever he led because this was her partner, this was the man she would protect with her life. His billed cap went onto the desk. He sat. She shut the door.

"There is nothing to see here, Cori," he said. "No reprimand. Nothing."

"That's good."

"And there is nothing that happened inside that house that shouldn't have."

Cori had raised her chin and held onto his ice-blue gaze. He was choosing his words carefully, but his gaze was clear – too clear. She dropped her chin and gave him one nod that told him she understood the way it was going to be.

"Okay, then. I'll be heading home unless you want to do some work? Maybe we should—"

"No, Cori. I'll be finishing up a few things here and then I'll go home too," he said.

"See you in the morning." She reached for the door.

"I'll not be assigned on Cinco de Mayo. Just so you know. I'll be having desk duty."

"I'd say you lucked out," she answered, trying to make the assignment palatable. Everyone would know this for what it was, a hedge against a lawsuit and formal internal investigations. She could only hope there wouldn't be criminal charges again. Just when he was seeing the top rung of the ladder, here he was sliding down the damn chute again.

"Captain Fowler was speaking to the chief and the mayor as I left. They saw the press conference too."

"Yep. No getting around that."

Cori thrust out her hip and leaned against the door. The bill of her hat scrolled through her fingers, the blue wool blouse stretched over her breasts and clung to her small waist. There was something incredibly intriguing about a woman in a man's uniform. She looked both powerful and vulnerable. She didn't falter. "Don't worry about it, O'Brien. Folks in Los Angeles have the attention span of donut holes. Give it a day and some celebrity will knock off his wife, and then you're yesterday's news."

Finn smiled a little, just a mere tip of his lip, the smallest breath of amusement. She could hardly look into his eyes anymore because they both knew she was spinning tales and that he had done what that attorney said he had. His innocence was in the knowledge that it was deserved. Cori didn't need a video or Fidel Andre Hernandez's testimony to know that Finn O'Brien had lost it at the sight of those children, at the gruesome line-up of bodies, at the useless waste of it all. But what she felt in her gut was not true until it was proven.

"See ya," she said.

"Night, Cori. Take care."

"You too, partner."

That was it.

Now here she was, fetching a spoon, thinking that she needed to move the refrigerator and clean behind it, thinking maybe she should give Finn a call, thinking about tomorrow and whether they would be frozen out by their colleagues just when things were thawing. That's when she heard the front door open.

"I'm home." Amber called out exactly two seconds before she walked into the kitchen. She looked at Cori and the baby spoon she held. She looked at Tucker. "Sorry. I've been trying to get him to stop doing that."

"No worries." Cori straightened up and her knees clicked. "If he keeps it up, he can pitch for the majors."

Amber kissed the little boy on top of his head. He chattered at her and batted his arms in the air. She snuggled back at him, cooing as she unslung her purse, dropped it on an empty chair and then put herself on to the one next to it. Her face landed in her hands and she sat there slump shouldered.

"Hard shift?" Cori asked as she gave the spoon back to Tucker.

"Not really. We're shorthanded. I don't know. Just kind of boring all around I guess."

"I'll get you something," Cori said.

She puttered around, fixing dinner for her daughter: mac 'n cheese, a salad, peas and a glass of milk. Long ago Amber had admitted that access to unlimited pizza was not all it was cracked up to be. Usually she loved her mom's dinners, a mix of Tucker food and adult fare, but tonight food held no allure. She was exhausted. Tucker reached out and took Amber's hair.

"Come here, pumpkin."

Amber pushed aside her plate and took Tucker out of his highchair, snuggling into him, kissing his fingertips when he reached for her. Cori sat down opposite her daughter. It was time she reached out, too. There was no delicate way to ease into the conversation, so Cori didn't try.

"Amber, honey, I know about Pacal."

Amber's shoulders fell. The last ounce of energy drained out of her. She put her head against Tucker's while he giggled thinking it was a game.

"Oh, crap. I thought Finn was a good guy."

With that, she raised her head and looked at her mother and, for the first time, Cori felt that she was eye to eye with another woman. Full-fledged, filled out with sadness and fear, and resolute in a way only a woman can be.

"He is a good guy, baby cakes, and he didn't tell me."

"Don't try to protect him, Mom," Amber said. "Seriously, you've got to get over it. He screwed me over big time."

"No, he didn't," Cori said. "I just happen to be a great detective. Not to mention I have friends in the right places. He made a mistake, and it came back to me. I can tell you right now that he's lucky he's still a bull and not a steer. When I found out, I went at him with everything I had."

Amber chuckled but just a little and it looked as if it wore her out to do that.

"Who told you?" she asked.

"Sheila Barnes, missing persons. You and her kids went to school together. Finn showed her the picture."

"I don't remember them," Amber said. "Whatever. I'm not going to fight with you about it. I'm not going to get crazy on Finn." She hitched the baby, gave him a hug, and then put him down so he could play. "Then I guess that's it. You two are just going to let it go, huh? Pacal is gone and nobody cares except me."

"I didn't say we were going to let it go."

"We?" Amber sat up a little straighter. "You mean you're both going to help? Have you found out anything yet? Do you have any idea where Pacal is?"

Cori let her head swing, giving Amber a no to every

question. At the same time, she was trying to decide exactly how much she wanted to tell her daughter. It might be safe to tell her there were others missing, but what would be gained by letting her know about the dead man in the shallow grave? The body at the morgue?

"Okay, honey, here's the deal. We took this to Captain Fowler and asked him to let us look into it because Finn found there's another young man gone missing. Maybe four altogether, including Pacal." Cori paused to see how that set. There was no panic and that was a good sign. "He told us we could check it out but no jacket, no big investigation. That means we have to fit it in between our regular work, so don't expect miracles. Got it?"

"Okay. Sure, that's fine. You guys will be able to do something every day, even if it's a little something. It's not like you're going to wait for a couple weeks or anything, right?"

"I don't know. It's a play-it-by-ear thing. Finn's already checked out the day labor sites. The corners are going to take a whole lot more time. So far, nobody remembers seeing Pacal."

"He's quiet. He's super polite. He probably wouldn't have stood out," Amber said, excited to be talking about the boy to Cori. "He's a really good guy, Mom. He's so—"

"Yep. I'm sure."

Cori felt the color rise to her cheeks. She didn't want to know about Pacal. She didn't want to see how the mere mention of him made Amber's eyes shine and the sound of his name made her smile. Cori wanted Pacal to be a name on a missing person's report. She wanted to know his height and weight, hair and eye color, not how it felt to hold his hand or that he loved his mother or that he was good with Tucker. Luckily, Amber was on to the next question.

"Did Finn try the hospitals? I couldn't get them to tell me anything when I called."

"You called the hospitals?"

"Someone had to do something," Amber shot back and Cori saw her hackles go up.

"Okay. I get it," Cori said, not wanting the fight her daughter was ready for. "Anyway, yes, he's been in contact with the hospitals—"

"And?" Amber prodded.

"And the morgue. Finn checked the morgue." Cori sat back in her chair. This was the time to tell her about the two bodies if she was going to do it. She wasn't. "And nothing. He's not there."

"Thank God." Amber fell back, her hand over her heart, her eyes closing for just a second.

"Amber, listen to me," Cori said. "You need to wrap your brain around the fact that we might never find him."

"Un-huh. Nope. Not going to happen." Amber stood up, her chair scratching against the linoleum. "I want you and Finn to stop telling me that. Until you know for sure, you are going to at least pretend everything will be okay. That's it. That's the way I want it."

Cori was up too. She couldn't sit still for this. She had tried to understand, she promised Finn she would, but there was a line to be crossed that Finn didn't have at his feet – the parent line.

"Amber Lynn Anderson, I swear I don't know how you managed to miss out on the men smarts. Didn't you see enough misery brought down on my head by men, to learn anything?"

"Oh Christ." Amber threw up her hands and did a quarter turn and another and another until she was back facing Cori again. Her hands were on her hips. "What's wrong with you, Mom? I hardly remember Daddy, but you never let me forget that he left us. And when Randy left after he found out I was pregnant? You don't think I learned anything after that? I learned plenty. I'm not as dumb as you think I am, Mom."

"Amber, I don't think you're dumb," Cori wailed, her arms flying up in frustration. "I think you want loving so much you just can't help yourself. You keep giving that heart away to the wrong guys. Guys without a future."

"That's the difference between you and me, Mom. You gave up," Amber snapped. "At least I keep trying. I really believed that someone was out there for me. You're so afraid of what might happen, you don't do anything. I mean look at Finn. He is so not available, and he may never be which means you want him because it's safe to want him. Tell me that isn't true; I dare you, tell me."

"Not true. Not." Cori eyes narrowed. Her daughter was treading on dangerous ground. "He needs to work things out on his own, and I'm not going to be waiting for him to do it. I'm taking care of my own self. I'm moving on."

"Oh, yeah." Amber threw her head up and her hair rippled down her back. She swept Tucker up from the floor and put him back in his highchair. "Lapinski? That's what you call moving on? He's like having dessert when what you really want is dinner. You'll devour that sweet little guy."

"He's a friend and I would never hurt him."

Amber turned around and faced her mom. She looked sad and wise and all the spit and fire went out of her.

"You wouldn't intentionally. The same way Finn wouldn't hurt you intentionally. But you're going to just keep putting your toe in the water because you're afraid to jump in."

Amber took a step around the table. She held her hands out, palms up as if pleading for Cori to really listen.

"Not all men leave, Mom. They don't. Pacal doesn't. And if I'm wrong you can say I told you so, but not until after you find out what happened to him. Just because you're disappointed in me, don't give up on him. He doesn't deserve it. He's fought his whole life just to eat and he's never complained. That's got to count for something."

Cori leaned back, her rear end up against the counter, her arms crossed as she looked at her daughter. There was no going through her, no going around her, so there was only one thing to do.

"Okay," she said. "I hear you. I believe you. This isn't a crush. I'm sure he's a good guy."

"More than you can imagine," Amber said.

"But, baby, you're going to ruin your life even more than you already have and for what? A Mexican kid? How are you going to build a real life with him? Have you thought about it? Have you?"

Amber blinked. She inclined her head. Her beautiful lips parted and then she turned to Tucker, took off his bib, set aside his dish and picked him up. When she turned back to Cori, she was holding her child tight, one arm under his rear end and her other hand cupping the back of his head.

"I didn't know you thought my life was ruined," she said. "I really didn't."

With that, she walked out of the room leaving Cori to wonder how she had made such a mess of things and how she could ever go about making it better.

* * *

It was midnight when Finn stepped foot in Kimiko's *sento*.

He had come home late, and she found him sitting on the bench under the pepper tree just outside the bathhouse, the stray kitten in his lap. He had wished her and her daughter good evening as they passed.

Finn sat there, thinking of nothing except how soft the kitten was and how wool was not a good choice for an LAPD uniform. It wasn't more than a half an hour when Kimiko came out of her house with the key to the *sento*. She went inside and Finn saw the soft lights go on. He imagined her looking at the garden to make sure the pebbles were raked, looking at the towels to make sure they were stacked just so. He thought of the husband who loved her so dearly that he had built her such an extravagance just so she wouldn't miss her native Japan. That was beautiful love. The man had made sure every detail was perfect, from the *noren* and *tatami sheets* that hung across the entrance and in the changing room, to the shoe locker, the dressing room, the small garden and the deep hot tub. While Finn O'Brien was thinking of how wonderful it is to be in love like that, Kimiko returned, and she bowed in front of him. She handed him the key.

"You give back later," she said.

"Thank you, Kimikosan," he answered.

"You no worry." She said and then went back to her house.

That elegant, beautiful lady knew of his troubles, knew the 'black dog' was surely sitting beside him even as the kitten sat curled in his lap. How could she not? That newscast had gone viral already. Some people were calling for his head and some were offering to kill those who wanted it. But if they had seen what he had seen, everything would be different. They would understand what he had almost done. They would wonder why he had not followed through.

He set aside the kitten, went up to his apartment, changed out of his blues and hung them up carefully. He put on a tee-shirt, sweatpants and sandals and went to the *sento* where he washed before easing himself into the hot water in the deep tub.

Finn put his arms out and his head back. He closed his eyes and blessed Kimiko. He blessed Officer Shay. He damned Fidel Andre Hernandez's lawyer, David Torres, because the lawyer might bring him down if truly, he had some evidence that would show Finn had lost his mind for that moment. He damned the man because, if Finn went down, that meant Fidel Andre Hernandez – Marbles – would walk free. That was the sin, that a killer might escape justice because a good man had lost his mind.

When Finn was done with his prayers and his damnation, he gave himself over to the water and the silence of the *sento*. He would need all his strength now; he would need to be in command of his wits. This was a race against time. Finn was determined to find out what was happening to the men from the corners before Marbles and his lawyer claimed him as their next victim.

CHAPTER 19

APRIL 30

Captain Fowler's Assistant, Tina: This is the roster. We've got six officers unable to participate. Five out on disability, O'Brien's on desk duty and you put Reese on suspension last week. Unless you want to bring him back to duty?

Captain Fowler: No, we don't need anyone going off half-cocked. Leave him home.

Tina: Okay, that means we have five teams of ten officers. All with body cams. Do they want us to break out the riot gear?

Captain Fowler: Make sure it's all checked out in case we need it. I know it will be tight.

Tina: It's not like the chief gave us a whole lot of lead-time. **(pause. sigh)** Don't worry. We'll be ready.

Captain Fowler: I know we will, Tina. Thanks. **(grabbing jacket)** I'll be downtown in a planning meeting the rest of the day. Anything else I should know before I go see the head honchos?

Tina: Actually, yeah. **(Fowler waiting)** I just hate to be the one to tell you.

Captain Fowler: (wearily) I won't hold it against you. Shoot.

Tina: We've only got three stars on Yelp. **(shrugging)** Sorry.

Captain Fowler: **(shaking his head)** Text me if you need me.

"Saw that lawyer last night on the tube. Tough break."

Detective Crane shook Finn's hand as they met up once again, this time in the Baldwin Hills precinct rather than standing over a shallow grave in the field of oil wells.

"'Tis a crock. There is no video," Finn assured him.

"Doesn't matter. People see and hear what they want," Crane said matter-of-factly. "If that guy has a video of an elephant doing handstands that has a passing resemblance to you, they'll have your hide. I swear, you can't go to the john without a camera pointing up your ass these days." Detective Crane gave a nod to Cori, unconcerned that he might have offended her. "Anderson. Good to see you again. "

"Back atcha, Crane," she answered. "What have you got for us?"

"Not as much as I would like which means nothing at all really. My bad for mentioning you. After the news, I got the word that I can't play with you guys until you are in the clear. So…" he drew out the word like he was singing. "If you want our files, you're going to have to look through the stacks yourselves. I had already pulled a few before I got shut down, but it isn't much."

"What was the official explanation?" Finn asked.

"My captain says we're already putting way too much time into this 'subset'." Crane snorted. "That was a new one on me. Latinos are now a subset but then you have to ask yourself, to what? I mean, if you really want to look at a subset check out us poor old white males."

"My heart breaks, Crane," Cori drawled.

"I'll just bet." He grinned at her. "Anyway, I think they're frustrated. We've got an uptick in the gang activity and our captain is trying to figure out how to budget for all the overtime to address it. Cinco de Mayo is going to eat up whatever's left, and we've got new immigrants acting like idiots so regular folks are calling in suspicious activity every three seconds. Somebody should explain that if they're just cool and don't run every time they see a cop we'll leave 'em alone. We can't ask them about their status. Anyway, pretty much my captain has just had it. She says we've got to look out for our other cases. The problem is that if we look at one of our South of the Border friends the wrong way, the media's got us in the ringer or La Raza's on our backs. If we ignore them—"

"The media has us in a ringer or La Raza's on our backs," Cori finished for him.

"Pretty much. Anyway, come on with me." Crane led them down a long hall. Finn and Cori took a look around to see how the operation stacked up to Wilshire Division, but Finn was still focused on the task at hand.

"That leaves our missing men and your John Doe on nobody's radar except ours which, at this point, leaves us exactly nowhere."

"Chin up, O'Brien. You might find something good here." Detective Crane threw open the door to an interrogation room. "This should keep you busy for a while – like a week."

Finn and Cori stuck their heads inside the room. Cori whistled. "I thought you said you pulled a couple of files for us," Cori said.

"The four files back there are the ones I pulled." Crane pointed to a small table in the corner of the room. "When I got called off, I just grabbed an armful. Figured if you were really interested you wouldn't mind sorting them out. If you don't want to, say the word and I'll put 'em back where I found 'em."

Cori looked at Finn.

"What shall we give it? Forty-five minutes?"

"We have to meet Gregorio in an hour and a half," Finn answered. "We can get a lot done by then."

Cori nodded.

"Okay then, folks, enjoy yourselves." Detective Crane said as he turned to leave. But Finn caught him before he left. "Any chance there might be some coffee around here?"

"I'll rustle you up some. I just won't promise it's any good."

"We're easy," Cori said.

Detective Crane shut the door while Cori and Finn rolled up their sleeves and started sifting through the files looking for assaults and murders committed against Hispanic men between the ages of fifteen and twenty-five.

* * *

The man sat on the running board of the truck, one of his hands pushed through the open window and holding onto the doorframe, the other resting in his lap, fingers curled in on themselves. His chest hurt. His head was swimming, and his good eye pulsed. He was thinking that he shouldn't have worked today.

He had been so tired when he got out of that child's bed that he didn't think he could drive, much less lift a shovel or a pipe. He sat on the edge of that bed, trying to catch his breath, hobbled by his failing health. Knowing that he would need all his strength to see the day through, he made a concession and took the gun from its hiding place.

Not that he needed to hide it. The woman downstairs never came into his room. All she cared about was the order of things: sign in, sign out, eat, sleep. He was a name on a list. Once he had managed to disappear for quite a while, but then they found him and back he went. Happily, because of the new laws the system spat him back out almost as soon as it took him in. They kept an eye on him, he kept an eye on them and it all worked. Still, he had a few secrets, and the gun was one of them. It had proven to be a godsend, for his strength had been used up just getting to this place and dealing with that boy.

He shook his head knowing he should have aborted this one. This place was the wrong choice from the get-go. It was too far away for one thing. Then the worker he picked up caused a ruckus when they got on the freeway, banging on the back window, afraid to sit in the bed of the truck. The man couldn't chance anyone calling the cops, so he pulled over and let the boy into the cab. Let him sit right beside him. It made him sick to have him so close, but there was no turning back.

No llores.

Don't cry.

Now he dropped his eyes and looked at the gun. The little noise he made came close to a laugh while he thought about the comedy of errors. Still and all, it ended up okay. Justice was done. Not like what had been done to him. His lawyer said 'show remorse and it will go easier'. Well he had shown true remorse, but the judge called him a liar. Bullshit, that's what their justice was.

Lo siento.

I'm sorry.

He had tried to make it right.

No llores.

He cut his eyes to the grave and the boy lying in it and shook his head. Damn if that kid didn't have a sixth sense. He knew something was up and that's why he turned his head when he did. What the man wouldn't have given for a sixth sense all those years ago. He could have protected himself if he had known what was coming and none of this would be necessary. Instead, they came out of the blue like vultures, like sharks, surprising him every damn time.

Ah well.

He let his hand drop away from the truck door. He needed to get on with it. He would have to buy a new shirt somewhere 'cause that boy had come at him like he wanted to fight, like he didn't know he was dead. That's why the man was all bloody. He couldn't go to the house with a bloody shirt, but he couldn't be late either. Nor could he leave things unfinished here. He would never sleep if he shirked his duty.

Pushing himself off the running board, he left the gun in the car and shuffled over to the grave. He walked through piles of pine needles, lifting his feet over fallen branches. The trees around him weren't faring well in the drought. Some had a few sprigs of greenery. The pines shed their needles if you breathed on them. He hadn't really noticed the sad state of things the first time he came here but it had been winter then. He thought it would be beautiful in the spring, but it wasn't. It was just a dead place.

The ground, while not hard, was laced with heavy roots that had made it impossible to dig the hole properly, but the boy had done the best he could. The man bent down to check for a pulse, but he moved too fast and the blood rushed through his body making him light-headed. He lowered himself to the ground, concentrating on his breathing while he considered what he had to work with. The top of the hole was shallow, the boy's head rested sideways on a big old root that looked like a brown and gnarly pillow.

One breath.

Two breaths.

Three breaths.

The corpse's butt was nice and deep and the feet deeper still. He looked very strange. He would not be laid out properly but there was nothing to do about it now. The man got to his knees. He would do what he could, and God would know that his intentions were honorable.

Very carefully he got to his knees, reached out with one hand, and arranged the boy's arm. He wasn't able to reach the other one since he had fallen on it, so he put that one hand over the boy's now-still heart, placed a card under it and then sat back. He didn't bother with the boy's feet. Instead, he paused and caught his breath again. When he had filled his lungs as best he could he reached for the shovel. Taking hold of the shaft, he was pulling it toward him when a foot slammed down on top of his hand.

The man cried out in pain. He pulled away in terror, lost his balance and tumbled into the grave. The pain in his body was excruciating and when his head fell back, he was looking up the bloody nose of the dead man. He could not open his lips to scream so he made the same sounds he had made so long ago when he lay helpless on a cold concrete floor. He threw his arm over his eyes and waited for arrest or death or something worse. Instead, the day went a little dark as a shadow fell over him. Tentatively, he moved his arm. He opened his eyes, the one good one and the one that looked like milk. Above him stood a man the likes of which he had never seen. This person had planted the shovel in the earth and was leaning on it like it was a silver-tipped cane. He was smiling.

"Whatcha doin', old man?" he asked.

CHAPTER 20

"Come on. Come on, now. Let's get you out of that stinky pot."

The man didn't move because it was hard to know which was the worse: to be in a grave with a dead man or standing upright next to a crazy one.

The fellow reaching for him was a mess from the top down. His dark hair was short but not shaved, and it looked like he had taken scissors to it himself. There was a round spot of white-blond that made it look as if he had slept with the left side of his head in a pie tin of bleach.

His face was an impish triangle with its broad forehead and pointy little chin. There was a scabby sore above his left eye and he used the stubby, dirty fingers of his free hand to pick at it. There were teeth in this person's head, but they looked none too healthy. His face was deeply lined and old before its time, yet there was a youthfulness about him that made it seem as if he was wearing a mask.

He was dressed in old clothes, dirty clothes: a work shirt, over a tee-shirt with a picture on it, a wool suit coat of black and brown checks. The coat pockets sagged; the back rode up his skinny bum. His jeans were so worn and faded that they looked as if they had been fashioned out of a baby's hide. His shoes were thrift shop specials, the cast offs of some businessman partial to wingtips. One shoe had a lace; the other was fastened with wire.

Despite the man's disarray and the face that looked like a tulip bulb waiting to be planted, he was quite the dandy, full of cocky energy and good humor, an odd thing considering. The man with the tulip bulb face stopped picking at the sore above his eye, tossed away the shovel and put both hands out to the live man in the hole. He wiggled his fingers.

"Come on. Up you go."

"I can do it," the man mumbled, struggling to extricate himself from the narrow hole and the sticky blood.

"Aw, shit, you can't," the man laughed. "I been watchin'. You can't hardly move. Come on. Come on now. Give me your hand."

"You've been picking at yourself," the man groused.

"What?" The younger one put his wretched dirty fingers behind his ear. "You mumble, buster. Can't hardly hear ya." He put his hands down on his knees and looked a little closer. "Oh, say, sorry man. Looks like somebody tried to carve you a new mouth and sewed 'em both up by mistake. No wonder you can't talk proper."

The man turned his head, not wanting to be looked at that way or to have to explain his scars, his eye, his body. He didn't want to touch the man's hand because he'd been picking at himself, but he had no choice. This guy wasn't going away. He had his hand out and was popping his lips: *comeonupcomeonupcomeonup.*

The man reached out and the young one pulled him up and over the top of the grave, so that he felt like he was flying. The young man caught him, held tight with one hand, and dusted him off with the other.

"What did ya think? You gonna get cooties from me? Hell, man you been laying in somebody else's blood…" he twirled the old man like he was dancing with him and swatted at his shoulders. "…that's skanky, know what I mean…skankier than anything I got…"

He swatted the man's behind and that's when the tables turned. The old man snapped his hand out of the younger man's. He was on the shovel faster than a cat on a mouse. Raising it above his head, blind with rage, he brought it down, hoping to deliver a deathblow, but the younger man scuttled out of range. His hands were up, but not defensively. It seemed he wasn't afraid of the old man – even with the corpse lying in a grave.

"Whoa, whoa, you old dude. I'm cool. Sorry. Didn't know your butt was sensitive." The younger man turned his palms upward and curled his fingers in a come-on gesture. "My bad. Come on. Come on. I'm 'bout the only person in the world who don't care 'bout your butt or that body."

The tulip-faced man ogled the corpse and then threw back his head and cackled, showing his broken teeth.

"Man, that was good. Gotta remember that one. Butt. Body. Hey, I'm a lover not a fighter." He stopped moving, dropped his hands to his hips, scooted over and checked out the grave. "Looks like you're the fighter, man. Good to know. Yeah, good to know. I ain't gonna tangle with you and I ain't gonna do you wrong. I keep my mouth shut. I'm in the brotherhood. Yep, your business is your business 'cause I don't want to get involved. Everybody knows my lips are zipped, my eyes are blind 'cause that's how I roll. I'm a pragmatic fellow, you see. If my time has come then it's come, but I don't think it has. That's why I don't have fear of you or pretty much anyone else. Last thing I want is the man coming down on my head, so whatever this is, it's your business, brother."

The old man stood with the shovel high on the shoulder again. He was breathing hard but at the ready, distrusting and upset that he could not finish his job in peace. But he was exhausted too, and the tulip-faced man kept grinning. What was he to do? He hadn't the strength for another fight.

"Adolph, man. Name's Adolph."

The vagrant raised his eyebrows and that made him look very young, indeed. Twenty-one? Twenty-two? The old man lowered the shovel. He knew a meth head when he saw one and Adolph was one.

The old man mumbled.

Adolph leaned forward and cupped his ears again.

"Didn't catch it. Sorry, man, you gotta work on your pronunciation."

The man said: "It's not deep enough."

"I see that. Yes, indeed I do."

Adolph turned to the grave and nodded. He pulled up his chin in contemplation; acting like this was business as usual. Suddenly he swooped down and looked close, seeing what was underneath the hand. He swiveled his head and gave the man a glorious smile.

"That is such a nice touch." Adolph put his hand over his heart. "And I mean that sincerely."

"Necessary," the man said.

"Yeah, well, I wouldn't know about that. But, hey, you look worn to a nub. That's what my mom used to say. Worn to a nub. Always wondered, a nub of what?"

Adolph stood up straight and held out his hand for

the shovel. The man pulled it back. Adolph kept coming, talking like he was going to take a bone from a big old ornery dog.

"I'm not stealing it, man," Adolph soothed "What would I do with a shovel, man?"

He went for it again, all gentle like. The old man pulled back again but not so fast nor so far this time. He was tired. The tumble had hurt his hip so bad that he wasn't sure if he could stand one more minute. Adolph's fingers were on the shaft of the shovel. Yep, the big old dog was ready to give it up. Just a few more steps, a few more words.

"Come on, man. I'll finish it up for you, and you give me a ride back to the city. Sucks out here. Killed me a squirrel two days ago, but that's the last real food I had me. Come on, I earn my keep. I'll do it right. Promise, man. Just a ride back to the city is all I'm asking."

The old man thought about this. He was tired and it was getting late. He would give the man a ride. He gave up the shovel and Adolph was pleased.

"There you go. Not so hard." Adolph scooped up a shovelful of dirt and heaved it over the corpse's feet. He looked back at the old man and wiggled his eyebrows. "Huh? Huh? Didn't I tell you? Tit for tat. Quid pro quo. You go on and rest your bones."

The man mumbled. What he said was that, yes, Adolph could do the work. Yes, he would go rest. Yes, he would take him back to the city. Even if his words were understandable, Adolph wouldn't have heard. He threw himself into the chore with gusto, as if happy to have been hired.

He heaved a few more shovelfuls over the feet and legs and then looked over his shoulder again. The old man was in the truck and his head was back. He looked like he was asleep.

Adolph began to whistle, a thing he did very well. He whistled a beautiful song. A tune written by Bach that he learned when his mother made him take piano lessons. She said it was restful. Most people turned to see where the beautiful sound was coming from when Adolph whistled, but the man in the truck did not so Adolph got on his knees and rummaged through the dead guy's pockets.

He almost stopped whistling when he came up with some damn good treasure. In the dead man's jean pocket, way down deep, Adolph found jewelry. Good stuff, too. A narrow chain with a gold disc and inside the disk a diamond – a carat at least. Gold bands set with rubies and sapphires interspersed with diamonds.

Adolph whistled louder, checked to make sure the old guy was still out and then went in once more. He found a chain and a locket in the brown boy's pants. There was nothing inside the locket except some initials, almost worn away. The thing wasn't worth much, Adolph was sure, but the other items were pricey. He would be having some very fine food as soon as he could unload this stuff.

Satisfied that he had what there was to find, that the old man was none the wiser, that if he didn't hurry it up they would get caught in hellish traffic and he'd have to spend more time than he wanted with mumbly-peg, Adolph pocketed the goods and picked up the pace. He switched tunes. *I've Been Working on the Railroad* seemed more appropriate.

A few minutes later he was done. It was a decent job. The night critters would eat away the guy's face because it was impossible to cover it propped up the way it was. All that dirt kept rolling off.

"Let's get this show on the road, old man!" Adolph hollered as he swung up his pack, tossed the shovel into the back of the truck and then hopped into the passenger seat. He sat down on the gun, pulled it out from under him and put it in the glove box while the man woke and centered himself. It took a minute, but Adolph was patient. He had done a bit of work and it had paid off handsomely. There was some good food coming and a bed to sleep in once he found a pawnshop. Yes, indeed, he had been lucky that day.

When the man had figured out where he was, what he was doing and remembered who Adolph was, he put the key in the ignition and drove over the forest path to the highway that led back to the freeway that would take them to Los Angeles.

Neither of them looked back.

Neither of them saw the earth move.

* * *

"You doin' okay there, Gregorio?" Cori asked.

Paul and Finn were already through the door that led to the cold room where the bodies lay. Cori pulled up the rear, stopping when she saw Gregorio hesitate. This room was hard to take for a seasoned pro; a normal person found it freakish. She put her hand on Gregorio's back as much to guide him as support him.

"It's tough. I'm not going to lie to you."

"*Si*," was all he said.

Cori gave his back a pat, threaded her arm through his and walked him into the room.

"Point the way boys," she said, and Finn gave her a wink, grateful for her help when she was personally conflicted by the situation.

Paul led them down an aisle to the gurney in question. Finn stood on one side, Paul at the head of the body and Cori and Gregorio on the other side.

"Doctor Craig is going to uncover the body, okay?" Cori said.

Gregorio nodded. Cori let go of Gregorio but stayed close in case she was needed. After Paul unzipped the body bag, they all stood silently for a minute. Finally, Finn said:

"Gregorio?"

"No. I don't know his name. I may have seen him. It's hard to tell. His face." Gregorio's hand circled his own. "It is hard to know."

Paul zipped the bag and they moved two tables back to the next one, going through the paces again. Gregorio shook his head once more. He knew neither of the victims.

"Well then, I'm believing we're done here. Thank you, Paul," Finn said.

His voice reflected the disappointment and frustration they all felt. Cori and Finn pivoted to leave. Paul adjusted the table, but Gregorio didn't move. He was looking over his shoulder, seemingly deep in thought.

"The first one," he said to no one in particular. "Did he wear a red jacket? A red jacket with blue?"

"We have his clothing," Paul said and left them. He returned with a plastic bag holding the dead man's belongings.

"Jeans, boots, socks, underwear, a shirt, a hoodie and…" Paul pulled hard on the last piece and held it up to show them. "A red jacket with blue designs."

Everyone looked at Gregorio. The man nodded as his lips curled in an expression of remorse.

"I seen him once. Maybe a few times. Always with the jacket."

"Where, Gregorio?" Finn asked, but the man shook his head.

"At a house. I seen him at a house."

"Which house?" Cori asked, confused as to why he didn't understand that they needed a specific location. Before Gregorio could answer, Paul interrupted.

"Sorry, folks, but I've got to finish up now. I've got a couple of meetings."

"We appreciate the time, Paul."

Single file, they left the room and went their separate ways: Paul back to work, Finn, Cori, and Gregorio to huddle on the sidewalk outside the building.

"You did a good job, Gregorio. We just need to know exactly where you saw that young man," Finn said.

"No. I'm sorry," Gregorio said. "I cannot."

"Okay, then, can you take us to the place you saw him? We'll go right now," Cori suggested.

When Gregorio began to fidget, Finn tried to reason with him.

"We should let his people know that he's here. You would want us to find you if it were you son, wouldn't you?"

"*Si*," he said. "If it were my son, *si*. But these people, in this place, they won't want to talk. No *policia*. No, I cannot do that."

"Okay, how about this, you point us in the right direction. Don't be specific," Cori said. "Nobody will ever know the information came from you."

"I will know," he answered.

"Gregorio," Finn stepped in, "it is looking like your community has a pretty big problem, so let us do our job. Whoever knows that young man in there might know things that will help us find your son and Pacal and the others who have gone missing. We don't want any other father to go through what you're going through."

Gregorio's black eyes met Finn's blue ones. It was like

looking in a mirror, not because they resembled one another but because there was truth behind them. What was amiss was bigger than the two of them, but both men had something to protect: Finn, the people in his jurisdiction; Gregorio the people in the shadows. It was Gregorio's decision to make and he did so by splitting the baby.

"I will go to the house where I saw him. I will ask first."

"Fair enough," Finn answered, "but better sooner than later, my friend. We're not wanting another boy to visit this place."

Gregorio nodded and turned away. The detectives didn't offer him a ride. When he was out of sight, Cori asked:

"What do you want to do now?"

"I'm feeling like it's time to visit McDonalds."

"You're hungry after all that?"

"No, but I'd like to have a chat with the person that served this boy from Baldwin Hills. Then I want to talk to the men on that corner."

* * *

"Amber! What's wrong with you? Table five has been sitting there for twenty minutes."

"That's not true," Amber shot back. "I looked at the clock. It's been seven minutes since they came through the door."

"They say twenty," Mr. Romero muttered and pulled the lever to refill a glass with Vitamin Water. Amber wondered what douche drank Vitamin Water with pizza, while Mr. Romero complained. "That damn boyfriend of yours. I tell you, I'm never hiring one of those people again. They can starve for all I care."

He slammed the glass onto the tray and the Vitamin Water washed out over the side, puddling on the plastic.

"Damn, damn. I swear if I ever get my hands on his neck…"

Amber snapped the order she had just taken on the stainless-steel ring that would let the cook know an extra-large pepperoni and sausage pizza was next up. She twirled toward Mr. Romero and put both hands on her hips.

"What, Mr. Romero? What are you going to do to Pacal when you get your hands on him? What could you do that hasn't already been done to him?"

"What are you talking about? Jesus, Amber, get to work and keep your voice down."

"You get to work," Amber growled. "I quit. That's right. I quit because you don't even have the decency to be worried about Pacal. He worked his butt off for you, and now you talk like he stole from you or something."

"Don't you talk to me like that," Mr. Romero hissed. "Pacal stole from me when he walked out the door without notice. I've lost business because we can't keep up."

"That's not his fault," Amber argued. "And if you're so ticked off, why didn't you just hire someone else? I'll tell you why. It's because nobody in their right mind would work for what you paid Pacal. You only got away with it because you knew he wouldn't complain."

"I paid him under the table. He didn't have to pay taxes. He made out okay."

"Oh yeah," Amber drawled. "He worked two jobs to keep his brothers and sisters fed. Big heart, Mr. Romero. Really big."

"Amber, this is not the time." He wiped up the spilled drink, refilled it with a quick spritz, picked up the tray and held it out to her. "Table two."

Amber glared at him, reached behind her, and pulled the apron ties. She wadded it up and put the ball of white cotton on the tray. His eyes went wide.

"What are you doing?"

"I told you that I quit. I quit because you don't have the decency to even wonder what happened to Pacal. Good luck finding replacements. I'm sure all those people who aren't 'like Pacal' are going to be beating down the door to get in here to wash dishes and clean up tables."

With that, Amber walked through the double doors and got her purse out of the cubby in the kitchen. The cook gave her a smile. She walked past her ex-boss, flipped her hair, and then held out the wide skirt of her uniform.

"I'll get this back to you," she said. "And here's a tip, let the next waitress wear jeans cause this dress looks really stupid."

Head high, Amber Anderson went through the dining room, stopping at table five long enough to inform the two people sitting there that they had been waiting all of nine minutes and that Mr. Romero would be taking their order. Once inside her car, she put both hands on the wheel and let her head fall forward.

She was so screwed. Her mom was going to go ballistic. How would she care for Tucker? Why...

Snapping her head back up, sitting tall, she slapped the steering wheel and felt better for it. She had done the right thing and there was nothing to do but head home. She pulled away from the curb calculating how long her pitiful savings would last and exactly how she was going to tell her mom she had quit, when she spotted three Hispanic men sitting on a retaining wall, talking under the shade of a tree in front of a house that was being remodeled.

Without thinking, she pulled up to the curb and rolled down her window. When she leaned over the passenger seat like she wanted to talk to them, one waved her away.

"No trabajamos," he said.

Amber knew that meant no work. She had heard that from Pacal but only when he lamented, he had not found work when he had a day off from the restaurant. These three meant they already had work and wouldn't take more.

"No. No," she called to them and gestured with the picture to get them close.

They looked at one another, shrugged and hopped off the wall.

"Do you know him? Have you seen him? *Se illama* Pacal Acosta."

She pushed the picture as close as her arm would reach. One man took it from her and showed it to the others. She didn't need to speak Spanish to know the answer to her question. They didn't know Pacal. She didn't know anybody who did. Los Angeles was big maybe even too big for her mom and Finn to do any good.

Amber thanked the men. They went back to sit on the wall. The radio was playing a song she hated so she turned it off, almost breaking the knob as she did so. Tears burned behind her eyes. She sniffed but she was too tired to cry, too sad and confused. She didn't know what she was doing anymore.

Amber put the picture back in her purse and drove home, wondering what she was really doing, but that was a silly question. She was trying to find the man she loved.

CHAPTER 21

Marjorie Landly, Internal Affairs: Detective O'Brien, this is Detective Vincent, CID and Detective Rodriguez FID. We appreciate you making time for us today.

Finn O'Brien: Happy to oblige.

Detective Vincent, Criminal Investigation Division: Detective O'Brien, this meeting is to inform you that a criminal complaint has been filed against you by the attorney representing Fidel Andre Hernandez. This complaint will go through proper channels. You will not be relieved of duty unless or until there is evidence that suggests this complaint has merit.

Detective Rodriguez, Force Investigation Division: I will be coordinating my investigation with Detective Vincent. We are also investigating Sergeant Van's actions the night of the incident.

Finn O'Brien (raising a brow): Sure, why would you be investigating Sergeant Van? I was the only one inside.

Detective Rodriguez, Force Investigation Division: Force Investigation is charged with looking into any law enforcement related injuries including those of animals.

We have to determine whether the dog was a clear and present danger to anyone on scene.

Detective O'Brien: Pity you can't ask Officer Shay for her testimony on that point.

Detective Rodriguez, Force Investigation Division (no reaction): Is there anything you can think of that we should know before we begin our investigation? Anything at all? **(no response)** For instance, in your original report it isn't clear why you shot at that particular time. Specifically, what indication did you have that you were in danger at that point in the operation?

Finn O'Brien (attempting to suffer fools): The suspect had a pistol in his belt. He was pointing a sawed-off shotgun at me. To his right there were four bodies, two of which had holes in their head and two more had their heads blown off. There was a fifth body sprawled in the doorway of the room from which the suspect emerged. That victim was shot in the back. Outside, an officer lay mortally wounded. It was these things that I perceived put me in danger given that I was the only person breathing in that house – other than the suspect. **(thinking)** Oh, and when I asked if he'd like to discuss things over a cup of coffee he declined and that just pissed me off, so I shot him.

Marjorie Landly, Internal Affairs (head bowed, hand to her brow)

Detective Vincent, Criminal Investigation Division: (unruffled) The further allegations that you threatened Mr. Hernandez with the shotgun after he was subdued will also be investigated. We'll have a formal interview after we get a response from the lab regarding fingerprints and the DNA test on the weapon. We have requested that the attorney, Mr. Torres, provide us with any video, audio, or personal witness statements in his possession, but, as you know, he is not required to do so.

Marjorie Landly, Internal Affairs (handing Finn a sheet of paper): This is a copy of the notification from the union that you are being represented by Jonathan Andrews. He should be contacting you shortly.

(Finn taking the paper. Marjorie Landly smiling her encouragement)

Detective Rodriguez, Force Investigation Division and Detective Vincent, Criminal Investigation Division (gathering files, pushing back chairs).

Detective Rodriguez, Force Investigation Division: You're done, O'Brien.

Finn O'Brien (taking his leave): I've heard that before, sir, but I fear I am still here.

Marjorie Landly, Internal Affairs (watching the closed door long after Finn O'Brien has left. Still wondering if he is single).

"Ah, Cori, haven't I had enough of these people! Cold as fish, they are. It was a righteous shooting. There was nothing more for me to do and they are asking what specific little twitch of the man's nose caused me to pull the trigger."

"You know this isn't about the shooting. It's about whatever went down after that." Cori said. "That attorney's been spouting his nonsense to any network that will give him airtime. He's getting people pretty riled up saying that you weren't polite to Mr. Marbles."

"'Tis a bluff. There is no way anyone from the houses on either side could have recorded us in the gloom of the morning. Not to mention, if they have video of me doing my duty in that house then they have video of

Hernandez killing those people. The lawyer wouldn't dare introduce such evidence."

Cori resisted the urge to quip that it would be a Mexican standoff between the defense and the prosecution. Instead, she slid her eyes his way to see if there was any reaction when she said:

"That doesn't mean something didn't happen. If it did, you'd tell me, right?"

Finn put an elbow on the car door and drove with one hand. Only a tightening of his jaw reflected his aggravation. He had no guilt for what he had done. It was only a moment's madness and had resulted in no harm. The same couldn't be said for what Marbles had done.

"If there had been, you would be the last person I'd be talking to. I'd not be bringing you down," Finn answered, his frustration born of the secret he kept and the truth he was telling. He cast her a glance and gave her a small smile. "No worries, Cori. There is nothing coming down the road. And there's nothing we can do about the lawyer. Let him talk. That's what they do."

"You got that right," Cori said. "Sometimes, it's good for a cop to talk, too. So, you just feel free to beat your gums, my friend."

"Now there's a delightful invitation." Finn laughed as he exited the 91 Freeway, driving into Compton. Cori changed the subject.

"Have you ever been in this place before?" she asked.

"I didn't even know it existed," Finn answered. "Sure, 'tis like going back in time."

"I would have been down here just to breath in the smell of country if I'd known. It smells like Texas."

Finn looked over at his partner. She was sitting forward, her big hair all teased and curled, glinting gold each time they drove under a streetlamp, excited to find a rural patch in the middle of L.A. Even with the windows rolled up, Finn could smell both American farmland and the Irish countryside. He supposed you couldn't take the girl out of the country any more than you could take the Irish country out of him.

From what he saw, this was a part of Los Angeles as alien as Mars and it was called Richland Farms. Finn's eyes scanned the neighborhood as he drove. Modest homes sat on lots the size of small parks. There were garages and barns and hitching posts. The area was originally set aside as a haven for black farmers migrating their families from the south in the early nineteen-hundreds. The man who owned the land, a preacher, had ceded it to Los Angeles with the caveat that it should always remain farmland. The city had honored his request all these years but now it was mostly Hispanic migrants from South America who farmed here.

"This is it," Cori said.

Finn pulled to the side of the road in front of the address Gregorio had given him. The one-story stucco home sat a fair distance from the street. There were raised garden beds overflowing with greenery and a chicken coop. Behind the house was a barn; its doors open to reveal three stalls. On the wide swath of dirt that served as a driveway, there was a small tractor, an old car and a dog that had come to stare at them. Four horses were tied to a hitching post in front of the house and Cori went for them as soon as she was out of the car.

"This is a paint, O'Brien." She put her hand on the horse's muzzle and spoke to it. "You are a beauty, you are."

She looked over at her partner and gave him a brilliant smile. Had it been another place, had they not been here on serious business, he would have knocked on the door and begged a ride for her.

"I'm thinking you and I need to come back on our day off for a good look around." Finn walked up and put a hand on the horse's flank. It snorted and danced back a bit, not thrilled with his attention but nuzzling into Cori. She laughed and said:

"I'm moving here. Tucker would love this. Can you imagine a city kid growing up like this and still having the city around him?"

"I can. I just can't imagine my partner chucking it all for a life mucking out the barn," Finn said.

"Who said I'd chuck the PD? I've got a kid to muck out the stalls."

"Sure, isn't that just Amber's life's ambition," Finn laughed. "Let's go. Remind me what this lady's name is that we're seeing?"

"Aurora Rosalis," Cori said. "Pretty name."

"And she knows about her son? Where he was found? What happened to him?" Finn asked.

"Both Paul's office and Crane contacted her after we gave them the contact information Gregorio gave us."

"Did he say how she took it?"

"No, but I imagine she took it pretty much like any mother would."

Finn didn't point out that mothers reacted very differently to tragedy. Some fell apart, some went into denial and some, like his mother, took things in hand and kept their grief private. He did not look forward to finding out which of these Mrs. Rosalis was. He also wished he could have brought her son's red and blue jacket but there were rules. She would claim the jacket along with the body. They stepped onto the porch and knocked. The door opened immediately, and Gregorio greeted them with a somber, '*hola*'.

"Hey, Gregorio," Cori said.

Finn shook the man's hand.

"*Senora. Senor O'Brien,*" he responded. "We are all here."

He opened the door wide to reveal a modest living room. It was exactly as Finn and Cori expected. What they had not expected was for the room to be filled with people. They sat on a long sofa, on chairs, on the floor. They hung in the doorways and facing these people were two empty, straight-backed chairs waiting to be filled by the *policia*.

* * *

Adolph liked the mac 'n cheese a whole lot.

"I like this damn mac 'n' cheese," he called out, unable to contain the joy he felt at eating an honest-to-God great big helping of the stuff. The men at the long, long table kept eating. A few looked up when he spoke and then went right back to their dinner.

Adolph also liked the pie.

"I love this damn pie," he hollered and two of the men at the long table looked his way for quite a while. One of those guys was across the table, eight chairs down on the left. The other one sat three chairs away on his right.

"I love this damn pie, too," called the one on the right and the one on the left laughed a little. Adolph thought that made dinner much better.

One guy got up and put his tray at the spot near the kitchen where there was a trolley and a sign over it that said PUT YOUR TRAYS HERE. You couldn't eat at St. Peter's outreach unless you followed the rules, and the tray thing was in the rules. Since Adolph liked the pie and the mac 'n' cheese and he didn't want to be asked to leave, he put his tray where it was supposed to go. He liked the guy who laughed, too. That man was still working on his pie, but it had been good to hear a happy person. Most times when the men piped up like that they were off their rocker, unlike Adolph who piped up just to hear the sound of a happy voice even if it was his own. He appreciated quite a few things unlike most of these sour pusses. Adolph liked a nice warm day, a good sunset, and the sight of a pretty lady. He just didn't have the energy to get himself back to where he would need to be to make a pretty lady turn her head. He'd fallen off life's bike and hit the ground hard. The bike had just rolled on without him. But that was going to change. Now that he had the resources, he might just be able to get a new bike, and a new life, and maybe a pretty lady to boot.

He made the tray all nice and neat on the trolley and followed another man out of the dining room. It was still early, but St. Peter's liked to lock the doors early, so he went right to the sleeping room instead of outside to see if he could bum a cigarette off somebody. Having a bed would be a good change from sleeping on the ground. The happy man finished up his meal, said a few pleasantries to the men at the table – all of whom were too tired, ornery, or crazy to talk back to him – and went to find a bed too. When he had chosen his, Adolph went to the one next to it.

"This one taken?" Adolph asked. The man shook his head.

"Adolph's the name." He put out his hand. The other man took it.

"James. Your head looks bad."

James pointed to the sore on Adolph's head. Adolph touched it. The memory of the man in the grave – the live one – flashed across his brain. Silly old man worried about a little pus when he was covered in some dude's blood.

"I've seen worse," Adolph chuckled. "Hell, I've had worse."

"Ain't we all," James said.

Adolph laughed again. Adolph laughed a lot. In another life, James would have thought Adolph sounded nuts but here his nonsense was refreshing.

"So, what's the drill?" Adolph stashed his knapsack under the bed.

"Not much. Doors locked by nine," James said.

"And no girls, I'll betcha."

Adolph put out an elbow and did a Groucho Marx thing with his eyebrows. James smiled and chuckled and lay down on his cot. He put one arm under his head and the other across his stomach.

"Yeah, guys like us are in demand."

Adolph took off his jacket and bounced a little on the cot. "Not bad."

"Don't get too used to it. They rotate. We can only bed down once a week. Gotta be out by six-thirty tomorrow. We get a bag to go. A bagel, some coffee."

"I can live with that." Adolph untied his one shoe and took it off. He untwisted the wire on the other one and then carefully twisted it back through the hole so he wouldn't lose it.

"I think they'll give you some new laces. They got stuff like that here. Go ask for some laces," James said.

"Naw, I'm good. I'll get some tomorrow."

James leaned up on his elbow and lowered his voice. "You got money? They won't let you stay if you got money?"

Adolph smiled. He put his jacket over the pitiful excuse for a pillow, wanting his head on it just in case someone thought to see what he had in the pockets. Then he lay down and laced his hands behind his head.

"Naw, I ain't got money."

"Good, 'cause they won't let you stay if you got money," James said and he settled back in too. "Ten bucks. That's all you can have on you. Ten."

"I ain't got ten," Adolph assured him.

They didn't talk anymore. James went to sleep. He didn't snore which Adolph wouldn't have minded, but he was equally happy that the man slept silently. The quiet made it easier for Adolph's mind to wander and tonight that mind of his wandered merrily over the last few weeks. The mountains had been interesting. He had slept next to a tree and covered himself with leaves to keep warm. He missed toilet paper in the forest. It was damn hard to catch a squirrel, but he had done it. That little guy looked kind of pitiful roasting over the fire Adolph had built, but he tasted just fine. Adolph couldn't remember exactly how he got left-and-then-lost in that forest but that was fine 'cause no one was asking. And there was the old guy. That was a blast of interesting right there.

That scarred up face of his had a doozy of a story to tell but even if the old guy had told it Adolph wouldn't have been able to understand what he was saying. He was curious to know what the dead man did to rile the old man so bad, but not curious enough to rile him up again. When he gave Adolph five bucks and his bloody shirt in trade for an old tee-shirt Adolph had, that was very cool. Adolph would wash it out somewhere and it would be good as new. All in all, it was a fine deal. Adolph got to the city and he got to the church. Not that he wasn't disappointed when his new buddy didn't ask him to stay at his place, or at least invite him over for a hot meal. Then he thought that maybe the old guy didn't have a house or there was an old shrew wife waiting for him. Hell, there could be a zillion reasons why he didn't take Adolph home. Like all things in Adolph's life, he rolled with the punches and enjoyed the place he found himself in.

Now the room was filling up. One by one the men had left the dinner table and come in to claim a cot. Some of them read – one had a Bible, one had a magazine, and one was reading an owner's manual for a chain saw. Some had backpacks, others had bags, some had nothing but what they carried in their arms. Shopping carts had to be left outside, locked up in an old garage that belonged to the church.

At ten o'clock a lady with cottony hair came in with the man who looked like a zombie. She sang a little good night song. The man advised that lights were going out. Then, even though the man didn't wear a collar or nothing, he blessed them. That was fine with Adolph. He was already feeling pretty blessed, but you could never have too many good wishes.

Tomorrow, he would reap the benefit of those blessings. Yes, indeed, tomorrow he would be ineligible for this cot because he would have a lot more than ten dollars in his pocket.

CHAPTER 22

Maria Gonzales.
Alberado Luca.
Cristian (no last name).
Elodia Cruz (daughter Estella, age one).
Emilio.
Eminilada.
Hector.
Herminia…

On and on the introductions went. Seventeen people in all said their names, some in voices that were small and fearful, others strong and almost defiant. Cori and Finn lost track of who was who, but they nodded and smiled at each person as they spoke. The last person to introduce himself was:

"Father Patrick. I minister at Our Lady of Tears. These are my parishioners."

Finn rose and shook the priest's hand.

"You've a good grip there, Father," Finn said.

"You better have a good one around here if you're going to help your neighbors with the chores."

The priest was the only white face in the sea of brown ones, but each brown face was unique, representing many nations. Finn saw the Spanish influence in those from Mexico, and the darker skinned South American Indians in others. Father Patrick sat on the floor between Finn and Cori. When they both offered their chairs, he waved them away.

"My parents were hippies. The floor was where we ate, slept and sat," he said happily.

"I would have expected you to turn into a guru instead of a priest," Cori said.

"God works in mysterious ways." He chuckled before turning his attention to Gregorio who was standing in the center of the room.

Gregorio had arranged the meeting and it was he who would take responsibility should it go badly. He spoke in a measured voice. While Finn and Cori could pick a few words out here and there, Father Patrick had to translate in full. He did so quietly, obviously fluent in the language.

"He's telling them to be honest. He's telling them that you and your partner are trustworthy and want nothing else but to help them find their loved ones."

Suddenly, the people around the room moved, and muttered. Two women with babies held them closer and raised their voices.

"He's telling them how Aurora's son died. That it is true he was killed and did not have an accident or run away."

Cori and Finn looked at the woman who sat center on the couch, staring in front of her, tears in her eyes. A woman on her left held her arm; the woman on the right dabbed her own tears. While they bore witness to her suffering, Aurora Rosalis sat strong, accepting of what had happened.

"Gregorio is saying that you will help them find all their men and will not stop until you do."

Cori tapped the priest's shoulder and kept her voice low so she wouldn't disturb what was going on.

"What does he mean all their men?"

People had started to talk to Gregorio, and it was clear there were some things to be worked through before they shared anything with Finn and Cori. Father Patrick unwound his long legs and stood up.

"He means the ones in Mexico," Father Patrick whispered. When Gregorio looked their way, the priest apologized for interrupting.

"*Perdonanos. Volveremos.*"

Father Patrick motioned for Finn and Cori to follow him to the front porch. The horses whinnied at their arrival and then settled down again. The priest left the door open so that he could still hear what was going on inside.

"I told him we would be back in a moment. I didn't want to disturb him, but you should know that what has happened to a few of the young men in the last year – them disappearing and all – well, it brings up some very bad memories."

"Of what?" Cori asked.

"*Asesino fantasma* – the ghost killer."

"Seriously, Father, if the supernatural is at play here you'll not be needing us," Finn said.

"No, that's just what they called the person because he appeared and disappeared so quickly. Unfortunately, when he disappeared so did the young men."

The priest laughed a little, but it wasn't a happy sound. He leaned up against the porch post.

"A while back – maybe three years or so – young men started disappearing from a small village in Mexico across the border from San Diego and just past Tijuana. I think there were maybe six in all. Only two were ever found. Those two were buried in shallow graves out in the desert. But not far out. A mile or two from the town."

"Much like the man we found a few days ago," Finn said.

"Sounds like it," Father Patrick answered. "Anyway, because the people were poor and had no money to bribe the police, nothing was ever done. By the way, half those people in there brought money with them to bribe you."

"I hope you told them that isn't a dandy idea," Cori said.

"I told them, but it's a cultural thing. Very hard to un-learn," the priest said. "So, onward. One day some older men saw a white truck with a pale man inside. He was talking to the young men, trying to get one of them into the truck with him. The men didn't like that, and they ran him off. They knew there was no work to be had like the man promised and some of their people were already missing. The old man in the truck was probably no one but people were afraid, nonetheless. The white truck, the way this man looked, well it snowballed into a legend. The old men swore they had come face to face with a ghost. The women went to church to pray for God to protect them and their children. For insurance, they went to the *Curandera* who took their money and—"

"And that would be?" Finn interrupted.

"Oh, sorry. That's a witch doctor. Lots of potions and spells to keep bad things away," Father Patrick explained. "Or potions and spells to make good things happen. It sort of all depends on what you're expecting."

"A little like praying to a patron saint," Finn said.

"A little. The difference is that faith is placed in a man dressed in feathers and gold chains instead of God. Any-way, the young men armed themselves but, after that, no one disappeared again. The old men took credit for being strong and scaring the ghost man away, the women took credit for their prayers, the *Curandera* took credit for the spells, and the young men took credit because the ghost knew that they would kill him if he came back again, and send his soul to hell."

Father Patrick opened the door.

"Some of them believe that the ghost has followed them here. It's kind of a 'just when you thought it was safe to go back in the water' thing."

"Yeah, well, I think we can pretty much rule out any spooks," Cori said.

"Although, whatever is going on is pretty scary," he said. His ears pricked when he heard his name called. Father Patrick stepped aside and held the door for Cori. "Ladies first."

She shot him a big grin as she stepped over the threshold.

"Bummer you're a priest, Father."

* * *

It was ten-thirty and Finn and Cori had learned a few things: tired babies looked like rag dolls when they fell asleep in their mother's arms, yet a mother's grip never faltered, old men snoozed and woke throughout a long night, strong men huddled, shared opinions under their breath, weighed words and intentions and, in the end, were looked to for final truths.

In all, five people had spoken about *Asesino fantasma* – the ghost killer, and three had told their stories about their men who had recently gone missing.

The young bride of Santos – a name Gregorio had given Finn – clutched at her little daughter and talked about her good husband who worked in a lumberyard and on the corners so that he could take care of her. They had only been married a little while and he had never missed a night away from home.

Pacal's mother was not there. She worked nights cleaning offices, but her friend spoke for her. And others chimed in. Many of these people knew Pacal and thought highly of him as a quiet young man dedicated to his family. He went to church. He was a handsome boy, and he was *valiente*.

"Courageous," Father Patrick translated.

"Why do they say that?" Finn wanted to know.

"...his brother is big in the Dogtown Rifa."

"That's not good," Cori muttered.

Father Patrick nodded and tried to keep up with the stream of Spanish coming from the woman.

There is bad blood between them.

The brother brought his homies to the house...

Everyone in the neighborhood knew that they wanted to jump Pacal. For a while people thought Pacal would...

Father Patrick held up a finger. He twisted his head a little as if that could make him hear better.

"...Pacal wouldn't do it. His brother finally gave up. Until he found out Pacal was dating a white girl. The brother was angry about *la chica blanca*. Now that Pacal is missing, the mother is afraid to even speak his name for fear of angering her oldest son..."

The priest listened again, translating it all in his head, delaying his translation by only a few seconds.

"The older son predicted that Pacal would come to a worse end for dating a white girl than he would for being in a gang. She says everyone knows that's true. She says the police should talk to the white girl."

Cori listened. She made notes. She took all this in without comment, but the way the woman spit out the words 'white girl' cut her to the core.

Just before eleven, they called an end to the meeting. Finn and Cori thanked everyone. They accepted the pictures pressed into their hands. Only two were relevant – Santos and Esteban – but others were added to the mix. In the end, Cori held pictures of men who had disappeared into the desert in Mexico, men who were known to have deserted their family, and one of a man who had died but the old lady wanted Cori to take it anyway. What the detectives heard did not warm their hearts, especially the information about Pacal's older brother, a gangbanger, a guy pissed off that his bro ran with a white girl.

"Cori?"

She looked up to see that she was standing alone on the porch. The horses were gone. She could hear the clop of their hooves echoing down the deserted street as their riders made their way slowly home. Finn and Father Patrick waited for her halfway between the car and the house. She went down the stairs and joined the two men.

"And on it goes. They run from one misery to another. Such trials. We are blessed, aren't we?" Father Patrick sighed and put his hands in the pockets of his worn black pants as they wandered toward the road.

"There are all sorts of miseries, Father," Finn said, "but in the grand scheme of things, yes, we are blessed."

All three turned toward the house as the lights went out. The dark and the silence settled upon them. Cori kicked at a stone, Finn ambled, and Father Patrick's eyes were on the moon. Each was thinking of another place: Finn of Ireland, Cori of Texas and Father Patrick of his hippie family, no doubt. When they reached the edge of the property, Finn spoke.

"So, Father, do you think you can draw up a timeline

for us starting with the disappearances in Mexico?"

"I'll try," he said. "Before you go, there is one more thing I should probably mention. I was at an Archdiocesan conference three months ago. I heard some stories. I sort of dismissed them until now."

"Like what?" Cori asked.

"There are two kids – well, young men – who went missing up Palmdale way about a year and a half ago," the priest said. "I knew about Santos, but now with the other three the Palmdale situation is looking a little freaky to me."

They were at the car. Finn had the keys in his hand.

"You know, Father, I can understand those people in the house not reporting these things, but what about you and the Palmdale priest?"

"What would I have reported, Detective O'Brien?" Father Patrick laughed. "Even my own bishop dismissed this all as folklore and family problems. If God's head man was uninterested, what luck would I have with a man of the law?"

"You could have tried," Cori said.

"Hindsight is a wonderful thing and so is context. Considering what we heard tonight, everything looks just a little different. Gregorio was lucky to find you both. I'm not sure that if he had walked into a precinct anyone would have given him the time of day." Father Patrick gave them a lovely smile. "And with that, I'll say goodnight. Up at five for the six o'clock mass."

"We'll be in touch, Father," Cori said.

"The sooner we can get this squared away the better." Father Patrick shook his head. "It's a pity, isn't it? Not too long ago, Santo's wife was in my church getting married, and now she'll be back for her husband's funeral if things go like I think they will. All in the course of a year."

Father Patrick raised a hand. Finn went to shake it. Instead, the priest made the sign of the cross and blessed the detective. Finn colored. Not that he wasn't appreciative of the gesture, he simply wasn't public about his faith.

"I'll be thanking you, Father," Finn said, not wanting to embarrass the man.

"You're more than welcome. He turned to Cori, but her palm went out.

"I'm good, Father," she said. "O'Brien will share."

"Good to know." The young priest smiled. "Good night then. And thank you for listening. Thank you for wanting to do something."

They said their goodbyes, but the priest turned back once more.

"One more thing. The Mexico matter? It might be superstition or even stories told to keep the young men close to home, but it was pretty colorful. It was said that the bodies that were found were buried in God's grace."

"How would anyone know?" Cori asked.

"They say the corpses were laid out like they were in a casket. Someone had put holy cards under their hands." Father Patrick shrugged. "Go figure, huh?"

CHAPTER 23

MAY 1

Margaret O'Brien: Hey, you still coming to dinner Sunday? Mom wants to know. Just FYI, she's acting like everything is fine, but she's worried because of that guy on TV talking about you. Dad, too, but you know him. Please make sure you come on Sunday. Call me back. Text. Four o'clock unless you can make it for mass in the morning and spend the whole day with us. See you soon.

When the door of the office opened, Cori swiveled around, smiled at the clerk who brought the mail and took the pile of interoffice envelopes from him. She rifled through, took the one she wanted and put the rest on Finn's desk. He didn't bat an eye, absorbed as he was in the report the lab had sent over on the paper sample.

"...Corollary 1. Some characteristics retained by the smaller pieces are unique to the original item or to the division process.

Corollary 2. Some characteristics retained by the smaller pieces are common to the original item as well as to other items of similar manufacture.

Corollary 3. Some characteristics from the original item will be lost or changed during or after the moment of division and subsequent dispersal; this confounds the attempt to infer a common source.

In particular, the principle of divisible matter and its logical corollaries have a profound effect on the forensic process of individualization. Therefore—"

"God, O'Brien, this is dryer than a popcorn fart. Can't we just skip to the good parts?" Cori whined.

"And sure, isn't this what they get paid for over there in their laboratory? The least you can do is pay attention." Finn grinned. Cori gave him a look flatter than a pancake. He laughed and started to read again.

"Alright, here we go. Bottom line, they cannot definitively say what this shred of a thing is – and I quote – "The physico-chemical traits present in the undivided object except those (size and shape) that define it as intact cannot be determined. Of the identifiable properties that might be inherited by the progeny fragments are color, elemental composition, and micro-crystalline structure."

"English please." Cori stretched an arm out on his desk and let her head fall upon it.

"The fragment," Finn said, "was viewed under a stereomicroscope and examined for color, porosity, shape and range of size. Because there was an edge to analyze, it appears they can give us a range of anywhere from three to six inches in length and a width of between two inches and six. They looked at both the torn and cut threads of the fabric used to make the paper. The paper is thirty-pound stock."

Cori sat up. "That would make it card stock, right?"

"Yes. It has a very high wood fiber content, and it is

bleached. The conclusion on the stock is that it is expensive and not inconsistent with greeting cards, high end business cards, or cover stock."

"Like on a book cover?" Cori speculated.

"Or a holy card," Finn said. "Sure, I can't get Father Patrick's little story about what happened in Mexico out of my mind."

"Don't get bogged down," Cori warned and then she added, "But don't let that thought go either. So, what else?"

"It was printed both sides. Three colors identified: red and blue but the interesting thing is the gold. It's gold leaf, not printed but overlaid. Just a trace. That's fancy. And real ink was used on the colors, no high processing Xerox. Someone spent some money on whatever it is," Finn mused.

"Could be a greeting card," Cori said. "How sick would that be, putting a greeting card on a corpse. Or maybe it's like a condolence card. *Sorry for your loss* kind of thing or, yes, a religious angle. Given how he lays them out all nice, that's not so farfetched. What else do you have?"

"Ink analysis concluded that the ink was first manufactured by RGX and June 30, 2016 is the date is was first commercially available. They confirmed with gas chromatography, mass spectrometry—"

"Spare me, O'Brien," Cori warned.

"Okay, they confirmed the deterioration showed the ink had been laid on the paper within the year. So we're looking at this year and we got the name of the manufacturer and a number. Ready to copy?"

Cori picked up the phone and dialed as Finn read off the phone number.

"Hello. This is Detective Cori Anderson from the Los Angeles Police..."

Finn half listened as she talked and fell silent while she was transferred at least twice. Finally, Cori was having a real conversation. She made notes, paused, and wrote again. "Yep. Thank you. Yep. We'll call again if we need anything."

She hung up.

"What have you got?"

"Mr. Tenaka is the VP of production. He confirms that the ink we're looking at is a fairly new product. His customers are liking it because it holds the color and won't fade and has a kind of hand painted, acrylic look. The gold is actually gold leaf that can be used on a press."

"That explains the trace metal elements," Finn said. "We've got red, gold and royal blue. Plus, there is a watermark. Hard to make it out from the piece we have. It looks like a half circle with a line through it."

"Let me see," Cori wiggled her fingers and Finn turned the screen her way. He enlarged the image. "You're right, I can't tell. Amazing what they can do. It looks like fabric when it's under that microscope."

She wiggled her fingers again and he turned the screen away while she kept talking.

"Tenaka gave me seventeen printing companies in the western region that have purchased the ink, so let's get on it. You take eight; I'll do the heavy lifting and take nine."

"I fear I'll be leaving you with the whole task, Cori." Finn finished the last drink of his coffee and grabbed for his jacket. "And if you have the time, can you take a look at the security footage from McDonald's, too."

"You having tea with the queen so you can't stick around and do the grunt work?" Cori kept her eye on him even as he opened the door.

"I'm off to have a word with Pacal's brother."

"Well, why didn't you say so?" Cori started to get up, but Finn stopped her.

"I'm wanting to see him on my own."

"Oh, come on, O'Brien. That's not smart. After what went down in that house with Marbles, the press is going to be on your back if you even look at this guy cross-eyed. Not to mention every internal oversight committee the LAPD can throw at you. Why buy yourself trouble?"

"I'm intending only to talk to the gentleman in the light of day. Nothing to hide," Finn assured her.

"And what are you going to do if a few of his homies are there and don't care what time of day it is? You won't have backup much less a witness."

"All true, and with my last breath I'll bear witness to the fact that you were right to caution me," Finn laughed. "You run down the printers on that list and take a look at the McDonald's security footage. By the time you're done I'll be back, and we'll see where we stand."

"I hate it when you pull rank." Cori leaned back in her chair and bounced a little as she eyed her partner. "You know, it occurs to me there's another reason you don't want me around."

"And that would be?"

"You don't want me to get in this guy's face because he called my kid a white girl."

"That's what she is, Cori," Finn pointed out.

"I don't need to speak Spanish to know they weren't bein' kind when they said it." Cori flipped her hair and righted herself. She picked up her phone and dismissed him. "Go. Go on. Git."

"Glad to have your permission. I'll be back after lunch," Finn said.

Cori held the phone to her chest and called to him before he was fully out the door. Finn stuck his head back in.

"Where are you going specifically?" she asked.

Finn walked back to the desk, picked up a piece of paper and handed it to her.

"Father Patrick must have been up at the crack of dawn. This was waiting when I got in."

Cori ran her eyes down the information.

"A timeline of the disappearances he knows about starting with the rumors out of Mexico all the way up to Pacal. Addresses for Pacal's mother and brother." She drew a line under the latter address. "And the woman who spoke last night. If he ever decides not to be a priest, he can come work for us."

"Happy now?" Finn asked.

"Ecstatic." Cori drawled. "If I don't see you right after lunch, I'm coming for you."

Finn went on his way but before he closed the door, he heard Cori raise her voice again.

"You just remember a worm is the only animal that can't fall down, O'Brien."

Finn shook his head, not at all sure what it was that she was trying to tell him but positive it was well intentioned. While he headed to Dogtown, Cori worked the phones. All the while her eye wandered back to Father Patrick's report, specifically the third paragraph down; the name and address of Maria Acosta, Pacal's mother.

* * *

It was eight-thirty, and the man was getting nervous. He should have been at work an hour ago. If he didn't go to work today, they would report him for sure because he had already missed one day. The first time no one cared. His supervisor was used to people like him not exactly following the rules, so he only said, 'don't let it happen again'.

But he had to let it happen again because Adolph was weighing heavily on his mind. So heavily he hadn't slept a wink. Adolph, the man was sure, was going to the police. He would tell them about the body. He would spill his guts. He would cackle and laugh that the old man had been a fool for trusting him. Indeed, if he had not been so nervous about getting checked in at the house, he would never have given Adolph a ride to the city. He would have used his gun again and left him to lie with the brown boy in the grave. But he didn't do that because he had been surprised and because he had been anxious. You couldn't think when you were surprised and anxious, you couldn't fight back. You were at the other person's mercy when you were surprised, anxious and terrified.

Now it was morning, and the man was thinking straight. He had a plan. He would surprise Adolph and take care of him proper. Finding Adolph was worth getting written up at work. That was why he was sitting in his truck outside the church, waiting. It stood to reason the man had spent the night inside, but seven people had come out already and there was no Adolph. The woman with the white hair and the tall, lanky man stood outside the door, smiling as they handed each man a paper bag with food in it. There were more bags on a small table next to them, but no one had come out for a good long while. The worry made the man's face ache. Suddenly two more men came through the door and then five after that. If they had been full up the night before there would be six more vagrants inside. He leaned into the truck's steering wheel, watching. One more came out and one after him.

Adolph.

Adolph.

Adolph.

The man thought the name, hoping it would be like a spell and conjure him up. One more and then there he was.

Adolph.

The man in the truck narrowed his eyes. Adolph was happy, well fed, and rested unlike the man who was annoyed, tired and worried. He started the motor and waited until the woman had given Adolph the sack lunch and the lanky man had blessed him. The man in the truck watched the church people pack up their table and go inside while Adolph and another man walked down the street. The man pulled out and followed along behind, waiting for the moment when Adolph and his friend would part ways. It wasn't long before they did.

Seeing his opening, the man parked his truck and was about to get out to greet Adolph, to invite him to take a ride, to offer him a meal, when Adolph turned into a shop. It was a worn-out place, its windows filled with coats and musical instruments and stuff so small the man couldn't see most of it. It just looked like junk – which it probably was – because in the corner of one window the man saw a sign: PAWN.

While he waited for Adolph to reappear, he wondered what the man had that was worth pawning. Then he thought this was a blessing in disguise because as soon as Adolph pawned whatever it was he possessed, he would have money. When the man disposed of Adolph, then he would have money, too. Yes, the man thought, Adolph's money would be most welcome.

He was thinking these pleasant thoughts when it suddenly dawned on him that Adolph had been gone a very long time. He couldn't imagine that Adolph had something so valuable that it would have to be negotiated or evaluated. In the next second, he had his answer.

A police car drew up alongside the curb and stopped in front of the shop. Two officers went inside. When they came out, they had Adolph between them, his hands cuffed.

They dipped Adolph's head as they put him in the car. Adolph was smiling. Adolph was a stupid man. He was also a talkative one. When the police car drove away with Adolph in it, the man started his truck once again. He went to work, and the supervisor was angry that he was late. The man listened to his supervisor berate him, wishing all the while that he had his shovel. If he had his shovel, he would have bashed the man's head in. Still, it wasn't the time to be angry.

It was time to worry.

* * *

The William Meade Homes consisted of twenty-four buildings and four hundred and forty-nine units of what Los Angeles County called affordable housing. It was a rectangle of brick blocks that had more in common with a work camp than a neighborhood. In between the buildings there was space where brown grass clung to life under the L.A. sun. There were a few bushes in the beds but no flowers. The community gardens, playgrounds and recreational facilities had been shut down long ago due to the high crime rate within the projects. In its wisdom, the government decided to close the three things that had at least a snowball's chance in hell of bringing the community together. That decision left the residents no choice but to shoot, stab and assault one another in stairwells, apartments, and the abandoned recreational facilities. So, all in all, this was not a great place to live.

To be fair, it was hard to imagine that a housing project like William Meade could be anything more, wedged as it was between the L.A. County Jail and the Los Angeles River, a concrete trough that ran with graffiti instead of water. While the sign at the edge of the complex heralded it as William Meade Homes everyone called it Dogtown. It was here Finn O'Brien would find the headman of the Dogtown Rifa gang, Santiago Acosta. He carried the handle El Tigre. He may not have known that Finn was coming but he was always ready for a cop. Today he was sitting outside his apartment, sunning and wasn't surprised when the detective appeared.

The two men eyed one another as Finn closed the distance. Santiago Acosta saw a man bringing trouble; Finn saw a man comfortable in his kingdom. *El Tigre* sat in a lawn chair, slouched a little, his legs splayed in front of him, a beer in his hand, boots on his feet, a pristine wife beater baring a well-muscled, awesomely tatted chest and arms. Even from a distance, Finn could see the quality of his ink and the narrative of it. He had not disfigured himself as Marbles had, but rather used the art to glorify his body and underscore his power.

His hair was razor cut and slicked back from a broad forehead. The skin of his face was taut but there were deep wrinkles at the corner of his eyes. Those eyes were small, and they glittered. His mouth was wide, his nose slightly curved. He was a handsome man, tall and powerful and lithe. Two pit bulls – one the color of tar and the other a tan – were by his side. The black one was sitting, its pink eyes on Finn, tongue hanging out as if it were salivating over the prospect of sinking his teeth into something – anything. The tan slept on its side, its massive chest rising and falling with each breath. The door to the unit was open and

Finn could see a woman moving around inside; he heard children. There were others out in the common area. Some were sitting and watching like Santiago Acosta, two were arguing, an old Asian lady dragged a wheeled cart behind her on the way to the grocery and in the far distance more children played. The two people arguing paused to look at Finn as he cut across the brittle grass, but they got back to it when it was clear the detective had no interest in them.

"That's far enough unless you got a warrant," Santiago said just before he took a drink from his bottle. He sounded sure of himself, intelligent, unruffled.

"Sure, it's just a chat I'm wanting, Santiago."

"I don't think you and I got much in common," the man answered.

There was a slight rise in the edge of his lips, a tap of his forefinger against the amber colored bottle in his hand. At the moment, his conscience was clear so there was no fear or apprehension – not that Finn thought this man was ever fearful. From inside the house, a woman's voice rose in anger. A slap was heard and then the sound of a little girl's outraged scream. Finn looked toward the open door, but Santiago's gaze never wavered.

"I'm here about Pacal." Finn turned his attention back where it belonged.

Santiago snorted. He motioned with his beer to another lawn chair. When Finn hesitated, he growled at the black pit bull in Spanish and the animal moved, sauntering away proudly as if to show that it went of its own accord. Finn sat. The tan didn't move, the warm sun on his belly making him lazy.

"You tellin' me Pacal's in trouble? What, he was late for church or something?"

"He's missing and your mother's worried. Actually,

quite a few people are worried."

Santiago slid his eyes Finn's way. "Nothing to do with me."

"I understand you had a falling out."

"We had a difference of opinion," Santiago answered. "I haven't seen him in more than six months now. I haven't been to my mother's house. I have my own house. My own woman. Kids."

"And you don't worry about your family?"

"They don't worry about me." Santiago pushed himself up, set aside the beer and rested his elbows on his knees. "Look, I know you don't come here not knowing who you're gonna be talking to. You know I done time. You know I am Dogtown for life. I appreciate you don't try to con me on that score, so I'll give it to you straight.

"I tried to help Pacal, but he didn't want none of it. Easy money. He wouldn't want for nothin'. My mother wouldn't be cleaning rich ladies' houses if they let me help but they don't want it. My mother got afraid. My brother," Santiago shrugged. "He's gonna die washing dishes, working day labor. Pacal believed all that shit about a better life. Maybe for the fancy dreamers, not Pacal. Stupid to think he could be more. Bullshit."

He sat back and watched the old Asian lady who was walking back the way she'd come, still pulling her still empty cart.

"So, you have no idea where he might have gotten off to, then?" Finn asked.

Santiago shook his head. He laughed a little. "You know, way back when, Dogtown Rifa was Micks and spicks. You and me, we'd be homies."

"That must have been some time ago."

"Like in the fifties, man. Before you and me. Everybody

hated Irish and Mexicans, now they hate Mexicans. Everybody thinks brown skin means Mexican. It's all good. It's history, you know. I like the history of this place and my people. All Latinos," Santiago said. His hand fell to touch the tan bull's belly. "They call this place Dogtown 'cause it was right near L.A.'s first dog pound. Hah, history. Now nobody knows this place 'cept us who live in it. It's a shithole but I like it. Know what I mean?"

Finn nodded. "That I do."

"I could have given Pacal money even if he didn't want to join up. They never would want for nothing," Santiago finally said.

"Except honor," Finn said. Santiago snorted.

"We all got our honor," he said. "I got honor from my homies and I give it back. And no matter what my family thinks, I give it to them too. I don't bother them none. That's being honorable."

"So you don't go to your mother's house at all?" Finn asked.

Santiago shook his head. "No, but I seen Pacal. I seen him standing on the corner. I keep up. I hear stuff."

"When was the last time you heard something?" Finn asked.

Santiago shrugged, moving his shoulders like he was itching to lift some weight. "Maybe two months ago."

"Did you hear anything that would lead you to believe he was in some sort of trouble? That maybe he was under some sort of duress?"

"Duress? Good word. You mean someone beatin' on him?" Santiago asked.

"Something like that. Maybe F13?"

"No, no duress. He was just being dumb foolin' with a *gringa*." Santiago shook his head. "No *gringa* going to want a guy who works the corners and washes dishes."

"I think you'd be surprised."

"Don't matter. He's gone missing. Maybe he's gone for good. The corners suck, man. You never know who's picking you up. Or maybe the white chick had a boyfriend that took Pacal out. Ever think of that?"

"Nope. We checked," Finn said. "How about a guy in a white truck cruising the corners. A white man. Old. Have you been hearing anything like that?"

"I hear there's an outfit downtown on Flower. That big tower they're building? Don't know the name of the builders. They're taking people to work and paying shit under the table. You go there. You look there for white trucks—"

Just then, a little girl ran out of the apartment, pushed forward by an angry stream of Spanish that was followed by the woman speaking it. Santiago scooped up the little girl and set her on his lap. Finn smiled at her. She looked pretty in a pink dress three sizes too big for her. On her feet were green tennis shoes. Her legs and arms were stick thin, her hair long and straight and falling around her eyes. She snuggled into her father's arms and Finn thought it a beautiful picture, the little scruffy princess engulfed in those tatted arms. Acosta's embrace made her strong and her delicate, bony body made him soften. When she didn't smile back, Finn glanced at the woman in the doorway. She didn't smile either and Finn saw that the little girl would grow up to be her mother: a gang woman, fiercely protective of her territory. This one was wide-hipped and heavily made up and Finn thought she would have no trouble taking him out if he did her man wrong.

"You've a fine family, Santiago," Finn said.

The woman turned away. Santiago Acosta hugged his daughter tighter.

"I'm sorry for Pacal," Santiago said. "He's a good kid. My family must be afraid without him. He took care of them all. I'll send money."

"He isn't the only one," Finn said. "There are more that are gone."

"I don't give a shit about no one else," Santiago said. "I don't believe you give a shit neither."

"It's because some are dead, Santiago. Heads bashed in, buried in the scrub." Finn moved in the lawn chair. It was old, the aluminum tubes felt fragile beneath his weight. "They are all young men who are gone. They all looked like Pacal. I know this is not the work of gangs. Even if it were, I wouldn't be looking at Dogtown Rifa. You've nothing to lose if you talk to me."

Santiago gave his daughter a kiss and set her on the ground. He sent her on her way with a pat on her rear end. She scampered off on her colt legs.

"He's dead then," Santiago said. "You should have said that straight out, man."

"He's not dead until I have his body. I have hope."

"Then you are *loco.*" Santiago squinted into the sun that seemed to hang low in the sky. "They all missing from day work?"

"Yes," Finn said.

"How were they taken out? The dead ones."

"Hit with shovels, pipes maybe. We don't know for sure yet. We do know they were struck one or two well placed blows. Not beaten. Whoever is doing this knows where to strike," Finn said. "The bodies are buried in remote areas. They are buried holding cards. Perhaps religious cards."

"That's no good," Santiago said. "That's a freak."

"'Tis that." Finn pulled out the pictures. Santiago took them and looked through. Finn had left out the picture of

Pacal. He did not want Santiago Acosta to know who the 'white girl' was. "Do you know any of them?"

"No. Maybe this one. I think I remember him when I still lived in my mother's house. I didn't know him good. He wasn't a homie." He handed back the pictures. "Sorry, man."

"Thank you." Finn got up.

"You want my boys to watch? You want us to help you out?"

"Watch out only. Tell me if you see or hear anything. Don't be taking the law into your own hands," Finn said. "And if I find Pacal in a bad way, I'll tell you first. Your mother will need you then."

Santiago raised a brow and Finn understood that it was too late. His mother would certainly need help; she just wouldn't need him. Finn turned but before he could walk away Santiago stopped him.

"They say Pacal was working to buy a ring for the *gringa*. I would have got him a ring for the right girl. Big as Baja."

"For the right girl?" Finn asked.

"Yeah, the right one," Santiago reiterated.

"And the white girl wasn't the one."

"No," he said.

"Did you ever meet her?"

"No need, man. I know the score. Maybe she was a do-gooder, you know, want to save Pacal from being a poor immigrant. Maybe she just wanted to see what it's like with a brown boy. "

Santiago slid down in his chair. He spread his legs wider and grinned with those beautiful white teeth of his.

"She got the wrong brown boy if that's what she wanted. She should have been lookin' my way."

Finn nodded. The man was talking about Amber, but Finn took no offense. He was talking concept, he was talking about a nameless woman, and that was no disrespect to his wife only to the *gringa*. Finn put his hands in his pockets, found a card and handed it to Santiago Acosta.

"In case you hear anything," Finn said.

Santiago took the card. It disappeared into his big hand and with the other he swiped up his beer again. The black pit bull wandered over to sit beside him. Finn walked halfway across the grass, paused, and looked back. Times changed and yet they remained the same: micks, spicks and *gringas*. Someone was always getting the short end of the stick and it was usually someone just one rung up who was swinging it.

* * *

It was near noon when Cori finished calling printers. She had a ton of notes as well as promises to fax customer lists and to messenger samples. She also had made a dozen little squiggles on the paper Father Patrick had faxed over. Those squiggles made a circle around one address: that of Pacal's mother.

Twice Cori had gotten out of her chair. Once she even put her jacket on and picked up her purse intending to drive to that address, knock on the door and introduce herself. Now she was doing it again, but this time she didn't get as far as her jacket. This time she just scooted her chair back up to her table and picked up the phone to make another call to another printer.

She just wasn't ready to meet the in-laws. Not yet. Maybe not ever.

CHAPTER 24

Detective Morrow: (looking at Cori, blinking behind his glasses. Cori sitting on the edge of his desk) Is there a reason you're here, Detective Anderson?

Cori: Just taking a break **(pause);** I'm trying to run down a company that printed up some kind of card and now it's hurry up and wait, so I figured I'd come brighten your day.

Detective Morrow: You are simply bored, Detective Anderson. **(pushing up his glasses. Cori picking up a pen and clicking it.)**

Cori: Morrow, do you have more than one shirt and tie? I swear, every time I see you it's the same old shirt. You know, it's just the color of puke. You want me to take you around some lunch hour and get you something with a little more pizazz?

Detective Morrow: **(taking back the pen)** As nice as that sounds, Detective Anderson, I don't think our taste is compatible. I…"

(Morrow and Anderson turn toward the sound of raised voices)

"For God sake, someone like that would have caused a riot if he even showed his face in the neighborhood, much less inside the building. It was my cleaning girl and her boyfriend. They took the jewelry. She tried to wiggle out of it, so I told her that building security had her and the boyfriend on video. They were the only ones in my apartment. The only ones. I have no idea who that person is you arrested."

The woman who was chewing the ear off Detective Grady, burglary, was as obnoxious to look at as she was to listen to. Her hair was cut in a fashion that was just on the wrong side of cool. Someone had tried to make her face match her hair and only succeeded in making her eyes too high, her cheeks too tight and her lips too big. Her jeans, shirt, jacket, and boots were expensively fashioned to look old, worn and ever so chic. Cori thought she looked stupid and, by the glance the woman cast Cori's way, it appeared the feeling was mutual.

Cori gave her the cop nod: pleasant, businesslike. Morrow blinked behind his glasses when she slid her eyes his way. She lost interest in both detectives when Grady offered her a seat. She took it without missing a beat.

"I demanded he return the jewelry, but she said she hadn't seen the boyfriend since then."

"The man who was trying to pawn the jewelry said he found it in the woods," Detective Grady persisted. "How do you think your jewelry got in the woods?"

The woman threw up her hands. "You're supposed to figure that out. I just want my jewelry."

"We'd like the contact information for your housekeeper so that we can interview her."

"I'm telling you, it's a waste of time." When Grady

stayed silent, she grabbed a pen and wrote the number on the first piece of paper she found on his desk. "I don't know where she actually lives, so if you can't get her at that number then I can't help you. Now, can you just let me identify my stuff? I've got to get back to work."

Detective Grady pulled a clear plastic bag out of his desk drawer and placed it in front of the woman. She poked at it.

"It's all there. The necklace, both rings and the locket." She dropped her hand hard on the desk and gave her fingers a drum. "What do I sign so I can get out of here?"

"We're going to need to hold these as evidence."

"Don't be ridiculous. The boyfriend is probably back in Mexico by now, and the guy you arrested at the pawnshop looks like a loony-tune. I don't want to charge anyone, so what do you care?"

"It's still a felony, ma'am. The D.A. will have to make the decision whether or not to prosecute."

"Oh, for God's sake," the woman snapped. "Just give me my jewelry. Give it to me."

She held out her hand and riffled her fingers. Detective Grady, knowing this was a lost cause, showed her where to sign the inventory. She made two quick slashes of the pen and finished with a practiced flourish.

"There." She slid the paper back at him.

"There." He put the baggie of jewelry in her hands. She put it in her purse. "The D.A.'s office will be calling you…"

"Tell them not to bother," she huffed, pushing back the chair, and starting for the door. "Honestly, you give someone a job, someone who probably shouldn't even be in this country, and this is what they do to a taxpaying citizen. Next time, I'll use an agency. You pay more, but…"

Nobody found out what you got when you paid more

because the door closed behind her. When she was gone, Cori slid off Detective Morrow's desk and ambled over to Grady's.

"Anderson." He looked up at her like a beaten dog. "Where's your other half?"

"Got rid of him a long time ago." Cori took a chair next to him. "But if you mean O'Brien, he's out on a top-secret mission."

"The kind that's going to get him tossed in jail or the kind that's going to piss the rest of us off?"

Cori shrugged, "One and the same, Grady. Hey, listen. The lady who was just in?"

"Yeah, what about her?" Grady asked.

"Just wondering who you picked up at the pawn? He wasn't Latino, was he? Young?"

"Nope. White guy. Why?"

"Just curious," Cori said. "But the guy who took the stuff, was he Hispanic? Him and his girlfriend were Hispanic, right?"

"What? You think the housekeeper was Swedish?"

Cori ignored that and said, "We've been looking for a couple of Hispanic males. This might be a long shot, but do you happen to have a description of the guy who took the jewelry?"

"The condo that broad lives in is like a movie studio. I've got good video." Grady jotted down a file number and handed it to her. "Knock your socks off."

"And what about the guy you picked up? He still here?"

"Yep. Got him in a holding cell. I'm going to book him on stolen goods. Waste of time these days, but I go by the book," Grady said.

"Where is he?"

"He's in three. Name's Adolph."

"As in Hitler?"

"As in Zuckor. Spells it with a 'ph'. That's according to him."

Cori pulled up her chin and wagged her head as if to say six-of-one-half-a-dozen of the other to her. She sauntered back through the bullpen, stopping long enough to say:

"Hey Morrow, want to come to dinner tonight? You look like you could use a home cooked meal."

"Thank you, Detective Anderson, but—"

"Awe, come on. Lapinski and O'Brien are coming. We've got a puzzle going on and we need an adult in the room."

"Might I ask what you'll be serving…"

"Excellent. See you at seven."

Cori went on her way knowing a little dinner party was just what Amber needed to buck her up and new eyes were just what she and O'Brien needed on their problem.

* * *

Cori found Jerry Haliwell sitting amidst thumb drives, tapes, CDs and even a few eight tracks. She handed him the reference number Grady had given her and then stepped back as he rolled his chair the length of the room before twirling to a stop, getting what he wanted and then rolling back to the console. He plugged in a thumb drive, hit a button, and rolled out of the way so that Cori could move closer to the screen.

"It's fifteen-seconds in," Haliwell said. "Back in a minute, I've got to hit the John."

Cori waved him away and narrowed her eyes, watching the tape for the first motion. It came as he said, fifteen seconds in. Haliwell was back a second after that.

"You're quick on the draw," Cori drawled as he took his

seat again. "Hey, Haliwell, stop it now."

The video was paused on a three-quarter profile of the man coming out of the apartment: right age, right build, definitely Latino. Behind the boyfriend was a young woman dressed in jeans and a tee-shirt, her long black hair pulled back in a ponytail. Cori said:

"Can you give me a printout of the man? Full face and profile if you have them."

Haliwell took care of business and Cori went away happy. In her office she laid the Richland Farms photos next to the prints, stood back and put her hands on her hips to look for a match. It was then Finn came back. She looked at him and smiled.

"Don't you look like the cat who ate the canary," he said as he hung up his jacket. "Did you get something from the printers?"

"Samples are being overnighted. I've got a bunch of customer lists faxed. I'm waiting for two more," she said. "But looky here."

"Where did you get this?" Finn asked as he moved the Xerox of Grady's thief for a better look.

Cori filled him in and then said:

"Sure, this picture looks like all the rest of them. I'd say whoever is showing an interest in these young men has a type."

"But this one was making his money the old-fashioned way, so we may be just wishing there's a connection to the day laborers."

"Then I think we should find out. Let's talk to Grady's collar."

Cori picked up the pictures. Finn stood back to let her pass.

"What's the man's name?"

"Adolph," Cori said as she went into the hall.

"Like…" Finn began.

"Nope…" Cori said. "Oh, and you're coming to dinner tonight with Morrow and Lapinski."

"Life can be so good, Cori."

"Don't I know it, O'Brien."

* * *

"Adolph Fritz Wilhelm, III."

Cori read from the rap sheet Grady had pulled. She tilted her head this way and then that as if she were gravely considering his list of transgressions. She flipped the first page, looked at the second and then flipped back to the first page as she took the chair across from Adolph. Finn lounged against the wall.

"No relations to *the* Wilhelm family," Adolph said, picking at his head, antsy in the silence.

Cori said, "Good to know."

She didn't bother asking which Wilhelm family he was referring to since she couldn't bring one to mind that had any prominence. Nor could she find anything on Adolph's sheet that would lead her to believe that he could mastermind the disappearance of a handful of strong, young, healthy men, nor did he have the psychotic demeanor of an insane killer.

"Mr. Wilhelm—"

"Adolph. Yep, Adolph will do the trick."

Cori slid the picture of the jewelry he had tried to hock across the table.

"You were arrested for trying to sell stolen goods. Are these the items you were attempting to sell?"

"Yes. Yes, they are. But I didn't steal those pretties. Nope. Found 'em. Free and clear. I told the officers that, but they cuffed me anyway. They took me in even though I'd done nothing wrong. Finders keepers. Possession is nine tenths of the law. Everybody knows that." Adolph shot Finn a grin. "Are you the muscle? I bet you're the muscle. I think she's the bad cop so who's going to be the good cop? Oh, maybe you're the good cop until I act up, then you're the muscle."

"Sure, there's only good cops here, Adolph," Finn said, charmed by the scruffy gentleman.

If Adolph were three feet shorter and had been found sitting under a shamrock, Finn would have believed him to be a leprechaun. The marvelous mischievous glint in his eye, the cropped hair, the country-gentleman-gone-to-seed attire, and the bright certainty that whatever was to come could be wiggled out of, endeared him to Finn. Satisfied that he had made his mark with the big man, Adolph attended to Cori with all seriousness. His hands were clasped on the table, his lips were pulled tight together, and his eyes were on her as she picked up where she left off.

"Adolph, you found stolen goods, so you couldn't keep them."

"How was I to know that?"

Cori lifted her shoulder.

"Maybe you really didn't find them. Maybe you were working with the person who stole them."

Adolph guffawed. "Well, that's just the silliest. I don't work."

"What do you do?"

"I just…am. Yes, I just am."

"And where have you been doing all this?" Cori asked.

"Here and there," Adolph answered.

"How about most recently?" she insisted.

"I was up in the mountains. You know, local."

"Big Bear?" Cori asked.

He shook his head. "No, lower."

"Crestline?" she asked.

He shook his head again and waved both arms over his head to indicate east.

"Adolph." She crossed her arms on the table. "Do you know where you were?"

"Not exactly. Not the name or anything. But I know I was pretty near the freeway."

"Adolph?" Finn called. "Is that where you found this jewelry? In the mountains?"

"Yes, I did find the jewelry there."

"When was this?"

"Yesterday? The day before?"

"It's not for us to tell you," Finn said. "Why don't you tell us exactly where you found the jewelry?"

"In the ground. Yes, I found it in the ground."

"Can anyone corroborate that?" Cori asked.

"What's that?" Adolph answered.

"Can anyone vouch for you?" Finn clarified.

"Well, maybe," Adolph said.

"Who would that be?"

"The guy who gave me a ride. He could. But I don't know where to find him," Adolph said.

"If he was with you when you found the jewelry, we only need his name. We'll find him and he can say that he saw you find it."

"I don't know his name." He saw the skepticism and bounced around his chair trying to convince them. "I don't. Well, I know his first name but, there's no way you can find him with that. His name's John and he was sleeping when I found the jewelry."

"Okay, cool your jets," Cori said. "Why don't you tell

us where you found it. Was it just laying on the ground?"

Adolph shook his head.

"Did you find it under a rock?" Finn asked.

Adolph's head shook and shook, and he said, "*Nothat'ssillynothat'ssilly.*"

Finn pushed himself off the wall and came to sit on the edge of the table right near Adolph. The man looked so small now, like a weird little doll with his bizarre two-tone hair, his pitiful clothing, and his bad teeth. Finn lowered his voice.

"Perhaps you found all those pretty things in a man's pocket, Adolph. Perhaps a Mexican man who had been in possession of them? Am I getting warm, Adolph?"

Cori sat back and put her pen to her lips. She saw what she had expected to see, and Finn saw it too. Adolph's color rose. He giggled. His head swung between the two of them as he lied through his teeth.

"That would be robbery and I didn't rob nobody. Not a living soul. I swear." Adolph held his fingers in the Boy Scout sign and smiled and jiggled his shoulders – and then he started to sweat. Finn and Cori were not amused, disarmed, or put off task by his antics. It was Finn who leaned into him as if he were sharing a confidence.

"We're not talking about a living soul, Adolph. You see, we know who took that jewelry and we are thinking you killed him for it."

"Killed! Killed!" he was out of his chair when Finn's big hand landed on his shoulder and pushed him down.

"We have a whole lot of reasons to believe that man is dead," Cori chimed in. "And, since there isn't anybody to tell us different—"

"But I told you. John was there. I didn't kill anybody. *Okayokayyeshe'sdeadandI foundallthatstuffon—*"

Adolph ran his mouth like a motorboat and Cori was thankful she was sitting far enough away that the spray didn't reach her. Unfortunately, he ran out of gas pretty darn quick. His brain had kicked in and he was starting to understand that he could be in a whole lot of trouble.

"Oh, no. I didn't kill nobody, and you can't say I did. You ain't got nothing. You book me for possession, and I'll be out in two weeks. You go do that because there is no way you can hang me with murder. No way, huh-huh."

Cori put the picture of the boyfriend in front of Adolph. The man looked at it for a long while. He started to get up. Finn's hand was on his shoulder again.

"Adolph, I think you'll be wanting to tell us everything about what happened in those mountains. If you do that now, things will go easier for you. Because you see, my friend, there are a few more we'll be looking at you for."

"More what?" Adolph asked.

"More murders. A man has been killing off these young Hispanic men. Picking them up off the corners and killing them. Burying them in strange places around the county. Places like those mountains you say you were in. And, Adolph, we think it's a man who travels around. Yes, travels about and picks them up and takes them to these places and then kills them. You travel, Adolph."

"But I don't have a car."

"Maybe you just meet up with these people," Finn suggested.

Cori took over.

"Now, Adolph, we know the man in the picture robbed the woman of the jewelry, but he's gone missing, so the logical conclusion is that you probably killed him."

"And maybe," Finn said, "you buried him up there in the mountains. Is that what you did? Steal the jewelry that he stole first, killed him, buried him and thought no one would be the wiser?"

Adolph snapped his eyes up and away from the picture. He looked right at Cori. They stared at one another for a minute and then Adolph shook his finger and spoke like a normal human being.

"You guys are guessing. I mean, how are you going to prove that something happened to him if you can't find him? Answer me that, will you? Got you, don't I?"

"Ah, Adolph, I wouldn't challenge the lady," Finn said. "Best thing would just be to tell us exactly where you 'found' the jewelry or, if you relieved this gentleman of it, where exactly you did that. Because if you don't tell us, Detective Anderson there will be booking you for murder."

Adolph crossed his arms and said, "You got nothing."

"Detective Anderson?"

Finn looked at Cori as he slid off the table. Cori got up and left the room. Adolph watched after her.

"Whereshegoingwhereshegoingwhereshegoing?"

He kept it up until the door opened again. When Cori came back, she was wearing disposable gloves and had Adolph's pack. She put the pack on the table, unzipped it and, when she found what she wanted, she put it on the table in front of Adolph. His mouth fell open as he stared at the shirt, stiff with dried blood.

"Cut yourself shaving, Adolph?"

CHAPTER 25

"Potluck tonight, boys."

Cori put a platter of cold fried chicken on the table. Next came a bowl of coleslaw and a basket of bread. Amber followed with a tub of pre-made mashed potatoes in a plastic container and grocery store gravy. Cori surveyed the small table as she announced, "And we've got ice cream for dessert."

Detective Morrow, Thomas Lapinski and Finn O'Brien were seated in the space that the real estate agent had said was a dining room. In reality it was a no-man's land of square footage between the kitchen and the living room.

"'Tis a feast," Finn said as Cori took her seat.

"You should see me when I put my mind to it," Cori laughed even as she realized that one chair was empty. She looked over her shoulder. "Amber, honey, come on out. Time to eat."

When Amber didn't appear, Finn started to get up to fetch her, but Cori waved him down.

"I got it."

Cori put her napkin on the table and disappeared into

the kitchen. The men filled their plates and made small talk, none of them envious of the position she was in.

"It's a feast for me," Finn said.

"It's been a long while since I've had fried food," Detective Morrow noted. "I tend to prefer eggs and yogurt. Vegetables. I do like a good steak now and again. Sometimes I add a bit of honey to the yogurt."

"It's a wonder no woman has snagged you, Morrow," Thomas said as he reached for the potatoes.

"Thank you, Mr. Lapinski," Morrow answered. "The joke is not lost, but there was never a chance I would be snagged by anything. I was destined to be a perpetual bachelor. Still, I can appreciate the draw of matrimony. There are exceptional women in this world."

"Kind of you to say so, Morrow." Cori was back but she was alone. She took her chair and put her napkin on her lap. "Amber doesn't want Tucker to get all excited with the company or she'll never get him to sleep. They'll eat in the kitchen."

The men nodded and fell silent, all fully aware of the strain the two women were under. Cori took a drumstick from the platter, a spoonful of potatoes and a deep breath.

"Okay, enough of that. We're not going to do her any good moanin' like a cow needs milking, so let's figure out how we can do some good."

"Have you ever noticed that, when the three of you are together, it means something really bad has happened," Thomas said.

"Mr. Lapinski, I think you were involved in the Little Ethiopia matter before I was, so that makes your point moot."

"That just might be, Morrow, but this time I can't do you any good. You don't have a picture I can track through my facial recognition software. The guy you've got says he knows a guy who killed a guy and the killer's name is John." Thomas stripped the meat off the chicken leg he was eating and waved the bone. "An incredible unique moniker, I might add. The man in custody doesn't know where John lives. He knows he drives a white truck and he's holding out to tell you where all this took place until you cut him a deal. You don't even know whose blood is on that shirt and, if it's not your guy's, then he's right. You've got nothing. Is that about it?"

"'Tis." Finn motioned for the potatoes.

"But that's why you're here," Cori said. "I wouldn't have popped for dinner if I didn't think the four of us could make something out of nothing. Come on, this guy's the best lead we've got. The only lead."

"While I certainly appreciate this fine meal and your incredible company, I am like the proverbial third wheel, folks," Lapinski said, "and I really don't see how you are going to find a man who's preying on day labor unless you're planning to put a cop on every corner."

"We know he's taken two from the same corner," Cori said.

"And the first time you get close he's going to bolt because he can find those folks in any city in the country," Lapinski argued.

"Does that mean we shouldn't try, Thomas?" Finn put aside his fork.

"No, of course not. But I can see your captain's point. You could spend every waking hour on this and come up with nothing. He doesn't want your billable hours going down a black hole. No return on his investment, you know?"

"And so we do this on our own time while we negotiate

with Adolph," Finn said.

"It is an intriguing problem," Detective Morrow said.

"Okay, if Morrow's in then I'm in." Thomas pushed his plate away.

"Let's look at what we do know," Finn said. "We know the killer has a ritual. Shallow graves, some kind of card under the hands, bodies laid out all nice. We've got the victim in Baldwin Hills that we've seen with our own eyes. One other man who arguably was taken out in the same manner and buried but not identified. Palmdale has reported one in the same circumstance, and then we have Father Patrick telling us of the killings in Mexico. Counting Mexico, this seems to go back about three years."

Thomas held up a finger. "It seems to me that the ritual indicates the killer knew his victims. Isn't that the general consensus? That when care is taken there is a personal relationship?"

"That's a general rule of thumb, Mr. Lapinski," Morrow answered. "I don't think it applies here."

"According to the people we talked to in Richland Farms, the men who saw the victims say they didn't seem to be singled out. In the course of any given day people needing workers drive up, point to someone, and the job is accepted," Finn said. "Usually that person is dropped at the same corner but, in this case, they never came back. Add to that, the incidents are spread across Southern California. Even the location in Mexico was literally across the border from San Diego. So it's Palmdale, San Diego and now here."

"Which suggests what?" Thomas challenged them.

"That the man we're looking for travels? A truck driver?" Cori offered.

They had all finished dinner, and Amber came to pick

up the plates even though Cori told her to leave them. Finn knew the girl needed something to do to keep herself from jumping out of her skin, and soon her comings and goings were forgotten as they talked.

"I'm not thinking so," Finn said. "The bodies are scattered. If it were a trucker, I would think we'd be finding them tossed off the freeways or at rest stops where there's easy access. And what cause would he have to come into the city? Finding an isolated place in the city takes time. A truck driver is on a schedule."

Cori reached for an envelope on the credenza. She opened it and distributed Xeroxes as she told them what they were looking at.

"We've identified the printer who manufactures the paper put in the Baldwin Hills grave. That company makes religious cards: Mass cards, condolence cards, saint cards—"

"Holy cards," Finn interrupted. "Those are sort of like religious trading cards. They are often given out to school children for being good or they are available at Mass on the individual saint's holy day."

"We believe they are the smaller, two sided ones," Cori went on. "There appears to be a watermark embedded in those that we think we can match with our piece."

"It looks like a Eucharistic symbol," Finn said. "They'll be sending samples over to the lab for confirmation. So, might it be that we're looking for a priest?"

"I like that idea," Morrow said as he scanned the information. "Priests are transferred to different parishes quite often. As we know, the Church has had its share of criminal problems of late."

"The collar would be great cover. These men would trust him," Cori added, warming to her theory. "So, he's a priest psycho, and he gets the urge, drives to the corners – who wouldn't get in the truck with a guy in a collar? – and off they go. But when the deed is done, he feels so guilty that he defaults to his training, buries them, and blesses them. Or maybe he's not psycho. Maybe he has these urges, but he really is a man of God and there's some underlying reason for taking them out."

"And that would be?" Finn asked.

"Maybe he's saving them from earthly pain and sending them to their reward."

Morrow stepped in. "We could narrow a search to parishes in a five-mile radius of the victim's last known place of work and find out how many Father John's there are."

"Or just radiate from where Adolph says the man dropped him. There can't be more than one or two Catholic churches in that area," Finn suggested. "But it's not feeling right. We have the shirt this man gave Adolph. It's a normal shirt and Adolph mentioned no collar."

"But there was a Bible in the truck. He said that," Cori reminded him.

"Okay, so not a priest," Lapinski piped up. "But didn't you say the man in custody was dropped at a church rescue? A priest would live at the church, right?"

Finn nodded. "In a rectory, but Adolph wasn't taken to a Catholic church."

Detective Morrow raised a finger. "Are Catholics the only ones to use holy cards?"

"I'm Jewish; what do I know?" Lapinski said.

"Let's assume they are. If that's the case, where Adolph was dropped makes no difference. Anyone working in liturgical circles would know where the outreaches are," Finn said. "But if we limit this to Catholics, then that wouldn't rule out a deacon. The Church has had problems finding enough priests to staff the parishes. It could be a lay minister who lives in the parish."

"I prefer that option," Morrow said.

"I prefer people weren't getting killed," Lapinski quipped.

"Okay, let's expand then," Finn went on. "What about a mortician? Wouldn't a mortician also be trained to lay out the bodies just so?"

"You think a mortician is drumming up business?" Cori smirked and then held up her hand. "Sorry, kidding. Anyway, do Catholics have their own mortuaries?"

"There are some that cater to Catholics, but that would be assuming we are talking about holy cards. There are also remembrance cards given at all mortuaries," Morrow said. "And there's the question of movement. I further assume morticians can easily travel to different jurisdictions and work. But would they go so far?"

More shrugs and murmurs. They all knew about the coroner's work but precious little about the people who took the bodies off their hands.

"We've a good list going. What else?" Lapinski asked.

"Could this be a political statement?" Morrow suggested. "The rhetoric against undocumented immigrants has been rather heated in the last year."

"It could be an alt-right group." Lapinski's agreement was tepid at best. That didn't deter Morrow from playing out his theory.

"Perhaps this isn't being done by one person. Perhaps the anti-immigrant movement is making a statement and there are people in each of these regions carrying out a central plan. That would account for the bodies being found so far away from each other. There is no traveling, only a methodical execution of a plan."

"To what end?" Finn asked.

"Education? Extermination?" Morrow answered.

"Simpler than that," Cori said. "Maybe it's plain old terror. Scare the shit out of these folks and send them scurrying back to where they came from."

"Then why murder anyone in Mexico? Those men were already there." Lapinski piped up. "I'm not feeling it. Nope. Nope. Besides, those crazies would want it publicized and the white power groups have been quiet of late."

"But neither have we been looking for such activity so we cannot say that definitely," Detective Morrow reminded them.

"But we can find out. That's an easy search," Thomas said. "I'll put it on the list."

"Keep it far down on the list, Lapinski. I'm not thinking this is some elaborate scheme by the Hitler Youth," Finn said. "The perp is consistent. It's hard to get a group of people to bash a head in exactly the same way. This man seems to methodically stake out his prey and then fairly decapitates his—"

Finn stopped talking and his eyes cut to a place over Cori's shoulder. Amber had come back in the room and was leaning against the wall, holding her sleepy child. Listening to him, the girl had gone white.

"Amber, honey," Cori said when she saw her daughter, "don't you think it's time you put Tucker down for the night?"

"Do you think..." Amber began but she didn't finish her question. She didn't have to. She wanted to know if they thought that's what happened to Pacal. She looked at each of them in turn and had her answer: they thought exactly that. She muttered a goodnight and left them to their work.

"Damn, this is hard," Cori said quietly.

"She knows we're doing what must be done," Morrow assured her.

Finn cleared his throat and began again.

"What if we have a sleeper who has done this before. The killings go without notice for a while, he's found out and fades away and then surfaces somewhere else only to move on before he can be caught."

"Definite possibility," Cori agreed.

"I've only sent local bulletins because the captain hasn't given us an official go ahead. That means all I have back is local. It's a line from Mexico to Palmdale to Los Angeles." Finn looked across the table. "Have you your computer, Thomas?"

"Always." He slid his chair back, retrieved it and then set it up as the conversation continued.

"But that's not a straight line. Wouldn't it make more sense for him to stop in L.A. and then go on to Palmdale?" Morrow asked.

"Wouldn't it make more sense for him not to kill people along the way?" Finn laughed darkly. "Sure, I'm thinking we aren't going to find much sense in any of this even when we finally know the truth. Not to mention the Palmdale victim's report made no mention of a card found with him and talk of them on the bodies in Mexico could be nothing more than myth."

"Then let's throw caution to the wind and see what we can come up with. I'm open for suggestions. Where shall I start?" Thomas asked.

"How would you go about finding out if there were other murders that involve religious items? Shall we start there? And start with Mexico. Let's see if there's anything solid about the 'ghost'."

"Do you have a name for the village where the men

disappeared from," Thomas asked.

Finn shook his head and got out his phone. They all waited while he dialed and said:

"Gregorio. Detective O'Brien. Do you know the name of the village where people say the ghost took his victims?" Finn listened. "Thank you, my friend. No, nothing. Just trying to piece together the person's movements."

He ended the call and said to everyone:

"Puerto Nuevo."

Lapinski started to type.

"Nothing," he said.

"Can you find me a police station in the place?"

Again, Lapinski typed.

"It doesn't show up."

"Road trip?" Cori raised a well-shaped brow.

"'Tis a possibility," Finn said. "So what's next?"

"What about the modus operandi? One blow to the head? Using a tool of some sort?" Morrow suggested.

"People bash each other's heads in all the time with tools. I think we'll have more luck with the card thing," Thomas said. "We'll have more luck with specific words. Murder, holy cards – what else could they be called?" Thomas asked.

"Mass cards," Finn said. "And put in Palmdale."

"Mom? You guys want coffee?" Amber was back, standing in the doorway. Her color was high, and her chin was up.

"I can get it, sweetie," Cori said.

Amber answered, "I'd like to do something to help. I'll get it."

"I've got the history of mass cards," Thomas said as soon as she had gone back to the kitchen. "I've got murder and the Catholic church. I have information on a number of attacks in churches, but these were done in public by a shooter."

"Could you add something to your search. Assault, perhaps. Our man doesn't use a gun."

"That we know of," Cori reminded him.

"Well, let's get back to assault," Lapinski said. "If I search that it will expand the universe quite a bit and it would take a lot longer."

"We need to narrow it, not widen," Finn said. "Cori, did you see anything on the security video from McDonalds?"

She shook her head. "I saw our victim go in and come out with a bag. I went through the entire thing. No white truck in the drive-through. The camera doesn't catch the entire parking lot or the corner where he was standing."

"It was a long shot," Finn admitted as he drummed his finger on the tabletop. It was getting late and they were all getting tired.

"You know, the one thing Adolph did say was that our guy is way old." Finn picked up a spoon and let it run through his fingers.

"Adolph could consider thirty way old," Cori said.

"True," Morrow said. "According to you, he said the man could hardly catch his breath. It was hard for him to walk so the man could be any age but appear old because he's sick. He also said the man's face was disfigured and that he was Caucasian."

"Then why the fixation on Latinos?" Cori's question was garbled because her chin was resting in her upturned hand. With the other, she was twirling the saltshaker.

"Easy pickings," Lapinski said offhandedly only to stop typing for a moment. He sat back and spoke almost to himself. "Here's a question. What kind of old guy suddenly becomes a serial killer?"

He looked around the room and was met with blank stares.

"Okay, okay, okay, the answer is no old guy becomes a serial killer. They may grow old killing, they may take time off if things get hot, they might have to move on to keep from drawing attention to themselves. Or maybe they try to go straight – you know, get married, have a family – but it doesn't work, and they start again when they get older. But from what I know – and granted, I'm no expert – there is not one instance where someone over, say, the age of fifty just up and became a serial killer. Is there? Can anyone think of one?"

Heads shook, shoulders shrugged, and Lapinski was emboldened. He typed furiously talking all the while.

"Okay, okay so hang in with me. Maybe they peak when they're older, but they start when they are younger. So why else would a guy like that be off the market, huh?" Thomas grinned and pumped his hands to encourage them to think hard. Finally, Finn had it.

"Prison," he said.

"That's it!" Lapinski pointed a finger at him.

"And let's establish old," Morrow chimed in. "Perhaps fifty-five? Sixty? That would certainly be a place to start."

Thomas's fingers were flying over the keyboard. He scrolled up and down and then typed in some other key words as he spoke.

"And let's say he's been out of commission twenty-five to thirty years."

"That would make him late twenties or early thirties when he was incarcerated." Finn leaned forward and crossed his arms on the table. He was grinning from ear to ear.

"And to that end, given the parameters of time and

the religious card and the shallow grave, I have come up with this!" Thomas opened his palms and pointed to his screen. "The Desert Trail Newspaper out of Twenty-Nine Palms—"

"A barren place if there ever was one, " Morrow noted.

"Be that as it may, the date is twenty-seven years ago, and the story is buried on page four. A Hispanic girl was found in a shallow grave, on her back, hands crossed over chest and a holy card tucked beneath them." Thomas grinned. He looked at each of them for approval. "Huh? Huh? Lapinski does it again. Right?"

"Dare I point out it is a woman who was the victim?" Detective Morrow said.

"Go with me here, Morrow," Thomas answered. "It's what we've got."

"How did she die?" Cori asked.

"Hyperthermia. She basically cooked to death. Oh, and her blood alcohol was off the charts so that didn't help any."

"Hyperthermia," Cori repeated and then chuckled. Morrow blinked behind his glasses and Finn put a hand to his jaw and raised his brows, but Thomas was on a roll and ignored their skepticism.

"Her name was Martina Nuevas. Sixteen years old—"

"A baby," Cori muttered.

"Indeed," Morrow said.

Lapinski kept at it.

"Her mother was a citizen, her father illegal. According to the reports, she went out with friends but never came back. Read between the lines and you get the feeling she was a wild child. Anyway, the family was large, they were used to her going her own way, but when she didn't come home that night for a family party, they called the cops.

The police found her buried in a shallow grave, laid out like your guy does it."

"I think you're hugging a rose bush, Lapinski," Cori said. "That is a one-off. If the person who was with the girl was even found, arrested, and convicted, then why would he turn on Hispanic men? If he were released after serving his time as you speculate, and if he were a serial killer, then it would stand to reason that he would go after young girls. Right?"

"I tend to agree," Finn said. "The card is interesting, to be sure, the shallow grave isn't that impressive. What person with a body to hide doesn't love a shallow grave? But I'm having a hard time extrapolating."

"Okay, here we go." Thomas's finger went up to stop the naysayers. If he got any closer to the computer screen, he'd be kissing it. "Someone was arrested nine months after the death and then it was another two months to get it to trial." His head popped up. "So much for the speedy trial thing, huh?" His head went down. "John Spears is the man's name. He was a construction worker in his late twenties. The story sort of fizzles out from there and they go straight to sentencing. The judge gave him twenty-five to life. If he's out, he would be in his mid-fifties now."

"Adolph says the man was old and infirmed," Finn reminded him.

"Prison isn't exactly a health spa," Detective Morrow said. "And Adolph did identify the man he met in the mountains as John."

"Do you have a picture, Lapinski?" Cori asked.

"It's not great, but I'll email it to you unless I can hook up to your printer."

"I'll do it." Cori went to him, leaned over, and connected his computer to her printer. They could hear the whir as it kicked in. "At least we'll have something to show Adolph."

Finn picked up the phone and called for a rundown on John Spears.

"Amber?" Cori called. "Will you bring me what's in the printer?"

A second later, just as Finn was reaching for a pen and paper, Amber came in with a black and white copy of the newspaper article and the picture of John Spears. She hung back, not wanting to disturb anyone, fixated on Finn as they were.

"Just give me the bottom line and then fax the read-out over," Finn said into the phone. "Yes. Sure, that's very good. Thank you."

When he hung up, he was pleased.

"There are sixty-four men by the name of John Spears registered with the DMV, but there is only one who drives a white Toyota truck. His full name is John Jamieson Spears. License plate is GRS692. He's got the original black and gold plates, so he'll stand out. The truck was registered to an address in Palmdale two years ago, but it's since lapsed."

"And before that?" Cori asked.

"San Diego," Finn said.

"Awesome." Cori breathed.

"Eh? Eh?" Thomas gloated.

"You're the man, Lapinski." Cori laughed, but her voice was tinged with admiration. "Amber, do you have that article?"

Amber took a step forward and Cori turned around, her hand out but Amber didn't let go when her mother took the paper in hand.

"Is it him?" she whispered. "Did he take Pacal?"

"It's only a hunch," Cori whispered back.

Just then, they heard the printer start again. The DMV information was coming through.

"I'll get it." Amber left before anyone could stop her. When she returned she had copies for each of them. She handed them out and then said, "I'm going to go to bed if that's alright."

Everyone wished her a good night and thanked her for her help. Amber smiled and wished them luck. Then she went to her room where she undressed and got into bed. Before she turned out the light, she took one more look at the copy of the DMV report and the newspaper article that she had made for herself. Folding both, she put them under her pillow for safe keeping because you could never be too careful when your mother was a cop.

CHAPTER 26

The boy's name was Neil, and he hated his job, but he especially hated having to work the night shift. He was only doing it because his parents said he had to have a job if he and Cindy were going to live in their house. He didn't want to be living in their house. He didn't even want to be living with Cindy, but there was no choice now. He was going to be a father and he was only eighteen. He should have been going to college or something. Instead, he was working at a gas station. He was a stupid idiot for knocking up Cindy even though he thought she walked on water for a while. She was so pretty and sweet. Then it turned out she was dumb too. What kind of idiot can't figure out how to take a pill every day? Then her parents kicked her out and they didn't want Neil to even come by to say how sorry he was. Now he was stuck like a pig on a spit and the only job he could get was at this miserable truck stop where he sold air-fresheners shaped like Christmas trees, and candy, and nuts, and cigarettes, and lottery tickets. He was on the waiting list for a job at Costco two towns over. If that came through, then he'd move out of his parents' house as soon as the baby was born. Once that happened,

Neil was sure Cindy's parents would take her and the baby back, Neil would promise to see the kid on weekends, and everything would eventually go back to normal.

Yeah, that was the plan. Costco, his own place, back to being the guy he should be.

He snapped a finger at the air-freshener card hanging on a display near the register. It swung on its hook, the flick exploding a sickening smell of fake pine scent. He glanced at the men's magazine he had taken off the newsstand. Then, bored out of his skull, forty-five minutes from the end of his shift, he looked out the big window, past the gas bay to the highway and the hills.

Traffic was picking up, and in an hour, there would be ten times more cars. He yawned and was about to get back to his magazine when he caught sight of something weird. There was a guy trying to walk across the highway.

Now, it wasn't bumper to bumper or nothing. There was plenty of time between cars if you were going to, say, sprint across four lanes, but this guy was nowhere near sprinting. Neil was pretty sure he was drunk. Neil set aside the magazine and started for the door to go yell at the guy to stay put when the man stopped on the side of the highway. Neil breathed a sigh of relief but then the guy started to walk again. Neil pushed through the door and dashed to the edge of the road, waving his arms, and hollering through the still morning.

"Stay there. Don't move. Don't move."

The man on the other side took a minute, but finally he seemed to notice Neil. He smiled and started staggering across the highway. Neil pumped his palms, trying to get the idiot to stay where he was.

"No! No! Don't!"

It was too late. The guy was on the move and obviously

out of it. He was dirty from head to toe like he'd been sleeping out in the brush. He didn't carry bags, he had no jacket and he seemed happy to see Neil.

Neil screamed again but this time it was in horror as the car hit the man and sent him flying toward the gas station.

* * *

The picture of John Jamieson Spears was presented to Adolph Wilhelm who took his own good time hemming and hawing over it. It could be the man he had met in the mountains, but he was older and different, and it was hard to explain really so he asked for a pencil and made some changes. Unhappy with his first attempt to capture the visage of the man who had killed the boy in the mountains, Adolph tore it up and asked for more copies of the picture. He marked those up, trying to age John Spears.

Kindoflikethislikethislikethisomygodyesitismorelikethis.

Cori and Finn sat at the table listening to him babble, watching him draw and then finally – thank heaven – come up with a version of his artwork that he found acceptable. Once he had done that, he handed it over to the detectives, saying he would rather cooperate than be charged as an accomplice to murder. For, no doubt, with the picture he had drawn in hand, John Spears would be found in no time and the truth would come out.

Finn and Cori had taken the picture and studied it for some time. Neither could make heads nor tails of it but it appeared that Adolph had drawn a hat atop John Spears' head and the map of Mississippi across the man's face. Still, they thanked him for his cooperation and made arrangements to transport him to the site where he would show them the body.

It had taken an hour to put some things at the office right and to have Adolph prepped for transport, but they were on their way before noon. They drove to the Angeles Crest Highway, through La Canada/Flintridge and headed toward Wrightwood. They were in the middle of nowhere, on government forestland, with nothing between the two cities other than Newcomb's Ranch, campgrounds, and a visitor center. During the winter, folks went to Mount Waterman for skiing. But it was not winter, nor was it camping season, and few people would be in this part of the San Gabriel Mountains. Mount Wilson was also in the vicinity as well as the Mount Wilson Observatory. It was the sign at the junction of Mount Wilson Road and Los Angeles Crest Highway where Adolph told Finn to:

Turnturnturnturn.

Finn pulled onto a fire road and started to drive into the forest.

Stopstopstopstopstop...

Finn did. Cori unsnapped her belt and muttered:

"Thank God. I was going to have to stuff a sock in him pretty soon."

Finn laughed and got out of the car. He waited for Cori to join him before opening the door for Adolph. Cori helped him out, keeping a firm hand on him.

"Hands out, Adolph," Finn said.

"I ain't going nowhere," Adolph insisted. "If I wanted to stay here, I wouldn't have hitched that ride. See what I mean? See why I'm telling you the truth? I could have just stayed here you know. Right? So, no need to cuff me 'cause I do not want to stay here."

"Your logic is awesome," Cori said. "You should be grateful he's cuffing you in front."

Finn put on the flex cuffs and gave him a nudge.

"Lead us to the pot of gold at the end of this dirty rainbow."

"I like the way you talk, I certainly do," Adolph giggled.

As he walked on, he whistled *Somewhere over the Rainbow* to the dead trees and the still air. On either side of him walked the two detectives. Cori slightly back, Finn slightly ahead. Finn's heavy boots cracked the twigs, her rubber-soled shoes shuffled through the leaves and needles. They each tracked the walk in their own way: Cori with half an eye on Adolph, Adolph seemingly with an eye on nothing in particular, and Finn's eye on the prize. He only wished he were feeling it, that excitement within that let him know he was close to the end of a journey. Perhaps this was not their man. The filament that tethered John Jamieson Spears to the two missing men was tenuous at best: a common name, a crime against a Hispanic, a conviction of second degree murder which was a far cry from the brutal premeditated attacks they believed their victims had experienced. These things bothered him greatly and yet here was Adolph leading them to a missing man, one who had ties to the corners, one who had been murdered. This one, though, was shot according to Adolph. So, yes, the connection felt…

"O'Brien!"

Cori's cry jolted him out of his reverie, and he looked up just as Adolph bolted past.

"What the…"

Finn was after him, but Adolph was like a rabbit, weaving and dodging between the trees. Cori was running too, fanning out to Adolph's right to try to cut him off. Just when they thought he was going that way he pivoted and went left.

"Adolph, you've nowhere to go!" Finn called.

Ahead of him, Adolph laughed and held his cuffed

hands over his head. They chased on for no more than a minute when Adolph came to an abrupt halt. Finn and Cori were on him: Cori taking an arm, Finn stepping in front of him.

"We've no time for games. Do that again and we'll cuff you behind and we will book you for everything we possibly can. No favors. Do you understand?" Finn barked.

But Adolph only grinned and nodded. He shook his head.

"I ran into a cobweb."

"Then don't run," Cori groused as she brushed it away from his eyes.

"Now, have you brought us on a merry chase or are you going to do what you said you would? We want to see the body."

"I said I would take you to where he's buried," Adolph reminded him.

"Then do it," Finn growled.

"I did. It's there. Right there." He raised his hands and pointed. "Where the gnarly roots are."

"Where?" Cori asked.

"There, under that tree."

"I see nothing but a hole?" Finn said.

"Me, too," Adolph answered. "But two days ago, there was a dead guy in that hole."

Finn and Cori looked at one another. Either Adolph was lying or the man who had been in that hole in the ground was named Lazarus.

* * *

One hundred sixty-three dollars and forty cents. That's how much money was laid out on Amber's bed. It was all she had in her fun money jar from tips she had made at Romero's Restaurant. She had three thousand in the bank, but she wouldn't touch that unless she absolutely had to. For now, she figured she had enough to pay the sitter for four days plus what she would have to spend at Kinkos.

Gathering up the money, she set aside forty dollars thinking that should be enough for the sitter today. She might be home earlier than expected but at least the money was budgeted. She put on an old, boxy jacket and buttoned it up. Her jeans were loose, and on her feet she wore black high-top tennis shoes. She grabbed a baseball cap and went into the living room. Tucker and the sitter were on the couch, Sesame Street was on the television and toys were already strewn around the room.

"Don't let him watch T.V. all day, okay?"

"I won't. We're going to go down to the park and swing for a while."

"Good. Tire him out." Amber swooped in and gave her son a nuzzle. He giggled. She drew back and put her hands on his face. "You be good."

He answered with a litany of unintelligible promises only a two-year-old can make, and Amber gave him one more hug for good measure. She closed her eyes briefly, trying to imagine him older, on his own, working, missing. If she had anything to say about it, he would never grow up and never be put in harm's way.

"What time are you going to be back? I've got a class at six tonight."

"I'll be home by four, maybe sooner," Amber said, sure that would be enough time. "If anything happens, you have my number. Call me and not my mom. Okay?"

"Sure. But everything will be fine."

"Yeah, I think so too." Amber gave Tucker one last kiss before she left the house and got to work.

* * *

"Mr. Spears. Mr. Spears." The woman who ran the house banged on the bedroom door again. "I know you're in there. Open up. Let me see you."

She pounded with her fist one more time and then stood back with her hands on her hips. She would give him to the count of three and if he didn't open that door then she was going in. She got to two when the door opened a crack. He put his good eye to it.

"All the way. Let me see you," she demanded.

He mumbled something and it made her think she'd been on the job too long because what he said was clear as a bell to her.

"You think I don't know sick? There ain't been no toilet flushing in the middle of the night. You ain't called for a doctor and I saw you yesterday and the day before that. Not to mention you were late the other day. If something funny's going on, I want to know about it now."

He mumbled again.

"So you say. Open up and let me see. It's the rules. You gotta open up."

She waited until the door was all the way open.

"Step back."

He did. She went in and looked around. The woman may be unmemorable in looks but she was well suited to her job. Her eyes were as sharp as a woman with twelve children who knew what each was up to at any given moment. Her head barely moved while she scanned the room.

"You've torn the wallpaper," she said. "Don't do it anymore. I'll patch it up later. I think I have some extra."

He mumbled that he liked it that way.

"Suit yourself." She was facing him, looking him over

the same way she had scanned the room. "Work called. They said this is the second time you haven't been in. I thought you said that's why you were late getting back here the other day. Because they kept you late?"

He stared at her with that one milky eye and the other dead as dead could be. There was nothing to see behind it but there was no threat there either. The man was beaten down but good. Beaten down and a Bible thumper too. You'd think that after all he'd been through, he'd be praying at the altar of the devil 'cause it was a sure bet, in his case, there weren't no God.

"Okay. Whatever," she said. "Look, the bunch of us? We ain't got a pot to piss in. We're here on this earth, in this circumstance, and we gotta make the best of it. Know what I mean?"

He kept looking at her and she looked away. Being close like this gave her the creeps. Still, she had a job to do.

"And I get that there's damn little pleasure in the world for you. I also get that a little hooky now and again is needed. But not two days, okay? You're fit. You got a job and that's more than I can say for the rest of them. You've got wheels. You need to hang on to what you got, okay? There's that good old light at the end of the tunnel for you so hang in there. Keep your nose clean."

He mumbled. She shrugged. He nodded. She was happy that her pep talk got her somewhere 'cause sure as shootin' she didn't want no trouble: not from him and not from the system that put him in this house. She put a big, rough hand on his arm. He looked at it thinking it felt like a man's hand. He looked back at her and realized her face could be that of a man. That's how hard her life had been.

"Okay, then. Go on. I told 'em you were late 'cause I had you doing something for me. You go now."

He nodded and she started out the door only to pause. He'd forgotten to take off his shoes when he came in and now there was dirt on the rug. She shook her head, words of reprimand on her lips. Those words were never spoken because she had a heart and wouldn't pile shame on shame. Maybe she would come back up later when he was gone and clean up some even though they were supposed to keep their rooms themselves.

She gave him a little nod and went back downstairs. The door closed behind her. Three minutes later she heard the upstairs toilet flush. Two minutes after that, he was out the door. She smiled and went back to making the chili she would serve for dinner. She would even grate some cheese for the top, maybe make some cornbread, because she was feeling good. She was feeling like she'd made a difference to that poor soul. Maybe one day, he would go out into the world and make a difference for someone else.

That was exactly what John Spears was thinking as he started his little white truck. Yes, he would make a difference in someone's world. It just wouldn't be today.

CHAPTER 27

MAY 3

By the time the computers came up with a hit on the status of John Jamieson Spears within the penal system, Adolph was charged and incarcerated for theft and selling stolen goods. It would be days before a public defender got the case and a judge got it on the calendar. That gave Finn and Cori breathing room. Adolph was off their hands but within reach if they needed him, and they just might need him in the next few hours to identify John Jamieson Spears. The man had, indeed, been incarcerated, served time, and been released. It was the release information that caused some confusion because he had bounced around a bit.

John Jamieson Spears was tried for second-degree murder citing depraved indifference. The trial was held in the San Bernardino Courthouse after the defense attorney requested a change of venue. Due to local publicity, it would have been impossible to seat a jury in Twenty-Nine Palms.

Spears was convicted when he was twenty-eight years old for the murder of Martina Nuevas, sixteen, and sentenced to twenty years to life serving time first in CIM, California Institute for Men, in Chino and the last four years of his incarceration in California State Prison in Lancaster, near Palmdale. Spears was first paroled three and a half years earlier. First to a Palmdale halfway house since it was deemed dangerous to locate him, as was the norm, in his home area of Twenty-Nine Palms.

He failed to return to the facility and was off the radar for almost a year until he was picked up on a parole violation near San Diego. He had crossed over the border and been in possession of a weapon. He was tried and sentenced to additional prison time in Chula Vista and then transferred back to Chino.

The California governor, under a Federal order to alleviate overcrowding in California jails and prisons, reclassified certain felonious criminal activity as victimless making it possible to release hundreds of one-time felons either to the general population or to halfway houses and parole. John Spears was paroled for a second time, now in the county of Los Angeles to the care and feeding of one Nicholas Ellis who was employed by Central Adult investigation on Temple Street in downtown Los Angeles.

He was a gentleman of impressive bulk, bald, and put upon. Cori and Finn seemed to be the straw that broke this camel's back, and all their prodding, kind requests and outright demands for information did nothing to switch Nicholas Ellis's track. He was on a roll of angst, so Cori and Finn let him barrel down the track for a while.

"Here it is. Here you go. This is the L.A. County Governance study. DOJ undertook it so it's the real deal. No holding back, I'm telling you."

Nicholas waved a hard copy of a lengthy report. Finn could only hope he wasn't going to read it word for word but determined to read he was. He snapped the pages until he found what he wanted.

"Understaffing impedes the Department's ability to carry out a number of tasks, lowers staff morale due to staff feeling unsupported. Hiring, procurement etc. appears to move extremely slowly, reducing the availability of staff and service providers to work with clients."

Nicholas hit the last twelve words with a verbal sledge-hammer. Having worked himself into a tizzy, he was breathing hard by the time he finished.

"So, I just wanted you to know that I am not making excuses about why I might not be able to get you all the information you require. We are seriously understaffed here, and I will do my best, but I just want to be up front."

"That is something we truly appreciate, Mr. Ellis," Cori said in her most honeyed voice. The man was not charmed, and Finn didn't really care to coddle him. Every agency in the world was underfunded, he needed no report to tell him that.

"While we sympathize, Mr. Ellis," Finn said, "we are in a bit of a bind. We understand that John Spears was assigned to your caseload."

"Spears? Spears?" Nicholas blinked behind his glasses.

"John Jamieson Spears?" Finn leaned forward and put his read-out on Nicholas's desk. He pointed to the final entry. "It says Spears was assigned to your caseload a little over a year ago. Does this look right?"

Nicholas scooted up to the desk, put out a pudgy hand and pulled the report his way.

"I don't know. I don't know. I have hundreds of cases, but if he's low risk for criminal activity, and they say he's in Los Angeles, then he would be assigned to me."

"You don't know Spears?" Finn asked.

"I'm not sure. I'd have to see a picture."

Cori whipped the Xerox of the booking photo out of her purse and put it on his desk. "This was twenty-five years ago but it might jog your memory. We understand his face might be a bit disfigured."

Nicholas perused it and shook his head.

"I don't know. I'm not getting anything from that. It's like trying to hold water in a sieve. They come and go. I'll look though." Nicholas struggled out of his chair and went to a file cabinet. "I don't trust computers. I use them when I have to, but I like paper. They're always after me to get rid of the paper. But we had the whole system go down about six months ago and everyone was going crazy. Me? I just kept on working because I had paper files. They should give me a commendation."

The babbling brook of protest, moaning and grumbling continued until he found the file he wanted. This he tossed on his desk before centering himself in front of his chair and lowering his bulk gingerly into it. *Fffttt* he sputtered as he fell the last two inches.

"Okay. Spears," he said. "What do you want to know?"

"Whatever you've got," Cori crossed her legs and settled in for the long haul. Concise did not seem to be in Ellis's vocabulary. He flipped open the file, ran his finger down it, and muttered to himself before sharing the information.

"Okay. Yeah, I remember him. It looks like your boy has quite a history. Convicted twenty to life."

"We know that; we're looking for something a little more personal. Insightful. You being the shoulder he leans on, we thought you might be able to tell us if he has some issues with the Hispanic community."

Nicholas ran a finger down the information, stopping now and again. Finally, he spoke.

"Yes, indeed, I should say he might have issues with Latino men. You know the girl he killed?" Nicholas waved his hands as if erasing a thought. He started again. "Not really killed. He let her die. Yes, I remember reading this now. She was very young, and he picked her up thinking she was much older. They both get drunk and, when he tries to get it on, the kid starts crying for her mother and he freaks. Anyway, long story short, he's drunk, she's passed out in the back of his truck. It was hotter than hell that day. He started to drive her home but stopped off for a drink to calm his nerves. He locked her in so nobody would mess with her while he's in this place 'cause it was pretty seedy. When he comes out, she's dead. At least that's what the transcripts say. They say he was shocked, that he had only been trying to protect her."

"What do you think?" Cori asked. "After talking to him, I mean."

Nicholas shrugged, licked his finger, and turned a page and then another.

"Not for me to say. He didn't talk much as I recall, but according to this she was pretty much broiled in the back of that that van. He panics, drives her into the desert, buries her all nice. He lays her out and finds some religious stuff in her backpack. He puts that stuff in her hands. In court his attorney argued that showed his good intentions, and he was drunk, so he didn't know what he was doing, but that's not the way the judge saw it. Look, see here?"

Nicholas held up the file but then pulled it back before the detectives could see anything.

"He opted for a bench trial. What a fool. A jury probably would have bought that story."

"That's about the time the Supreme Court ruled that drunkenness was no excuse for death due to depraved indifference," Finn said. "The man's timing wasn't good on that score. Still, we're looking at him for murder of a number of Hispanic males not women."

"Oh, *fffttt*," Nicholas waved away Finn's confusion. "That's easily explained. Have you seen this guy? I mean really?"

Finn said, "We've heard he's a bit worn."

"Hah, that's a good one." Nicholas threw himself back and his chair groaned. He was actually smiling. He pulled a picture out of the file and showed it to Finn and Cori. "Here's what he looked like when I got him. The man could barely speak. He's almost impossible to understand. You can see why."

"He looks like his face got caught in a cotton gin," Cori said, thinking that Adolph's drawing hadn't been so far off the mark. "What happened?"

"What he did was a big story in the Latino community, so when Spears got to Central, the gangbangers used him for a punching bag and just about everything else you can imagine. It got so bad that they transferred him to Lancaster. He gets paroled but he's picked up on a violation down in San Diego. They put him back in Chino and that's where it gets bad. Here. Medical reports."

Nicholas passed those across the desk to Cori.

"*Los Papi Chulos* runs Chino and it turns out the girl's cousin once removed, or some such nonsense is *the man* there. A real thug. Sociopath. Sadist. Son of a bitch doesn't even begin to describe him. What happened to his cousin all those years ago is family legend, so the guy has a bone to pick."

"And he acted out on Spears?" Finn asked.

"*Ffffttt.* Not just the cousin. The whole gang used him, and they were brutal. Harnessed him like a horse and literally split his face in two. He lost all his teeth; he had internal injuries. They sodomized him, one of them tried to cut off his testicles. Anyway, the poor sod would have been better off dead in my opinion. You want to read the particulars?"

Cori and Finn declined, and they handed back the pictures and medical reports. The parole officer put the file back together and said:

"This guy is a mess so, yeah, I guess you could say he has some issues with Hispanic men."

"Nobody stopped what was going on?" Cori asked.

"I wasn't there." Nicholas shrugged as if to say 'the guards can only do so much'.

"Is he disabled, or could he swing something hard enough to bash a man's head in with a pipe?" Finn asked.

Nicholas shrugged. "I guess he could."

"Well, what's your assessment?" Finn said, frustrated and tiring of this posturing.

"I don't know." Nicholas threw up his hands and whined back at Finn. "He seemed okay at the intake. I mean he could walk. He could move his arms. Maybe he shuffled a little. He had a hard time talking when I saw him, but, yeah, at the intake he seemed fit enough. I see that I recommended him for work. I haven't heard any complaints, so I guess I knew what I was doing now, didn't I?"

"No, no." Finn waved his hands, open palmed, crossing one another. "The last time you saw him, man. How was he then?"

"That was the last time I saw him," Nicholas sniffed. "And if you're going to take that tone—"

Cori started to say something, but Finn leaned forward, eyes narrowed, and spoke first. His voice was low and measured.

"He's been on your caseload for over a year, Mr. Ellis."

"Yeah, well, what do you want from me?" Nicholas shot back.

"I want you to do your job," Finn said. "I want you to keep tabs on murderers. I want you to earn your keep."

"I do my job," Nicholas complained. "And a lot of thanks I get. Look, Spears was low risk, or he wouldn't have been on my docket. I did the interview and now he checks in at the kiosk. As long as he checks in at the kiosk, then I don't have to look at his ugly puss. That's my job. To make sure he checks in at the kiosk."

Nicholas ripped a sheet of paper out of the file and tossed it Finn's way.

"See for yourself. He hasn't missed a month. If he does then I'll put out a warrant and he'll be your problem."

"Holy Mother Mary." Finn let his head fall back and he prayed to the ceiling for patience. When he looked at Nicholas again, he said, "Fine then. If you'll give us his address, we'll be on our way."

"*Ffftttt,* I'll have to check on that. I'm not sure if he was moved. I think he might have been early on so this may not be the right one." He looked at the front of the file, perusing it as he talked. "You haven't got a warrant so obviously it's not urgent and it's almost lunchtime, so you'll have to…"

Before Nicholas could make another excuse, Finn rose, put his fingertips on the cluttered desk and rested his weight upon them. Nicholas looked up, his face blushing with anger and then going pale with fear.

"The address, Mr. Ellis. In the next few moments, if you would be so kind."

Without another word, Nicholas Ellis opened the file, rifled through it and came up with the information Finn wanted. Finn thanked him and the two detectives went on their way leaving the man with a newfound sympathy for the likes of John Spears. It was a hard thing to admit you were at the mercy of a stronger man.

* * *

"*llama a la policía*. Here. See?"

Amber pointed to Finn O'Brien's phone number. She knew that she probably shouldn't be handing out his cell, but she would apologize later if someone actually called. She smiled at the man who seemed nervous to be talking to her. She pointed to the truck's description. "A white Toyota truck. Um, *blanco. Blanco. Este carro.*" She looked down at the note she had made from Google translate and hoped her pronunciation was okay. "*No te metas en el auto.*"

Don't get in the car.

Call the police.

That's all she wanted these people to know and she was nearly hoarse from trying to explain herself to the men on the ten corners she had visited. She pressed the flyer into the man's hands. She was pretty sure that it said what she wanted it to say, but she tried to speak to each and every person anyway. Amber would point to the fuzzy booking picture of a young John Spears hoping that the years hadn't changed him too much so that they would know who they were looking for.

"Do you understand?" Amber snapped her fingers and closed her eyes searching for the right word. Finally, she had it. "*Entender?*"

She smiled, pleased that she had remembered the word Pacal had spoken so often to her. Did she understand what he was saying? Did she understand he loved her? Yes, she understood.

"*Si. Si.*" She had said then. Now a man was saying the same thing to her.

Amber shook her head. She had almost forgotten where she was. She pressed the paper into his hand. He nodded and went to share it with another man who waited under a tree.

She had done what she could. All the information any of them had was on that flyer. The only thing that wasn't was Pacal's picture. She didn't want to confuse the issue. Besides, if any of these men saw the white truck and called Finn, then they would find John Spears. If they found him, Finn and her mom would make him tell about Pacal. And if they couldn't make him tell, she would.

CHAPTER 28

Doctor Brand: (probing head wound, watching screen to guide his hand). One more millimeter and this guy would have been toast. **(slowly pulling the bullet out of the skull, depositing it in the pan.).** You say he walked a couple miles like this?"

Nurse Cairns: That's the word, Doctor. ER says he was pretty chatty when he came in.

Doctor Brand: God works in mysterious ways. Guess somebody up there has a plan for him **(buzzer sounding)** Damn. No cardio output. Let's get to it. Don't want him to have walked all that way for nothing.

The house was a block of beige stucco. There was a concrete walk that intersected with a vertical slab that butted up against the front of the house. There were two vertical windows on either side of a cheap front door, two larger horizontal windows beside those and three narrow windows upstairs. There were no abutments nor was there a garage, but there was a driveway. Finn went for the driveway and Cori to the other side of the house. They met up on the sidewalk when they were done looking around.

"Only one car in the back," Finn said. "Late model Camry. Blue."

"Nothing on the side but a fence. There was a gate. Trash cans on the other side. Looks like a small yard in the back so there's probably a backdoor," Cori answered.

Finn pivoted and let his eyes travel up and down the street. Cori did the same, double-checking in case he missed anything but there was nothing to miss.

"Pity, no white truck," Finn muttered.

"Since when is anything that easy?" Cori answered.

He started up the walkway and Cori followed a step behind since whoever laid the cement walk had only made it wide enough for one.

"Let's hope Mr. Ellis has given us the right address," Finn said as he reached the door. "He said he wasn't sure if he was still here. Given the kiosk system Spears could be anywhere."

"Ellis has low level offenders. He's a clerk, not a parole officer," Cori said.

Finn knocked on the door and when it was opened, he had no doubt that, even if John Spears wasn't in residence, Nicholas Ellis had sent them to the right location. This halfway house was as gloomy and stale as its gatekeeper. Finn showed his identification.

"I'm Detective O'Brien and this is Detective Anderson."

"Which one do you want?" she asked.

"John Spears."

"He's not here. He's at work."

She turned on her heel and walked inside. The detectives went after her. There was one man in the living room. Cori tipped her lips and dropped her chin as if to say 'no, not you'.

"Where would work be?" Finn asked.

"He's over at the Goodwill in Long Beach."

"'Tis a long way for him to go for work."

"They take a lot of our people," she said. "He's almost ready to cycle out and they'll take him on permanent. They'll even help him find a place to live."

"When is he scheduled," Cori asked.

"Next week. Maybe sixth or seventh depending on when the paperwork comes through."

"Does he have plans?" Finn asked.

"He keeps to himself. I don't know. He's never given me any problems."

"Nothing?" Cori asked. "Late to check in? Contraband in his room?"

"No…" she began and then paused. "Well, not really trouble. He was late a few days ago. He was really upset when he came in. I felt bad for him. I mean it could have been anything that kept him."

"What day was it?" Finn asked.

"Day before yesterday."

"And did you notice anything different. Was he hurt?"

"Nope, but after that he was telling me he didn't feel good. Reminded me of my kids. They always had stomach aches if they hadn't done their homework or someone was bullying them." She put a hand to her mouth and her eyes got wide. "Oh, gee, maybe someone was being mean to him 'cause of his face. And I made him go to work. But what was I supposed to do? We guarantee them and the placement keeps them on a tight leash."

"Where's his room?" Finn asked.

"Upstairs on the right," she answered.

"He has no problem walking up the stairs?"

Finn kept his eye on the flight as he asked this. It was steep with a hand railing only at the bottom.

"Nope," she answered. "He's slow but he can walk. Are

you taking a look?"

"Yes," Cori started for the stairs.

"Go ahead," she said. "I've got something cooking. Call me if you need me."

Finn started for the stairs and then stopped. He called her back. "Missus, is there anyone else up there this time of day?"

She shook her head. "It's just me and Doolittle in the other room. Knock your socks off."

* * *

He had worked with Glen before and he didn't like Glen. Glen was a halfwit, slow and loutish. He babbled constantly about the clothes they were picking through and then, when he couldn't think of anything to say about the clothes, he would ask stupid questions.

Did you get your face caught in a lawnmower?

Did your mother croak when she saw you?

Then he'd laugh and his one lazy eye would get bright, and John Spears would want to kill him. Wanting to kill a white halfwit upset him. He never wanted to kill for the sake of killing and now look at him. All because of Adolph, he was sure. Adolph had disturbed the rhythm of things. No, he had changed the very essence of things and that disturbed the ritual. That's why everything was going to hell. The boy in the mountains had been taken to the wrong place. He had been killed in the wrong manner. His grave had been poorly dug and he had not been laid to rest properly and Adolph had appeared.

Yes, John thought, that is why there was an itching under his skin, a pressure in his bladder, a spin in his brain that signaled things were amiss. He wanted to be back in his room. He wanted to say his prayers and be alone and get ready for tomorrow. He only needed one more day, after all. There was just one more boy to send to his reward.

Payback for what had been done to him.

Payback for the violations.

Payback for the humiliation.

No Illores.

He would not cry.

The season was almost over.

* * *

The room was ten by ten, a standard bedroom in a tract home. There was a small closet, a dresser, a bed, and a window.

"Just once I want to walk into a room and find the pictures of victims with stickers and crazy writing all over the place – oh and a confession written in blood. Bam, we're done just like CSI. Know what I mean?"

"'Twere it only that easy, Cori," Finn opened the closet door. "Nothing in there."

Cori went for the dresser and started with the bottom drawer and worked up.

"Empty."

Slam.

"Empty."

Slam.

"Clothes. Two shirts, a pair of pants – dirt in the drawer and in the cuffs," she said. "Three pair of underwear, one pair of socks, pajamas. This guy travels light."

Slam.

She opened the top drawer.

"Emp–" Cori pulled up short. "Wait a minute. What have we here?"

She dug in her purse and snapped on latex gloves before reaching into the drawer and pulling out a manila envelope and a cell phone. Finn had already put on his gloves by the time Cori tossed him the phone.

"The envelope is addressed to a Judge Franklin. L.A. County Superior Court but no street address." Cori looked up. "Do you know him?"

"No, but we'll find out who he is," Finn said. He turned on the cell. "I don't think this belongs to Mr. Spears. The language is set to Spanish. We'll have to get it unlocked."

"Nice," Cori said as she crossed the room, digging in the envelope and pulling out maps. Finn set aside the phone and took one of the maps from her.

"'Tisn't a roomful of pictures but this is starting to look promising." He turned his map over and looked at the front. "Mine is forest lands in the county."

"Mine is a map of utilities and rights of way. The other's a county map, all roads including freeways," Cori said as Finn spread his out on the bed.

"Interesting. Neatly done but hardly inspired. Red ovals, green circles and black crosses." He pointed to a large, sandy colored expanse clearly labeled Baldwin Park. "This is good."

"Do you have Mount Wilson?" Cori looked over his shoulder.

"I have a green circle in the general area but no black cross. These are strange things to send to a judge." Finn folded his map, took Cori's and did the same. She gave him the envelope when he asked for it and then watched as he put it and the phone back in the drawer.

"What are you doing?"

"We're leaving everything as we found it for now. He'll be back by five-thirty and we'll talk to him in this room and see what he's willing to show us." Finn opened the drawer below and looked at the clothes.

"Did you see the dirt, Cori?"

"I did and I'm going to just scoop me up a little. There's some in the carpet, too." She stepped forward, bringing a baggie out of her purse. "I'm betting this matches the stuff that came off at least one of our bodies."

Finn snorted a laugh as he felt behind the dresser. Finding nothing, he went to the bed and lifted the mattress. A second later he dropped it onto the frame as something caught his eye.

"I think he's back," Finn said.

Cori was by his side in the next minute, leaning over the bed to get a look at the white Toyota truck turning at the corner.

"He's early," she muttered. Then Finn heard a sharp intake of breath before Cori pointed out the window. "He's made us."

The white truck had slowed, stopping when it came upon the unmarked unit.

"Damnation," Finn muttered as he ripped off his latex gloves and ran for the door.

Cori heard him pounding down the stairs, but she stayed kneeling on the bed, head stuck through the open window. The white truck was still idling beside their car and she saw that the back plate was black and gold. Strike one. Pipes and a shovel were in the truck bed. Strike two. Strike three would be—

Just then Finn O'Brien burst through the front door running full tilt. The man behind the wheel of the truck was alert and saw him coming. He hit the gas and the truck shot down the street just as Finn ripped open the door of his car and threw himself behind the wheel. The last thing he heard was Cori screaming out the window:

"South. Turn right. Right!"

Seconds later the unmarked unit pulled out and gave pursuit leaving Cori to call for air cover and guess which sector Finn would end up in. Since there was nothing to do but wait, Cori gave the room another shot. This time she collected evidence because it was a sure bet John Spears was not coming back to this room. When Finn returned with more evidence bags, she would be ready to fill them.

Cori stripped back the sheets, dumped the pillow out of its case, pulled in a chair from another room and searched the top of the closet. She found nothing until she went back to the dresser and checked the clothes. She set aside one of the shirts after seeing three pinpoint rust-colored stains on the front. But it was what she found in the pocket of the pajama top that really made her smile.

"Cori Anderson, you are cooking on the front burner today," she muttered.

Carefully, she laid the holy card showing Saint Stephen looking toward heaven on top of the shirt with the blood specks. No need to worry about a warrant since – until the middle of May – John Spears was a parolee whose life was controlled by the state. Right now, Cori Anderson was the state.

She couldn't wait for Finn to get back with Spears. Together they would go to Fowler and tell him there was no need for a task force. All that was needed to wrap up this mess was O'Brien and Anderson, thank you very much.

* * *

Finn was in the Toyota's wake, but Spears had a good head start. He also knew he was being pursued because he took chances, cutting off a Mini Cooper in the right lane before swerving back into the left in front of delivery truck. The Mini Cooper slammed on its brakes and the truck's horn blasted long and loud as it swerved to miss the little car. Spears' recklessness caused the other drivers to stop cold, forming a cube of automobiles that boxed Finn in.

"Out of my way!" Finn screamed.

The Mini Cooper moved first, pulling over to the side of the road giving him room to move into the right lane and back into the left after he made the pass. Finn was still hearing the angry blast of the delivery truck's horn even though he was a block away. The white truck, though, had vanished. Slowing, Finn looked right and left, down the side streets that led to neighborhoods like the one he had just left. A helicopter circled in the distance.

"This way, man. This way," he muttered.

Cori, good woman, had called in the pursuit, but she had no idea where they had gone after that first turn. Finn reached for the radio to tell them specifically where he was but, in that split second, the white truck loomed in the rearview mirror. Finn saw it just before it rammed into his tail and spun him into the intersection.

Spears was around him and gone before Finn could turn into the spin and stop. He bounced off a light pole and took the fender clean off a Prius that had been waiting at the stop. Everyone was out of their cars: the Prius driver was spitting like a wet hen, the delivery truck driver was laying on the horn, ticked off to be caught again and a pedestrian was taking a video. Ten cars were lined up behind that truck and Finn was rushing into the intersection, dodging the cars that were trying to get around the mess.

He shouted into his radio, advising that officer was unable to pursue a murder suspect. He gave his coordinates. He watched the helicopter turning, and then he scanned the streets hoping to see a flash of the white truck or get a glimpse of a black and gold plate, but Spears was gone, and Finn was marooned.

There was nothing he could do now except deal with the mess on the street. He calmed the Prius driver and waved the truck through. He called for a traffic officer and a tow truck. Finn took pictures of the incident, assured the Prius driver that someone from the precinct would be calling to speak with her and set things right. He gave the driver his card and called Cori to let her know that he would soon be back to pick her up.

Then he heard from dispatch advising him to return to the precinct, stat.

The day was about to get a whole lot worse.

CHAPTER 29

Captain Fowler: That's the way the chief wants it. I spoke to him at length yesterday.

O'Brien: But we are so close—

Captain Fowler: No, O'Brien. I'm reassigning. You screwed up when you didn't make that meeting. You've become fixated on this problem at the expense of your other responsibilities. That was not the deal. The chief does not want you to be the only law enforcement face the Hispanic community sees.

O'Brien: If I could just speak with him—

Captain Fowler: (ignoring O'Brien) And that's why I'm putting Anderson in charge. You are not to speak to reporters; you are not to initiate any action on any of your jackets without Anderson's permission. Is that understood, O'Brien? Anderson?

Anderson: Yes, Captain.

Captain Fowler: (giving Finn the once over) You will reschedule that meeting ASAP, is that clear?

O'Brien: Crystal.

Captain Fowler: O'Brien. Just so you know. They were

going to give you the results of the test on the shotgun. It was damn important and it's about time you start treating procedures with some respect. You do not leave your desk until that is taken care of.

O'Brien: Yes, sir.

Finn O'Brien had heard his captain well enough the night before and now, here he was, chained to his desk. He had enough to keep him busy, but he bridled at the restraint. Cori was downtown at the meeting with the chief as one of the lead detectives in her division. Fowler was gone too. Tina had her door closed. Morrow was out as were half the detectives in the division as they prepared for May five.

Finn had finished writing the report on what went down at the halfway house where they had found Spears. He had sent the soil samples from Spears' room to the lab for processing ASAP against soil samples taken from the gravesite near Mount Wilson, the Baldwin Hills site and the third body in the morgue that had yet to be identified.

By phone he interviewed the other men who shared a house with Spears. Those interviews were short. Spears never spoke to anyone. Finn contacted Nicholas Ellis, instructing him to call John Spears into the office. This he knew was an exercise in futility. The cell phone was with the techs in the hopes they could unlock it. He had begun to analyze the maps and was just about to tackle a document he had sent to the D.A. for clarification when the phone rang.

He had a visitor.

* * *

"It's good to see you, my friend." Gregorio stood up and took Finn's hand. "Come back to the office and we can talk. I'll fill you in on our progress."

Gregorio shook his head. "You can come outside?"

Finn asked no questions until they were well away from the building. "What brings you here?"

"I came to tell you a young man has died. I think he was taken like the others were."

"When did this happen?" Finn asked.

"They found him two days ago, lost and hurt. Now he's dead." Gregorio shook his head with sadness. "At church, they take up a collection to get the body of the man back. He die in the hospital, but the priest say he was shot in the mountains. He say the dead man work hard, standing with men to get work. So I ask who this man was and they send me to his..." Gregorio paused and searched for the English word but he couldn't find it. "M*oza amiga*. You understand?"

"His girlfriend?"

"*Si*, girlfriend," Gregorio smiled.

"Was she from Richland Farms?"

"No. She live on the Westside. She work for a lady who say this boy stole but the priest, he say he works."

"What did the girl say?"

"She say he work and he stole," Gregorio said matter-of-factly. "A hospital call and say he was dead."

"How did the hospital know who to call if he died?"

"He was shot, but he walk a long way even with a bullet in his head. They say he talk enough to give her name. The doctors say they ask what happen to him. He say he was in the forest and then he waking up. Dirt on him. Then he was walking. That's all he remember. A man in a gas station find him and call the police. They take him to the hospital, but he die."

"Where was this?" Finn asked.

"I don't know. That's all I hear. I write down the hospital and the girl's name."

Gregorio handed Finn a folded paper with the address of the Huntington Hospital and a phone number for a girl named Graciela.

Finn smiled and blessed Adolph's dark little soul. He had been telling the truth after all. Huntington Hospital was the closest one to Mount Wilson and now the package was complete. With this information they had Adolph's missing body from which he had filched the jewelry, a girl's missing boyfriend, and a day laborer who was also a thief and who had also managed to walk a mile to a gas station with a bullet in his head.

"Thank you for this, Gregorio. I'll see what I can find out about the body being released."

"You think this boy is like my son? Like the others?"

"I do." Finn put his hand on the man's shoulder. "This is getting us closer to finding Miguel."

Gregorio's head swiveled and he looked down the street.

"My bus," he said. He touched the paper with the address of the hospital on it. "Do not worry. Now we all watch. Everyone."

Before Finn could ask what he was talking about, Gregorio ran for the bus that had stopped a half a block away. Finn smiled, pleased with the turn of events but, when he unfolded the paper, he saw more than the scrawl of Graciela's name and number. What he saw didn't make him happy. He chased after the bus.

"Gregorio! Gregorio."

The man turned, his foot on the bus riser and his hand on the rails. Finn held up the paper.

"Where did you get this?"

"Gotta go," Finn heard the bus driver call and Gregorio

took the next step calling as the doors closed.

"They say a lady leave it."

"Who? Which lady?" Finn danced a few steps to keep pace as the bus pulled away, still shouting, "Which corner?"

Behind the glass, Gregorio shook his head and shrugged. When the bus was out of sight, Finn went back to the precinct, down the hall, and when he turned into his small office Cori was there with her big hair, big smile, and big hello.

"You're supposed to be grounded, buddy."

"You're supposed to be my partner, Cori."

Finn gave her the flyer. It took a minute for her to register what she was seeing. When it hit her, she said, "I didn't do this."

* * *

"I swear, I did not know that Fowler was going to reassign me, O'Brien; therefore, I couldn't have been making plans to run the investigation any different than you were. And, even if I did know, why would I keep something like this from you? Or didn't you notice it's your phone number printed here. Not to mention this isn't exactly on department paper."

Cori turned the flyer so that he could see it in full. He glanced at it and then he leaned forward and really took a look – a thing he should have done before suggesting she had ratcheted up the Spears investigation on her own before he had been told to step down.

"You're right." Finn bit his lip and then asked. "You don't think Thomas is behind this do you?"

"I wouldn't put it past him. Or what about Morrow? Did you ask him?"

"He's signed out. Holy Mother, if Spears sees this it will

drive him underground for sure. We'll never find hi…"
Finn's voice trailed off. He picked up the flyer, looked at
it and then at Cori. "Cori, it was Amber. She was the only
other one in the house the night we came up with Spears.
Gregorio said it was a woman handing these out."

"Aw, lordy. I'm sorry, O'Brien." Cori reached for the
phone. She punched in Amber's number and waited. "Not
answering. Damn. Damn."

"Call your land line," Finn said, and Cori was on it.

"Hello! Who is this? Where is she? Okay. Okay. If you
hear from her you tell her to stay put." Cori hung up. "The
sitter's at the house. Amber got called into work."

Cori shoved back her chair. It clattered against her desk.
She caught it before it fell.

"Grab that grubby jacket of yours."

"Where are we going?"

"To find my kid," Cori said. "God help her."

* * *

It was noon but he had been awake since three-thirty
because that was when he always woke. His prison years
taught him to stay up late and wake early, to stay vigilant
so he would see the Mexican boys coming. No matter
how he watched, though, some guard would open his
cell and turn a blind eye because it was easier to let the
Mexican boys have their fun than it was to protect him,
a man who had agonized over the wrong he had done,
who had tried to make amends. That judge could have
changed things, but he didn't. He damn near said John
Jamieson Spears was a cold-blooded killer, which he had
never been. Not even now. Now he was simply doing
what the justice system could not; he was punishing
those who deserved it.

He stretched out his legs. They ached. His shoulders did too. His chest hurt. His left arm was shot through with pain. He hated all the things that had been taken from him, but it was his strength he missed the most. He would like nothing more than to be in his child's bed, but they would be waiting for him at that house so he couldn't go back. And today was the last day of the season. Today he had to finish and, in order to do that, he must start the day.

First, he needed to piss and find some water. He wouldn't eat anything because his stomach didn't feel good. No surprise. He had slept in his truck in an alley, of course he didn't feel wel...

Suddenly there was a crack against the windshield. Spears threw himself down on the bench seat, feeling for the glove box where Adolph had stashed his gun, vowing not be taken without a fight. But it wasn't the police who had found him. The voices calling to him were young and the hands on the windshield were black.

He raised his eyes and saw enough to know that these were street thugs. They probably wore their pants around their ankles and talked like gangsters and such. One of them pressed his face against the passenger window. Behind Spears, another boy pounded on the driver's window. Both of them called him names: whitey, honkey, piece of crap.

Spears' heart lurched and when it settled it felt like an elephant was sitting on his chest. Still, he wouldn't show weakness. That had been his mistake with the brown boys, and he wouldn't make it again with the black ones.

Slowly, amidst the screaming and pounding, John Spears pushed himself to an upright position and gave those boys a good look at his face. They stopped pounding on the windows and stepped back. Then the first boy said something that Spears couldn't hear but it was clear he had leveled a challenge at his friend. That boy accepted the challenge and bent down to pick something up off the ground. When he reappeared in John Spear's window, he was holding a rock.

Surprise.

John Spears was holding a gun.

CHAPTER 30

"I'm going to kill her. I am serious, O'Brien. This is the last straw. Quit her job? That move is just dumb enough for twins."

Cori paced the parking lot of Romero's and railed against her daughter. Now and again Mr. Romero looked through the window and glared at them. He had been clear about how he felt about Amber when he informed Cori that it was true, her daughter no longer worked there. He also had a few choice words for the no-good boyfriend of hers, but when he called Amber stupid, Cori got in his face. What Amber had done might have been stupid, but the girl was not.

"She's still not answering." Cori shut the phone down, crossing in front of Finn again as she paced. "What was she thinking? What is she thinking?"

"She was thinking that the boy she loves is in trouble and that we aren't moving fast enough to find him. Sure, we weren't exactly careful what we said in front of her the other night," Finn reminded her.

"I know. I never realized there was a need." Cori sighed.

"There wasn't until now," Finn said. Cori's chin clicked up an inch as if to say *ain't love a bitch*. He gave her a minute and then asked, "What do you want to do now?"

Cori took a turn. She looked at the restaurant. Finn glanced over in time to see Mr. Romero turn away from the window.

"We have work to do. Let's head back to the office," Cori said, "After I try Amber one more time."

* * *

Amber sat in her car, leaning against the door, one foot up on the console as she scrolled through her phone, looking for nothing in particular, continually defaulting to her screen saver – the picture of her and Pacal, the one she had printed and given to Finn. Her flyers were gone and this corner on North Sepulveda was her last stop. She looked at the men waiting for work. Some looked bored while others appeared anxious. None of them looked like Pacal. Pacal always stood straight and strong while he looked for an opportunity. He was never ashamed that he stood for work. That was why he was often chosen, he told her. Amber had smiled and said that's why she chose him. When she asked why he chose her he said because she was a *buena mujer*, a fine woman.

How could she not love a man like that?

How could anyone give up on a man like that?

The answer was, they couldn't, and she wouldn't. But the day was done. She would start again tomorrow. She sat up and had the key in the ignition when her phone rang. She looked, hoping to see Pacal's name. Instead, she saw her mother's. Amber let it ring. She didn't want to hear her mom ask, 'How's your day going?' like this was just another day.

Amber hung her arms over the steering wheel, put her head down and closed her eyes. The phone was ringing again. Again, she let it go. There was no reason to answer it. What would she say if her mom asked how she was?

Gee, Mom, I'm sad and lonely and scared.

Bullshit.

Sure, she might be all those things, but she was not defeated. If there was no body, there was hope. If she was the only person who believed that, so be it. Picking up the phone, her thumb hovered over the button that would place a call to her mom, but she never pushed it. There in the street, heading for the corner, was her worst nightmare: a white Toyota truck. She laid on the horn with one hand while she started the car with the other.

"Stop. Stop! It's him…"

She was screaming at the top of her lungs: screaming at the men on the corner to pay attention. Screaming at the man who was stopping across the busy street from where Amber was parked. That truck could only be driven by one man, the man who knew where Pacal was.

* * *

John Spears was agitated.

His nerves tingled and his bad eye was pulsing. He knew he wouldn't be able to grasp a pipe or the shovel properly, and that meant he would have to use the gun again. He hated the gun, but this would be the last time. After this one he would move on, find a quiet place, and get some rest. This season had taken a toll on him.

But it wasn't just the season and the turn of events that was making him anxious. It wasn't the prickle of his nerves along his arm and in his hand or the shortness of breath that never made it all the way into his lungs. His agitation was also fueled by frustration. He had driven by two of the usual places where men gathered but no one was there. He went round one block three times and the corner was still empty. He drove by another one. Empty. Perhaps he had slept through a day and it was the fifth. Perhaps everyone was downtown celebrating instead of working but that couldn't be. He turned on the radio and the announcer said it was the fourth of May.

Becoming more anxious by the minute, he went up Sepulveda and finally found a few men, but they weren't to his liking. They were old and ugly. What good was it taking out men who had one foot in the grave already?

Then he looked again and decided the one in the green shirt might do. The one in the green shirt would have to do. He stopped the truck, rolled down his window, pointed at the man in the green shirt and made a shoveling motion.

"Diez dólares por hora," he said.

The man smiled and then lost interest. He looked around to see who was honking so loudly.

John Spears looked too. The other men stood up straighter and turned their heads, curious about the sound that was now one long blare. Through his one good eye Spears could see that sound was coming from the car gunning across four lanes of traffic, causing the oncoming cars to split and swerve. He could see that car was coming for him.

CHAPTER 31

Amber was almost across four lanes when her luck ran out. A car going north couldn't stop and clipped her rear brake light. She hung on tight and turned into the skid the way her mom showed her when she was learning to drive. She pulled out of it in a split second and found herself pointed due north. The man who hit her was cursing up a storm. The door of his car was open. The other traffic was cutting a wide swath.

She snapped her head the other way. The driver of the truck was gesturing for the man in the green shirt to hurry. Amber stepped on the gas determined to use the only weapon she had to stop this man – her car. But Amber was going too fast and when she reached for her phone she veered and hit the curb. The three men scattered. John Spears saw his opening and sped away.

"Damn it," Amber cried as she scrambled for her phone.

When she had it, she threw her car into reverse, shot backward, slammed it into drive and took off after Spears, chasing him up Sepulveda until he made a sharp turn. Amber followed, her heart beating as she dodged one car after another. She hit speed dial to call her mother. Cori answered almost before it rang.

"Where in the hell—"

"Mom—"

"—quit your job–"

"Mom!" Amber screamed. "I've got him. Come help, Mom. The man who took Pacal, I've got him."

Amber heard sounds on the other end of the phone. Tussling. Moving. Voices.

"Mom. Mom. Finn!" she called, driving with one hand and speeding after the white truck, praying that a police car would appear and stop him. But it didn't happen. Spears blew through stop signs and lights. Amber barely kept up.

"Mom!"

"We're here. You're on speaker. Where are you? God damn it, what are you…"

"I'm headed to the canyon. The canyon. Mulholland, I think. Mom, I'm…"

That was when the line cut out.

* * *

"Amber! Amber!" Cori cried.

"Cori." Finn kept one hand on the wheel and the other clamped over his partner's arm. She tried to shake him off, but he held tight. "Cori, sit back. Now."

"Don't you dare tell me to stand down." She snapped her head his way, hair flying and nostril's flaring. Her mouth was twisted into a snarl that promised to unleash all hell if he didn't back off, but he wouldn't have it.

"The only person I need in this vehicle with me is a police officer." He loosened his grip a little to test her. "I swear, Cori, I will put you out if you can't bring it. Choose, for I'm headed to Mulholland either way."

"You bastard."

Finn let loose of her and put both hands on the wheel.

"That's better," Finn said. "Now get her back."

Cori dialed. She listened.

"Not answering. Going straight to voicemail."

"Sure, she's in the canyon then. Keep the line open. The reception comes and goes and we need her back."

"We don't need phone reception." Cori shut down the line. Her fingers flew over the phone. "That car she drives belongs to me. It's got a GPS tracker so step on it, O'Brien."

* * *

Amber Anderson was not in a good place. There were no bars on her phone. The main road was a mile back. She had ripped something on the undercarriage of the car, and she couldn't make it go straight anymore. Not that it mattered because there was nowhere straight to go.

She had followed the white truck up Mulholland, a windy canyon road, and almost hit another car head on when she passed a van. She had turned off Mulholland when the man had and followed without thinking, running the car into the ground. Isolated, unable to call out, surrounded by scrub and trees and hills that kept her from hearing the traffic on the main road, Amber was now officially scared. She opened the door. It was only a mile back to the road, maybe less. She would walk it and flag someone down. She would...

"Oh shit. Oh my God."

She would do nothing because there he was, emerging from the brush. John Spears was headed straight for her, limping fast, his face nearly covered by a floppy hat and he was carrying a shovel.

Amber slammed the door and hit the locks. She started the car and threw her arm over the back seat and stepped on the gas. The back wheels spun out and the front end didn't move at all.

"Jesus. Mom. Finn. Help me."

Frantically, Amber tried again. Forward. Back. Forward. The car rocked. The car moved an inch. Amber spun back around, her breath coming hard and fast as she tried to put the shift into drive.

"Come on. Come on," Amber pleaded, but it didn't move.

She grabbed her phone and shook it. She held it up, whimpering, praying to see the bars that never appeared. She dropped her hand and that's when she saw that John Spears was standing right beside the car, looking at her. She stared into his milky eye and the other one filled with hatred. She saw that his lips weren't lips at all but a map of scars that radiated from both sides of his mouth. Amber opened her mouth to scream and that's when he swung his shovel and shattered her windshield.

* * *

"Another hundred yards and turn left."

Finn looked ahead and saw there was a traffic break coming just after the spot where Cori wanted him to turn.

"You missed it," she snapped, swiveling to look behind. "I told you left."

"I got it, Cori. It was faster this way rather than to wait for the traffic to pass."

Finn made a U-turn, scraping over the shoulder before swinging back onto the road. A second later he was crossing a wide turnout from which a small road – a path really – went into the canyon. Finn slowed, both to get the lay of the land and to search for any sign of Amber's car.

"Still not answe…" Cori began only to pause. "Wait. I've got the signal again. Straight on. We're good. Jesus,

O'Brien, go. Go now."

Cori unlocked her seatbelt, leaned forward, and grabbed her purse. By the time they found Amber's car, Cori had her gun in hand.

* * *

There was a bird singing. He thought it was a strange sound in a place as desolate as this with its scrub and water-starved trees. He couldn't tell where the bird was, but it was nice that it was singing. He raised his face to the sun. That felt good. He rested against the open bed of the truck, his body alternately shot with pain and dancing with tingles. The singing bird helped him to relax. He wondered if it was the same bird that had been at the other place. Wouldn't that be something? Wouldn't that be like a blessing? Not really, because this wasn't like the other place.

That day the boy was handsome, his skin smooth and brown, his hair black. That boy dug like his life depended on it and smiled when he completed his task.

Now he was holding a gun and watching a blonde, fair-skinned girl angrily dig in the hard ground. He could see sweat stains on the back of her shirt and under her arms. Even though it was a mild day, she would burn easily.

No matter.

Soon she would be out of the sun forever.

He would shoot her in the head to be nice. He didn't want her to see it coming but that might be difficult since she kept cutting her angry eyes his way. He couldn't fault her. He would be angry too if he knew he was going to die, which surely, she must know.

No Illores.

Don't cry.

He would tell her that if she turned at the wrong time, if he couldn't move fast enough to take her by surprise.

"I'm not doing this anymore."

John Spears, lost in the moment, enjoying the song of the bird and the warmth of the sun on his face, was surprised to hear her voice. When he realized that she had stopped digging, he tilted his head and waved the gun barrel to indicate he wanted her to continue.

"No. I won't dig anymore, and I don't think you're going to shoot me if I'm looking at you." Amber raised her chin and grasped the shank of the shovel with both hands so he wouldn't see her shaking. "I think you're a coward that way. You kill people who aren't looking at you."

When he didn't speak, when the hand holding the gun fell to his lap again, Amber took a step up, standing just at the edge of the hole she was digging.

"You won't shoot if I look at you because you only kill people when they aren't looking at you," she said again. "Isn't that right? Isn't it?"

The mutilated man stared. The barrel of the gun waved but this time he didn't raise his hand. He didn't feel well. He wanted this done and she was still talking.

"I want to know where Pacal is?" Amber said. "Pacal Acosta. Where is he?"

The man mumbled something, but she didn't think it was words. Amber thought he was making a noise to try to hurry her on and that's when she knew the truth: she would never see Pacal Acosta again. Either he was dead, or she would be, so it was over. Hope shattered, flying away in shards, tearing her insides to shreds as she came to this realization. And then she came to another. She would not die without a fight, without knowing what had happened to the man she loved. Amber raised that shovel over her shoulder. Holding it with both hands, she took a step toward him and then another, all the while screaming.

"Where is he? Where? You tell me, you fucking bastard. You…"

She was no more than three steps from him, the perfect distance to swing that shovel, when he raised his arm, leaned forward off the edge of the truck bed, and put the cold, hard barrel of his gun in the middle of her forehead.

"No illores."

CHAPTER 32

Cori's hand was on Amber's car. The front windshield and driver window were both destroyed. The other windows were cracked. The front end had been pounded and the back lights were taken out. Finn was walking toward a stand of bushes. Both of them froze when they heard the shot. It reverberated through the canyon, fading fast, swallowed up by the surrounding hills. They drew their weapons, bent their knees, and swiveled in opposite directions, unable to tell exactly where the sound had come from.

"Northeast," Cori whispered.

Finn pointed at the ground. The dirt was disturbed, delicate branches from a long- dead shrub were scattered a foot or two ahead. Northeast made sense.

"I go." Finn waved her back.

Cori opened her mouth to argue. It was her daughter out there after all. Then she thought again. There was every possibility that they wouldn't find her alive but, if she was and Cori was leading, she might do something to compromise them both. She sent him on ahead.

Finn found a hat. He held it for Cori to see. She nodded. It was Amber's baseball cap. He tossed it aside, needing no encumbrances. Cori looked at it as she passed and then stayed on his heels. Finn gestured, indicating a clearing. He could see footprints where the scrub ended, and a berm of earth rose up: one smaller set of prints was ahead of a larger set. Finn could see beyond the berm. He fell back and stayed low.

"The truck is there."

"Do you see Amber?"

He shook his head and then they both stayed quiet, listening for any sound that would tell them where John Spears was. Finally, Cori whispered:

"We've gotta go, Finn. Please."

Finn nodded, wishing there were something more to go on. It would do them no good rushing into the open, running toward a man with a gun and a hostage.

"Stay put," he said and dropped flat.

Using his elbows to propel him, Finn inched forward until he was almost at the top of the berm. Before he reached it, he turned his head and put his cheek against the dirt. He raised his hand and positioned his weapon. Only then did he lift his head enough to peer over the edge of that rise and what he saw made his heart sink.

Amber lay on the ground, one foot in an indentation in the ground. Her arms were out in front of her and both hands still wrapped around the shank of a shovel. Her hair had fallen over her face. She wasn't moving but Finn knew that could mean any number of things. She could be wounded, knocked out or she could be dead. Two things convinced him she was not dead: first he saw no spread of blood near her body and second, John Spears was standing over her pointing his gun at her as if he meant to use it again.

Finn could waste no time. Without looking back, he

motioned for Cori to follow him. In the next second, he burst into the clearing gun high, arms locked.

"Police. Drop it. Drop it and step away from the girl."

If John Spears was surprised, he didn't show it. He kept his gun pointed at Amber while he turned his head slowly toward Finn. His face was expressionless, his strange eye seeming to lock onto the horizon.

"Leave it on the ground, Spears. Drop it," Finn ordered and the man seemed to bend as if he was, indeed, going to put it upon the ground. Finn called his partner up to be ready to retrieve the gun.

"Cori, if you would…"

The man smiled a little and inclined his head as if to say he was sorry. Finn's mouth went dry. No one looked at the barrel of a gun like that if they weren't thinking they could beat it. That's when Finn knew Cori did not have his back; that was what made this man bold.

"Just us two," John Spears mumbled.

Spears words were barely audible, but Finn O'Brien understood their meaning. The man had nothing to lose and so the detective's threats were unimpressive. Finn also understood how smart Spears was because his gun was aimed, not at Finn, but still at Amber.

"The girl's done nothing to you. Let me see if she's all right."

Spears shook his head. Finn tried again.

"She's a *gringa*, Spears. No good to you," Finn insisted. "We know about prison. We know about what was done to you. We understand."

The man tossed his head a little. He snorted. The good eye sparkled and the milky one stared at nothing. His lips tipped up and this time the effort pained him. He seemed to list left, his shoulder dropped an inch and that took the gun just a shade left of Amber's head. But it almost seemed as if he was not there for a moment. Still, that was not something Finn could count on.

"You're a man of God, Spears. Sure, I've gone with God my whole life too."

Like a dog hearing its master at the door, Spears ears pricked, but when he didn't respond Finn pushed on.

"God understands vengeance but not the taking of innocent life. Don't all the saints attest to that? The saints you carry with you? They would want you to spare this girl."

"She gave herself," Spears mumbled, slurring his words. He swallowed as if saying too many at one time was painful. "To one of them. Gave herse—"

"No. No, she didn't. I know this girl. She is a mother, Spears."

Finn moved slowly into the clearing, his weapon as steady on Spears as Spears' was on Amber. Silently, he cursed Cori. It was dangerous that she had gone off. It was dangerous for all of them. There was nothing for him to do but keep the conversation going until he determined where she was.

"The boy she is looking for was her friend only. She worked with him. She is innocent."

Spears eyes flickered toward Amber for a minute and then he looked back at Finn. He shook his head.

"Lie," he said.

Finn was about to try to reason with him again when he saw Cori coming silently upon Spears from behind, her weapon raised as if to execute him and Finn knew that this would not end well no matter what he did.

Before he could fire, before he could call out to Cori, before Cori could murder the man who had taken so many lives and was threatening another most precious one, Amber rose to one knee and swung that shovel. With a primal cry, she caught Spears at the back of his legs. The man went down hard, and she was upon him, flailing and screaming.

"Where is he? Where is Pacal?"

She scrambled to her feet, beating John Spears with the shovel. He raised his hands across his face and rolled in the dirt, unable to escape the attack. In a matter of seconds, Amber brought the shovel down again and again, losing her footing, stumbling as she wept and raged. With a harrowing scream, she raised that shovel high but, before she could smash the shovel into his head once more, Cori was on her, pushing her daughter back and struggling to take it away.

Finn threw himself at Spears, ripping the gun out of his hand, pulling at Spears' arms, using his legs to stop the man from kicking. Then, as suddenly as the fight had begun, it was over and Finn was left spread eagled, pinning the man to the ground. Breathing hard, he waited for a struggle to continue but it never came.

"O'Brien?" Cori said.

He pushed himself up just as Amber broke free and threw herself at Finn, trying to roll him away from John Spears.

"It's a trick. He knows where Pacal is. He…"

Finn pushed her back.

Amber went at him again, this time kicking Spears.

"Get up, you bastard," she screamed and kicked him once more before Cori grabbed her. She wrapped her arms around her daughter, pulled her back and then held her head against her shoulder until Amber's frantic wails became inconsolable sobs.

Slowly, Finn pushed himself off and rolled onto the dirt.

He got to one knee and holstered his weapon.

"Is he…" Cori began.

But Finn wasn't listening. Spears' lips were moving so Finn swooped down, his hands on either side of the man's head as he lowered himself to listen.

"Finn," Cori said again.

"What did he say?" Amber asked.

Finn pulled back, hardly believing this is how things would end. He put a hand over the mangled face and drew it down across the eyes. When he looked at Cori and Amber, he said, "'Twas a woman's name. Delores."

Amber shook her mother off and came to stand next to Finn. She put her hand on his shoulder.

"*No illores.* That's what he was saying."

Finn and Cori looked at her, but she never took her eyes off the mutilated face of John Spears.

"It means don't cry."

CHAPTER 33

MAY 10

O'Brien: (surprised, holding the door open) I'm here for the committee. Have I got the time wrong?

Marjorie Landly: Come in. It's only me today.

O'Brien: (closing the door, sitting across the table) I am sorry for missing it the other day. 'Twasn't my intention to be disrespectful, but there was a matter—

Marjorie Landly: (hand up) The union is well aware of the matter, and we would also like to wrap up the other matter. Fidel Andre Hernandez…Marbles.

O'Brien: I'll not be making any kind of deal if that's why you're here.

Marjorie Landly: I wouldn't have expected you to even if this thing went into overtime. The reason no one else is here is because the investigation into your actions in that house is closed. Fidel Andre Hernandez was beaten to death in his cell last night. Members of *Nuestra Familia* are the leading suspects. **(waiting)** Detective O'Brien, did you hear me?

O'Brien: I did.

Marjorie Landly: Poor guy wasn't ready for the big

time. He should have learned something in juvenile incarceration.

O'Brien: I'm just sorry his victims won't get their day in court. I would have liked to see Officer Shay's family have some justice at least.

Marjorie Landly: (standing, picking up her briefcase) I think you managed to hand out a little in that house, Detective. I mean, you did take him down. That's something. **(puts her hand out)** It was good to meet you. **(O'Brien taking her hand)** Let's not make a habit of it, okay.

O'Brien: I'll do my best. **(Landly heading for the door. Finn stopping her)** The test results. On the shotgun? What came back?

Marjorie Landly: The file is sealed, Detective. **(small smile)** Have a good one. **(gone).**

"She wouldn't tell you? I can't believe it," Cori said.

"It's not that she wouldn't tell me, I simply didn't push it," Finn answered. "The file is closed, and we go forward."

"I couldn't take it. I'd have to know what they found on that pump. But you probably know already. I mean in your heart you know, right? That's right, isn't it?"

Cori tossed a wad of paper at him, but he batted it away and then picked it up and put it in the trash. The woman was a pain and a half trying to get him to tell what had happened the night he had collared Marbles, and he was as much a pain for refusing to tell. Fidel Andre Hernandez meant nothing in the grand scheme of things. Just as John Spears was nothing. What they had done loomed large but the men themselves? Finn would not speak their names for fear of giving them any legacy, nor would he burden his partner with things that would pain her.

"I'll not be dignifying that with an answer," Finn said. "How is Amber these days?"

"Sorrowful for sure. It's going to take her awhile to come to grips with the fact that Pacal is gone. If they don't find him, she will always have a shred of hope. That's going to be hard to live with. The girl is brave, though. She's got more guts than you can hang a fence on," Cori said, twirling toward her computer only to turn back again. "Do you know what she's doing? She's looking into schools. She got a new job waitressing, and she wants to go back to school."

"Sure, that's wonderful," Finn said. "She'll be fine, Cori."

"I know that, and I know why she's doing it. That boy took her up a peg." She waved her hands across one another. "I'm not changing my mind about legal and illegal, mind you. I'm just saying he taught her something about responsibility that I couldn't."

"Is she going to visit Pacal's mother?"

"Not now. Maybe never. She doesn't want to cause the woman any pain, and she wants to figure out what purpose it would serve," Cori said before she fell silent for a minute. When she spoke again, it was with a tone Finn had never heard before; soft and intimate. "You know how lucky she was, O'Brien? I mean, lucky that that man didn't kill her? Another couple of inches and he would have shot her in the head."

She looked Finn straight in the eye then. He tipped his head. He understood. The thought of losing Amber grieved her almost as much as the reality of it would have.

"But he didn't," Finn reminded her. "His heart was probably already giving out already. His sight must have been affected or he wouldn't have missed at that close range. She was smart to play dead for as long as she did."

"I don't know if she was smart or stunned or both.

Whichever, I'm grateful she stayed down," Cori said. "God, when I thought she was dead I was going to kill him."

"I wouldn't have let you," Finn said.

"Then I would have killed you first," Cori answered.

Before Finn could ask if that was the truth, Tina interrupted.

"Detective Anderson? Captain Fowler is waiting on you for the Cinco de Mayo recap."

"Sorry, forgot." Cori was up, putting on her blazer, flipping her hair out of the collar as if nothing dark had passed between them. She laughed when she said, "Cinco de Mayo. Didn't that just rile the wagon masters for nothing? I swear, all that money preparing for Armageddon and all that happened was a bunch of people had a damn good time picnicking in the park."

"Better safe than sorry," Finn said. "And since we're not the wagon masters, it matters little."

"Hah, I'm not even sure we're allowed in the wagons on this train." Cori picked up a note pad. "I shouldn't be more than forty-five minutes. Want to grab lunch when I get back?"

"Can I be having a rain check for tomorrow?" Finn asked.

"Sure. Anything important going on?"

"Just an errand to run," he said.

"Okay. See you."

When Cori was gone, Finn picked up the coroner's report on John Jamieson Spears and noted the cause of death. Heart attack. A bit of poetic justice, Finn thought. He was just glad that the injuries Amber inflicted on the man had not done him in. Finn wouldn't wish that guilt on her conscience. Although, given what he had probably done to Pacal, Amber might have been honored to be the

SECRET RELATIONS | 335

one that dispensed such justice.

He filed it along with the preliminary report on the scene investigations. They had used Spears' maps to identify areas where he might have buried his victims. They had found skeletal remains at one site but so far had come up empty at others. Captain Fowler had told Finn and Cori not to hold out hope that they would be able to cover all the areas indicated on the maps.

They had found a journal along with a Bible in Spears' truck. The marked Bible passages were self-serving to the man's mission of revenge. It was a pity the system hadn't done a better job, sending him for treatment instead of to halfway houses. Perhaps then he would have understood the difference between individuals and an entire culture.

The journal was filled with the ranting and raving of an angry, bitter man whose pain – physical and psychological – colored every waking minute of his day. On those pages were the words John Spears himself could not speak, and his hatred of the Hispanic community was nothing less than epic. While it would take better minds than his to follow the dark tangle of the man's narrative, there was one thing that was clear: John Spears wanted someone to pay for what was done to him. If it couldn't be the men in prison, it would be men who bore a resemblance to them. At the front of the journal was a letter to Judge Franklin blaming him for setting these events in motion.

Finn put aside the reports to file later, checked the time and realized it was getting late. He grabbed his jacket and was on the road five minutes later.

The day was beautiful, bright, and sunny, and he drove with the windows down. Making good time on the freeway, he exited at Compton, drove into Richland Farms, and pulled up in front of Our Lady of Tears church just as the noon mass was getting out. He sat in the car and watched the women and old men stream out of the building, recognizing one or two of them from Gregorio's meeting. Their young men would be back on corners, waiting for work, safe for now. The peace wouldn't last. Someone else would take Spears' place and there were other men like Marbles waiting for their turn to exploit people like this.

Finn shook his head. If he wasn't careful, the 'big black dog' of depression would be coming back to sit on his porch and that was the last company he was wanting. He got out of the car and decided to be happy for what they had accomplished.

Finn took the low-rise steps to a plaza that surrounded the church and then walked through the big double doors and down the center aisle of the old building. It was cool and quiet inside. Christ on a crucifix loomed over the altar. To his right and left were the Stations of the Cross. Beyond the communion rail in the sanctuary, on either side of the altar, were statues of St. Joseph and Mary. Kneeling in front of the Blessed Mother was the man Finn had come to see. He took a seat in the front pew and waited until Father Patrick was done praying. It was only a moment later when he turned and saw the detective. He had his hand out and his vestments were flowing as he came to the communion rail and Finn got up to greet him.

"Detective O'Brien. I'm happy to see you."

"'Tis happy I am to see you also now that the circumstances are better."

"You did a fine thing, Detective. No one else would have gone to bat for these folks the way you and Detective Anderson did. Gregorio filled me in on the details. I'm praying that you're able to find Miguel and Pacal."

"I am, too, Father," Finn said and both of them knew it

would never happen.

"Now tell me what brings you here?"

"I'd like to talk with you, Father," Finn said.

"Of course. Just let me change." Father Patrick turned toward the sanctuary, but Finn stopped him before he got too far.

"You're dressed just fine for the conversation I'm thinking of having," he said.

Father Patrick's brow furrowed, his mouth opened and then it dawned on him what Finn O'Brien had in mind. The detective hadn't come to see a friend; he had come to see the man of God.

With a nod the priest opened the little gate in the communion rail and joined Finn. He gave the detective's arm a pat and then led the way to the carved wooden structure nestled beneath a stained-glass window at the back of the church. Each man opened a door that led into the confessional. When Father Patrick was seated and Finn O'Brien was on his knees on the other side of the ornate privacy screen, they began.

"Bless me Father for I have sinned," Finn said.

"How long has it been since your last confession?" Father Patrick asked.

And with that, Finn O'Brien began to tell his secrets and his sins to the only person he knew on this earth who would keep them.

A LOOK AT: INTIMATE RELATIONS (FINN O'BRIEN 4)

A woman in a window. A cop out of his element. A crime of unimaginable passion.

It's two in the morning when a domestic disturbance brings Finn O'Brien to an artists' colony on the frayed edges of the City of Angels. Housed in an abandoned brewery, the concrete fortress looms like a dystopian portal to hell. Inside the detective finds a bizarre gathering of Los Angeles elites, a man in a rage, and a young woman beaten to death, her face obliterated.

As he hunts a killer, Finn finds himself in a surreal world where art and science create strange bedfellows, money and desire birth shameful descendants, and the deadliest relationships of all are the most intimate.

AVAILABLE MAY 2021

ALSO BY REBECCA FORSTER

ABOUT THE AUTHOR

Rebecca Forster started writing on a crazy dare and is now a *USA Today* and Amazon bestselling author with over 40 books to her name. She lives in Southern California, is married to a judge, and is the mother of two grown sons.

Made in the USA
Las Vegas, NV
31 July 2021

27303554R10201